The Sage of Canudos

THE SAGE OF CANUDOS

A Novel

BY

LUCIEN MARCHAL

Translated from the French by
Charles Duff

E. P. DUTTON & CO., INC.
New York   1954

Library of Congress Catalog Card Number: 54-8849

CONTENTS

PART III

THE BATTLE

MAPS

TRANSLATOR'S NOTE

Not all maps of Brazil show the little place known as Canudos, the center of the amazing drama presented in this novel. Canudos is situated in the hinterland region of the northeast, about 400 miles inland from the port of Bahia in the state with this name. This hinterland region of Brazil is known as the *sertão*, a word used almost exclusively in reference to it and of frequent occurrence in this book. The reader will also make the acquaintance of the word *jagunço* (pronounced almost as it would be in French, but with stress on the *u*). *Jagunço* was first used to mean bandit, robber, or ruffian. In time it came to mean simply an inhabitant of the *sertão:* a "hinterlander." This is the sense in which it is used throughout Lucien Marchal's novel.

C.D.

AUTHOR'S PREFACE

THE episode in the history of Brazil called to mind in this novel is known as the "Canudos Campaign" and occurred between the years 1886 and 1897. At the time, it gave rise to many violent polemics; at one moment it compromised the stability of the republican government. Later, it became the subject of various studies in human geography, the most remarkable of these being Euclides da Cunha's work with the title *Os Sertões* ("The Hinterlands").

Canudos is undoubtedly a unique ethnical phenomenon. It is, at the same time, an astonishing demonstration of the action of a physical environment on the temperament and mentality of men, and a curious example of the disappointing results which can be produced when the principles of civilization have been badly assimilated by a simple-minded population.

❖   ❖   ❖

It is advisable to note clearly that the Canudos events are related exclusively to the northeast of Brazil. They could not have taken place in any of the other regions of the country, for in them conditions are utterly different. One must not forget that the surface of this vast country equals ten times that of France; and that a line drawn diagonally from Manaos to Porto Alegre represents a distance the equivalent of that from Copenhagen to Timbuktu. Hence it will be realized that each region has its own peculiar features and develops along its own line of evolution: all the more so because the human material resulting from the mixing of races is not the same in the south, center, and north.

L.M.

The Sage of Canudos

Part I

THE MACIEL FAMILY

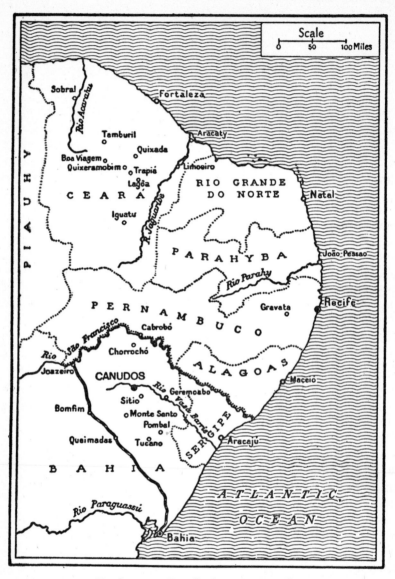

Northeastern Brazil, showing Canudos

1. The Hatred

FOR MORE than a century the rivalry of the Maciel and Araujo families besmirched the Brazilian state of Ceará with blood. The Araujos prided themselves on their descent in direct line from the *bandeirantes*—the first Portuguese pioneers—and were reckoned among the biggest landowners in the state. Their domain extended to the south of the Quixeramobim River over more than 75,000 acres, reaching as far as the sources of the Jaguaribe and to the outskirts of Iguatu. Their residence with its vast roof of thick tiles darkened by the rains, its wide veranda, flanked on the right and left with sheds and ranchos—rustic huts in which the laborers lived— was built on the right bank of the river and had been named "Boa Viagem." It dominated a broad plain surrounded by the line of hills, the sierra.

Allied to some big families which shared among them almost the whole of the state territory, the Araujos enjoyed a considerable political influence, which is to say that they could contrive the appointment to all the important posts in the administration of those men who were devoted to them and knew how to utilize public funds in the interests of the family. They were so powerful that they even had granted to them the right to dispense justice on their own estate.

At this period slavery still existed throughout the whole of Brazil, but the abolitionist campaign had just been initiated by some intellectuals who were convinced that Negroes were men. Certain *fazendeiros*—great landed proprietors—whether for sentimental reasons, or in hope of retaining their working staff by attracting their sympathies through a gesture of generosity, began to liberate colored families, to whom they granted small farms on leases for which payment was made in kind. But the Araujos were not a party to that baneful policy. They did not free a single slave. As for the free half-castes to whom they had granted this or that allotment on lease, they kept them under their sway; for they were responsible

13

for administering justice among them. The Araujos liked order, wealth, power, force, and harbored against colored men a fierce hatred, a hatred which came from the depth of centuries.

Furthermore, they had resentfully seen grow and develop from year to year north of the river a farmstead created by a family of crossbreeds: the Maciels. Originally from Pernambuco, the Maciels were the issue of a crossing of Dutch with Brazilian Indians, re-crossed later with Portuguese and Negroes; they were of a race which blended the strong muscular system of the redskin natives with the suppleness of the black and the will power of the white. It is often said that the man of mixed breed accumulates the faults of the races of which he is a product, but has lost their good qualities. This is true only of the man of mixed breed living in a milieu consisting almost exclusively of whites, which develops in him an inferiority complex by reason of the hostility and contempt which he comes up against. The hybrids of the Brazilian *sertão*— the northeastern interior or hinterland, with its center in the state of Bahia—are of quite another stamp. The Maciels were men of initia-tive. They had obtained from the state government of Ceará a con-session of some hundreds of acres of "lapsed" land which formed part of a fazenda or estate abandoned by some Spaniards who had returned to their own country. They were mostly poor lands, apart from the slopes of a sierra to the north which gave a good yield of maize, cotton, or sugar cane.

The Maciels settled themselves in the Spaniards' old farmhouse which they had reconditioned: it stood on the left bank of the river at a place called Formosa, about five miles from Quixeramobim, the first important village one meets to the east, and at about ten miles from Boa Viagem, the residence of the Araujos, situated to the west. There were three Maciels: Joaquim, João, and Luis. Only one of them, Joaquim, took a wife and had two sons by her (Vicente and Miguel) and a daughter (Helena).

At first they did not cultivate the land and kept to raising cattle. They quickly became involved in disputes with the Araujos, who said that the Maciel beasts were crossing the river to graze on the fertile pastures to the south. When João went into the vicinity of Boa Viagem to verify the facts, he was found two days later in the river with his chest perforated in three places by knife wounds.

A fortnight later a cousin of Araujo was getting married in the little hamlet called Villa. At the moment when the procession was moving forward to the church, the bridegroom was killed by a shot which came from the corner of a house. The murderer, who had fled on horseback, could not be identified; but it was understood that he was one of the Maciels. Then it was war. The Araujos massacred without pity all the Maciel cattle which crossed the river. In awe of the power of those whites, who were rich and related to the state governor, the Maciel brothers beat a retreat. They drove their animals away toward the sierra. But hatred was tenacious in the heart of Araujo. Two years later, weary of seeing the half-breeds' farm prosper, he paid a hired killer—a *capanga* such men are called—to rid him of the half-breeds. In the *botequim,* the little café bar and store at Quixeramobim, the capanga picked a quarrel with Luis Maciel. There was a free fight. Luis was killed, but the capanga received a knife wound in the belly from which he did not survive.

A short time afterwards Joaquim's wife died of a pleurisy and he was left alone with his two sons and his daughter, all of whom were by this time past the age of twenty.

Vicente was a tall thin fellow, indolent but intelligent. He had the vague look of men who lack will power. Miguel, on the contrary, of medium height, had the build of a Hercules. He had a round face, black eyes, a penetrating look, a broad back, and enormous buttocks. His complexion was very bronzed by the sun, his hair flat like an Indian's, and his biceps standing out under his shirt gave him a look of habitual brutishness among men of decision. He it was who killed old Araujo with gunshot one evening when he was returning from Quixada.

This murder was to have tragic consequences, because in Araujo da Costa, who took over the management of the fazenda of Boa Viagem, hatred was even stronger than in his father.

He was then fifty-one years old but, with his head of thick white hair, his white beard and mustaches, his deeply lined brow, and two heavy pouches under his eyes, he looked at least sixty. He believed that his blue eyes were enough to prove that he belonged to the race of the masters. His whole countenance expressed vicious ill temper, for he had a swollen liver and could no longer drink alcohol.

From the time when he passed through colleges at Rio de Janeiro he had maintained an air of superiority and aristocratic manners which made him feared and hated by the slaves, the tenant farmers, and all members of his family who had not had the honor of being molded in the capital. On the other hand, neither his studies nor his sojourn in an ordered society had in the least deprived him of his wild animal instincts. His pleasures were those of a wild-cat. Thus, when a slave had committed a grave fault, he had him brought into the field behind the dwelling house. There he read him a lecture and then, as if getting angry, he would say: "Out of it! Get out of my sight! I'm going after you!" The slave began to run. When he had gone fifty yards Araujo shot him down. It was only on such occasions that he could appreciate the meaning of the word joy.

He had married the daughter of Sylvestre Vegas, a big land-owner of Iguatu, but, after two miscarriages, it was certain that she could not give him an heir. On many occasions in his rage he beat her, to the point that one day she fled with two slaves and took refuge with her father. He declared on all sides that the Vegas were a rotten lot and that he was going to ask for a divorce. In the region they did not know what that meant, but people added that Araujo was well educated and that he had relations with the Pope who, they said, was going to authorize him to take another wife. Soon afterwards it was learned that Padre Julio of Fortaleza had declared that the laws of God could not be broken and that Araujo had bowed to this opinion. For the only authority that he respected was that of the Church. From that moment onward he set about begetting children by negresses, but refused to recognize such off-spring as his, and liberate them, as nearly all the fazendeiros did. At six o'clock every morning he appeared on the veranda alone with his vile temper. He would give orders and then stretch himself out in an armchair to ponder over his hatreds.

It was there on the veranda, during a cloudless afternoon in April while the birds were chirping in the mango trees, that he conceived the project of finishing with the Maciels for good. Those people were becoming dangerous. Thanks, no doubt, to those re-publican elements which were beginning to infiltrate into the imperial administration (the empire of Pedro II was in course of disintegration), they had succeeded in obtaining a new concession of plots of land to the west and now they had two fazendas: that of Formosa, occupied by Vicente; and that of Tamburil, managed by Miguel and his sister Helena.

Every time he went to Quixada or Quixeramobim, Araujo da Costa made inquiries about the half-breeds. In this way he had learned that Vicente had married the daughter of a businessman in Massapé, while Miguel had decided not to marry at the moment but, with his sister, to go and settle on the new concession at Tamburil. Vicente already had in his service at Formosa about ten colored laborers, stolen—so Araujo thought—from the fazendeiros who had been stupid enough to liberate them. No! *He* would never free his slaves: he would not give them the opportunity of leaving him to go and work elsewhere.

There was something more serious: at Quixada, at Quixeramobim, and even at Fortaleza, the state capital, one could see that the Maciels had many people in sympathy with them, even among the whites. They were beginning to have political influence—half-breeds! Former cowherds! It made Araujo da Costa's stomach turn. Yes indeed, as his friend Ribeiro used to say, you could feel the republic coming! . . . It would not be proclaimed before he had avenged his father. He was going to act; and without delay. He could see in the distance the bare line of hills which surrounded Vicente's dwelling house, and his heart rejoiced at the idea that soon a thick cloud of black smoke would rise into the sky over there, announcing that the fazenda of Formosa was no longer anything but a heap of ashes. His mind was firmly made up. The same evening he sent a herdsman off to Pernambuco bearing a message for Siqueira de Menezes and Theotonio, the most famous professional killers of the northeastern hinterland. For he had no intention of undertaking the operation himself. When one has the title of magistrate, it is preferable, in order to maintain one's reputation, not to lend oneself to assassination and banditry—apart from the fact that the Maciels were formidable people. He feared them, in spite of all his contempt for mixed blood.

It was only three months later that the killers reported one evening at the fazenda of Boa Viagem. It was raining in torrents. The summer season was well advanced. The sky streaked with lightning and vibrating with violent detonations was rolling enormous clouds against the sierra.

The two capangas tethered their horses in the big iron shed.

"For the last two hours we've been traveling in the rain," said Siqueira as he went up on the veranda where Araujo was waiting to receive them.

"You might have chosen another date," said the fazendeiro. "Why didn't you wait for the dry season? I wrote saying there was no need for haste."

"Pooh!" replied Siqueira. "Killing is done at any time of the year."

The servant girl brought each of them a shirt and a pair of trousers, into which they changed on the veranda, and then Araujo da Costa led them into the dining room. This was a vast rectangular hall with whitewashed walls and having as its only adornment a long, massive table, the legs of which had been patiently carved by slaves who were artists. After having again talked about the weather, then of the state of the crops and cattle in the direction of Pernambuco, they tackled the main subject.

"I want the work well done," said Araujo. "I want this to be final."

"What do you take me for?" replied Siqueira, who was proud of his seventeen jobs of murder, all efficiently carried out.

"I know you, I know you," Araujo hastened to say, "it's because I know who you are that I called you. Here in Ceará, we have nobody of your stature."

"At your service, colonel . . ."

Siqueira de Menezes was a small thin man with a hooked nose and a great wisp of hair which fell over his right eye. He had a wide mouth but thin tightly pressed lips and, stuck on this head of a bird of prey, were two enormous ears. Theotonio, on the other hand, was tall, strong, and well set up, and had the slow, heavy motions of an athlete. He was a tough fighter when things went badly.

They sat for a moment without speaking. Araujo snuffed the two candles which lit up with a yellow reflection the bronze faces of the capangas. Then Siqueira said:

"How about the money?"

"Half before, half after," replied Araujo.

"That suits," said the capanga. "Pay up."

Araujo took from his pocket a roll of filthy bank notes and set out ten in a line in front of Siqueira, and ten before Theotonio.

They picked them up as if they were old scraps of paper, crumpling them in their big hairy hands, and stuffed them into their trouser pockets.

"The execution will take place tomorrow, at dawn," said Siqueira.

"May God protect you!" replied Araujo who, for all that, was not a humorist and did not like people to abuse the prestige of God.

At that moment the black servant brought them three very small cups of coffee and three glasses of water.

They drank and remained silent as if they were savoring a rare and precious drink. Then Siqueira said casually:

"To be absolutely sure, we ought to have had six men. *Men.* Not just fellows with cactus juice in their veins."

"I have Negroes," said Araujo.

"Not up to much. Unless you can put fear into them."

"I'm going to show them to you. They can handle a gun. They're my hunting men."

He clapped his hands and the black servant girl in a white dress appeared in the open doorway.

"Call João," he said.

João was the foreman, a one-eyed half-breed whose right cheek formed a large fold resulting from a gash received in the course of a brawl. Araujo gave him his orders and soon afterwards six Negroes were led into the dining room. Araujo pulled a face more disagreeable than usual to speak to them. He was not unaware that, in order to dominate these black men, one must put on the mask of a brute.

"Tomorrow," said he, "you'll give these men a helping hand"— he indicated the two capangas with his finger—"it's a matter of doing away with the Maciels. You understand? Once and for all. If you back out, I'll take every one of you into the corral. Understand?"

The Negroes bowed their heads. It is the slaves' sign of assent. They were being asked to kill: they were ready to kill, like soldiers.

They were shut up in a rancho to the right of the fazenda, a wretched hovel where farm implements were kept, while the capangas went to sleep in the open shed. The latter had no difficulty in falling asleep, for professional criminals sleep well, the thought of human life being foreign to them.

It was nine o'clock in the evening. The rain had ceased and the sky, now cleared, was glittering with stars. Here and there in it were seen those light white patches in which certain southern constellations are blurred. It was a sky which imposed silence.

On the veranda of the Formosa fazenda, Vicente Maciel and his wife were chatting with Miguel and Helena who had come to assist with the hoeing.

"Tomorrow," remarked Miguel, "we'll finish with the valley that runs toward Massapé and the day after we'll go back again to Tamburil. We'll expect you on Monday next week. There's much work to be done."

"We can't complain," said Vicente. "It's a good year. We've had plenty of rain. The cotton plants are magnificent. I've counted up to three hundred flowers on one stem."

"The cotton's giving a good yield," said Miguel. "And it sells well. It's a pity that there's red worm in the sowings. I've a whole heap of plants which haven't come up because of that."

Next they spoke of the maize, the manioc, and sugar canes. The women discussed things among themselves in an undertone, because Vicente's *senhora* was six months pregnant and women's views on the question of reproduction are inexhaustible.

It was nearly eleven o'clock and all were getting ready to go to bed when the barrier of the corral creaked. The women gave a start of fright, but Miguel's masculine voice reassured them.

"No doubt it's some stranger who's come to ask for hospitality."

"It's not a horseman," said Vicente. "It seems to me to be a Negro."

"A Negro? What can he be coming to do here at this hour?"

There was a moment of uneasiness and the Negro went up on the veranda.

"Good evening, Aristides," said Vicente.

Immediately everybody became calm. This was a Negro whom

they knew. Only Vicente did not appear to be reassured, for Aristides was his spy in the Araujo household and it must be something particularly serious for him to slip out at night, with all the risks this meant for a slave.

Aristides had a skin as black as coal. He was a full-blooded Negro. Tall, well-built, with an open look, he must have been of Senegalese origin. He could read and write. He was one of the best elements among the Araujos, but he carried on in their midst an underground campaign tending to incite the slaves to revolt. He liked the Maciels because they employed free laborers.

"Well," Vicente said to him calmly, "is there anything new?"

The Negro wiped his forehead, took some time and said:

"They're coming to kill you; tomorrow, at dawn."

"What?" yelled Miguel. "Who's going to kill us? I'm waiting for whoever it is."

"Keep calm, Miguel," said Vicente. "What's going on, Aristides?"

Aristides gave an account of the arrival of Siqueira and Theotonio and of everything that the servant girl had told him.

"It's arranged for tomorrow, at break of day," he concluded. "They're going to come and kill you and set fire to the fazenda."

"We'll see about that," Miguel growled between his teeth. "Fortunately we're here with Helena. They'll see who they've got to deal with."

"Siqueira has already done a lot of killing," said the Negro.

"I've heard him spoken of. But Miguel Carlos has no fear of a capanga. I'll shoot him down; I won't miss the opportunity."

"Come with me," said Vicente to the Negro.

He led Aristides into the *sala* or principal living room to reward him.

"Be off, quickly," he said to him. "They mustn't become aware of your absence."

"No danger," said the Negro. "They think that I've gone down Pedra Branca way to bring back mules. I won't return by Boa Viagem. I'm going to cross the river and go down directly by Moraes."

"May God come to your help!"

When the Negro had gone Miguel turned toward Vicente:

"You're sure of him?"

For he knew the wiliness of certain Negroes who bring you false information in order to get money.

"Quite sure," replied Vicente, adding: "It surprises me all the same. For more than two years we've had no argument with the Araujos. I thought it was all finished."

"That's never finished. Don't forget that I struck down his father, that old blackguard. Besides, Araujo well realizes that the good days are past: soon all the Negroes will be free, and there's not one who'll remain on in his service. He won't have any more farm hands and his cattle will croak. When we have the republic, he'll be on the same footing as ourselves, but it's to us that the Negroes will come to work. That's why he wants to eliminate us: so that he'll be alone here in this hinterland. In that way the Negroes would be driven to go and work for him."

"Possibly so," said Vicente without conviction.

"In any case, since you're certain that your Aristides is not telling lies, we must get ready to receive these rascals. Put your men in the kitchen. We'll close the doors and shutters. How many firearms have you?"

"Three."

"Good. With three we'll manage. Tell your wife to go and lie down. These troubles are no good for pregnant women. You'll stay at the window to the right: I'll keep behind the door and Helena will be at the window on the left."

For Helena could handle a gun and pistol as well as the dagger. She had already been involved in two free fights, at Tamburil and Sobral. Her amazon temperament was well known in the hinterland.

When all preparations were made, Miguel declared that he would like to have a nip of rum. Helena brought him a bottle and a small cup. Vicente did not drink. For several months he suffered from his stomach and drank only infusion of wormwood.

"You're going to sit up and watch?" Helena asked.

"Naturally," said Miguel. "Go and have a rest. When they're outside I'll call you."

The women shut themselves in a room. In the kitchen the Negro laborers were lying on the ground. One of them was snoring. Miguel and Vicente were in the main room seated on stools at the table on which was burning a candle with a very yellow flame. The silence was charged with menaces. The night was hot, humid, and enervating. From time to time a violent beating of wings could be heard —an owl changing its perch in the mango trees. Toads began croaking in the direction of the river. Miguel stood up and partly opened the door to glance out into the night. The moon had risen and her golden crescent seemed to be posed on the top of the palm tree which grew on the top of the sierra bordering the road to Quixada. Over the corral and around the shed some bats were tracing sporadic flights at a right angle.

Miguel shut the door again and returned to his seat to pour out a drink of rum. Vicente was silent: he had the fixed look of those condemned to death and awaiting their execution. He was a man who hated fighting. On the table the flame of the candle died in a big patch of grease. They were left in the dark.

When a long time had elapsed, Miguel said:

"It must be getting on toward five o'clock. If your Negro hasn't been telling lies, they must be about to arrive."

"Supposing we take up our positions to await them."

"That's a good idea. Call Helena. We mustn't be taken by surprise."

They installed themselves at their posts. Miguel could easily keep a general eye on the whole corral through an opening cut in the bottom of the door to allow cats to pass through during the night. And so they waited.

A light morning mist filled the valley but did not go beyond the sugar canes. The gate of the corral was clearly visible. A cat appeared in front of Miguel's face and fled, scared as if it had seen a ghost. Miguel called it. After a moment's reflection the cat decided to go through and it ran off toward the kitchen.

They remained waiting.

All of a sudden a red clearness came into the sky. The line of hills became violet and the sun stood above the mountain as if it had come up from Quixada. It was daybreak.

"Your Negro was telling us stories," said Miguel.

And he got up to go and drink a glass of rum.

"Aristides wouldn't do that," replied Vicente firmly.

"Good. I'm waiting."

They did not have to wait very long. The sun had not yet come out fully when a man on horseback wearing a broad Bahian hat appeared at the barrier.

"Fire! All together!" Miguel commanded.

"Wait, wait!" shouted Vicente. "Maybe it's not him. There ought to be two of them."

"You know this person?"

"No."

"Then we must down him."

"And supposing he's not our man?"

"We needn't care a damn; it's our skin we're defending. It could be him and then you're a dead man. I know the capanga game."

The procedure of the hired killers was extremely simple. They presented themselves as visitors. Sometimes they were received by the servants. In that case they asked to speak to the boss: they would try to entice him out into the plantations under the pretext of seeing the crops, and there they executed him. But, if the boss should himself put in an appearance on the veranda, they struck him down immediately, flight being easy for the killer who did not even have to get down from his horse.

Vicente continued to hesitate, for he had respect for life. The rider advanced unconcernedly to the middle of the corral. Perhaps he was a peaceful traveler on the way to Maranhão?

Two shots rang out. Theotonio sank on his horse. Immediately there was agitation in the sugar canes.

"Fire into the canes! Fire into the canes!" roared Miguel.

This time Vicente in turn began to fire and they spattered the field of canes with bullets.

But everything suddenly became calm again. The sun was shining in a deep-blue sky. A flock of birds were chirping in a mango tree; a parrot was swaying on a leaf of banana tree.

Theotonio's corpse had rolled under the horse, but remained caught by the foot to a stirrup. The horse had dragged him in under the shed. A rattlesnake, frightened by the fusillade and having no doubt lost its way, crossed the corral. Miguel killed it with a shot.

Although the incident seemed to be ended, the Maciels dared not go out of the house. They were keeping their eyes on the outskirts of the fazenda.

"You see that it was him all right," said Miguel to Vicente.

"I should say so."

"If you had gone out on the veranda, you wouldn't have come back on your feet. He's a worthy man, your Aristides!"

Helena had returned to Vicente's wife to reassure her, to tell her that it was finished. In the kitchen the Negroes were now talking it over in a loud clamor.

Taking precautions, the Maciels did not decide to go out until almost nine o'clock. It was already a long time since Siqueira de Menezes had abandoned the field with his black assistants. He had again taken the road for Boa Viagem in a rage like a wild animal caught in a trap. It was the first time that he had failed in an undertaking.

On arriving at the fazenda he saw Araujo da Costa walking nervously back and forth on the veranda. Siqueira jumped down from his horse, went up the steps in a few strides and took a stand in front of the old man. He looked him straight in the eyes.

"We were given away," he said slowly.

Araujo gave a start of astonishment and looked at him as if he doubted his statement.

"We were given away," repeated Siqueira. "We were received with gunshots and Theotonio was killed."

"Who could have told about you? Nobody could have betrayed you. Nobody knew about this business."

"We were given away," Siqueira repeated once again with a menacing calm. "Come now, you old scoundrel, pay up! Three contos (1,000 milreis). Straight away."

"We agreed on two."

"Three, or I'll down you. Theotonio has been killed."

Siqueira put his hand on his pistol.

Araujo looked down, turned his head right and left as if seeking a weapon with which to defend himself or some way of escape. His hands were shaking slightly. He led the capanga into the main room. There he produced a roll of dirty bank notes and counted out the money. Siqueira seized it, stuffed it into his trouser pocket and went out without a word.

"Open the barrier," he shouted to a Negro.

He jumped onto his horse, drew his pistol to show clearly that any attack would in a flash get a reply, spurred his mount and made off at a gallop.

Araujo stared at him until he disappeared behind the sierra, and then let himself collapse into his wicker armchair.

He was chilled to the bone, humiliated, and wondered how he could still breathe while his body was filled with so much rage. Then he recalled to mind what Siqueira had said to him: "We were given away." Who could have betrayed them? Only the servant girl had heard a few fragments of their conversation; and the Negroes who had taken part in the expedition had been locked up. Of Maria, the servant, he was sure. She was the woman most devoted to him. He would not have liked even to put a question to her on this subject: he was afraid of losing her. More and more he felt himself abandoned by his staff, who were corrupted with abolitionist and republican ideas. Not for one moment did he think that Aristides could have betrayed him. He was one of his trusted men and, besides, he had sent him to the south. Who, then? Weary of turning over these thoughts, he set about reckoning accounts. He must sell at least thirty mules to pay the cost of the capangas. A gang of bandits, he said to himself, nibbling at his mustache in a fury. But it wasn't finished, he mused. He would have his revenge, cost what it might! In a year, two years, in ten years' time: but have it he would.

He spat at his fox terrier as it was coming to bother him.

2. Monte Santo

WITH GOOD REASON Araujo da Costa postponed his vengeance for five or ten years. When pluck and will power are lacking, one likes to put off settlements of accounts for as long as possible. Savagery does not take the place of energy.

Some years passed, excellent years from every point of view for Araujo and the Maciels; because, anyhow, peace is preferable to war. Vicente's wife gave birth in the normal way to a son, whom they baptized Antonio.

Three negresses had sons by Araujo da Costa, who obstinately set himself against recognizing them.

The abolitionist campaign developed on a large plan with the symbolical slogan "Freedom of the Belly." The fazendeiros everywhere were setting free their mulatto children. A blast of human solidarity was blowing over the whole of the state of Ceará. Blacks, whites, mulattoes, half-castes or *cafuz* (the mixture of native Indian and Negro) were holding out the hand of friendship to each other. A new race was going to be born, one which would be a synthesis of three continents: Europe, Africa, and America.

Araujo da Costo remained insensible to this movement which was sweeping the whole of Brazil. He remained a traditionalist and slavemaster. Nevertheless, this formidable progressive pressure had the effect of calming him. By taking away from him the right to administer justice on his estates, the governor had deprived him of fifty per cent of his prestige. He submitted to it, promising a terrible revenge: for, although he had studied at Rio, he had not read Condorcet and did not believe in progress.

The Maciels consolidated their position during this period. They did not greatly develop their farmstead: for at this time they were trying to make a living, not a fortune. Vicente tried to have another child by his wife and had not succeeded.

"May God's will be done!" Miguel Carlos had said. "The main thing is that we have an heir."

"Why don't you get married?" Vicente had asked.

"I have my reasons," said Miguel.

He was never frank with his brother about it, but he once stated that he had an infectious disease and had too much family sense to father corrupted offspring.

This being so, Vicente, his wife, and the whole family brought all their love to bear on the only child, the hope of the Maciels: Antonio, who was reared in cotton wool.

He was a strange child with green eyes. He cried very little and slept through whole days. On seeing his broad, high forehead, Miguel Carlos had remarked: "He'll be an intelligent boy."

When the child reached his tenth year, Vicente engaged a mulatta from Fortaleza who taught him to read and write. Antonio seemed to have much aptitude for study. For hours he was absorbed in an old breviary printed in big type, the only working tool which the "governess" had brought with her. But the more he progressed, the more he became a dreamer and taciturn. At first Vicente had been very satisfied to see the child isolate himself at one end of the veranda and plunge himself into reading. He had even bought a second breviary for him, one printed in smaller type (these were the only books to be found in the region). At the end of some months, however, he began to be uneasy about his son's meditative bearing to the point that one day he said to him: "Just because you can read and write isn't a reason for ceasing to work."

Antonio had read in his breviary that children owe respect to their parents; and he obeyed. He would jump on a horse and go out to inspect their cattle in some valley. He became tired quickly. Then he would settle himself at the foot of a palm tree or boulder and for hours remain there in thought, looking at the blue expanse of sky and the arid immensity of the earth. What could be turning over in that brain nurtured on odds and ends of philosophy—some proverbs and a few elementary precepts? At times he was vexed with himself for feeling such horror for work, but how could it be otherwise if he preferred the litanies of the Virgin to the most beautiful horse on the fazenda? He was terribly clumsy at castrating calves, but he could recite from memory all of the *Gloria in Excelsis Deo* in Latin. He loved Latin; he did not understand it, but he had the impression that this strange language was opening horizons to him in the Kingdom of God. He had the feeling that it was the real language of the divinity. Could anyone conceive that God could speak in any other language but Latin? He certainly did not speak in Portuguese. Antonio worked unceasingly to learn Latin psalms in the hope that this would more easily throw open the gates of paradise to him. How could he occupy himself with those bulls and cows, those sugar canes, the cotton and manioc, while he felt himself irresistibly attracted by the mystery of this world? He would have liked not to eat or drink any more so that he could surrender himself to complete contemplation. All arid lands have produced beings of that kind. The prophets of Islam were emanations of the sands of the desert. Fertile regions produce the poets of love; but the desert is philosophical. In zones of abundance, there is the cult of life: in the arid zones, man asks himself why he lives.

When Antonio reached the age of sixteen, Miguel Carlos asked Vicente without beating about the bush whether the boy "had it."

"Why shouldn't he have it?" replied Vicente testily.

"His voice hasn't even changed."

"It will change," said Vicente, who had faith in his son.

Generally, when the son of a boss reached the age of puberty, he began to go with the negresses to blow off steam. Alas! Antonio did not appear to be inclined toward the pleasures of sex. Even the little daughter of the servant, so pleasing and pretty, did not seem to interest him—a fine girl, nevertheless, with well-shaped breasts. Miguel Carlos would have taken her if he had not been afraid of passing on his malady to Antonio. There was no danger: Antonio remained as lifeless as a cipher.

"Take away his books and throw the lot into the fire," said Miguel Carlos to Vicente one day, "or he'll become completely mad. These church things will turn his head."

Vicente was opposed to violence and brusque action and declared that Antonio would improve with time.

"He'd be much more in his place in a monastery than on a fazenda," Miguel Carlos insisted.

"All young men have dreamed of being a padre," replied Vicente.

Neither Vicente nor Miguel who, throughout their whole lives, had no other preoccupations than the breeding of cattle and the making of rum or flour or manioc, could imagine what was happening in that soul of Antonio, who was turned topsy-turvy by the enigma of the world and floundered in a hodgepodge of Christian principles without succeeding in establishing a logical hierarchy. In spite of many hours of prayers and reflection, Antonio did not yet know which was the gravest of the deadly sins. Was luxury more reprehensible than gluttony? Some of the deadly sins such as pride and sloth, did not hold his attention because he was guilty of them. He became terribly vain and professed a deep contempt for the men of the hinterland who spent their lives making the bulls mount the cows, coupling asses and mares, extracting the juice of sugar cane and in begetting children between two outings in the fields. Those people never had a moment in which to pray to God. He was always alone in the evening in front of the little rustic altar which he had made in his room and on which was enthroned a plaster statuette representing the Virgin with the child Jesus in her arms. Even his mother never thought to replace the candles.

The more he advanced in age, the more worried he became. All those problems, which presented themselves with increasing sharpness and remained without a solution, exasperated him. He would have liked to find other books which would have provided the key to his difficulties, but all that he discovered in the village was a little pornographic work with the title *How should one behave in marriage?* He was revolted by it. What did it matter to him whether or not a woman made water in front of her husband? How could human beings debase themselves to such discussions? He was as much nauseated as he was bewildered by it.

It was while all this was going on that an event happened which was to have a very great repercussion: he fled.

He did not go away for good but merely to take part in the pilgrimage of Monte Santo. It was nevertheless a flight of some importance, for it lasted nearly a month as it is a journey of twelve days on horseback from the fazenda of Formosa to Monte Santo.

It was in Quixeramobim one evening that he had heard about this ceremony at which were present, so they said, tens of thousands of people from the hinterland. At it the prophet Sylvio Silveira harangued the crowd and brought the annual message from the divinity.

The gathering took place every year on May 16th. It was now April: Antonio had time to get ready. He did not speak to anybody about his decision. He had a strong suspicion that his father would have forbidden him to go on this journey, but his mind was made up to act in full independence and to thumb his nose at paternal authority. God, he told himself, comes before parents. He was beginning to become fanatical.

On May 3rd in the afternoon he had a horse saddled. Vicente had gone out. Antonio did not go to take leave of his mother for fear of raising the alarm. He set out at a trot toward the river as if he were going to make a tour of inspection in the campo. At the place where the river could best be crossed by wading he met a herdsman from the fazenda busy rolling a cigarette in a piece of maize straw in the shade of a gigantic umbuseiro tree.

"When you get back this evening," Antonio said to him, "you'll tell my father that I've left for Monte Santo."

"Very good, senhor," replied the Negro humbly, rolling his eyes in astonishment.

Antonio drove his horse into the water and took the road for Pedra Branca. He was not easy in his mind, for he was on lands owned by the Araujos and, had he met a foreman of the fierce master of Boa Viagem, he might have been asked what he was doing in those parts. Fortunately he had prayed hard and found himself under the high protection of Providence. Neither that day, nor the next, nor the day after did he meet anybody. He avoided the sharecroppers' dwellings, slept in the open air, and reached Iguatu without let or hindrance, but with a great void in his stomach. One can scorn food with impunity: but the flesh has its requirements. He regaled himself with a good dish of beans and six bananas at the *botequim,* the little village store and café bar.

Half a day's journey to the south from Iguatu he joined two horsemen who also were on their way to Monte Santo. They were sharecroppers from that neighborhood: one was called Pedrosa, the other Ferreira. They were true hinterlanders, taciturn men: they could travel for miles and miles without uttering a word and, when they spoke, it did not interest Antonio, who did not understand how it was that men could discuss cattle, ants, bees, and cotton while following a sacred way. Nevertheless, they were obliging companions and they knew the route. They knew where to find fazendas which gave hospitality to pilgrims. This was the third time that they were going to Monte Santo.

"Is it beautiful?" Antonio asked.

"Magnificent. It is the most extraordinary pilgrimage in Brazil."

"You never saw the like," added Ferreira.

"And Sylvio Silveira?" inquired Antonio.

"He's hardly to be seen. There are too many people."

Antonio swore that he would see Sylvio Silveira at close hand. He wanted to know exactly what a prophet was, to see his bearing, his features and eyes, and to hear his voice.

In reality this Sylvio Silveira was a remarkable person. He was the son of a sharecropper of Chique-Chique, and also a natural mystic—one of those meditative offspring of regions of quartz and white sand which reflect the sunlight in a way to cause hallucinations. He had begun by preaching the gospel to the street Arabs in his own village, then to the men, and next he set out over the country to propagate the good word. He had never been ordained a priest and had never been received into any of the orders; he wore a homespun habit which he had made for him by a Turk at Joazeiro. He gave himself out as a prophet and for ten years assembled the hinterland people at Monte Santo. The official Church tolerated him because he fostered mysticism, for there were not enough monks to bring the benefits of religion to those populations of the vast northeastern regions of Brazil. In short, he was a bastard prophet; but he was recognized.

Coming from Bomfim, Antonio and his companions crossed the saddle of the sierra de Itabiuba late in the morning of May 15th. They stopped to contemplate the holy place. They caught sight on a little plateau framed in the mountains of the important little village with the two spires of its colonial church and the giant tamarind tree in its "Commercial Square." On the other side of the plateau the Sacred Way stood out, about a mile and a half in length, lined with twenty-five chapels gleaming in the sunshine: it went up the flank of the sierra making a contour of the highest peak in order to reach the *Alto de Santa Cruz* ("Height of the Holy Cross"), where the big chapel is, and in front of which rises an immense wooden cross standing out sharply by itself against the immaculate blue of the sky.

"It's up there Don Silveira preaches," said Pedrosa: "only those who get as far as the Height can hear him."

"I'll hear him," thought Antonio, "I'll go right up to the Height."

Down on the plain to the north of the village along the Cariaca River an enormous crowd was already encamped. The three pilgrims began to pick out the leather hats of the men of Ceará and Maranhão, the broad straw hats of the Bahians, the white, green, or red turbans of the women. As he did not notice any horses, Antonio asked:

"They didn't come on foot, did they?"

"The horses are on some pasture land over yonder in a hollow of the sierra," said Ferreira.

"And they can be caught again easily?"

"There's no stealing here. These people are penitents."

"I don't mean that," replied Antonio, "but the horses have to be found again."

Ferreira looked astonished. He could not know that Antonio had not the slightest aptitude as a herdsman and that he was very awkward at what they call there "doing the campo," that is, rounding up animals that are out grazing.

"I'll see to this matter. You can trust your animal to me," said Ferreira.

Antonio had never seen so many men and women gathered together. They were of all colors and races: whites, blacks, half-breeds, Indian-Negro hybrids, Indians, mulattoes. They were squatting in little round groups, chatting in the sunshine. Antonio saw two half-breeds walking among the groups telling their big beads which consisted of strung beans. He was very impressed by this. He had always been moved on seeing great strapping men at prayer. Further away he saw a group of Negroes in fits of laughter as they ate oranges and kissed the women. He spat. Ferreira had gone to lead the horses to the pasture.

"How will he find us again?" asked Antonio who had the feeling of being lost in this crowd.

"That's easy," replied Pedrosa. "People are in groups. Those from Ceará are recognized immediately."

They sat down on the hot, stony ground. A great calm filled the valley for, in spite of a child's whining here and there or an occasional burst of Negro laughter, the crowd was rapt and silent as they waited for the great event. From time to time urchins went past with baskets of oranges, bananas, or pineapples; for on that day the pilgrims ate only fruit. You do not take part in a procession of penitents gorged with food. The Cariaca River, with its crystal-clear water, sufficed to calm enervated stomachs.

"What a mix-up there is on that pasture land!" Antonio said.

"It's the same every year," replied Pedrosa, a fatalist. "They'll sort it all out."

And they settled down to sleep. As for Antonio, he contemplated the Sacred Way, the little white chapels strewn along the route which boldly mounted toward the *Alto,* the Height. What a man, that Silveira! he thought. What a labor to create that road! Truly Silveira had great vision. What he had done at Monte Santo could not fail to strike the imagination of the crowds which flocked there from every corner of the hinterland to travel the "Road to Heaven." Confronted with this grandiose work, Antonio felt himself very small and saw his dream of evangelization fade away. He would never achieve Silveira's stature.

He lay down on his back and slipped his hat over his face. As if the supine position favored the flight of his imagination, he resumed his daydreaming. More than ever he intended to follow a spiritual and religious career. In the state of Ceará, there was no Silveira. . . .

At that moment he heard near his ear a sound as of whispering which grew in volume. Puzzled, he raised his hat. An unknown man was urinating just beside him. He replaced his hat over his face, disgusted by the lower depths of the flesh.

When he awoke again the night cold was coming over them: the blue of the sky had become overshadowed while a vague red gleam was still trailing on the crest of the sierra de Itabiuba. The crowd had become completely silent. A star shone above the Alto de Santa Cruz. Soon afterwards the moon rose in the sky, enormous and near. The big chapel was resplendent in its whiteness and the little ones along the route in turn glittered as the moon was reaching the middle of the sky. Antonio experienced a tremor of emotion and enthusiasm, for under the moonlight the Sacred Way looked even more grandiose than in the sunshine. He was ready to yield himself to God, to the Virgin, to the Holy Spirit, or to any saint whatever in order to gain Paradise. He would like to have cried aloud his faith to all that crowd, but he feared the silence. As he was in a state of great excitement, he felt himself on fire and he went to the river to drink from his cupped hands. The water was cool: it had already been freshened by the night air. Antonio felt an appeasement of the flesh. He went back to his companions, stretched himself on the ground and fell asleep under the stars beside Pedrosa.

He woke up before daybreak, for his impatience was working within him even during sleep. He felt highly strung: his head was heavy and his intestines were rumbling in a disturbing manner. He felt a weakness in his limbs and wondered whether he would ever reach the Height of Santa Cruz.

He was the only one on his feet while dawn was coming and he looked around at the sleeping crowd: he did not see a face; one would have said that here thousands of parcels of rags were scattered along the bank of the river. Then the sun rose. All those rags shook themselves and out of them came men and women who began talking and gesticulating.

Suddenly a big colored man from Bahia shouted:

"He has arrived!"

The news spread from one end of the plain to the other.

"He has arrived! Look!"

The doors of the big chapel had just opened. The prophet was there. The crowd became jubilant as if all hopes had been fulfilled. A Negro began to sing a *choro*—one of those popular Brazilian folk songs with a lilting tune—but one of the men who went around telling their beads (they had reappeared) made him be quiet. The time was not one for rejoicings but for penitence. The ascent of the Holy Way is not made by dancing and singing. It is made by walking with bare feet on burning stones and reciting litanies.

Antonio would have liked to begin the ascent immediately so as to get to the head of the procession, but Pedrosa told him that this was forbidden. He must walk with his group and their time of departure was only given at half-past eight by two of Silveira's acolytes who were at the foot of the mountain.

"I will see Silveira," Antonio kept repeating to himself. "I'll see him at any cost."

When the procession began to move forward, the group of people from Pernambuco were at the head. It was their turn this year. But the people from Ceará followed after them.

"I should like to go to the head," Antonio said to his companions.

"Don't be backward. Go ahead," he was told, "we'll find each other in the Ceará group after the ceremony."

He slipped forward toward the head of the procession. The sun was oppressive and the slope was steep: heavy beads of perspiration ran down his body. At each of the little chapels a halt was made and they recited three *Ave Marias*. Antonio regretted not having eaten a few bananas before setting out on this climb. His stomach was crying out and his bowels were going into all sorts of contortions. At the third chapel he could not hold out and he relieved himself noisily at the side of the road as the litanies of the Virgin Mary rose to the limpid sky. He would certainly have reached the head of the column at the sixth or seventh chapel had the stones on the route not been so burning hot and the crowd not been so dense. At the twelfth, however, he was almost reaching his goal when he had a fainting fit. He felt dizzy and collapsed. On recovering his senses at first he saw nothing but blue, the intense blue of the sky. He realized that he was stretched out on his back on the threshold of one of the white chapels and, beside him, the tide of pilgrims still continued to move upward. Some of them looked at him with astonishment, others with eyes full of fright as if they were seeing a damned person struck down by the arm of God. Gradually he again got a grip on his thought. "I want to see Sylvio Silveira." He turned over, rose to his knees and straightened himself up. He felt his limbs weak, a feebleness in the joints, but in his head an iron will was affirming itself. He flung himself like a madman on the stony road to take his place again: he jostled the penitents, scorched his feet on the pebbles. He was allowed to pass: he had such a look of hallucination that the pilgrims expected a miracle.

He did not rejoin the Pernambucans until shortly before reaching the Height. He was sweating like a dock laborer and, with his crazy look and disheveled hair, was taken for a man possessed.

The procession reached the Height. It was a narrow platform at the very top of the peak with the chapel on one side and the great wooden Cross on the other. At the foot of the latter some stones had been piled up to form a little mount. It was this spot that Antonio chose for his observation post. From there he would see Sylvio Silveira face to face. In fact, to the left of the chapel door some planks had been placed on two trestles. This was the prophet's platform: it was hardly a dozen yards from the Cross and stood opposite to it. The crowd massed as best they could on this small space, but the majority of the pilgrims remained on the road. The last of them had not come farther than the fifteenth chapel.

Antonio was eagerly watching the door of the little church whence the prophet was to loom into sight. A triumphant radiance came

from the sun full in the sky. Far away in the depth of the valley
was the gleaming-red Cariaca looking like a golden ribbon casually
abandoned on the reddish soil. And farther away the sierra showed
against the sky its row of sharply rugged teeth.

All of a sudden *he* loomed into view. He was a small rotund man
almost bald, with a smooth round face like a watermelon, little eyes
under thick eyebrows, a very small mouth with something astonish-
ingly sensual about it, a nose like a ball and as red as a radish. He
was clad in a thick brown homespun habit, gathered in at the waist
by a knotted cord. He walked toward the platform, tucked up his
habit, put one knee on the planks and hoisted himself up in the
everyday manner of a mason. This entrance on the stage disappointed Antonio. Before then he had in his mind a picture of Sylvio
Silveira as a tall, thin man with a long face, a big forehead, and
inspiring eyes. Yet he was a tubby little man who looked rather
comic. And that way of his of climbing onto the platform! Antonio's
sense of dignity received a shock.

But already the prophet was lifting up his arms toward heaven.
"My very dear brethren in Jesus Christ!"

He had a low hollow voice, so deep that Antonio felt its resonance
right down to his stomach.

"On this solemn day," said Silveira, "on the threshold of the formidable events which are being prepared for us, I invite you first
of all to render homage to the Virgin Mary who remains as the
supreme hope of the men of the hinterland. *Ave Maria!*"

The chapel hand bell began to tinkle as the crowd recited the
prayer. That set the pilgrims going; it prepared them to hear a
discourse lasting one hour under the sun.

When the bell stopped tinkling, Sylvio Silveira rolled up his
sleeves and began to thunder against the country which was rotten
and about to make the acquaintance of fire and flood; against those
who propagated republican ideas, directly inspired by Satan;
against those men who slept with thirty-six women who gave their
bodies for a pineapple or a handful of beans; against the urchins
who lent themselves to the desires of men fallen into the most degrading vice. His eloquence became more and more violent as he
continued speaking. He attacked everything with a savage energy
which compelled the penitents to bow their heads. Then he de-

scribed the tortures of hell, the tongues torn out, the men and women burned alive, the bodies flogged with leather thongs furnished with nails. In order to escape these terrible punishments there was one method only: sacrifice, privations. "Blessed are those who suffer," said Christ. He expanded at great length on the need for suffering.

Antonio did not lose one of those words, and the ideas crushed into his brain in a deluge. He would have liked to put some questions to the prophet. He would have liked to retain, to fix in his memory all the speaker said, but Silveira spoke of so many things that one became utterly bewildered.

The prophet perspired steadily. From time to time he seized his homespun habit and on several occasions raised it to cool his chest. At last, after having dealt severely with them and threatened them for more than an hour, he held out his arms to give them a blessing.

"You, only you who are here today," he cried out, "have merit in God's eyes. You only who are here today will be forgiven your sins because you have imposed the sacrifice on yourselves. Blessed be ye, my brethren! *Gloria in Excelsis Deo!*"

The pilgrims raised their heads: they knew it was the end of the discourse. Every year Sylvio Silveira ended with the same words. Antonio wanted to rush toward the prophet, but was prevented by a crowd so dense that no kind of movement was possible. When he succeeded in getting through to the door of the chapel, after elbowing his way vigorously, Sylvio Silveira had disappeared: the folding doors were closed. Against them had been placed a big packing case into which the pilgrims threw their trifling contributions of money. All the penitents, a tall Negro informed him, must pass in front of that case. He who gives nothing does not benefit from the forgiveness. Antonio had only a milreis—about a shilling—in his pocket: he threw it in shamefacedly. He had not foreseen that indulgences were bought. That was not written in the breviaries. Now he dared not try to see Sylvio Silveira: he felt himself more ignorant than any one among all those penitents. He was humiliated by not knowing the conventions.

He dug his way into the column of pilgrims which was going down (the one which had paid) while another went up (that which had to settle the account).

As he unfortunately did not know the pasture ground and, furthermore, could not have found his horse again among thousands of others, he had to await the return of his companions. He sat down on the bank of the river. The plain which bordered the Cariaca now presented an extraordinary animation. The Negroes, once their sins were forgiven, had again begun to laugh, sing, and dance: men on horseback surged up from all sides. Antonio wondered where they had gone to find their horses.

In the end, after nearly two hours, Pedrosa and Ferreira appeared. They had followed the upward procession at their ease without hurrying; and in the same way they had come down at their ease. Ferreira was not long about bringing back the horses. All three men jumped into the saddle and set out again.

The north route was already congested with a multitude of horsemen who ambled along slowly, like people who have completed their task and have nothing further to do. It was very necessary to take one's place in the queue.

"Well!" said Pedrosa. "You saw Sylvio Silveira? What a man!"

"Yes, indeed, what a man!" replied Antonio.

They did not speak again until they came to Bomfim. At that point Antonio declared that he was going to stop for a day or so, because his belly was on fire like a thatched roof under the sun, his stomach was contracted, and his head a vacuum. But his companions declared that they would wait for him: he could not undertake the journey alone in the open country in that state. Next morning Antonio said that he felt well enough for another stage. They gave him some lime juice mixed with bicarbonate of soda to calm his dysentery, and set out.

It was a journey without incident under an exhausting sun. His companions took leave of him a little before reaching Iguatu and went back to their farms. He finished the trip alone, a prey to apprehension which was perhaps of death. He felt discouraged, his mind unbalanced. Never had life seemed so stupid to him.

Sad news awaited him on his return to the fazenda. He arrived there toward ten o'clock in the morning. The moment he pushed open the barrier of the corral, a Negro ran to notify Vicente who appeared on the veranda, looking grave. Antonio did not fear his father: he knew that he was gentle and conciliatory. So he went forward calmly, his soul at ease.

"Good morning," he said.

"Good morning. Where do you come from?"

"From Monte Santo."

"Your mother died while you've been away," said Vicente in a hard voice.

"What?" cried Antonio, staring wide-eyed. "My mother?"

"She is dead," Vicente repeated. "She has had a complication."

Appendicitis. At that time in that place it could not be treated.

Antonio threw his riding whip on the ground and collapsed on the bench holding his head between his hands. What had he done that God should inflict such a blow upon him? He had never spoken very much with his mother. In the hinterland, men paid little attention to women. He experienced the suffering which wrings the heart the first time misfortune is met. Then, during that same night, a bright spot shone out: Sylvio Silveira's pronouncement: "Blessed are those who suffer."

Because of that, because he was overcome by great suffering, Antonio did not weep.

3. Sobral

FOR SIX YEARS life flowed on without change at the fazenda of Formosa. Peace seemed to have been finally established with the Araujos. As for the death of Vicente's wife, it did not bring any change in the course of their daily existence (women take so small a place!). It had, however, the effect of greatly increasing Antonio's mysticism; he became more and more of a hermit, more and more taciturn, and less and less of a farmer.

"No doubt about it, he's mad," said Miguel Carlos to Vicente. "You'll have to have another child besides that one."

"Why don't you yourself marry?"

"Me, it's different. I'm suffering from a malady which rules out children."

"You haven't yet got over it?"

"It never finishes. You think you're rid of it and back it comes. So, there's only one thing to be done: you must get married again."

"It's easy for you to talk of it."

"Yes, yes! Not with an old woman. With a young one. Matured women have soft children. One such is enough for us."

Some weeks after this conversation Miguel Carlos had returned to Formosa with his sister Helena to help in marking the cattle. It was in June. They had spent the evening working out the number of beasts they would take into the town, the number of those which must be marked. They had gone to bed toward ten o'clock so as to be fresh and ready for the next day's work.

It was a little before daybreak when an unknown voice in the corral called out several times:

"Vicente Maciel! Vicente Maciel!"

The hard authoritative voice did not announce anything good. Vicente went out on the veranda, for he was not lacking in courage. Through the very dense fog he saw in the middle of the courtyard the silhouette of a horseman:

"Who goes there?" he said.

"We come on behalf of Araujo da Costa. You know what that signifies?"

"What do you want?"

"Don't try to resist. Vicente Maciel! the fazenda is surrounded. Give yourselves up and we won't do you any harm. We are merely charged with evicting you."

"Damned scoundrels!"

"Keep calm, Vicente Maciel. Otherwise Siqueira will give the order to attack. And there's a hundred of us!"

Vicente partly opened the door and called Miguel Carlos.

"What's going on?" the latter asked.

"The Araujos have encircled the fazenda and are asking us to give ourselves up."

"I'll show them who I am," Miguel shouted in a rage.

He seized a gun and appeared in the doorway. Vicente barred his way with his outstretched arm.

"No! No!" he said. "Hold on. Don't fire. They're a hundred and we'll be massacred."

"You'll be massacred anyhow!"

"No. They say that, if we surrender, our lives will be saved. They only want to drive us out of here. We must yield. We can have our revenge later."

"The gang of bandits! Wait. We'll shoot down one. We'll see whether there's a hundred of them, as they say."

But Vicente drew himself up in front of Miguel.

"You'll not do that!" he said. "You're not alone. Stop! Wait!"

Miguel pushed him aside roughly and was about to put his gun to his shoulder when Vicente, carried away by an irresistible force, threw himself on him, tore the gun from his hands and threw it into the corral. Miguel sprang on his brother and tried to catch him by the throat.

"Coward!" he yelled in his face.

Vicente tried to push him off with his long arms.

"Shut up!" he said, panting. "You don't know what you're doing."

During this brief dispute, the horseman had called out "*Vamos!*" and now there were at least ten horsemen in the corral.

"It's all up," said Miguel Carlos letting his arms fall. "We're done for. You wanted it."

"You see quite well that there was nothing else to be done. Look."

Vicente pointed to the corral full of horsemen, each with a weapon in his hand.

"If they had wanted to kill us, they'd already have done so," he added.

Antonio had just appeared like a specter on the threshold of the door.

"Well, are you agreed?" shouted one of the horsemen.

"We're coming," replied Vicente.

He told Antonio to call Helena and they went down the veranda steps to give themselves up to the assailants. Two half-breeds approached them warily, fearing one of those desperate leaps so frequent among men of the tropics.

They felt them to see whether they had any weapons, removing the knife each man had in his belt. When it came to Antonio's turn, they did not find a knife.

"You're hiding it!" one of the half-breeds said in a threatening tone.

"I haven't any knife," Antonio replied calmly.

The hands of the captives were tied with leather thongs.

Siqueira had arrived and was proudly cutting capers on his horse. He was gloating over his revenge. This was going to cost old Araujo a nice sum. For so successful an operation he would have to be forthcoming with his money.

When the group set out walking, preceded by a dozen horsemen and followed by about fifty armed Negroes, the morning mist had dispersed and the sun was filling its place with light. The birds disported themselves against the limpid sky, wheeling about in joy and freedom.

When they reached the fork of the roads to Boa Viagem and the northwest, the caravan took the northern direction on an order from Siqueira.

"I told you, I did, that they'd get us," said Miguel to Vicente.

"No doubt they'll leave us in the sierra," Vicente replied with confidence.

Helena's face was savage and resolute: "The gang of rascals!" she muttered between her teeth. "Blessed are those who suffer!" Antonio was thinking. "They're going to kill us," thought Miguel Carlos. "It all might have been worse," Vicente said to himself.

They marched all day under the sun without food. On arrival at Sobral toward nine o'clock at night they were tired out, aching all over and almost at the end of their tether. They stopped at the entrance to the town.

"Sit along the side of that ditch. You're going to be given something to eat," Siqueira said to them.

They did as they were told and sat down in a line; first the four Maciels, then the twelve Negro laborers and the two servant women.

Vicente was groaning. Miguel Carlos and Helena were silent. Antonio was praying.

Four men with weapons in their hands mounted guard near them. The others had gone into the village.

An hour later two Negroes brought cooking pots and served each of the prisoners with a ladleful of maize flour mixed with some black beans: a consistent paste, which was poured into their hands.

It was a very starry night but there was no moon. From the village came a hullabaloo of voices, with a burst of laughter rising in it from time to time. No doubt Siqueira was regaling his troops with rum to celebrate the success.

Miguel Carlos was wondering why they had been taken to Sobral. He himself had always been a man who favored immediate settlement of accounts. The uncertainty in which they were being kept about their fate set his nerves on edge: he suspected some sadistic maneuver on the part of the capanga. Turning toward one of the sentries who stood a few yards from him, he asked casually:

"Comrade, where's the boss taking us to?"

"Don't know," the man said in a tone of voice which did not invite conversation.

Miguel went back to his reflections. Looking at his tied hands, he felt a rebelliousness of terrific violence rise within him. He was ready to spring on the sentry. Oh, if only there had been four men like himself! But there were only Helena and himself who would have dared to attempt an escape. Nevertheless, he did not give in; he persisted in his efforts to find a plan to get out of this trap.

The night rolled on with a terrifying slowness. They had the feeling that the stars were fixed, that they themselves would never budge again and that they would be frozen stiff there in that icy-cold night.

Then Siqueira turned up again accompanied by a dozen men. He was reeling and the men were chattering loudly among themselves.

"Stand up!" he shouted at the prisoners. "Get into line along the ditch."

"I was right that he would have his own revenge on us around the corner," Miguel thought as he felt his heart shrink. As he got up, he touched Helena's elbow.

"This is it," he muttered.

"Good-by, Miguel," she said calmly.

"Good-by."

Siqueira's ten men had already lined up in front of them. He felt the need to justify himself somewhat:

"As for me," he said to them in a thick voice, "I'm carrying out Araujo da Costa's orders. You know Araujo da Costa? He's a damned old fool, but he pays well. Last time you beat me. This time I've got you. Anyhow, I'm going to get you. Come on, men!"

The ten men brought their guns to their shoulders as best they could, for the rum had softened their limbs.

"Fire!" roared Siqueira.

The night was shot through by a flash, torn by the bursts of flame. There were four more reports: this was the sentries who were lending a hand; they shot down the Negroes who remained standing after the first volley.

"That's something like work," Siqueira wound up. "Araujo may well pay for it. Zeca," he added, turning to his "second in command," a thin, lithe little man from Pernambuco, "See if they're all dead."

After which he led his men toward the village.

Miguel Carlos had allowed himself to fall backwards like an inanimate mass but he had not been touched. He merely felt his shoulders hurt. Helena had fallen on him. She must have been well hit, for he felt a warm liquid running on his belly. Miguel forced himself not to make the slightest movement; he had heard Siqueira's order to finish off the wounded. A few steps away some Negroes were emitting the death rattle, but the rattles faded one after the other. That's Zeca finishing them off with the dagger, he thought. What was he to do when this man Zeca reached him? He would have liked to push Helena's body aside in order to have a little freedom of movement. Even with his hands tied, he felt himself strong enough to kill that fellow Zeca by felling him unexpectedly with his fists. But the body was heavy and he saw his approaching shadow. He felt rather than saw him turn over the bodies of Vicente and Antonio. Then Helena's was rolled over his face. He closed his eyes: he felt himself being pulled by the legs and he let himself loose like a rag. There was a moment of awful silence. Some stones rolled down. "He's climbing up on the embankment," thought Miguel. He waited with beating heart; he could hardly breathe now with Helena's dead breasts crushing his face. At last, after a long pause, he decided to push the corpse gently aside and ended by turning it over. He gave a quick glance around him. The place was deserted. He got up on his knees. At that moment a very feeble voice called: "Miguel!" It was like a voice from the beyond, almost unreal. Nonplussed, he remained still. Then the cry

was resumed in a very faint voice: "Miguel!" He recognized
Antonio's voice. He crawled over the body of Vicente and saw
his nephew under a Negro.

"Are you hit?" he asked.

"No."

"Let's get out of here. Come quickly."

He helped his nephew to free himself; he shook Vicente, who
was quite dead.

"Follow me," he said to Antonio. "They've tied their horses over
yonder under the shed at the entrance to the village. We've each of
us to take one and make off, but we must move quickly."

Antonio had not Miguel's physical strength, but the fear of death
and the instinct of self-preservation filled him with the energy of a
cowboy. A great clamor of voices was still going up in the village.
The gaiety still continued: the conscience of the hired killers was
at peace; their task had been accomplished.

It did not take Miguel and Antonio long to untether two horses.
They sprang into the saddles and sped into the night at a gallop.

Two of the hired assassins who were standing on a doorstep
caught sight of them just as they were making off.

"Siqueira!" they shouted. "Somebody has stolen the horses!"

They all ran to the shed. Two animals had in fact disappeared.
This was an unusual occurrence. It caused Siqueira to sober up
immediately.

"Are they all quite dead?" he asked in a threatening manner.

"I examined them, boss," said Zeca. "I finished off six who were
slightly hit."

"You're certain?"

"Absolutely certain."

Siqueira hesitated for a moment, then he went toward the ditch.

"You can't see anything in that," he said, after glancing over it,
"take them out on the ground."

The men set to work. They were drunk and they fumbled with
their hands. They had to work together—three of four at a time—
to heave the corpses out. When they were all out, Siqueira counted
them.

"Fourteen," he said. "Two of them have cleared off."

"Impossible," said Zeca. "They were all dead."

"That's a good story!" Siqueira spat at him. "Where are the Maciels?"

When they had ascertained for a certainty that Miguel and Antonio had disappeared, Siqueira slowly drew a pistol from his belt, leveled it at Zeca and sent a bullet straight into his face.

"Three men to catch the fugitives," he directed.

Three Pernambucans whom he had taken with him to fulfill his sinister task stepped forward.

"In the saddle," Siqueira commanded. "And bring them back or I'll down you like this fool."

He kicked Zeca's body.

"Which way?" one of the Pernambucans asked timidly.

"Take the road for Tamburil," said Siqueira. "They'll go back home."

He had guessed correctly. After taking their bearings quickly— they were accustomed to do this—Miguel Carlos had led Antonio onto the trail for Tamburil. At the end of a quarter of an hour's gallop, they stopped and got down from their horses. It was still night. On hands and knees Miguel Carlos found a sharp stone with which he cut the leather thong that bound Antonio's hands. That took a fairly long time. Once freed, Antonio untied the thong which held Miguel's hands. They got into their saddles again and set off once more at a rapid trot. They did not speak. One might think that after so terrible an adventure anybody would feel the need to relieve his feelings. This is not true. A man is so flattened, so disintegrated by such happenings that thought is stunned. Great griefs are silent.

First they crossed a plain covered with thorny thickets, then they went over a little sierra, which was not very high, and down into an arid valley. In the east a red glow in the sky announced daybreak. The stars faded out. A filtered clearness invaded space. They found themselves on the bank of a river. The ford was quite visible: they went toward it. For the time of year there was still much water: it came up to the horses' withers. When they had reached the other side, Miguel Carlos glanced back at the road they had taken and it was then that he caught sight of the three Pernambucans out on their quest.

"Look," he said to Antonio, "we're spotted."

As Antonio did not reply, he added:

"We're going to wait for them here."

"We have no weapons," remarked Antonio.

"What about it? We're fit and well anyhow. We must fight for it, and the sooner the better. We must finish this business. Is that so, or isn't it?"

Despite his empty stomach, the emotional upheaval of that failed execution with the accompanying horror of those corpses lying in the ditch, and the fatigue of their journey across the sierra, Miguel Carlos had maintained all his composure and energy. He felt that he was about to play his last card. He was ready. One against three (he did not attach any importance to Antonio). It was all clear; he had no fear. He took cover in a thicket near the steep bank and ordered Antonio to keep behind him.

"Try to find yourself a piece of wood which would serve as a bludgeon," he said to him.

The horses were hidden in a thicket: "All right, so long as they don't whinny," said Miguel Carlos to himself.

The Pernambucans walked into the ford in Indian file, unconcernedly. They were still drunk.

As soon as the first man reached the steep bank, Miguel Carlos sprang on him like a panther and pulled the gun from his hands. Before the man had realized what was happening, a shot rang out and the second of the pursuers collapsed on his horse which reared in the water. The third fired at Miguel, but the latter had flung himself behind the first man's horse which received the full discharge in his belly. It fell with its rider in the water. With amazing agility the Pernambucan jumped on the bank; but Antonio, coming to the rescue, struck him a vigorous blow on the head with his bludgeon. In the river, the last of the pursuers tried to pull his horse half around: he did not succeed. Miguel had thrown himself on the man struck down by Antonio and had torn off his cartridge pouch and reloaded his gun. With one shot he killed the man who was trying to get out of the river.

For all that, the man lying on the bank was not dead. He recovered his senses and shook his arm feebly, still suffering from the blow of the bludgeon.

"Stop! Stop! I give in," he groaned.

With one blow from the butt of his gun, Miguel Carlos smashed his skull. He struck him two more blows by way of precaution.

"Die, you swine!" he said.

Antonio watched this spectacle with a look of terror in his eyes, but he had not dared to intervene. He was afraid of Miguel Carlos. Nevertheless, this ruthlessness against a fallen man revolted him. He did not understand hate, because his heart was not solid enough for hatred. Miguel Carlos sat down in the dust out of breath.

"Push him into the water so that I won't see any more of him," he said to Antonio, pointing to the Pernambucan's body.

Antonio did not budge: he felt an overwhelming horror about touching corpses. Then Miguel Carlos stood up brusquely.

"So what? You're afraid?" he sneered.

He was about to seize the dead man when Antonio yelled: "Miguel!"

He held his uncle by the arm. "Look out!" he said, pointing with his finger at one of the legs of the corpse. Miguel looked: a short thick snake was slithering along the trousers and its flat head appeared on the belly. For, in the Brazilian hinterland, man is harassed not only by man but by wild beasts, reptiles, insects, poisonous brambles, and mosquitoes which kill.

"Give me your bludgeon," said Miguel.

Antonio held it out. Miguel seized it and killed the snake. . . . He pushed the two bodies into the river and said:

"Let's get out of here. I've had enough of this."

Once on his horse, Miguel no longer felt any fatigue. He stirred his horse with his heel and set him at a gallop.

"We'll be at Tamburil before evening," he said.

Antonio kept up the hard pace with difficulty; he was utterly exhausted. All his limbs were aching and his raw buttocks compelled him to stand in his stirrups. He bent his will to hold out, to dominate exhaustion and pain. Blessed are those who suffer!

At nightfall they went into the corral of the fazenda at Tamburil. All the laborers, Negroes, and mulattoes, ran forward to welcome them. They looked inquiringly at them with anxious eyes. They were glad to see the boss return, but their apprehensiveness was greater than their joy. The foreman, João Pio, a half-breed from Maranhão, expressed what they all thought:

"We have heard about that affair at Formosa. We didn't know what had become of you. We thought you were dead."

"The others are dead," replied Miguel Carlos sadly.

"The others?"

"Yes, Helena, Vicente, and the laborers."

"And what happened to the laborers?"

"They lined us up along a ditch and shot us—at Sobral."

Negroes have an astonishing faculty for expressing horror with their eyes. Miguel could see that they were overcome with terror.

"And how did you manage to escape?" asked the half-breed, who was more composed than the others.

"I'll tell you that later. It's too long a story. I'm starving with hunger. I'd like to drink a glass of rum and eat."

They went up on the veranda and reached the kitchen. While the servant woman was reheating the black beans and *fubá* (a local cereal), Miguel was giving his orders to João Pio:

"Don't let us lose any time. We may be attacked from one moment to the next. How many guns have we?"

"Eight."

"And cartridges?"

"There's quite a lot. And we can make more. We have powder and grapeshot."

"Set to at once. Work quickly, for there are many of them."

When the foreman went out, the beans and maize were hot and the servant prepared two good helpings of the dish known as *feijoada*. Antonio had vanished and Miguel went to look for him on the veranda. He was not there. But on glancing into the dining room, Miguel saw him on his knees in front of the little Christ hanging on the wall.

"Come and eat," Miguel said to him. "You'll thank the saints when you've filled your stomach."

While they were eating, the foreman returned. He was curious to know how they had escaped the fusillade.

"They were all drunk," Miguel told him. "Some of them aimed too high."

The inhabitants of the fazenda at Tamburil spent the night awaiting an attack which did not come. Siqueira had waited in vain for the return of the three men and the escaped prisoners. All the others declared that they did not want to go on with it. They were afraid. They took Miguel Carlos for a sorcerer.

4. The Revenge

ARAUJO DA COSTA could not have conceived such a revenge. First of all, he did not believe that any retaliation on the part of the Maciels was possible. He considered that they had been well brought to heel and that they would not begin again so soon. He himself felt ready to give up this struggle, not because he felt any remorse for the crime he had caused to be committed, but because he had had enough of being hoaxed and exploited by the capangas. Siqueira had come and told him that the whole family of Maciels had been executed and he had paid up. He had paid royally. It was not until some days afterwards that he heard from a Negro that Miguel Carlos and Antonio had missed being massacred. The news put him in a rage and he had ordered the Negro to be given fifty lashes because he had not spoken up sooner. Then he had calmed down, trying to convince himself that after such a lesson the Maciels would lie low.

Furthermore, Araujo da Costa continued to refuse to acknowledge the evolution of ideas. He considered that social conditions in Ceará, as he had known them from the time of his youth, must remain unalterable. He was always an antiabolitionist and antirepublican.

Now at that period the republican and antislavery campaigns were in full swing at Fortaleza under the inspiration of Araujo's wife's own brother, Vasco Lima de Vegas. Some thousands of colored people and mulattoes had already been liberated by certain fazendeiros who put their ideals before their immediate interests; and the movement was proving to be irresistible.

Miguel Carlos followed attentively the growth of this movement.

In all the botequims (cafés) at which he called, he discussed with
ardor the problem of the liberation of the colored men. Many of
the Negroes and mulattoes, accustomed to slavery from childhood,
were afraid of freedom. They wondered what would become of
them, for they had no rule of conduct to guide them when left to
their own responsibilities. Hence Miguel Carlos was favorably
known, by name, to the Republican Committee at Fortaleza.

He presented himself there on June 14th.

Araujo da Costa would never have thought that Miguel Carlos
could put in an appearance at a committee in the state capital
and be received there, for he underestimated the intelligence of
the half-breed and underrated the importance of the political movement which was turning the whole country topsy-turvy. But under a
rough, gross and brutal exterior, Miguel Carlos concealed a wily
mind which was not lacking in subtlety. Nor in logic. His reasoning
had been simple: "I'm not strong enough to down an Araujo. But
Araujo has against him all the republicans and abolitionists. I am a
man of good reputation with these people. I'm going to stir them
up against him. I'll down him through politics."

Having made this decision, he jumped on his horse and set out
for Fortaleza. However, when the moment came for him to appear
before the committee, he wavered. He wondered whether he would
be put off with a few of those curt phrases with which they address
you in the government offices. If, as a consequence, Araujo became
aware of the step he had taken, it would be a war to the knife.

On several occasions he had passed by outside the committee
rooms, which were installed in a little house on the Rua Guaranis.
Through the open window he had caught sight of a young man
sitting alone at a table covered with papers: he was engaged in
enjoying a cigarette. When Miguel passed by again, he was busy
writing. "But where's the committee?" Miguel Carlos asked himself. This building seemed to be completely lacking in activity and
the street, under the torrid sun, was deserted. In the end he hitched
up his trousers and decided to go in.

Whenever he went into a botequim Miguel was full of go, his
demeanor was free and easy and often aggressive. But in this place
he felt ill at ease and awkward, and he turned his leather hat slowly
between his fingers.

"I should like to speak to the chairman of the committee," he managed to say.

"Who are you?" the young man asked calmly—an adolescent with a milk-white face the pallor of which was further accentuated by shining black hair and eyes.

"Miguel Carlos, of Tamburil."

"And what do you want with the chairman?"

"I want to speak to him about that Sobral business."

The young man gave a start of interest. He eyed Miguel distrustfully from head to foot.

"You have details about the crime at Sobral?"

"I was present at it."

"You were there?"

The young man did not conceal his astonishment, for at Fortaleza the story went around that all the prisoners had been shot. But surely the man in front of him could not be one of the band of hired murderers?

"And what were you doing there?"

"I'm one of the Maciel family."

"Just a moment."

The young man went through to the next room and came out almost immediately.

"You haven't a weapon?" he asked.

"My knife."

"Go in."

The room into which he introduced Miguel was cool: it looked on the garden. It was furnished with a desk and two chairs. A very thin man in a white shirt was sitting on the ledge of the window, through which came a heavy perfume of roses and orange flowers. The bones of his face were so conspicuous that one would have thought he had been suffering from hunger for weeks.

"Sit down," he said to Miguel.

He himself stood up and came and sat at the table.

The conversation lasted more than an hour. Miguel had to give an account of the attack on the fazenda and of the massacre at Sobral; he had to go over events leading up to the incident but, of course, carefully omitting to say that it was he who had shot down Araujo's father. When he thought that he had enough particulars, the chairman of the committee said:

"I'll need you again tomorrow morning to make a deposition before the chief of police. We must put an end to this series of crimes for all time. Either the supporters of slavery must submit or we shall kill them. Be here tomorrow at ten o'clock."

Miguel Carlos felt lighthearted as he left the premises. The sky was blue, the sun was glowing red, and he felt a sensation as if his whole being was penetrated by the light. He went to drink a pint of rum in a botequim in Tupys Street but, contrary to his habit, did not enter into conversation with anybody. He shut himself up with his thoughts. He dared not believe in the reality of what he had heard. So the chief of police was going to hear his deposition? Would the republicans be strong enough to arrest that man Araujo? All this gave him something to think about, and yet it was almost unbelievable to anybody who had known the power of the master of Boa Viagem. Nevertheless, Miguel could not but tell himself that, if he had come to Fortaleza, it was in the secret hope of having the man arrested. Now that he was achieving his aim, it seemed to him an enormity. For the republic was not yet proclaimed. Perhaps the chairman of the committee imagined that he was stronger than he really was. All these thoughts kept passing through his mind until ten o'clock next morning. When he put in an appearance at the republican offices, the thin man was taking a breath of fresh air with his secretary on the threshold of the front door.

"Very good," he said to Miguel, "you're punctual. We're going immediately."

He went to find his hat, a magnificent Panama, and they set out toward the police barracks. It was a one-story building, dreary and tumbledown, with a wide main entrance. They were taken into a dilapidated office and it was there, in front of a dirty table covered with inkstains, that Miguel had to make his deposition. The chief of police, a big stout man with hard eyes and the fists of a boxer, wore a navy blue uniform; his tunic was open, for the heat was already violent. He stood beside the chairman of the committee; a clerk sat at the table. It did not progress quickly, this deposition, because the scribe wrote it all out in longhand. Miguel did not like this. He liked to tell his story in one stretch. "Go easy, go easy," said the chief of police. At last the document was completed. The chief of police read it over again in a loud voice.

"Is that all right?" he asked.

"That's right."

"Sign."

When Miguel had signed, the chief of police turned toward the thin man with the document in his hand.

"Do I carry this out immediately?"

"At once."

While the chief betook himself into the courtyard of the barracks, Miguel and the chairman of the committee went out into the corridor.

"We'll wait and see the troop set out," said the thin man.

"They're going to arrest Araujo?" Miguel asked timidly, wishing for a confirmation of his thoughts.

"You just don't imagine that we're going to continue tolerating incidents such as that which occurred at Sobral! Are we civilized or savages? But," he added, "don't talk about it. This must be settled without any fuss."

In the courtyard there was a great bustle. Horses were being led from the stables: men were fetching saddles, others were slipping on their tunics. In less than ten minutes the troop was ready. The chief of police gave his final instructions and, with a lieutenant at the head of the column, the riders set out.

Miguel felt a sort of pride as he watched them file past. It was he who had put all that in motion. Fifty horsemen, all erect in their blue uniforms with beautiful well-furbished German carbines slung across their backs. And picked horses. All this gave an impression of order, strength, and justice. Miguel would have liked to accompany them but had to content himself with returning to the pal who had offered him hospitality and lived in a shaky little cabin on the Baturité road. At first he intended to return immediately to Tamburil but, on reflection, decided that it was better to wait for two of three days. Thus he could return by Quixeramobim and find out what the people there were thinking. So he prolonged his stay and then again decided to prolong it for a few more days until the troop of mounted police should return. By exercising patience for a few days, he should know for certain whether Araujo

had really been arrested and that everything was finished. He
wondered how they would judge him at Quixeramobim, where
opinion ruled that those who had recourse to official justice are
fainthearted people lacking the courage to stand up for themselves.

The troop did not return until seven days later and it arrived
during the night. On the morning of the next day Miguel knew that
they had brought back Araujo. His pal, who sold wood from door
to door, had come home with the report. He added that Miguel
must keep out of the way, for the partisans of the Araujos were going to organize a demonstration.

Miguel followed this wise advice and kept himself ensconced in
the shanty: he was thus unable to be present at the riot which took
place on Portugal Square where the demonstrators assembled. From
what his pal told him of it, the repression had been brutal. The
mounted police had straight off opened fire into the crowd and
dispersed it with their sabers. There were seven dead and twenty-
four wounded. On the day following Miguel once again took the
road for Quixeramobim. His horse was well rested and kept up a
brisk trot.

Miguel Carlos was now ashamed of what he had done. He ought
himself to have murdered Araujo. In having recourse to justice he
had succeeded in getting seven men killed. "Bah!" he said to himself after ripe reflection, "they were Araujists. It's better that they've
disappeared. They were partisans of slavery."

When he reached Mundico's botequim his conscience was at
ease. It was three o'clock in the afternoon. Some muleteers were
drinking rum at the counter, and three women, negresses, were looking at fabrics.

Mundico gave him a boisterous reception.

"How goes it? What a fine kettle of fish that business with Araujo
da Costa was! You arranged things very nicely!"

"And what do their friends say?" asked Miguel who wanted to
know quickly the state of opinion.

"Pooh!" said Mundico. "They daren't say anything. Araujo's wife is
already back at the fazenda and has liberated all the Negroes. See
those negresses," he added, indicating the women who were feeling
the fabrics, "they come from there. This is the first time they've
ever been paid."

Miguel experienced a feeling of pride. In spite of everything, he had compelled them to give in, those Araujos! In this mood he felt shame and pride. He was not fully aware of what he had done, nor, especially, how far his initiative had carried. He did not doubt that he had brought a weighty contribution to the work of revolution and of the republic. It gave him pleasure to hear that the colored people of Boa Viagem were no longer slaves; he really thought that, with this reform, and the departure of Araujo da Costa, peace would reign in that region, but he could not see any further; he did not perceive the political repercussion of the event.

He was now in a hurry to return to his own home, but he must pass by Formosa, where he had sent Antonio to put the fazenda in order again. How had he managed? Had he worked? It would be unfortunate if he had found his breviaries again, Miguel thought.

5. The "Batuque"

HE HAD FOUND those breviaries of his again. So, when Miguel Carlos reached Formosa, he caught a glimpse of Antonio sitting on the veranda in the act of saying his prayers and telling his beads. His face was puckered up and he looked as if he were the caretaker of an abandoned house, for the corral was empty and there was no movement in the sheds. There was not a sign of men, horses, cows, or oxen. All was calm and silent in the twilight.

"So there's not a single farm hand here yet?" Miguel asked as he went up on the veranda.

"No."

"All the same, you're not going to let the fazenda fall into ruin. You ought to have asked Mundico for men. He would have sent you some. You haven't been to Quixeramobim?"

"I was waiting for you."

"So you haven't budged from here and you don't know anything? You're unaware that Araujo has been arrested by the mounted police and that he's in jail at Fortaleza?"

"I don't know anything."

"Well! I'll tell you. We're rid of them and we're going to be able to work. It's now a matter of putting your back into it and leaving off all those prayers of yours for a while."

Antonio was impressed by his uncle's extraordinary dynamism: he was overwhelmed by this ardor and activity. But they could not serve as an example to him. He felt irresistibly inclined to meditation and reverie.

"Don't forget," Miguel Carlos continued, "that you're the last of the Maciels. You haven't the right to lose what your father won at the cost of a hard struggle. You must take a hand in the work yourself."

"I will work," said Antonio sincerely, so sincerely that Miguel Carlos saw a glimmer of hope. Perhaps the boy had understood?

"I'll send you my foreman tomorrow: João Pio. He's an honest man. You can trust him. But it's up to you as boss here to tell him what he has to do. You must know where you want to put your cattle and where to plant your cotton."

"I'll work," Antonio repeated.

"Give me a glass of rum. I'm going to be off soon."

"You're going to travel during the night?"

"It's better. I had too much of the heat coming back from Fortaleza. The sun was as hot as hell."

After taking a few drinks, Miguel resumed:

"There's only the foreman, and that's not enough. You ought to take a wife—get married."

"Oh! . . . but . . . (Antonio hesitated about how to reply) . . . I don't know anybody."

"There are girls on all the fazendas. It won't be difficult to pick one."

"Ought I to get married immediately?"

"Straightway. You must get all that moving. You must increase the number of cattle, and start planting again; a wife is needed in the house, and children. This must become a real fazenda, what!"

Antonio was utterly crushed. He had a horror of women—they chatter too much, prevent us from thinking and praying and, in their conception, were at the root of all sins of men. A wife! He felt shame rising to his forehead.

"Think that over, my boy," said Miguel getting up. "Pay a few visits to the fazendeiros around here. You'll soon have found one. And if you don't find one, ask Mundico: women are constantly going to his store to make purchases."

Night had fallen and the air was cool: the stars were shining in a pure sky and a sharp white gleam on the summit of the sierra indicated that the moon was about to appear.

Miguel Carlos leaped on his horse, went round the house and took the north road which led to Tamburil.

Antonio was alone. Leaning on the balustrade of the veranda, he heard the horse's footsteps fade away on the rocky mountain path as the vast lunary silence filled the valley. He remained long in contemplation of the moon, the stars, and the line of hills, each in turn. The solitude did not frighten him, but it made him feel the need of God's presence. He went into the big room, lit a candle, and began to read the Gospel according to St. Matthew.

On the road to Tamburil, Miguel Carlos allowed his horse to amble along. Every week he came to see how things were progressing. Everything was going well. The cattle had been rounded up again, taken care of, and branded. Nearly ten acres had been prepared for planting sugar canes, five for manioc, two and a half for cotton, and nearly thirty for maize. But it was João Pio who took the initiative in all this. "Antonio always gives his approval," the foreman told him, "and he remains sitting on the veranda morning, noon, and night."

"So," said Miguel. "He hasn't altered. Does he travel around?"

"No. He doesn't budge."

"Well I'll be damned! All the same, he *must* get married. At his age I was running after every girl on all the fazendas, in all the villages, and even in the huts! I don't understand his indifference."

"It's because he doesn't know yet. He's a bit late in maturing. And then he never speaks of anything but God and the Virgin, like a monk. If I were in your shoes, I'd organize a *batuque** here. When he sees others at it, he'll get the taste: it will excite him. We could even give him a little *catuaba* in his beef tea."

Miguel Carlos knew that catuaba was an aphrodisiac which no

* An African fertility dance, brought to Brazil by the Negro slaves and now almost unknown there. It survives in many parts of Africa, especially in Angola.

man could resist; but he didn't wish to use it before employing other means. On the other hand, he was in agreement about the batuque.

"A good idea," he said. "We'll arrange that."

"But the woman must be brought during the fete," said João Pio.

"Naturally. I've got one in mind: the daughter of the Massapé fazendeiro. You know her: Paulina."

"Paulina? Yes. She's a beautiful girl."

"She's a lovely girl."

Miguel told João Pio to take all necessary steps for the batuque. As for the banquet, that was easy: they'd kill an ox and two or three suckling pigs and a dozen chickens. The important aspect of it was the music. Guitars, accordions, and mandolins would not be difficult to find. But a drum was needed. There was only one drum in the whole of Quixeramobim—that of the church orchestra and it belonged to the padre.

"If ever the padre hears that it was for a batuque that we borrowed his drum, we'll be excommunicated," said João Pio.

"Fiddlesticks!" said Miguel. "Padre Julio's a decent sort. He'll let out a yell but he won't do anything."

The festivity took place a fortnight later, on a Saturday. João Pio had invited more than eighty Negroes and negresses. For the batuque is of African origin and only Negroes can give it the stamp of authenticity.

"Saturday at six o'clock in the evening at the fazenda of Formosa," João Pio had called out to them as he made a tour of the fazendas in the region. "Don't miss the opportunity!"

They were far from missing it. Batuques were rare events. They were now hardly ever given. Under the influence of the priests and monks, the fazendeiros prohibited them on the pretext that they were immoral fetes. Yet, with or without batuques, the number of mulatto bastards remained appreciably the same. The Negroes did not understand how there could be anything in the batuque to which exception could be taken. Because in it one made love in public? And if so, what then? That doesn't alter the business in any way and it's more gay. They were all delighted with this idea of Miguel Carlos. They were going to have some fun! The never-ending work on the plantations, with clouds of mosquitoes and wasps which never stop buzzing round your head, and the ticks which stick to your legs and the ants biting your toes—it all makes you miserable. From time to time there must be a celebration at which a person can enjoy a good laugh and have a joyful release of feelings throughout a whole night. That sets you up again as a man, for months.

The corral had been carefully swept to receive those who were invited. In the center, three great logs had been set up in a tripod which held the half ox they were to roast. To the left, almost against the veranda, four small hearths arranged with stones had to serve for cooking the maize flour and beans. To the right, two other hearths had been prepared for roasting the chickens. Finally, on the veranda, three broached barrels of rum had been put in position. The iron shed had been thoroughly cleaned out, and installed there were three long tables on trestles covered with tablecloths of a whiteness to stimulate the appetite. In the background was the customary litter of maize straw for couples no longer in control of their passions.

From five o'clock onward the guests began to arrive in little groups: negresses in dresses of white cotton fabric; Negroes, some bareheaded, others with wide straw hats turned up on their foreheads, others with children's hats given to them in the town. But there were not only Negroes. Whites and half-breeds did not disdain this kind of merrymaking, though they might leave the principal role to the Negroes.

Miguel Carlos and Antonio welcomed those arriving. (Miguel had made Antonio go down in the corral to attend to his social duties as boss of the fazenda.) All the couples looked serious and rather solemn, for there must not be any laughing before the moment the fete begins.

The fire had been lit under the half carcass of beef hanging in the corral. Some women lit the hearth fires under the cast-iron cooking pots, others were beginning to roast the chickens, when suddenly at the moment when nobody was expecting it, and people were beginning to despair, the orchestra made its entrance to the tune of a military march. *Viva!* roared the guests, gesticulating. The orchestra drew up in the corral to finish their piece.

"And what about the drum?" Miguel asked of a big half-caste

who seemed to be the leader of the troupe. For you cannot have a batuque without a drum and Miguel saw only guitars, mandolins, and accordions.

"It's coming," the man replied, adding: "We've arrived a little late because it's better not to be on the spot before the fete, otherwise the public never stops shouting: 'Music! Music'—and that's never good; it makes a bad beginning."

"Good! Good!" Miguel agreed. "Ah, there's the drum. Settle yourselves over there. You'll have a small drink of rum and then we'll get going."

Miguel had placed Antonio at the head of one of the tables. He looked bewildered, serious, and disapproving. He wondered why this fete had been organized, why all those people whom he did not know had been invited. In the general jubilation, he assumed the mask of a lost soul, which did not in fact surprise anybody as it was rumored that he was touched.

While waiting for the viands to be cooked, the guitarists sang to their own accompaniment some nostalgic *choros,* popular folk songs. In the night under that shed, lit only by the yellow reflection from the flames of the fires burning on the hearths in the corral, those songs thrilled with a strange sadness which wrung the hearts of the Africans. They listened to them in deep silence. After each choro, sighs were heard; homesickness for African soil and freedom.

"We're going to begin," called out some person who could not be seen but who must have been near the veranda.

The feast began. Four men quickly served the food as there were neither plates nor forks. Pieces of beef or suckling pig or chicken were thrown at the guests who caught them in their hands. Then a dumpling of cooked maize mixed with beans was brought to them. And every man and woman set to and ate heartily. Their appetites were ferocious. A banquet in the hinterland is rare, and, when one's skin is black, it is not every day that meat is eaten; nor even every week. There were women who had been servants on the fazendas who kept asking their husband or man friend to cut some meat for them: the daggers were working steadily. However, others who had never served at the table of white people ate heartily with their teeth like the men, or nibbled their pieces in short spasms like cats.

Then the bottles of rum were passed around. Everyone had a

drink and passed the bottle to his neighbor. That helped the appetite and whipped up the spirit. They all began talking and laughing. A huge Negro stood up, a man well over six feet in height and built like a Hercules. He was brandishing two big bowls in his right hand and challenged another Negro who was seated at a nearby table.

"Will you take me on?" he shouted to the other.

"Cangica has never refused a challenge, David!" replied the other colored man.

"Come on then!"

They took their positions facing one another and David filled the two bowls with white rum. Everybody stood up to watch them.

"Attention!" shouted Miguel Carlos. "I'll be judge!"

He placed himself beside the two rivals and counted: "One, two, three!"

The two men lifted the bowls and began to drink greedily. The challenger's bowl was the first to fall back on the table.

"He's already down the drain!" he said with pride.

Cangica put down his bowl a few seconds later.

"You've won," he admitted. "Something caught in my throat at the start."

"Let's clear the ground!" shouted Miguel Carlos.

In a twinkling the big shed was emptied of the tables. Some were removing the soiled tablecloths, others the boards, others the trestles. They were all in a hurry to see the batuque begin.

The orchestra opened with a few *modinhas*—popular town songs —to get them in the mood. These are naïve quatrains set to music in a simple and always identical rhythm to old refrains:

> *Trepei num roseiro*
> *Quebrei um galho*
> *Segura, menino*
> *Senaõ, eu caio.*

All of a sudden a vigorous roll on the drum warned them that the real fun was about to start. The men got into a line which went from one end of the shed to the other. Opposite them, three paces away, the women in turn lined up.

"All ready?" the big guitarist called out.

"Rather!" shouted the Negroes.

Then a strapping young Negro raised his arm as if in a Roman salute and indicated one of the women who responded by raising her arm. They went forward to the middle of the corridor formed by the two ranks, posed themselves facing each other, and began to dance on the spot, springing higher and higher as the drum beat quicker and louder. Soon they leaped so high that the wind, billowing into the woman's skirt, exposed two magnificently shaped buttocks. All the men squatted down the better to admire these ebony curves, caressed by the reflection of the flames from the hearths. Suddenly the dancer cried: "Ready!" The dancing girl settled herself on the ground with her legs apart and her skirt drawn up as far as her navel. The man gave one more bound and fell on her, interlacing their legs like two crossed pitchforks. Then, with a movement of their backs, they brought their bellies together so violently that they hurled one another back to their starting point.

The orchestra, letting itself go, brilliantly and with *brio,* played a dance tune to do honor to this performance. And, immediately afterwards, two other dancers went forward on the dance track while the bottles of rum were being passed around among the men. At the fourth exhibition the crowd of onlookers had already reached a high point of excitation. The men, who were by now beginning to feel the effects of alcohol, began shouting:

"Strip! Strip!"

Neither the girl nor her partner needed to be asked: in a moment they were naked (clothing is light and simple in the tropics). They were a handsome couple with slim legs in harmony. The negress had pointed breasts like buds in spring: her oblong hips presented an exciting contrast to the geometrical roundness of the male's. The men, now warmed up, were uttering impassioned cries:

"What a girl!"

The dancers were springing with the suppleness of cats. One would have said that their legs were elastic. In the yellowish light which filled the shed the two black bodies rose almost to the roof like two enormous marionettes in a nightmare.

It was at this moment that the sensational act was produced. The gate of the corral creaked and a horseman appeared wearing a broad-brimmed hat in Spanish style. He was followed by a young girl clad entirely in white: she was seated like an amazon on one of those small Arabian horses that are well acclimatized in that hinterland, in which they find some of the conditions prevailing in their African desert.

Miguel Carlos welcomed the visitors in a dignified manner. He was really handsome in his black costume, with a big red silk kerchief around his neck.

"How goes it with Senhor Souza dos Santos?" he said in a highly polite manner, holding out his hand.

Then, turning toward the young girl:

"And Senhorita Paulina didn't find the journey too tiring?"

They exchanged a few compliments.

When the naked dancers had sent up the final belly smack, Miguel Carlos went forward toward the shed, followed by the young girl and her father.

"*Amigos!*" he called out. "I present to you Antonio Maciel's fiancée."

"*Viva!*" roared all the guests.

Thereupon the big guitarist elbowed his way through the crowd, went up and bowed to the young girl and improvised a song for the occasion. He accompanied himself with one of those passionate, sensual rhythms peculiar to South America. This man was the greatest improviser of songs in Quixeramobim; and never missed an opportunity of showing his talent.

All eyes were fixed on the young girl. She was white with a pink face and the black eyes and hair of an Andalusian. She was wearing a Spanish headdress with her hair parted in the middle and heavy plaits covering the ears. She maintained a serious, almost severe look.

When the singer finished his improvisation—with a final chord on the guitar—and the acclamations were bursting forth, Miguel Carlos looked for Antonio. He had disappeared. But he had not dared to take flight. He had gone to sit on the veranda near some barrels of rum, and had begun to pray, asking God to forgive the abominations at which he was present. It was there that Miguel Carlos found him.

"Didn't you hear what I said to you," Miguel rapped out at him.

"Yes."

"Well, well! You might have taken the trouble to come and introduce yourself to your fiancée. A wife is being found for you: she's been brought to your home. Isn't that enough?"

"I didn't know what I had to do. . . ."

"Come on, let's go down. And be quick!"

The introductions were made. Antonio dared not look at the young girl, but Paulina eyed him from head to foot as if he were a calf that she was going to buy. She attributed his awkwardness and dumbness to shyness. This did not displease her. She found him thin, sickly-looking, and weak. But he was a landowner, a fazendeiro. One must know how to make concessions in life and, besides, her father knew what he was doing. She had absolute confidence in her father.

"We'll take our places at a little table which I've had set up over there in the corner by the rancho," said Miguel. "In that way we can join in the fete."

The foreman had had this table placed near the litter of maize straw. When Miguel and his guests came to take their seats there, several couples were already engaged in satisfying the passions exacerbated by the dance. One heard the sighing of the negresses, like that of an animal in heat, interrupted from time to time by their strident little cries. A heavy odor of rum, roast beef, and sweat permeated the atmosphere in the shed.

A few rolls sounded on the drum, the guitars and mandolins twanged, the accordions wailed; men and women got into line again. The batuque continued, but this time it was not just two dancers who were leaping but the two ranks together, animated by a frenzy which gave the impression that all the guests were victims of collective nervous excitement. This was absolutely Africa, wild and impassioned, reborn on American soil. And the rollings of the drum and the despairing wails of the guitars mingled with the inarticulate cries of Negroes under the violent emotion of the infernal dance.

Miguel Carlos tried to see the effect which the spectacle was producing on Antonio. But Antonio was stiff and impassive like a block of wood, with a look of resignation in his eyes. Paulina was enjoying herself; this was the first time that she had witnessed a batuque. Souza dos Santos was sipping rum.

"Excellent, this *teimosa* rum!" he remarked. "You have some *cayana* among your sugar canes?"

"Not so much."

Cayana is the cane which gives the best-flavored rum but its yield is less. They continued discussing plantings and cattle while the Negroes danced and went into contortions. Several times they tried to induce a conversation between he engaged couple. Paulina herself put a few questions to Antonio. He replied only in monosyllables. She found him really stupid, uncommunicative, and disagreeable. But, since her father had decided in this way . . . In the hinterland, girls don't have any fantasies about bliss. Existence there is not in the right setting for happiness. It is a matter of keeping life going by bearing children and being owner of a piece of land, because land is the basis of life. Do not the philosophies which come from arid regions all say that life is a test? Bliss? It does not exist. One is happy only after death.

Paulina was to become mistress of a fazenda; that was the main thing. Her only fear was that Antonio was too feeble to be the father of her children, for he was really very thin and his eyes were too deeply sunken under his forehead (she didn't know that he suffered from chronic dysentery). She was not unduly worried by all this. If need be, she would see that she had a child by a robust man: there was no scarcity of them.

Miguel Carlos was driven to despair by Antonio's attitude.

"You mustn't be surprised," he whispered to Souza dos Santos. "He's never known a woman."

"*What?*" exclaimed Souza opening his eyes wide. "He's never . . . ?"

"No, I swear it to you."

Souza burst into laughter, then, turning to Antonio and pointing to the couples wallowing in the straw:

"Those are your laborers? They're in the right sort of condition!"

He began to laugh again and poured himself out a drink of *teimosa* in the little cup that had been brought to him.

They were no longer dancing. The orchestra was resting and drinking. The Negroes and negresses were squatting in little groups and telling erotic stories or tales of witchcraft. At that moment

Mundico, the trader from Quixeramobim, came up to the table. He was completely drunk.

"I congratulate you," he said to the betrothed pair in a thick voice. "I congratulate you. Come on now, kiss one another."

And as Antonio did not budge:

"You needn't be afraid. It's only me, Mundico. I know what love is. You must kiss. In the town, it's like that. You begin that way."

Antonio did not allow himself to be convinced. He was embarrassed.

"It's all right, Mundico," said Miguel. "They're keeping that to themselves."

Mundico went away reeling and threw himself on the straw.

"I'm going to show you over our house," said Miguel winking at Souza. "Let's go in."

When the Negroes saw the group move toward the veranda, they wondered if the festivity was finished and if they were not to get any more rum, but Miguel anticipated their thought:

"The fete's going on!" he shouted. "Don't bother about us. There's enough rum to last till morning and meat for those who want it."

Miguel showed his guests the various rooms in the house: he kept Antonio's room as the last to be shown. Without Antonio seeing it, the bed had been arranged with new sheets and a new bedspread which Mundico had brought.

"And this is your room, children," he said as he opened the door.

He went inside and lit two candles fixed on a little table placed against the window. "You can begin right away. The marriage will be celebrated when the padre comes on his next round of this region. Agreed, Souza dos Santos?"

"Agreed."

"Good night and may God favor you."

They shut Antonio and Paulina into the room and went outside to take part again in the festivity which had just recommenced.

"You think they'll make a go of it?" Souza asked.

"He can't do anything else," said Miguel. "He's going to be forced to comply."

"You say he's never done it?"

"Well now!" said Miguel Carlos coarsely. "And Paulina? It strikes me she must know something about it?"

"Paulina has never been mounted by anybody. She's a virgin," replied Souza who could never shed his cattle-breeder's vocabulary.

"Agreed, Souza, agreed. But a woman knows more about that than a man. It's a woman's business."

"Paulina's an intelligent girl, no doubt about that."

They returned and sat at the little table and resumed their drinking. The Negroes had begun dancing again to the rhythm of *modinhas* played on an accordion.

Gradually men and women, exhausted and worn out, lay down on the ground. When day broke on the dead fires in the corral, the shed seemed to be strewn with corpses. Jubilation was dead. It would not come to life again for perhaps several years.

6. The "Cegueira"

THE BATUQUE at Formosa caused a scandal. The Negroes who took part in it went about everywhere saying that it had been a magnificent festivity, but the abolitionist fazendeiros would have no truck with the Maciels. "The moment when they were getting ready to confer human dignity on the colored people, was not the right time," they said, "to recall to mind the bestial customs of Africa by an orgy of that kind."

When Padre Julio heard what had happened, when he learned that the very drum of his church orchestra had served to provide rhythm for the unspeakable debauch, he flew into a great rage. He celebrated mass in a state of agitation and without elation with the motions of a man wrestling with a problem, and then he mounted the pulpit and thundered against the lewd people who had abandoned themselves to this disgraceful exhibition. On all those who were guilty he inflicted a Novena of expiation and—for he was a practical man—a fine of ten milreis. Never had the little church at Quixeramobim heard such a violent and threatening discourse. For a long time after the mass, the faithful, dumbfounded by the savage eloquence of the priest, remained prostrated saying prayers and begging for forgiveness.

Nevertheless, Padre Julio well understood the need for joy and love. Every three months he himself replaced all his young black servant girls with others. But he had a horror of batuques, of obscene dances, and of all those African customs which, if tolerated, would quickly tear men away from the religion of Our Lord Jesus Christ.

After the mass he mounted his horse and left for Formosa. He intended to have an explanation from the Maciels. He was going to inflict an exemplary punishment, for the prestige of the Church was at stake.

While under the brutal sun following the track used by muleteers, Padre Julio wondered what could have impelled the Maciels to organize a batuque. Moreover, they were Christians and they were not of the Negro race. And this sacrilegious idea of having borrowed the drum belonging to the church orchestra for the filthy business! They would pay dearly for this. What would he ask of them? A hundred milreis? On thinking it over, he told himself that it would be preferable to make them hand over two good milch cows: his own were yielding hardly anything. He was satisfied with that solution. But, at the same time, the popular imagination must be stirred. Hence, he would insist that one of the Maciels should come to make honorable amends in public on the occasion of a mass in the church at Quixeramobim.

When he went into the corral his face looked as stern as when, in the pulpit, he asked the faithful for the subscriptions which they owed to the church. He leaped from his horse and went up on the veranda.

He was received by Paulina. He had not seen her for a long time as he seldom went in the direction of Massapé. She was wearing a red dress under which he pictured her body all white like milk. Ah, the white women! But they won't be the domestic servants of priests, so that the latter are condemned never to have any women but negresses or, at best, half-whites. Padre Julio concealed his flurry behind a smile.

"How are you, senhorita?" he said, bowing slightly. "I'm very happy to see you again. The last time I went to Massapé, you were still a little girl. And here you are, 'Dona'."

"Not yet. We must first get married."

"Whenever you wish. I'm at your service."

He looked her over so intently that she felt uncomfortable.

"Go into the big room, padre," she said. "I'll call Antonio."

Padre Julio was well acquainted with Antonio, whose devotion he had been in a position to appreciate during the offices on holidays of obligation, Easter, Christmas, and Corpus Christi, in the church at Quixeramobim. He remembered having heard his confession on several occasions, and that he was a strange young man who put unusual questions, to which he had replied that one must not seek to penetrate the mysteries of religion.

Antonio had much respect for those who wore the ecclesiastical habit. He greeted Padre Julio with deep humility. After some general remarks about life in the hinterland, the padre, who was not only a good fellow, but a realist in every respect, broached the main question.

"How about this marriage? It must not be long delayed, for I fancy that you've already had contacts?"

"What contacts?" asked Antonio, while Paulina turned her head away.

"No, no, I don't want any details," said the padre. "It's enough for me to know that you sleep in the same bed."

"But . . ."

"I'm not pressing you. I understand about that," said the padre good-humoredly. "But you know that the woman must not be impregnated outside marriage. Clearly there are compromises possible in all rules. In any case, we must do our best to respect the rules. Supposing we fix the date for next Saturday? What do you think of that?"

"But . . ."

"Is that all right, Senhorita Paulina?" the padre continued, noting Antonio's hesitations.

"According to your orders, padre."

"I advise you to have a mass. The simple benediction is not enough for fazendeiros. That won't cost you very much. I won't even ask for money. Two milch cows will amply pay for it. Look, for that price I'll even let you have the orchestra. Is that agreed?"

As neither of them replied, he concluded:

"Very well! That's settled. I'll make arrangements for it . . . Tell me now, in regard to that batuque you gave, who was it who had the foolish idea to borrow my drum?"

Antonio did not like to be reprimanded by the padre.

"Miguel Carlos," he said without hesitating.

"Indeed! I'm going to haul that Miguel Carlos over the coals. Doesn't he realize that it's sacrilege to have the church drum used in scenes of debauchery? Where is he?"

"He's gone back to Tamburil."

"Yes, once it's all over and done with, he's cleared out."

This time Antonio bridled up, for at that period the family sentiment was stronger in him than the religious.

"Miguel Carlos never clears out," he said so firmly that Paulina was taken aback.

"Never mind!" said Julio, who had come to settle the matter of the marriage. "I'll give him absolution when he comes to confession, but I shall insist that he doesn't ever do it again. He set a very bad example."

A servant woman brought three very small cups of coffee. They drank some, and the padre asked if he could have a small drink of rum to put heart into him. It was a long road to Quixeramobim. Paulina rushed into the kitchen and returned with a bottle. Julio drank several stiff drinks one after another and gave his blessing to the engaged couple.

"So it's understood; until next Saturday then."

He jumped on his horse and went down toward the river. When he had disappeared behind the sugar canes, Paulina said:

"He's a good sort, the padre."

"Yes," said Antonio.

Without another word, he, too, went down into the corral, crossed it and went off into the plantation. He felt highly strung. This marriage business aroused a spirit of revolt in him. He came near to hating Miguel Carlos. Paulina he held in contempt. He went down as far as the river, sat under a palm tree and began to meditate. Not marry Paulina? Flee? Where? He was conscious of his unfitness to live with other men: this he had well realized on the occasion of his journey to Monte Santo. Tell Miguel Carlos that he refused? Miguel would kill him; and Antonio was as much afraid of death as of life. He felt himself discouraged, overcome, dead beat—as if after walking for ten hours in the sun.

He was afraid to return to the fazenda, to find himself in the presence of Paulina. He began walking again. He followed a track which crossed stretches of white quartz. The reflection of the light was such that at one moment his sight troubled him, and he had to sit down. He felt his legs give way when he stood up, and he made haste to get home. He forced his pace, dragged on by a sort of anguish which caught him in the stomach, slipped indoors surreptitiously and went and threw himself on his bed. He declared he felt ill when Paulina found him. She offered to make him an infusion, but he refused it.

Next day he sent a messenger to Miguel Carlos to inform him of the day of the marriage.

The days passed without incident. He had resumed the reading of his breviaries while Paulina busied herself with the foreman in the work of the fazenda. She was the daughter of a fazendeiro and knew all the work on the farm. She knew that cotton is planted on a level with the earth, that maize must be planted deeper, that the young shoots of sugar cane are placed in a furrow five fingers deep, but that they must be covered with a very thin blanket of earth; she knew how to couple a donkey and a mare to breed mules—even when the ass was a small one.

She got on well with João Pio, the foreman. He pleased her. She had always liked men with broad shoulders and biceps which stood out, with strongly marked chest muscles. And that penetrating look of João Pio's, those eyes with all the perspicacity of the Indian! She was glad that he was neither a Negro nor a mulatto and that he was a real half-caste Indian, tough, true to race, and strong. Not that she had any hatred of Negroes, but she never went so far as to put them on the same footing with other human beings. All those colored people were still her father's slaves when she was younger. He had liberated them, but, for her, they always remained tainted by that slavery; they bore a mark of degradation which she did not succeed in eliminating from her mind.

She was well aware that João Pio would be her man when she wished, but she preferred to get married first of all.

The marriage took place on the Saturday as agreed. Paulina had again put on her dress of white cotton fabric. Antonio wore a black suit much too big for him and lent by Mundico who maintained that a fazendeiro ought to get married in black. "I know town customs," he added in a tone which did not admit of a reply.

Miguel Carlos was there with his red silk kerchief, but the star turn at the ceremony was certainly Souza dos Santos's wife. She had sacrificed herself to be present at the marriage of her daughter. Ten hours on horseback. With such a corporation as hers, one appreciated that it was a sacrifice. She had a midriff like a barrel; sagging, flaccid, gelatinous breasts; and an enormous fat neck. She oozed perspiration in great beads and exhaled an odor stronger than that of any of the Negroes present. She it was who had given the light of day to this flower of the hinterland whom Miguel Carlos had conquered for Antonio. It was not encouraging. She had put on a yellow carnival dress, with big red flowers, and had taken out her diamond necklace. The swarm of children and Negroes massed at the entrance to the church were dazzled by the spectacle.

The mass was short. Padre Julio had always been expeditious. When the ceremony was ended, the orchestra, which had formed itself in a group at the back of the church, played *Luar no Sertão* ("Moonlight in the Hinterland"), a melancholy song which, in the minds of the guitarists, encouraged tender affection and love.

Padre Julio lit a cigar and offered one to Miguel and Antonio as they were going out of the church. That was a great luxury: happily things were going well. Antonio stated, however, that he did not smoke. Julio led Miguel by the arm.

"I have been entrusted with passing this on to you," he said.

He plunged his hand into the deep pocket of his soutane and drew out a visiting card which he held out to Miguel. It bore only a few words, but how precious! "Dona Laetitia sends to the newly married couple her best wishes for their happiness." Dona Laetitia was the wife of Araujo da Costa. No doubt she was on bad terms with her husband, but, all the same, she belonged to the Araujo clan. Miguel was flabbergasted by it.

"I'm going to tell you some extraordinary news," he said, addressing the newlyweds. "Dona Laetitia sends you her best wishes."

"Dona Laetitia?" repeated Souza dos Santos. "The Araujo? Why, that means permanent peace!"

"It's peace," replied Miguel. "And not too soon. At last we're going to be able to work quietly. I did not expect that. This is a far finer day than I had expected. We'll celebrate it at Mundico's."

They turned their steps toward the main square to which the six arcades of its façade painted in garnet red gave a little artistic touch. They ordered pints of rum but Antonio refused to drink. Miguel Carlos, who was in a state of great elation, drank steadily. Peace declared in the Araujo camp! He had never expected a message like that from Dona Laetitia. It was necessary to thank her: they would send her one of the finest horses on the fazenda to seal the pact of friendship. Fortunately things were taking this turn, since Antonio was not the man to stand up to those neighbors of his, so full of hatred.

They returned to Formosa slightly tipsy. Even the fat mother felt a desire to dance. But there was no ball, although it was the custom. The batuque had already cost dearly enough.

What happened a month and a half after the marriage was bound to happen. Instead of going out on some rounds in the campo to keep an eye on the cattle, instead of inspecting the plantings, Antonio spent whole mornings and afternoons shut up in his room, leaving to João Pio and Paulina the responsibility of managing the daily work. He appeared on the veranda only in the morning for an hour or two; and in the afternoon toward five o'clock. With this regime, his eyes quickly became unaccustomed to the violent light of the hinterland. It is a treacherous light which cannot be endured except by those who have had long training. And no doubt the fact that Antonio, with his mania for thinking too much, constantly kept looking at the sun, had something to do with it.

It was on September 27th, toward six o'clock in the evening, that it happened. On that day Antonio had been to Quixeramobim to hear a mass celebrated by Padre Julio with the object of attracting the blessings of heaven on the next sowings. The trail which leads from Formosa to Quixeramobim runs across large areas of chalky, whitish ground, where the reflection of the sunlight is so strong that it causes an extremely irritating discomfort even to those used to it. The journey takes three hours on horseback. So Antonio had set out at seven o'clock to be present at mass at ten o'clock. He returned in the afternoon under a fierce sun—a thing which no plainsman would have risked—and he reached Formosa at half-past four. He ate a dish of beans and went to sit on the veranda.

An hour later, just at the moment when the sun was going down behind the sierra, and as Paulina was engaged in gossip with the servant girl under a mango tree behind the house, she heard a cry:

"Paulina!"

It was Antonio's voice. It was indeed the first time that he had called her, but it was a cry of pain, an appeal for help. What was happening? The cry came from the veranda. In a flash she pictured again the attack on the fazenda and the massacre at Sobral, of which she had been told. She dashed forward, followed by the servant. On reaching the veranda she saw Antonio standing upright with his arms stretched out, groping around him. His eyes were wide open but he did not look at her.

"Antonio," she said.

"Paulina," he replied in a sad, trembling voice.

She took him by the wrist.

"What's the matter?"

"Hold me. Don't let me go. I don't see any more. I'm blind," he said with a sob.

"Of course you're not," she said to reassure him. "You don't become blind like that, all of a sudden. It's a blackout. Come. Sit down."

She made him sit on the bench and continued to hold his hand. She passed her other hand in front of his eyes; there was no reaction.

"You don't see anything?" she asked.

"Nothing. It's night. Everything's black."

She felt helpless. Had she loved him, or if he were a man like the others, she would have caressed and cajoled him, for she felt compassion for him. That would not have cured him: yet, even so, it would have comforted him. But he was an odd kind of man. She did not know how to take him and did not find words to speak to him.

"You don't want anything?" she asked.

"No."

He was curt, hermetically sealed. She insisted.

"You wouldn't like me to make you some camomile tea to bathe your eyes?"

"I have no pain in my eyes. I'm blind."

And closing his fists and in an ill-toned voice he shouted in a fit of rage:

"Don't you see that I'm blind?"

"Don't shout," she said calmly. "As for me, there's nothing I can do. It may be necessary to go to Fortaleza: that's the only place where doctors are to be found."

"I don't care a damn about doctors! Not a damn! I'm blind," he roared, straightening himself up and beginning to gesticulate.

He wanted to walk but bumped against the balustrade. He turned around, wishing to go forward at any cost. Paulina barred his way.

"You're going to fall. Sit down again."

He consented to sit down again. At that moment the laborers were returning from the plantation. As the foreman was delayed in the shed, Paulina called out: "João Pio!"

"I'm coming," he replied.

She explained to him that Antonio had suddenly become blind.

"At what time?" he inquired.

"Just at the moment of sundown."

The foreman did not hesitate at all. In the tone of voice of a person who well knew what he was dealing with, he said:

"It's the *cegueira*, sun blindness. He'll see again tomorrow."

In the hinterland they give the name *cegueira* to a night blindness known in the world of scientists as hemeralopia. It is a phenomenon due to the violence of the light in regions where the air is very dry. Sight is lost at the exact moment when the sun goes down. It is recovered when the sun rises again.

"You're sure that he'll see?" Paulina asked.

"Quite sure. But he must remain indoors for a week in a dark room. It's the only way to cure it."

"You hear, Antonio?"

"Yes . . . Lead me into my room. Give me my book. It's there on the bench, unless it has fallen down. I'm bewildered."

They took him to his bed. He sent them away as soon as he was seated, adding:

"I don't need anybody."

He wished them to understand that he knew how to suffer alone, that he had no need of wifely consolation, that he was able to bear his misfortune without the help of anyone. He stretched himself on his back and began to recite the various prayers that he knew. Happy are those who suffer! But he was impatient to see the day breaking. Would he see again? Was the foreman right? Notwithstanding the fervor of his faith, he could not escape an anguish which gradually overcame him. He was seized with an imperious desire to see whether the blindness would persist. He got up and walked, groping his way toward the window, and found himself against the wall. He began to grope to find the opening, pressed lightly toward the right and collided with the other partition. How was that possible? For he had taken the right direction. He slowly retraced his steps. Wherever was that window? He bumped into another wall, followed it, groping along it nervously. Anxiety caught him in the throat; he felt a choking sensation like a person drowning. Quick, the window! He found it, pushed open the shutter with feverish hands (the windows were simply openings without glass). He looked at the sky: it was uniformly black. Antonio replaced the latch and returned to his bed. He found it without difficulty, threw himself on it, and rolled there as if he were in a fit of hysteria. No, he did not see. In his sky the moon and stars were dead. Would he see again? The foreman said that he would recover his sight with the sunrise. Was that true? He had never known anybody who was stricken with cegueira. He had heard this affliction spoken of, but it was said to be confined to other regions: it wasn't a malady found in Ceará. And supposing he didn't recover his sight? Supposing his eyes were dead? He dared not dwell on the thought. In spite of everything, it asserted itself and then he had the feeling of falling straight down into a yawning chasm. He writhed in despair on his bed and was no longer able to pray. Yet he must pray. What other resource had he but prayer? After a long spell, he succeeded in recovering composure and began to mumble litanies.

For a moment he thought of Paulina. She could have been near to watch over him: she could have bathed his eyes with a soothing infusion. That might have done him good. Immediately afterwards he felt angry for having had this thought; he was angry with himself for even having called her to help him. He did not want to have anything to do with women. He must keep to the line he had marked out for himself, the line of men who consecrated themselves to God. She had spent only one night in his bed, a horrible and degrading night. The next day he had made her arrange a room for herself. "Let her sleep!" he thought. "Let her not concern herself with me!"

She did not sleep. Soon after having put Antonio on the bed, she had gone back to sit on the veranda with João Pio. In the hot night there was something soft about the brilliance of the stars. When the moon rose behind the palm tree which stood out on the summit of the sierra, it lit up a dream landscape: fireflies without number fluttered in the sugar canes and one had the feeling of a vast silence in spite of the croaking of the toads and the deafening noise of crickets. One would have said that all these sounds were on the margin of the silence.

"So you don't think it's serious?" Paulina asked.

"It's nothing. In the hinterlands of Pernambuco and Bahia, many people are affected by cegueira."

"All the same, his eyes must be weak."

"No, senhora. But if I may give my opinion, he's not a very strong man."

"How could he be strong? He eats hardly anything. How different from Miguel Carlos! Yet it's the same family."

"That's no reason, senhora. The senhora hasn't traveled much yet, but those who have covered the hinterland know that there's nothing extraordinary in it. In our race—a mixture of Indian and white —some funny things happen. Thus, I've seen in the same family one of the boys who was as strong as a bull, while his brother was limp and lifeless as if he were short of blood. A half-breed has to be of a dark brown color if he's to be strong. If he's too white, then his flesh is soft. I knew a very dark-skinned half-breed who had a white child by a mulatta woman. But he was as soft as a ball of cotton wool."

"Then you think that Antonio is too white?"

"He's too white for a half-breed. That's why he's weak."

"In any case, *you*'re a good brown color. No danger of you lacking strength."

She moved closer to him and their shoulders touched.

"All by myself I load the black mule with sacks weighing a couple of hundredweights."

She felt his biceps.

"Your arms are hard."

He had understood. He knew already that neither of them would escape or try to escape the magic spell of that warm night charged with heavy perfumes. But he dared not play the game too quickly. He was only the foreman and a half-breed. She was white and the boss's wife. The boss was certainly a bit crazy and there was nothing to fear on his side; the danger, if he got to know about this, would be that he'd go and tell Miguel Carlos. Then there would be tragedy. But such prospects have never stopped any passion. At the mere thought of having a white body in his arms, João Pio was ready to risk anything. He put his arm around Paulina's waist and drew her to him: she did not offer any resistance. With a calm strength and enveloping gestures which one would not have imagined in that uncouth man, he took her on his knees and gave her a long kiss. When she straightened up, she said to him simply:

"Come."

At the end of the veranda there was a little room reserved for passing strangers who might ask for hospitality. It did not communicate with any other room and had only this door which opened on the veranda. It was furnished with a bed always made, a table on which a candle was stuck, a stool, and a goatskin bottle which was filled with fresh water when there was a guest. Antonio had hung on the wall a little wooden cross which he had made himself.

It was there that they made love for the first time. João would have liked Paulina to strip fully. He had a consuming desire to feel on his bronzed chest the softness of her white flesh, but she refused obstinately. He would also have liked to light the candle: again she refused. But a moonbeam which came in through a fairly wide chink caused by disjointed planks in the door revealed to João the milky whiteness of her buttocks.

"Be off quickly," she said as she was sitting up again.

"There's no danger," he said. "He won't budge as long as he sees nothing."

She pushed him toward the door with her arm.

"Go out!" she repeated. "I'm afraid."

He moved away tightening his belt. Then, turning, he said in a low voice:

"Good night."

"Good night."

He went inside the house again to reach his room near the kitchen. Paulina returned to sit on the bench on the veranda. She was both appeased and thrown into confusion; content and distressed. She congratulated herself on her audacity and feared the consequences. But she did not like plaguing herself. In her whole being she felt an assuagement, a satisfaction which invited her to sleep. She went to bed and slept until morning.

She was not yet awake when Antonio recovered his sight.

7. The Pieces of Rock Salt

THAT PARTICULAR YEAR, the season known as that of the "cashew rains" went by without the fall of a drop of water in the whole state of Ceará. All the planters and cattle raisers knew what that meant: the threat of drought, the most terrible scourge known to them. Oh, no doubt there was no need to despair: they could have good rains in December, but the old fazendeiros were skeptical. "When the cashew rains don't come," they said, "the danger is great."

Mundico's botequim at Quixeramobim was now always full of customers. All the fazendeiros went there to wait for the muleteers who brought news from various distant parts of the country. The news was bad. From one end of Ceará to the other there was great uneasiness: everywhere men were getting ready to fight the terrible scourge.

Miguel Carlos had come to stay in Formosa at Antonio's in order to keep himself informed about events. His fazenda at Tamburil

was too far from the centers of population. His arrival, his statement that "while waiting" he was going to remain temporarily at
Formosa, threw João and Paulina into a state of anxiety. This did
not last, for every day Miguel Carlos went to Quixeramobim. Hence,
they had the whole of the day to themselves, for Antonio had begun
again to pray throughout the afternoon.

Every evening Miguel chatted at great length with João on the
veranda. Paulina often came to join them while Antonio continued
with his prayers.

Miguel told them what he had heard at Mundico's.

"There's a muleteer from Itapicurú," he said, "who reports that
the *maryseiros* in that part have wept."

The *maryseiros* are sacred and mysterious trees of the hinterland.
They are consulted like oracles. If some delicate little drops form in
beads across their bark, it will rain: if the tree remains dry, drought
will inevitably sweep the country.

"We have a maryseiro in the second valley, on the Tamburil
road," said João Pio. "I had a look at it again yesterday: it's as dry
as deadwood."

"It still has time to weep. This is only November twelfth."

"Yes, but the ground is cracking very much in the bottoms. A bad
sign."

"The rivers haven't gone down much. There's still hope."

Every day the sun seemed to grow in strength and savagery. The
roads were covered with a thick bed of dust: the pastures became
yellow or took on a gray-beige tint. The colts and calves were no
longer seen gamboling. They grazed sadly, seeking obstinately for
some grass which was still green. The reflection of the light was
infernal and Miguel Carlos had forbidden Antonio to go outside.
"You don't want to have another attack of blindness at a time like
this," he added. The new plantation of canes, at which João Pio
had worked for a fortnight with his Negroes, was lost. The nights
grew colder—a sinister portent.

On November 27th, there was a faint ray of hope. Toward four
o'clock in the afternoon an enormous white cloud appeared above
the sierra in the direction of Boa Viagem. It rose in the sky with
astonishing rapidity as if it wished to blot out the sun. It became
gray at the base with an almost black border. Suddenly it blacked

out the sun. A violent wind arose which raised swirls of dust. It howled in the roofing of the shed. The cloud was seen to come down with great eddies of haze as if it were going to enshroud the fazenda. A formidable crack of thunder sounded, followed immediately by a second one. Two flashes of lightning stretched their cables of fire across the sky. Rain began to fall in a deluge. In the dining room the Maciels awaited the end of the storm, which lasted for a few minutes only. When they went out on the veranda, the sun had reappeared and the corral had become completely dry.

"That's bad, that is," said Miguel Carlos.

For those brief and violent storms were sure signs of great drought. They remained for a moment as if dumbfounded by the portent. João Pio said:

"There's nothing more but to wait for the night of Santa Luzia." *

Nobody replied. The night of Santa Luzia had already deceived people so often! And yet they maintained their hope. The man of the hinterland never despairs. After a time, Miguel Carlos said:

"In 1877 it was the same as this, but it rained in the month of January."

"We must wait for the night of Santa Luzia," João Pio repeated.

On the days which followed they experienced the heat of a fiery furnace. To breathe the burning air made them dizzy. They felt as if their eyes had gone dry: they kept them half-closed to protect them against the corrosive air. That did not prevent Miguel Carlos from going every day to Quixeramobim to get news about the progress of the scourge. However, when he put his hand on the pommel of his saddle at the end of an hour, the leather burned like red-hot iron. The sky was pitilessly clear and, as far as could be seen on the plain and along the slopes of the sierra, there was not the least trace of verdure. Shorn of all their leaves, the trees held up their skeletons in the terrifying light. Here and there bullocks could be seen standing motionless as if petrified. Life had completely disappeared: the whole region resembled a kingdom of the dead.

João Pio and Paulina had lost interest in love-making. They met again two or three times in a very hot little cabin but had to give up the idea of having their pleasure there. Their skins stuck like the bark of a rubber tree and, when their bodies were perspiring pro-

* The feast of St. Lucy, December 12th.

fusely, they gave off an odor so acrid that it was almost unbearable. Antonio remained in bed day and night, enfeebled by the morbid sweating of a weakling. The Negro laborers took turns to bring a little maize to the famished animals.

One day on his return from Quixeramobim Miguel Carlos said:

"A muleteer states that it's raining in the Sierra d'Araripe."

"That's a different zone," João Pio replied. "I've worked in the Araripe. In that part they don't ever know such droughts as we have here. I distrust the news brought by muleteers. I prefer to wait for the night of Santa Luzia."

"That's only four days from now."

As the date approached they became more and more anxious and were torn by their hopes in accordance with their anguish.

The day before the eve of Santa Luzia, João Pio came in from a round of the farm with bad news.

"Veado is on his knees," he said.

Veado was the finest ox on the fazenda, the most powerful and most docile. He was gray with big patches of white on his belly. Yet João Pio had looked after him well: he seemed capable of holding out for a long time. The sun had suddenly brought him to his knees. His heart could not hold out; and he was dead. As if to confirm João Pio's news, three *urubus,* black vultures, appeared in the sky and described two great circles above the valley where the corpse lay.

At last December 12th came. Anxiety and impatience were at their height among the colored workers as well as the bosses. On all the fazendas of Ceará the same test was about to take place, for everybody had absolute faith in it. "The pieces of rock salt never tell lies," they said.

João Pio had everything ready. The moment the sun went down he brought a plank to the middle of the corral and on it in line placed six pieces of rock salt, each as big as a hazelnut. Antonio, Paulina, Miguel Carlos, and all the Negroes had formed a circle and were looking at these pieces of salt with a sort of eagerness: as they looked their faces took on the intensity of spirit mediums. Would the pieces of rock salt respond to their hopes? Each piece was supposed to represent a month: January, February, March, April, May, and June.

If one of the pieces melted or became humidified in the course of the night, then there would be rain during the month which it represented. Nobody could look at them during the night for fear that one or the other of them might have the evil eye and divert the beneficent influences.

"Get indoors," said João Pio to the Negroes. "And no one is to go outside before sunrise."

"Supposing we were to go and say a prayer with Antonio?" proposed Miguel Carlos who was being drawn back to the practice of his religion by fear of a cataclysm.

Miguel was a man who would brave any dangers and face up to every difficulty but, confronted with the drought, he felt powerless and his faith returned. He knew how to defend himself on the human plane and feared nobody. But drought was not on the human plane. There undoubtedly existed a mysterious power with unfathomable designs. That must be God. There was nothing more to be done but to beg for His pity.

Miguel Carlos, who was the child of his endeavors, could measure better than anybody the extent of such a disaster. For the loss of his plantations he would find consolation fairly quickly, but the loss of his cattle meant the annihilation of the product of twenty years' labor and struggle with the land and men. At his age he could never again rebuild for himself; and he could not count on Antonio. It would be the downfall of the Maciels.

He did not sleep that night. His mind dwelt on that downfall. He pictured the valleys strewn with the corpses of beasts killed by the sun; he saw his magnificent bull Lampeao lying on his side with his eyes closed and his belly already inflated by the vapors of death. Horrified by this vision, he sat up on his couch, wiped his forehead, then lay down again telling himself that he must not shout before the blow came. Perhaps next morning he would find one of the pieces of rock salt wet?

How long the night was! How lugubrious with the shrieks of owls, the croaking of toads, and those distant lowings of famished cattle! Oh, Santa Luzia, see that at least one piece is wet tomorrow morning!

The dawn came. Miguel Carlos opened the window of his room. Not the least trace of mist was to be seen on the sides of the menacing sierra. Miguel's heart was beating fast. He went down into the corral. João Pio was already there, standing in front of the little pieces of rock salt aligned on the board.

"Well?" Miguel asked from a distance.

"They're all dry," said João Pio.

"All of them?"

"All of them."

Miguel Carlos went to the board to verify the sinister portent for himself. He examined the pieces most carefully one by one, hoping all the same to discover a trace of dampness on them. They were all as dry as if they had remained for hours exposed to the sun. He stood up and without a word went back on the veranda. Paulina arrived at that moment.

"What then?" she asked, already uneasy on seeing the despondency of the men.

"They're all dry," said Miguel, "every one of them."

Paulina let her arms drop and sat down on the bench, for her legs were giving way.

"What are we going to do?" she asked.

"I don't know. We'll see."

The Negroes had arrived in the corral. João Pio had informed them of the result. They could be heard discussing it. "We must get to the coast," one said. "We could find refuge in the direction of Teresinha," said another. Then Miguel Carlos stood up and from the level of the veranda shouted at them:

"You'll leave when you're told to. I know what I'm about. I'm the one who gives orders here."

He had already recovered all his energy. Setbacks were brief with him: they did not last. He turned toward Paulina.

"I'm off for Quixeramobim," he said. "I'm going to see what the others decide to do. This evening we'll make our decision."

As he went along the passage to reach his room, he caught sight of Antonio on his knees in front of two statuettes with a candle burning on each side of them.

"Blockhead!" he muttered, for he no longer believed in God's pity nor that of the saints.

8. The Nocturnal Cavalcade

WHEN Miguel Carlos went into Mundico's botequim, at about one o'clock in the afternoon, there was already a crowd of people in front of the counter as if all the fazendeiros of the district had arranged to meet there. There was old Mariano from Flores Novas, with his great white mustaches and the mane of a lion; tall Soarès from San Bernardo with his riding whip hanging from his arm; fat Macedo from Conceição with his gold watch chain across his belly and, on his fingers, three enormous rings set in emeralds, rubies, and sapphires; and Moraes from Cachoeira, a half-breed with a mysterious Hindu look about him; and little Oliveira from Riacho do Sangre, quite bald; and a tenant farmer of the Araujos, one Sodré, from Pedra Branca. Excepting Moraes and Miguel Carlos (it is not fitting for half-breeds to put themselves on a level with the whites) all were wearing the white suits of "colonels" and big hats of fine straw.

Conversation was general and well enlivened by the rum. They had all made the experiment with the pieces of rock salt and in every case the pieces had remained dry. So a cataclysm was inevitable. Macedo, the richest of them, was of opinion that no time was to be lost: he was going to drive his cattle immediately to the banks of the Jaguaribe.

"It's all right for you to talk," Soarès retorted. "You have the Oliveiras there, they're relations and they'll give you leave to put your animals on their pastures. I haven't a chance like that."

"There's much solidarity in time of drought," said old Mariano.

"You still have to find decent people," Soarès corrected him.

"And you must be able to pay," added Moraes.

"As for that, there's always some way of coming to terms. You pay in cattle."

"I know that," replied Moraes. "They take your best heads and you return home ruined. A lot of sympathy is shown to you, plenty of compassion: but you don't get help and, if you are helped, you must pay and pay well."

"As for me," said Soarès, "I intend to go down toward Goyaz and sell all my beasts. I believe that's safest."

"You'll never reach Goyaz," said Macedo. "You need at least five days to get across the parched country. The cattle will never stand up to it."

"If everybody goes toward the Jaguaribe, there won't be enough pasturage."

Miguel Carlos had ordered himself a rum, and, leaning on the counter, was listening attentively to all that was being said. He found that this conversation could not yield any result. It wasn't a matter of expressing opinions but of making decisions. He broke in:

"Before asking ourselves where we'll go to," he said, "we must first know whether we're to leave or to remain."

"I'm staying, I am," Moraes affirmed.

"You don't believe in the pieces of rock salt?" rapped out Macedo.

"No. Five years ago, you remember, they were dry and it rained in the month of January."

"Very little rain there was."

"It revived the pasture lands and the cattle were saved."

"Saved is only a way of saying it. Many head of cattle were lost."

"Fewer than if we'd left in an exodus."

"The fight against drought is hard."

"It's nothing if you win out. The laborers will stay behind in any case. They don't like leaving the country."

The discussion continued for more than two hours, becoming more and more long-winded as the rum took effect on their heads. Finally, they were all agreed—except Macedo—that they had better wait until the end of the month of January, even at the cost of some losses.

"We mustn't give in until the utmost limit is reached," said Soarès.

They were all of this opinion. They were hard men, descendants of pioneers, born for fighting, or half-breeds with roots in this unprofitable soil which was their land.

Miguel Carlos was satisfied, for he also was a fighter. He had made up his mind not to give in before exhausting his last resources.

Back at Formosa, he declared to João Pio that he was resolved to hold out until the end of January.

"Beginning tomorrow we must mark all the places where we can dig *caçimbas*."

Caçimbas are little wells a yard or two deep which are dug in the farm lands and yield a small quantity of water for a few days.

"The river has not run dry yet," said João Pio. "There will be water in it until the New Year."

"Good. We have a fortnight to dig the caçimbas."

"We mustn't dig them too quickly otherwise they'll dry up."

"Naturally. We'll start work when there's only a trickle of water left in the river."

A few days later it was Christmas. Every year this festival gave place to rejoicings. Cakes were usually baked for the farm hands. The herdsmen would provide an *encamisada,* an equestrian spectacle similar to the display which the Arabs give on their festive occasions.

That year they did not make cakes and there was no encamisada. Under threat of the scourge they all took refuge in prayer and concentrated their greatest hopes on Antonio. They no longer took him for a fool but as an inspired man, and were not far from believing that he had direct relations with God. Now they felt respect for his strange mystical demeanor.

It was Miguel Carlos who suggested going with the whole staff to hear Padre Julio's midnight mass at Quixeramobim.

When they arrived at the village it was a little after eleven o'clock. The night was icy cold, the sky sprinkled with stars and the moon cast the shadows of the two church spires as far as the middle of the square. There was already a considerable crowd of people, divided into little groups of five or six men (there were very few women. Paulina was one of the exceptions permitted to make this midnight trip). The conversations were animated, each person contributing some new detail regarding their chances of escaping the catastrophe.

Padre Julio's midnight mass was always a success but, when drought was threatening, it attracted many more participants. They consisted of people of all degrees and colors: fazendeiros, tenant farmers (sharecroppers, that is), farm workers, whites, half-breeds, Negroes, and mulattoes. It was one of those occasions on which they regained consciousness of their solidarity: they felt a need to support one another in the merciless struggle they were about to have against earth and sun.

When they all went inside, the church was full. The altar with its little silver-plated columns, gilt tabernacle, and copper candlesticks, was glittering with lights, for most of those present had brought their package of candles: and so the padre had no need to economize and could arrange a glowing red altar such as he liked.

About halfway through the service he went into the pulpit, a little pulpit of black jacaranda wood on a pillar to the right. He announced that he was going to try to move the Divinity to have pity on them; but he did not know how it would work out. God must be dissatisfied with the hinterland; he must have his reasons. There was nothing else to do but to beg his forgiveness and do penance. That was why nocturnal cavalcades would be organized in all the fazendas. On Tuesday he would go to Flores Novas, on Thursday to Riacho do Sangue, and so forth, to preside over the ceremony. Miguel Carlos noted that he would come to Formosa on the Monday of the week following.

After mass Miguel sent Paulina to Mundico's botequim where she could wait for him. With Antonio, João Pio, and the farm laborers, he remained behind to talk under the moonlight with the men from the surrounding country. They all had a feeling of the disaster which was hanging over their heads. All had the vague presentiment that the sun would crush them and drive them from their land, but they were so solidly attached to the soil of Ceará that they were determined to fight on to the limit of their strength.

"Padre Julio gave us a magnificent mass," said a half-breed who was still dazzled by the illuminations and silver-reflected lights and by the altar.

"He's a good padre: he takes care of the people."

"After a mass like that," remarked a Negro, "we ought to have rain."

"If it doesn't rain on my place within a fortnight of the cavalcade, I'm clearing off."

"Too quick. If it rains, it will be in the second fortnight of January."

At that moment a man in a white linen suit and wearing a Panama hat took Miguel Carlos by the arm.

"How are you?"

Miguel looked at him and then shook his hand.

"Why, Senhor Souza dos Santos! I hadn't seen you. Where have you come from?"

It was Paulina's father. He had arrived at the mass a little late.

"If you'd like to see Paulina, she's at Mundico's waiting for us."

"No need. I've nothing to say to her."

He added after a short silence:

"Nothing yet?"

"What do you mean, nothing?"

"She's not yet pregnant?"

"No . . . no. To tell the truth, I haven't asked her."

"And Antonio?"

"He's here."

Miguel looked around the group for him.

"Where is he?" he asked a farm worker.

"He returned to the church," said the Negro. "He asked to be advised when we were leaving."

"Always the same," said Souza laughing. "He's not a man; he's a monk. Give my regards to Paulina and excuse me for leaving you: I'm going back to Massapé with some people from Queixada: they're waiting for me."

The Maciels were home again a little before sunrise. They slept throughout the day but, toward evening, Miguel Carlos went out to inspect the sugar canes. The planting was destroyed: the canes were dry, down to the roots. Even a fall of rain would not have brought them to life again. The weeds had been burned up and the soil was greatly cracked. On returning to the fazenda he was somewhat enervated. No doubt he believed in the efficacy of the prayers and penances, but there was no denying the facts. The drought was beginning to rage brutally.

"We mustn't wait too long before digging those caçimbas," he said to João Pio.

"We'll begin after the cavalcade. There's still a thin trickle of water in the river."

"It's a good river all the same," said Miguel as if speaking to himself. "If only we could have made a dam, we'd be able to resist every drought. We couldn't save the plantings but we'd save the cattle."

Late on Monday afternoon, as he had announced, Padre Julio arrived at Formosa. They took him into the big room. Miguel Carlos, Antonio, and Paulina soon came to join him.

"You'll accept a cup of coffee, padre?"

"Ha! . . ." said Julio, wiping his forehead, "if only you had a glass of rum. . . ."

Miguel liked that about Julio. He did not care for padres who drink only water, coffee, and other spiritless beverages. He sat down opposite the priest.

"Frankly," he said, "do you believe that after this cavalcade we'll have water?"

"My friend," retorted Julio, "I am only a man like yourself. I do not know God's point of view."

"Ah! Ah!"

"But," added the padre having poured himself out a bumper of rum, "if you do not address your prayer to Him with faith and fervor, you'll get nothing. He'll see quite well that you're not so deeply interested. . . . Let us not delay. I've sent my two curates, one to Boa Viagem and one to Massapé, and I've fixed the meeting for six o'clock at the crossing of the Boa Viagem-Massapé and Tamburil-Formosa roads."

"The Boa Viagem people are coming too?"

"Naturally. The hatreds are finished, aren't they?"

Miguel Carlos hailed João Pio.

"In the saddle," he shouted, "we're leaving. Fetch the horses."

With the padre they were thirteen: Miguel, Antonio, João Pio, and nine Negro laborers. One farm hand remained behind to watch the shed. Paulina remained indoors with the servant woman.

When they arrived at the meeting place all the delegations were already there. From Boa Viagem there were about twenty people; from Tamburil, twelve. Souza dos Santos had brought nine men with him from Massapé. Padre Julio immediately unfolded the surplice which he had attached to the pommel of his saddle; the two curates followed his example. Two men jumped from their horses and cleared a little space of ground and placed there a candle which they lit. Padre Julio said a short prayer and then took his place at the head of the cavalcade with the two curates.

Night had fallen and the sky was full of stars; the air suddenly became icy-cold but there was no wind. The procession followed a track which at first went across the land belonging to Miguel Carlos and then that of Souza dos Santos. They stopped when they had progressed a little over half a mile. Again two men sprang from their horses, cleared a piece of ground, and planted on it a candle which they lit. And so on, at a distance of about half a mile from one candle to the next, they repeated the ceremony. When they reached the heights of Massapé and could look over the whole plain reaching as far as Formosa, they could see the road they had taken marked with points of light. They felt, as it were, a mystical emotion. How could heaven not respond to men who dressed the earth with candles? By becoming absorbed in the ceremony which they fulfilled, confidence came to them as in the case of a man who, at the end of a long prayer, begins to feel himself touched by grace. Antonio was participating in a nocturnal cavalcade for the first time and was moved by it to his innermost depths. His imagination, sensitive to mystical spectacles, was stirred: and he felt certain that it would rain in the second fortnight of January.

They wandered throughout the night until dawn marking the land with their little yellow stars. When the sun rose above the sierra, Padre Julio turned his horse toward the east and with arms outstretched cried: "Lord, deliver us from the sun!"

Then each man returned from there in the direction of his own land with the joy in his heart of regained confidence. They now felt themselves able to wait for the rain.

"I believe," said Miguel Carlos as he went into the corral at Formosa, "that Padre Julio has got rain for us. It was a beautiful ceremony."

The spectacle had impressed him very deeply and his faith, which often wavered, had been vigorously revived.

"I also feel that it will rain," said João Pio.

"It will certainly rain," Antonio interposed for once.

"May God will it! But while awaiting the water from heaven, we must take what there is in the earth. We must begin making the caçimbas tomorrow."

They began this work. It was the hardest, most exhausting, most murderous work they ever did in the hinterland. From six o'clock in the morning the men were at their posts in the place indicated to them by the foreman. Each man was to open a hole—one, two, of three yards deep—until he found water. . . . Thus, once the river was dry, the cattle could still be watered for a few days: poorly, but sufficiently to hold out. To open a hole of one or two yards in depth is not a herculean task, but to open that hole under a hellish sun in an atmosphere as dry as if it had come from a blast furnace, without ever being able to seek shelter for an instant (there is no shade: the trees are stripped) demands a certain effort. The Negroes were working in this manner for twelve hours daily with pick, shovel, and hoe. In spite of intense sweating, they could not remain naked: even the secretion of their skin would not have protected them from the murderous rays. So they wore their short leather jackets and hats. In normal times this kind of jacket, well-greased, keeps pliable: but in times of drought, under the brutal action of the sun it becomes stiff with horny points which wound and a hard rough surface which tears the skin.

While the Negroes looked for water, Miguel Carlos and João Pio were going over the farm lands on horseback to round up the cattle into one valley, where they could be fed with maize from the reserve, and water brought to an old stone drinking trough. Antonio had offered his services but the men did not want them: he would only have slowed down the work. All the more so as even now they could not make very quick progress. The horses had become weak and could not keep up a long gallop; and they were afraid, because at this time the snakes, for their survival, were moving toward the coast in mass. The ground everywhere was infested with them. It could no longer be a question of killing them, for they came in tens of thousands.

In the evening the Negroes in the shed, at the end of their tether, collapsed on the straw like men knocked senseless, but very soon the servant woman brought them *jurema* tea. A quarter of an hour later they were themselves again; although jurema tea wears out the system, it has the immediate property of banishing fatigue.

Fortunately, for there was now night work to be done at the fazenda. Every evening, as soon as they had drunk their infusion and swallowed their stew made with maize and black beans, João Pio took three men with him to drive off the bats. These fell in a mass on the cattle to suck their blood. They had to be dispersed with gunshots.

Thus, every day the fight against the drought and all its consequences expanded. They were few to endure such a battle. Even by working in relays at their task, they could sleep only for a few hours. Beaten down by the inhuman heat and light, by the snakes, bats, and the vultures which circled around stalking some dead beast, menaced by hunger and thirst, the men of the hinterland obstinately faced the situation in the hope that soon a liberating cloud would rise in that implacably blue sky.

Every night Paulina, enervated and distressed, went to lean on the balustrade of the veranda for an hour or so. She no longer thought of making love: she was unbalanced, and suffered from headaches, she was troubled by her stomach and irritation of the skin. She watched the sky for a long time to see whether she could find some indication of a change in the weather. The sky was clear, the moon shone brightly, the air was cold, and now she feared that great silence which enveloped the valley and was broken only occasionally by the shrieks of the owls and the distant shots fired by the men who were out dispersing bats.

9. The Exodus

On January 21st, full of a fierce hatred against heaven and earth, in revolt but powerless, Miguel Carlos decided that the Maciels were going to escape to the coast. João Pio had been in Quixeramobim the day before and had brought back sensational news from there. Many refugees, fazendeiros, and tenant farmers coming from the south, had already passed through the town in the direction of Fortaleza. There had been a free fight in Mundico's botequim:

a half dozen refugees on the way through had come to ask him for goods but declared that they could not pay and would pay him on their return. Mundico told them that he could not feed all those fugitives from the drought and refused to let them have the goods. Whereupon they drew their knives and wanted to attack him. He beat them off with blows of a machete. Two of the men jumped behind the counter. Then Mundico vanished through a door leading to the kitchen and ran to give the alarm to some men who were still in the street. While this was happening, the refugees pillaged his store, jumped on their horses and made off. However, two of them were still within carbine range when Mundico came out of Nico's house. Nico was good with a firearm and with two shots he downed the men. But Mundico said that he'd had enough of it. He hired an ox wagon for the next day and was leaving for Fortaleza with all his store of goods.

João Pio's account of what was happening had overcome the final hesitations on the part of Miguel Carlos.

"We won't go to Fortaleza," he said. "There are still people there who bear me a grudge because of the Araujo business. We'll go on the Jaguaribe. You'll leave this evening for Tamburil. You'll bring back everything: men and cattle. You'll load everything in my room and in Helena's on the wagon."

"What about the farm implements?"

"You can leave them. Take only a pick and a hoe, in case we get into difficulty with the wagon."

During João Pio's absence, which lasted three days, Miguel Carlos himself took over directing the work. Once again Antonio offered his help, but it was refused. Miguel supplied the cattle with water drawn from the caçimbas, and with maize which he brought from the shed on two mules; and he rounded back into the valley the animals which were trying to escape in search of water. He rested for an hour or two in the afternoon, and then in the evening went out again with three men to disperse the bats. His bronzed face, contracted by fatigue, looked like that of a convict doing forced labor. There were times when he felt overcome by a terrible lassitude. His sides pained him as if they had been compressed in a vise: his liver was heavy, and he had cramps in his buttocks. But he braced himself, drank some jurema tea and went back to work, braving the sun, his eye fixed on the south in the childish hope of seeing some sign of a cloud there.

Three days had elapsed since the foreman's departure. "He ought to be back," Miguel Carlos thought. "What's happening over there? Yet we haven't a minute to lose. The beasts are beginning to die like flies." He regretted that he himself had not gone to Tamburil.

A little before dawn on the fourth day, Miguel, tired out and his limbs aching, had just gone indoors to throw himself on his bed when he heard rising in the night the *aboiado*, the song of herdsmen driving their animals. He got up with a bound, went down into the corral, jumped on the horse tethered in the shed and sped to meet them. He had the herd turned into the valley where Antonio's cattle were penned in, and returned toward the fazenda with João Pio.

"Was it a hard job?" he asked.

"Hard enough. We collected the cattle and counted them, but I wanted to go around the pastures myself to see that nothing had been forgotten. Because forty-two head of cattle are missing."

Miguel Carlos did not wince: he opened his eyes a little.

"Forty-two!" he said.

"That seemed to me a lot, but it's correct: I saw it myself. Forty-two beasts and one man missing."

"A man?" Miguel was greatly surprised. "Where's he gone?"

"He's dead. He was bitten by a poisonous snake, a *cascavel*, and he passed away the same day. He urinated at least half a bucket of blood."

"Which one is it?"

"Leão Ferreira."

"A decent man. There wasn't his equal for castrating calves and cats. And his dog? His black fox terrier?"

"We've brought him with us. He's with the drovers."

They were now on the veranda: they remained for a moment without speaking. Paulina came to ask whether they would like a cup of coffee.

"Save your water," said Miguel. "Fetch us the rum."

She went to find the bottle and two little glasses, which she placed before them.

"When shall we leave?" she inquired.

"Tomorrow, when my cattle will be a little rested. We must go quickly. We're losing five or six head a day."

The sun rose and immediately imposed its fatal glaring light on the desolate landscape of the sierra. Miguel Carlos looked with hatred at the sky which had suddenly become blue. Antonio's and Miguel's Negro laborers were gathered together in the corral. They were arguing.

"It's a sad business," said one from Tamburil, "to leave a place where you've worked for so long."

"This country around here has no luck."

"It's better in the towns. You don't care a damn about drought there."

"Negroes work hard and earn little in the towns."

"They get more fun. To have a woman here, you must go to the village whorehouse and there's never anything but negresses. In the towns there are houses with white women."

"Old ones that the whites don't want any more."

"Yes, but they are whites."

Although they had been for more than two months subjected to the action of a pitiless sun, they conserved all their vitality.

"Go ahead with the caçimbas," João Pio called out to them: "It's the last day. We've leaving tomorrow. Try to draw as much water as possible so that the cattle will be able to face up to it. Let them have as much maize as they want."

While the Negroes were making their final effort to get the cattle fit for tomorrow's journey, Miguel and João Pio overhauled the axletrees of the wagons and Paulina collected what she wished to take with her. Left to himself, Antonio kept to his room and for hours remained seated on his bed.

Paulina was perhaps the only person who was not sad about leaving Formosa. She had her own reasons for this. Not being resigned to spend her life with that crackpot Antonio, she was hoping that this exodus would provide her with an opportunity to rid herself of him. Clearly she would no longer be mistress of a fazenda; but she preferred anything to that false situation at Formosa. She had tried to recapture a touch of life in her love adventures with João Pio, but, over them hovered at all times the menacing shadow of Miguel Carlos. She could not live a life divided between a crazy husband and a scared lover. She was conscious of her beauty; and she considered that she deserved better than that. The thought of town life enraptured her. She would never have been able to go to a big town but for the exodus. Fortunately the drought had come. Perhaps she would be able really to live.

She put in her trunk all her clothes and knickknacks, not omitting a single thing, as if she would never return. Meanwhile she assumed a sad countenance, for Miguel Carlos was gloomy and careworn and he believed—she thought—that everybody was like himself. In regard to him she harbored an indefinable feeling of fear mingled with admiration, hate, and confidence. He inspired respect in her; but she did not love him.

That evening the bosses and workers went to bed early: they had to be well rested for the morning. During the night the bats were able to have the time of their lives: there was nobody to disperse them.

The departure took place with the rising of the sun. All the herdsmen on horseback dashed off toward the valley, encircled the cattle and drove them on the road to Quixeramobim. The two wagons followed, each drawn by six oxen. Installed on the last one were Paulina and the negress servant. Women's bones are not hard enough to sustain—even on horseback—a march of twelve hours under the burning sun, and their skin is too delicate. They had put Antonio with them, for in the course of the night he had a recurrence of his dysentery.

"Get up on this wagon," said Miguel when he was told about it, "otherwise you'll die on the way."

Miguel Carlos and João Pio on horseback wound up the column. It was a long one. When the head reached the pass on the range of hills, the tail had hardly got beyond the plantations of sugar cane. In some parts of the road, the burned fields unfolded a gray-beige carpet as far as the foot of the mountain: here and there they caught sight of skeletons of bullocks or horses already bleached. A great anteater had come to die at the edge of the road: its swollen corpse was already covered with flies and ants. Flights of birds passed over them high in the sky moving in the direction of the coast.

"I wonder whether we'll still find a little water left at Quixeramo-bim," remarked Miguel Carlos.

"I doubt it," replied João Pio. "When Mundico left, there were not more than six caçimbas which gave any."

"If we don't find water, we'll lose many beasts."

"Many—especially bullocks. The bullocks have become very weak."

"If only we can save the three bulls."

"As for the bulls, there's no danger. They'll hold out. Besides, they've been better looked after than the others."

When they reached the top of the pass on the sierra, Miguel Carlos turned in his saddle to contemplate for the last time the Maciel domain. João Pio was expecting him to express some kind of regret, but he did not utter a word. He knew how to keep his regrets and hopes to himself.

On arrival at Quixeramobim early in the afternoon, Miguel Carlos had his cattle penned on the church square. The town was completely abandoned. Doors and shutters were closed. There was no longer a trace of life anywhere. Two or three men remained to watch over the herd: the others lay down in the shadow of the houses. But soon they had to get up. Every house was invaded by tens of thousands of fleas. Paulina, Antonio, and the servant went to lie down in the shade of the church.

The sun was terrifying. One's hand could not be held on the back of a bullock or a horse: it burned like a sheet of hot iron. Miguel Carlos and João Pio went to inspect the banks of the river. They found many caçimbas but they were dried up.

"Maybe we'll find some at the foot of the hill on the road to Quixada," said João.

"Let's go," said Miguel.

They spurred their horses and galloped toward the north of the town. There were some caçimbas there—all completely dry.

Miguel Carlos drew his hand across his forehead.

"We're going to advance by forced marches. By leaving at sun-down, we'll be at Trapia tomorrow morning."

"There's no water at Trapia," João Pio replied. "It's one of the most arid places I know. The beasts are very tired. There will be many losses."

"Whatever the losses may be, we must get out of this. If we delay here, it'll be worse."

When they returned to the church, Paulina was eating a pineapple.

"Where did you get that?" asked Miguel.

"I bought some."

"Give me a slice."

"It'll make you more thirsty, boss," said João Pio.

"No, the night will soon be on us. Cold calms the thirst."

They set out again at about half-past six, soon after sundown. Some exhausted bullocks were lying down. The drovers swooped on them armed with goads with which they prodded the beasts' haunches, necks, or bellies, shouting all the time. Thus roused, the bullocks at last got on their feet.

"That's good," thought Miguel Carlos, "we won't leave a single one at Quixeramobim."

He was in a hurry to leave, to reduce the distance which separated him from the Jaguaribe River. João Pio maintained that no water would be found at Trapia. What did he know about it? Water behaves in strange ways; sometimes you find it where least expected. Moreover, if their was no water, the march would continue during the day, whatever the cost. If they marched well, they would reach Lagoa in the evening and they would find water there. A second march under the burning sun would be hard; many animals would remain on the ground. But there could be no hesitating. The strongest would survive: this was the law of life.

They had hardly gone more than about a quarter of a mile beyond the last house in Quixeramobim when a cow collapsed. The Maciels had few cows: they devoted themselves almost entirely to raising bullocks. The cow that died on the side of the trail was one of their good breeders. João Pio had leaped from his horse and was examining her. He opened her eyes and felt her ears.

"If we could make her drink, she'd pick up," he said.

"Leave her," Miguel Carlos ordered. "There may not be enough water for us and the men. Let her die. There's nothing to be done about it."

Night had fallen. The column was advancing on a broad plain in the direction of a line of hills. The bats had appeared and were flying in thousands over the herd. It was necessary to disperse them and, while at the head of the herd the nostalgic notes of the *aboiado* rose toward the stars, at the tail end the night was broken by shots from firearms.

On the wagon Paulina and the negress had dropped off to sleep exhausted. Antonio was muttering prayers.

Before they had reached the sierra, two horses and seven bullocks had lain down, the horses silently, the bullocks lowing sadly.

"This is going badly," said João Pio. "The cattle won't stand up to a second march under the blazing sun."

"You get on my nerves," retorted Miguel Carlos. "If there's no water at Trapia, we must get to Lagoa in the evening whatever the losses may be."

João Pio fell silent: he knew that he must not insist when Miguel Carlos had made up his mind.

At sunrise they were in sight of Trapia, whose white gables added a bright patch to the grayish immensity of the parched plain. They arrived there an hour later. After crossing the sierra they had a further loss of two horses, two heifers, and four bullocks. Trapia is a little village with about thirty small dwellings: they were all abandoned. João Pio rapidly went over the ground as far as the foot of a neighboring hill. He found many caçimbas in it, large and deep, in witness to the energetic struggle of the men of that place against the drought. But there was no water: all the wells were exhausted.

"I expected as much," said João Pio, disheartened.

"Run ahead," commanded Miguel Carlos. "Tell them not to halt."

And under the hot sun the herd resumed the march on the plain in the direction of another sierra of which the reddish peaks with rugged outlines could just be seen.

"It's time we reached a place where there's water," said João Pio. "There's only a few cupfuls left in the skin bottles."

"Lagoa is over yonder on the other side of the sierra, two hours' ride from the saddle of the hill," said Miguel Carlos. "We'll get there."

It was eleven o'clock in the morning when the event occurred. Miguel Carlos gave the warning. It could not escape him for he had a quick sure eye and keen penetrating sight. He pulled up his horse brusquely and shaded his eyes with his hand.

"Look," he said to João Pio.

Very far away, almost at the foot of the sierra, they could discern a white cloud on a level with the ground like a patch of retarded morning mist. But at eleven o'clock in the forenoon there could not be any morning mist left there, because of the burning sun.

"What are we going to do?" João Pio asked in an anxious tone of voice.

"Get the men to make a half-turn and let them head the cattle at a gallop for the other side of the river."

A short time before this they had in fact crossed a dry river bed. In any case it would make a good rampart. The fire would come as far and die down on the bank. As there was no wind, it would not succeed in jumping across the stony bed of this river, which was more than twenty yards wide.

Thus warned, the cattlemen faced the herd and with their goads tried to make them turn aside from the route. But the animals, finding themselves on the way toward the water, refused to obey and wanted to charge ahead. The herdsmen drove their horses into the dense mass of bullocks and planted their goads right and left, letting out guttural shouts. Miguel Carlos had himself taken charge of the wagons.

"What's the matter?" Paulina inquired.

"Prairie fire."

The cloud of smoke had greatly expanded: it advanced with extraordinary rapidity.

"Hey there!" Miguel yelled at the herdsmen. "Get a move on. Pitch into the main body!"

Standing in their stirrups the cattlemen bestirred themselves like devils. They had at last forced the herd to move around in a half circle, but about fifteen horses had escaped and continued on their march toward the sierra.

"Leave them!" Miguel shouted. "As soon as they smell the tang of smoke they'll rejoin us at a gallop."

Behind the cloud, which seemed to progress with increasing speed, they now caught sight of short, bright flames. A tang of burned grass filled the air. The herd began to gallop, closely fol-

lowed by the herdsmen. The horses which had refused to come
back behind the river now joined them again, racing in panic.

The wagons had already crossed the river.

"*Vamos! Diabos! Andan!*—come, you devils, get a move on!"
yelled the men, meanwhile driving the animals.

The last bullocks were going into the bed of the river when the
cloud of smoke reached them. The heat of the fire combined with
that of the sun became monstrous, inhuman. Stifled by the thick
pungent smoke, exhausted by the effort they had just shown, the
men's legs were trembling. They took off their sweat-soaked shirts,
rolled them around their heads and threw themselves flat on their
bellies with their faces against the soil. It was the only way to
escape asphyxiation. Paulina and her servant had rolled themselves
in the blankets. Miguel Carlos had remained at the edge of the
river, his head rolled in his shirt like the others, but he was trying
to see whether the fire was going to leap across to where they
were on the left bank. Unfortunately every time he half-opened his
eyelids he was blinded by the aggressive smoke. How long was this
smoke going to stifle them? It rose and cleared only very slowly,
hanging about in the hot motionless air. All the terrified cattle had
continued their flight in the direction of Trapia.

In half an hour's time the smoke at last became thinner. Miguel
Carlos was able to make sure that the fire had not come across.
The herd of cattle was safe. It was now scattered all over the plain
as far as Trapia. They would have to get it together again quickly,
otherwise it was capable of returning to Quixeramobim.

"Go ahead, men!" Miguel shouted. "Let's not waste any time."

The herdsmen leaped into the saddle. Their black faces covered
with perspiration betrayed no weakening: they were hard, willing
faces.

"You haven't a drop of water, boss?" one of the men asked.

"Give them what's left in the skins," said Miguel to João Pio.

There was hardly enough to wet each man's throat and the water
was warm, but with a little liquid on their tongues they felt
refreshed. They set out at a gallop to find the herd.

It took nearly an hour to round it up again. The column, once
more re-formed, crossed the protecting river again and the song

of the herdsmen rose toward the sun as if in sheer bravado. The
men were not yet defeated.

On the black burned plain the atmosphere was so stifling hot
that it was no longer possible to breathe except with the mouth
open, which parched the tongue terribly. The men then licked the
perspiration which was running down their arms, to relieve the
pangs of thirst. But their burning thirst became worse.

Paulina had one more pineapple which she shared with Miguel,
João Pio, Antonio, and the negress servant. It was warm and did
not refresh them, and was also rather nauseating, being too sweet.

It was not until two hours after sundown that they reached the
saddle of the sierra. Twenty-three beasts had remained behind on
the plain.

"Now we're saved," said João Pio.

"You see that the cattle stood up to it," said Miguel. "Without
that damned fire we wouldn't have lost ten head."

"It's been a narrow escape."

They were pleased. They had the feeling of having won a
victory. They felt themselves capable of going on still farther than
Lagoa. The losses were heavy, though not irreparable. The bulls
had not shown any signs of weakening; the horses held out well.
Brave little Arabian horses with the desert in their blood! They
were getting near to the goal. Two or three more hours of effort
and the game would be won.

Never had Miguel Carlos known such a disappointment. For the
first time he was seized with despondency, a physical despondency
as if his nerves and bones did not want any more of it. He had got
down from his horse and was sitting in the dust on the side of the
road. The cattle were massed in the only street of the abandoned
village. It was already night. The sky was covered with stars. The
air was growing cold. The herdsmen were gathered together at
the entrance to the village some distance from Miguel. They were
awaiting orders from the boss. They did not speak: they were dumb
with anxiety. If there was no water for the beasts, there was none
for the men either and the water bottles were empty. From Lagoa
to the Jaguaribe River was a day and a half of good going. All of
them, even João Pio, were sadly chewing jurema leaves to abate

fatigue, but thirst was gnawing at their stomachs and entrails. One more day and a half without a drink of water! Oh yes, they could have jumped on their horses, set out at a gallop and would certainly have reached the Jaguaribe before dawn; but there are things which are not done. You don't abandon the boss in such circumstances.

When Miguel Carlos went up to them, they made way for him. Miguel's face was calm and his look had lost nothing of that vigor which so greatly impressed the Negroes.

"This is what we're going to do," he said to them. "Three men are going to leave for the river. Let them take good horses: they'll take with them six waterskins which they'll fill and come back to meet us. In this way we'll gain half a day. We'll have something to drink tomorrow early in the afternoon. How's that?"

"Very good, boss."

The three men detached the leather water carriers which were tied to the wagon, sprang on their horses and disappeared into the night. The others took their places again at the head of the column in the village. The melancholy song of the *aboiado* arose in the great nocturnal silence: a shot rang out announcing that the bat hunting had begun.

The cattle, which one might have regarded as exhausted, quickened their march as if carried along by a new burst of energy. The mass of bullocks went forward tumultuously with a great swinging of paunches and clashing of horns.

"They scent the water," said João Pio.

"May God will it," said Miguel prudently.

Carried along by the instinct of self-preservation, the animals had recovered an astonishing vitality. In the course of that night march not one of them faltered. It was only when the sun rose that the herd slowed down their gait as if they felt the presence of the enemy. All of a sudden the heat was torrid. The column was at that moment crossing a stony plain with heaps of gravel here and there: this had been turned over in colonial days by men seeking precious stones. During the forenoon only two bullocks had collapsed; which did not much matter. Miguel Carlos felt that he was master of the situation. At half-past eleven the men's effort was rewarded: the herdsmen were back with filled waterskins. Water at last. It was tepid, but it appeased the dried-up tissues.

"Don't drink too much at one go," João Pio ordered. "You'll get cramps."

The Negroes did not listen to him. They drank in long draughts and then holding their bellies with both hands let out a resounding laugh.

Paulina and the servant woman did not wish to drink more than a few mouthfuls. They said that this warm water nauseated them. Antonio drank greedily: the thirst tortured him more than the others, for his bowels were on fire.

It was nearly five o'clock in the afternoon when they crossed a little chain of hills and emerged onto a green plain. There were trees with leaves on it. Pasturages extended to the left further than one could see. To the right a vast cotton field and a plantation of sugar canes were seen. The bullocks wanted to rush in this direction, but the herdsmen drove them back into line with furious goadings.

All of a sudden, before anything could happen to forestall it, the herd whirled around vigorously a few times: it spread out and swooped forward. The herdsmen were overwhelmed and worked desperately with their goads over the tide of horns which surrounded them. At that moment the oxen drawing the wagon in turn swept forward. Shaken by the violent bumps, Paulina and the negress servant yelled in despair. Miguel Carlos hurled his horse forward and seized one of the leading oxen by a horn but the beast was almost mad. With an angry thrust of its head if forced Miguel to let go. The wagon gave a terrific lurch and overturned. Paulina, the servant, and Antonio were flung violently onto the ground with the trunks, waterskins, and farm implements. Paulina uttered a piercing shriek. João Pio rushed toward her.

"It's all right, it's all right," she said, pulling herself together. "I haven't come to any harm."

Antonio and the negress felt their limbs to see that none was broken. With its wheels in the air, the wagon had been carried forward by the unchained oxen.

The Jaguaribe River was just over a quarter of a mile away. It was about a hundred yards wide at that place and formed a bend which had created a shore, a little beach of gray sand. It was on the side where the cattle had dashed forward to reach the water. Some of the cattle had waded into the river; they had water up to their paunches. The horses, being harder to please, had gone upstream to a point where the water was clear. They did not stop drinking; they gorged themselves with water. When a bullock, its belly taut like the inner tube of a tire fully inflated, returned toward the bank, it looked at the men gratefully and then went off at a slow pace toward a bluish clump of the thick grass which could be perceived a few hundred yards away.

Having drunk their fill, Miguel Carlos, Antonio, Paulina, the servant, and João Pio had come to stretch themselves out in the shade of a giant aroeiro tree. They lay on their backs listening to the rumbling of their bellies and remained quite motionless to avoid cramps. The farm hands were lying further off under an umbuseiro tree: they had again begun chewing jurema leaves to combat the frightful fatigue which was contracting their chests and racking their joints. Two were groaning, tortured by cramps; they had drunk too much of the warm water when the men of the advance guard returned with the waterskins.

Nobody spoke: nobody wished to speak. It was first necessary to allow life to reinvigorate the enfeebled systems, to let the fatigue go out of their bones and muscles.

The cattle dispersed over the plain, concentrating in the grassy parts. The men did not trouble about them, knowing that they would not stray far from the river.

Men and women had sunk into a heavy sleep when night came. They had not seen the sun go down nor did they even feel the presence of the horses which came to nuzzle them in gratitude. They could not hear the lapping of the river water against the banks. They heard it only in a dream. From time to time one or the other of them gave a sudden start, a brusque movement. Anguish had so entered into them that it still remained even after their relief: it stirred up horrible nightmares just as, after having emerged from a storm, one is still pursued by seasickness in his hotel bed.

10. The Adventure

WHEN Paulina awoke the sun was already fierce, but here there was not that infernal reflection from the parched earth. There was the shadow of the trees. There were coppices here and the tall grasses of the fallow land which softened the light. There was the coolness of the river. The men had gone to the little sandy beach to wash their shirts and trousers, which were clammy with perspiration. She caught sight of their big black naked bodies standing upright in the faint light of morning. The negress had gone to fetch the cooking pots: she had built a little hearth of stones and was attending to the cooking of beans and maize. Miguel Carlos was seated a little further off with João Pio. Antonio was still sleeping.

Paulina got up and stretched herself.

"Feeling better?" Miguel called out to her.

"I feel as if my back's broken," she said.

"That's the wagon. The wagon causes more fatigue than riding a horse."

"And that upset yesterday; it gave me a turn."

"Tomorrow it'll be all right. We're going to find a fazenda where we can get lodging."

When the men returned to the river, Miguel had two horses saddled.

"We're going to look for a place to put up," he said. "We'll come back in the afternoon or in the evening."

"You're not eating before leaving?" asked the negress. "The beans are almost cooked."

"No time," said Miguel Carlos. "We'll eat in the village. There's a botequim there."

They mounted their horses and set out in the direction of Barra da Cunha which was about a mile and a half away. It was a village of some fifty dwellings, two of them having two stories. The church, of colonial type, with two little spires, was very modest:

it was built of puddled clay and whitewashed. There was a commercial square with an old iron fountain in the center. On this square was Nico Justino's botequim, a fine store and café bar with six arcades.

Nico Justino was Portuguese and had all the characteristics of the Portuguese merchant: a magnificent corporation, a head like a ball, thick eyebrows, a heavy walrus mustache, and big black eyes with a restful look.

There were only two women customers in the store: they were looking over some cotton fabrics in the manner of all the women who came to the botequim. When Nico Justino saw Miguel Carlos and João Pio come in, he went forward toward them with an air of importance.

"Well?" he said. "You've arrived from the hinterland?"

He had not lost his Portuguese accent and pronounced *s* like *sh*.

"We got here in the end," said Miguel.

"You're among the last. It's more than a fortnight since the refugees passed through here. You held out for a long time."

"It's a wrench to leave your land."

"I know, I know . . . what will you drink—a rum?"

"Some rum."

Nico placed two glasses and a bottle on the counter.

"When I left Portugal," he continued, "I was very upset. It's funny how you esteem your land, even when you don't make a living on it."

"We were comfortable at our place," said Miguel. "It's this drought which drove us out."

"Bah! It'll pass over like the others. In Venezuela, it's the earthquakes, in Peru, the volcanoes, here it's the drought. There's always something to cause trouble. That's life."

"Have a glass with us," said Miguel.

Nico took a glass and helped himself.

"It's good, this rum of mine, isn't it? I make it myself. I have a little fazenda and go in mostly for sugar cane."

"You haven't any pasture land?"

"Very little. It's not worth speaking about. Why? No doubt you've brought cattle with you?"

"Yes. We'd like to settle them somewhere while waiting for the end of this drought."

"My poor friends," exclaimed Nico Justino throwing up his arms. "I think you've come far too late. All the land is already occupied. There are too many cattle. We haven't enough pasturages to feed so many beasts. How many head have you?"

"About three hundred."

"Dear me, dear me! You'll never find land for them here. All those other refugees have already brought thousands of head. You must go further. You ought to have taken another direction."

"That's that," Miguel said to himself. "We haven't finished yet. And after such an effort! Damn it! Well, we're not yet worn out."

He drank a good bumper of rum.

"You might get settled at Hallum's," Nico Justino then remarked, raising his hands in a gesture of doubt.

"Who's Hallum?" asked Miguel, clinging to any hope however faint it might be.

"He's a strange fellow, a Dutchman. He lives over yonder in a hollow of the sierra. He never leaves his place, not even on feast days. He's not a Christian. Perhaps he committed some crime in his own country. In any case we never see him. His foreman deals with all matters of business."

"Is it a big fazenda?"

"I should just think so! And well looked after, with some fine cattle on it. Maybe you could have a shot at seeing him. In a case like yours, you must risk trying anything. There's nothing doing with his foreman. He's already told some of the refugees that Hallum didn't want cattle on his lands. But if you could only succeed in seeing the man himself . . . You never know. He's a funny fellow."

"What about it?" asked Miguel Carlos, addressing João Pio.

"We'll go there."

They had another good glass of rum and were off toward the sierra. In order to reach Hallum's estate, they had to cross a fairly high hill. When they came to the summit, Miguel Carlos and João Pio were able to take in with a glance the Dutchman's domain. It was a magnificent valley which stretched like a wide corridor between two chains of hills. The dwelling house was situated in the middle and seemed to be spacious with an enormous red roof of new tiles and glittering white walls. It backed on a great orchard. To the left they noticed a banana plantation; some cotton fields spread out to the right. The pasturages must be at the other end of the valley, further away than the orchard.

When Miguel and João reached the gate of the corral, some dogs began barking furiously. A young mulatto appeared on the veranda, went down into the corral, ran across it and opened the gate.

"We'd like to speak personally to Senhor Hallum," said Miguel Carlos.

"Very well, senhor."

The mulatto went into the house again and a few moments later a white lady, who was no longer young, appeared. She was short and stout: her pale blue eyes imparted a still more uninteresting look to an already dull white face the color of those stalks of vegetables grown in cellars. Haughty and scornful, she had a superior bearing that was very different from the prepossessing and ceremonious bearing of the Portuguese landowning class. She was so distant that Miguel Carlos wondered whether it was worth while asking for an interview with the boss who, no doubt, was still more forbidding. But he decided that this was his last card and he couldn't afford not to play it.

"Most illustrious senhora," he said, "we come from the hinterland and we should like to have a talk with Senhor Hallum."

She looked them over calmly from head to foot.

"Come in," she said.

They were ushered into a drawing room such as they had never before seen. A big carpet of Moorish pattern covered the floor. In the center of the room there was a round rosewood table: around it were four chairs so delicately made that one hesitated to sit on them. On the walls hung some very large somber pictures—a few portraits and foreign landscapes—in heavy gilt frames. At the end of the room there was a big figure of Christ. Between the pictures were blue plates of windmill pattern.

Although they were asked to sit down, Miguel and João remained standing. They felt that the conversation would be brief and that they would go out with nothing.

Hallum came in. He was a man about sixty years of age with a thick mop of white hair, a white mustache trimmed short on a level with his lip. His chestnut eyes set off a big red nose. Short and broad-shouldered, he had no corporation. His suit was quite white, without the slightest speck, and gave him the appearance of a superior personage.

Miguel and João were more convinced than ever that the game was lost. This was not a man of their class: one would have said he was a governor. However, in an engaging tone he invited them to be seated.

"Well now," said Miguel Carlos collecting all his courage. "The drought has driven us from our fazenda in the hinterland. We have succeeded in getting to the Jaguaribe with a part of our cattle, but Nico Justino told us that there were already too many animals on the fazendas around here. He added that you were perhaps the only one who might still have a little place to harbor us."

"I'm not taking any people but, as for the cattle, it might be arranged. In the village they spread the rumor that I don't want to do anything for the refugees. I told them that I was willing to let them have some pasture lands, but they wanted to install themselves in my huts. That I won't have."

"We don't ask to be lodged on your place," Miguel Carlos hastened to make this clear. "We're only looking for somewhere to settle our cattle."

"How many head?"

"Three hundred."

"That's not many. I'm very willing to take them, but I insist that I don't want any farm hands from outside on my estate."

This put new heart into Miguel Carlos, for he had only one thing in mind: to save the cattle.

"I understand you," he said. "To have strangers would lead to disputes. But if you take the cattle you'll be rendering us a great service."

"It's not a service: it's a matter of business for me as it is for you. It will cost you one bullock a month. Do you agree to that?"

"Agreed. We hope to return home in September."

"You can take your cattle away again whenever you wish."

A negress brought a tray with glasses and the traditional bottle of rum. They drank and then Hallum asked why they had waited so long before quitting their land. Miguel Carlos told him of the fight they had put up, of their exodus, and of the prairie fire which had driven their herd almost mad.

"What a very odd idea," said Hallum, "to go and settle in such places."

"We hadn't enough money to be able to settle in fertile and well-watered places," said Miguel Carlos. "We began in a small way. We're only half-breeds."

"I know what it is," said Hallum as if speaking to himself. "You start something, work hard, and then some event happens and everything falls to pieces. There's no justice; none anywhere."

He remained thoughtful for a moment: he was thinking of the terrible bankruptcy of his export business in Rotterdam; of all the bank sharks who had swept down on him, of his flight to Brazil.

"See here," he said brusquely. "I'm going to put your mind at ease regarding your cattle. I authorize you to leave one man here to look after the herd. Your foreman for preference."

"This is my foreman," said Miguel pointing to João Pio.

"Well, well! I'll take you into my employ," said Hallum. "But you'll build yourself a hut on the pasture land. Does that suit you?"

"If my boss agrees," said João Pio.

"Naturally I do," said Miguel Carlos. "We couldn't have wished for anything better. I thank you, Senhor Hallum."

"No, no thanks: I know what I'm doing."

They went outside on the veranda and Hallum showed them the boundaries of his property which here and there was bordered by the sierras.

"It's too narrow," he said, "and too long. But there's always water. That's the main thing."

They agreed to bring the cattle next day. Miguel and João Pio again took the road for Barra da Cunha.

"Nico Justino told us that he wasn't a Christian," said Miguel Carlos when they were some distance away on the fallow land. "Yet he has a big figure of Christ in his main room."

"Nico Justino also said that there was no chance of making an arrangement with him."

"He's a friendly, obliging man. His manners aren't the same as those of us Brazilians, but he's a decent man."

"Then you think that I ought to remain with him?"

"Clearly you must. We couldn't have hoped for as much. We must have impressed him favorably, isn't that so? Or he may even be thinking of making use of you."

"And what are you going to do with Paulina, Antonia, and the farm laborers?"

"We'll see."

They called again at the botequim and told Nico Justino of the success of their venture.

"You see," said the big fat Portuguese, "I gave you good advice. I thought it would be a good solution."

"You said that it wouldn't succeed."

"I said . . . I said . . . I didn't say that. I said he was a funny man because I don't know him! I couldn't give you a guarantee. But I did tell you to go there."

"All right, all right," said Miguel. "Give us a drink . . . Now I must find lodgings and work for the men."

"There's nothing doing here," said Nico. "You won't find anything. And there's no work. All the fazendas have their own personnel. You must go on to Aracaty. In that place there are government agents who look after the refugees."

"You don't say so! The government looks after *us?*"

"It seems that there's an employment office."

They had to spend that night under the trees again. Paulina was indignant. She took Miguel Carlos and João Pio to task for not having found a lodging.

"You're just stupid," she said to them. "Moreover no doubt you didn't look around. All you're good for is going drinking in the botequims."

"Go yourself and you'll see that there's nothing doing," replied Miguel.

"If I'd gone I'd have found something. And there's Antonio with another attack of his dysentery. He can't stand on his legs and he's going to have to sleep on the stones."

"Fiddlesticks! It's the last night. Tomorrow we'll be leaving for Aracaty."

"I'd have done better to stay with my father," Paulina grumbled to herself.

"What's that?" said Miguel in a menacing tone. "Be careful what you say or things'll get hot here. There's only one master, and that's me. You understand?"

Paulina fell silent, rolled herself in a bedcover and lay down at the foot of the tree.

A few steps away Antonio was stretched on his back holding his belly with both hands. A little further on the farm laborers had lit a fire of wood and were squatting around it. The flames lit up fiercely their black, set, expressionless countenances.

Miguel Carlos was too excited to sleep. He had sat down on a stone and, smoking a long cigarette of twist tobacco, was looking at the golden crescent slowly mounting in the sky toward the Southern Cross.

Next morning it was necessary first of all to drive the cattle to Hallum's estate. João Pio took charge of this with the men. It occupied them the whole morning. Miguel Carlos had retained a dozen horses for the journey to Aracaty. One could not travel a hundred yards on foot. But, if they were given work, whether in a town or on distant fazendas, they could not keep their mounts. He had therefore decided that João Pio should accompany them and take the horses back to Hallum's estate.

On his return from driving the cattle João called at the botequim. Nico Justino told him that it was better not to make the journey to Aracaty on horseback. There were in the village two Negroes who owned a boat and could take them: the trip by the river was easier. Paulina immediately declared that she would prefer to go by boat.

"How much does it cost?" Miguel asked.

"That doesn't matter," said João Pio. "I'll pay, as I'm staying here. . . ."

Before making up his mind, Miguel Carlos wanted to investigate for himself and he went to the village. He did not return until evening.

"It's settled," he said. "We're leaving tomorrow at break of day."

"I was almost of a mind," said Paulina, "that we'd have to spend another night here."

"If we had left on horseback," retorted Miguel Carlos, "we'd have been halfway there by now and no doubt we'd have been able to put up at Limoeiro. It was you who suggested going by boat."

"I don't want to arrive at Aracaty worn out by two or three days on a horse under this sun. My back's stiff and sore: I can't stand upright any more."

"Tomorrow evening we'll be at Aracaty, the Negroes told me. They hope to be there by about five o'clock in the evening."

"It won't be too soon. I've had enough of this adventure."

"You must thank heaven that it has taken a favorable turn. I've saved your cattle."

But Paulina was in a bad mood: her nerves were on edge.

"If we had left Formosa earlier, we should not have had all those difficulties and by now we should be settled somewhere. Men are too stubborn."

"A woman hasn't any sense of land. A woman leaves her father's hearth to follow her husband. But a man doesn't abandon his land without fighting."

Antonio was sitting at the foot of the umbuseiro tree and did not appear to be paying attention to this discussion. He was staring at the river. He looked like a corpse, with his drawn features and bloodshot eyes, which seemed to have sunk deeper under his forehead. Miguel Carlos was contemplating him attentively and wondered whether the dysentery wasn't going to kill him.

"Are you feeling better?" he asked him.

"No, it's still just the same. My inside is on fire."

"At Aracaty we'll find some ipecac. That'll do you good."

"Perhaps so," said Antonio in a fatalistic tone of voice.

Miguel Carlos asked the laborers, who had lit a new wood fire, to awaken him before daybreak as they ought to be at Barra da Cunha before sunrise.

"Right you are, boss," they said, "we don't oversleep, not us."

The boat in which they took their places on the following morning was a long open one made from a hollowed-out trunk of *gamelleira*—a light, fibrous native timber which does not absorb water. It was about thirty feet long and could take fifteen people squatting. The two Negroes who steered it were in the stern; one had a boat hook, the other paddles. Traveling was easy, for they went with the current. The boat shot forward rapidly between banks bordered with small trees with broad, thick foliage. On both sides of the river there was fallow or waste land: savanna. However, toward midday, they saw on the left bank some fields of cotton, manioc, and sugar cane, and then some little plantations of orange and lemon trees. Soon afterwards among the trees appeared the white gables of a village. This was Limoeiro. They did not stop there. They were in a hurry to arrive at Aracaty, to reach the end of their miseries. The sun beat down fiercely on the boat, but men who have dug caçimbas for forty days under the dry sun of the hinterland are not troubled by so little. Only Paulina felt ill. In spite of the big broad Bahian hat which she wore, her face was red and swollen with the heat: she had unhooked her blouse and allowed her arms to drop into the water. Antonio had been placed in the bow so that he could relieve nature in the river when his bowels contracted too violently: he sat on the boat's edge and a herdsman held him by the arms. Miguel Carlos sat silent in the stern: he seemed to be absorbed in his thoughts. He was wondering how it would turn out for them at Aracaty. Nico Justino had said that there were government agents there; but Miguel Carlos did not like such people. He preferred to settle his affairs himself; and still must do so, if possible. Would work be found for all the men? And for himself? And would they find a lodging for Paulina and Antonio? His success with Hallum kept up his morale. He told himself that he would solve the problem, somehow. He was a man who never lost confidence.

As the Negroes had announced, they reached Aracaty two hours before nightfall. They arrived at a little wooden landing stage to which was moored a river steamer whose funnel was smoking gently. Along the edge of the river stood half-a-dozen buildings with flat roofs and dilapidated walls—no doubt old dwelling houses transformed into warehouses. Sitting along the walls were some men in rags and tatters, smoking very small pipes.

Once landed, they took a narrow alley which led into a broad street covered with a thick bed of dust and having a few shops along it. A passer-by told them where to find the main commercial square which was just at the end of the street. For, in all those more important little colonial towns, you must first of all go to the commercial square, the Praça do Comercio: this is the center of everything, and here you will find the botequims and offices.

The moment they arrived there, they were stopped by a group of soldiers. One of them, with two yellow stripes on his arm, asked them where they had come from. "From the hinterland," replied Miguel Carlos. "Pass," said the soldier.

It was a square like all the commercial squares in all the localities created by the Portuguese pioneers: the church with two spires painted yellow, three or four botequims in arcades. There were also six very old tall trees which provided a cool shade for all the refugees who were to be seen in groups squatting in the square. They were Negroes and people of mixed breed with not a single white among them. Sharecroppers and farm laborers. Miguel Carlos was unfavorably impressed: he wondered what they were going to do with all this crowd. He realized immediately that there was not the least hope of finding a place to lodge in Aracaty. He was going to be driven to apply to the government agents; and he loathed the idea.

He learned the news from a mulatto, a short stout man with a kindly appearance.

"They've told us to wait," said the mulatto. "They say that we are being taken care of."

"And where's the office?" Miguel asked.

"Over yonder." The mulatto indicated a small building to the right of the church.

Miguel went there immediately. He wanted to know what he must be satisfied with. He was received at the door by a young man who said to him:

"We can't tell you anything at the moment. We are waiting for instructions."

When Miguel returned to his group, Paulina said to him that before anything else a lodging must be found.

"Don't bother me," Miguel retorted. "We can't leave the square. We have to wait."

"If you rely on those government people, you'll get some further surprises."

"I don't rely on anyone, but you see very well that we're caught in a trap. All the streets are guarded by soldiers."

"What are they going to do with us?"

"I don't know at all. We just have to wait."

An hour later there was some excitement in the direction of the church: the soldiers spread out to form the crowd into a column and then they set out down the street which Miguel Carlos and his party had taken on the way to the square.

"Where are they taking us to?" Miguel asked of a well-dressed man of mixed breed.

"I think that they're going to put us on board the boat which is at the quay. They don't want to leave us here. They say that the town hasn't enough to feed the refugees."

"I wonder where they're going to take us."

"Couldn't say."

They did in fact make them go on board the steamer. They packed them on the deck like cattle. By using their elbows, Miguel Carlos and his men forced their way to a place near the side on the deck. Paulina was placed between two farm laborers who served as a rampart to make her a little comfortable.

The sun was going down when the boat left in the direction of the sea. Aracaty is, in fact, a little river port for local trade. It is built on the Jaguaribe, a short distance inland from the coast.

As long as the boat followed the river it slipped forward quietly, but none of the passengers appreciated this smooth motion. They were all asking each other where they were being taken to. They had no confidence in the government. Some of them said they were going to be sent to work on sanitation schemes in places where there were fevers and epidemics. Others affirmed that they were to be deported to the Amazon region. Others believed that they were being sent to make roads.

All their reflections were put to an end the moment the boat crossed the bar and entered the sea. It began to pitch and roll heavily. None of the passengers had ever set foot on a ship. Hence, by the end of about ten minutes they were all stricken with seasickness. Miguel Carlos tried to overcome it but did not succeed: he felt his strength waning. Paulina had stretched herself out to make herself more at ease. The closely packed passengers were vomiting on each other. Their groans mingled with the sound of the water lapping against the hull of the vessel and the nerve-racking vibrations of the engines.

Never had Miguel Carlos made such a horrible journey. He would have perferred to wander for a week without water in the hinterland rather than undertake that trip again. The torture lasted five days, five whole days during which they never succeeded in eating even a bean or swallowing a mouthful of water. When the little coastal steamer at last entered the bay of Bahia, they were at the end of their strength. The rolling and pitching having gradually ceased, they began to come to life again, but they felt empty with a void in their stomachs which doubled them in two. They felt as if their heads were unsteady and, when they wished to stand upright again, they were immediately seized with the feeling of seasickness. They dared not make a movement for fear of again upsetting their stomachs.

The coast steamer went alongside the quay and the landing began. It was a disembarkment of waifs and strays. Paulina could no longer walk unless she was helped by two men. Antonio went forward doubled up like an old man. By a supreme effort of will Miguel succeeded in holding himself straight. All the other passengers held themselves as stiffly as possible, for they had the feeling that the least disturbance of their stomach would cause a return of that terrible desire to be sick.

It was four o'clock in the afternoon. The sun was still fierce, but to those who know the sun on the hinterland of Ceará, that of Bahia is mild. A mulatto wearing gold-rimmed spectacles came to count them and then requested them to follow him. He took them into a vast shed.

"You can spend the night here," he said to them. "There's enough maize straw for everybody. Tomorrow we'll tell you where you can find work."

11. Bahia

As THEY gradually recovered from their seasickness, the passengers from the river steamer were beginning to think things over.

"We've been caught in a trap," said Miguel Carlos to Paulina as she lay beside him on the straw.

"It could have turned out worse," Paulina replied.

For, the moment that Paulina had heard that they were at Bahia, she felt a lively satisfaction. She had often heard Bahia spoken of, that marvelous city with its two hundred churches, innumerable big shops, the city of beautiful dresses, jewels, and perfumes. How many times she had dreamed of seeing Bahia; and now she was there. She forgave the government agents for having inflicted on her that appalling journey by sea. She felt that a new life was about to begin and already she had the firm intention never to leave Bahia, never to return to that hinterland region, the *sertão;* and to rid herself of this man Antonio who got on her nerves in a way that was driving her mad. Miguel Carlos? She would end up nicely by brushing him aside also. This might perhaps not be so easy; yet her mind was firmly made up to do it.

Antonio was also pleased. During his pilgrimage to Monte Santo he had heard people speak of the marvels of the city with two hundred churches: he had intended to come and see it. Unfortunately his uncertain health had not permitted him to undertake this journey. He was convinced that, in thanks for his ardent prayers, God had permitted him to be taken to Bahia.

As for Miguel Carlos, he was in a rage for having been deported so far away from his land. He was resolved immediately to set about making a plan to return to that country.

And so it was that on the next day, when the mulatto with gold-rimmed glasses came to ask which of them wanted to go and work in the countryside and which ones preferred work in the city, Miguel put his name down for work in the city. But he advised his men to go into the campo. He preferred to see nothing more of them, for he knew that he would not be able to organize the return of a dozen people to their own part of the country. He would have difficulties enough about taking Paulina and Antonio with him.

A *mocambo*—a hovel in the Negro quarter—was offered to them by way of a lodging. This was not pleasant for Paulina. A white woman does not go and live in a Negro quarter. But she declared that she would try to find herself a situation as a servant. That would settle everything. More money would be earned and she would be well housed.

The little hut given to them had only two rooms and a tiny dark kitchen smelling of soot: there was no flooring, merely a level of beaten earth. They were used to that. In the first room there was a table and two stools: in the second, two wooden bedsteads.

The first days were difficult. They had to borrow cooking pots to prepare food. They had to obtain some sacks of maize straw for the beds. All the Negroes of the vicinity looked at Paulina with astonishment. Never before had a white woman been known to live in that quarter: it was an event.

Because of his impressively broad shoulders, Miguel Carlos was chosen as a docker: he drew a high wage. He would soon have some money in his pocket. Antonio had asked how he should employ himself, and Miguel told him to visit the churches and pray that they might all soon be able to return to their own country.

Every afternoon Paulina went out for a walk in the city. She did not fail to inspect the great avenues, the parks, the places with magnificent palm trees. In a few days she knew all the big stores of both the upper and lower towns. What caused her misery was her dress, her poor little white dress such as is worn by a hinterland countrywoman. As daylight was fading, at the time when everybody went out to enjoy the cool of evening, she looked with envy at the broad boulevards laid out with palm trees, at the mulattas walking arm in arm rustling their flounced dresses of all the colors of the rainbow. She felt deeply humiliated when she saw, passing in their landaus (driven by coachmen in livery), the white women of Society displaying their gorgeous dresses covering the whole breadth of the carriage and showing off effectively parasols embroidered in guarani lace. There were negresses who were better dressed than she. She would never become resigned to such a situation. Gradually two ambitions became clear in her mind: to have beautiful frocks and to go to bed with a white man. Her father had delivered her over to an impotent half-breed, she had given herself to a good strong one out of spite. It was a makeshift. She intended now to raise herself to the eminence of her race.

If Miguel Carlos earned good wages, he did as much work as three men. But it was not with these meager sums of money that Paulina could hope to realize her projects. It was a matter of urgency that she should be taken on as a servant in a wealthy household.

Nearly every day she went to the market place in the lower

town to eat a simple little dish of cereal. She began to make the acquaintance of the women in the shops. These mulatto women were well in the swing and knew about everything that happened in the city and even about what went on in the important families.

"You'll be able to pick your employment, senhora," one of them told her. "They're all looking for white servants, and they are difficult to find."

A few days later Paulina went into service in the house of the Secretary of the Interior. Miguel Carlos showed a lively satisfaction. "With this," he said, "we'll quickly save the money needed for our return." For he thought of nothing but that: to return to the country. He did not forgive himself for having been caught in that trap at Aracaty. Paulina promised him her co-operation.

"In the meantime," she added, "I shall have to spend some money on clothes. A woman employed by the Secretary of the Interior cannot go about ill-clad."

Miguel Carlos entirely agreed. All would be settled very nicely. Antonio was beginning to recover from his dysentery (a druggist had relieved it with a little tincture of opium) and he could take over the preparation of food for Miguel. In this way he would not be entirely useless.

The Secretary of the Interior lived in a *palacete*—a small palace —on the Avenida da Liberdade; in front of the house was a big garden with beds of roses and azaleas. As a crown for the rose bed in the center there was in bloom a Japanese camellia of which the secretary was particularly proud. The house was of one story with a flat roof and walls covered with *azulejos:* blue, green, and yellow tiles. The entrance door, to which there was access by a flight of a dozen steps, was in wrought iron and the windows were ornamented by grilles with bars in squares which ran along the lower part.

Paulina put in an appearance at eight o'clock in the morning. The morning mist had completely lifted but drops of dew were still sparkling on the leaves of the rose trees. In spite of her natural forwardness, Paulina could not resist a slight feeling of anxiety. She wondered what impression she would make on her masters: a futile thought, for she was not to see them before the evening. She was received by a negress who welcomed her with that most engaging smile of colored people. She was led straight to the kitchen through a vestibule tiled in black and white. From there she was taken by a young mulatto woman, whose gestures were awkward and restrained, and accompanied to a room situated over the outbuildings. There she was to live. It was a much bigger room than any seen in the farmhouses in the hinterland. The windows were provided with panes of glass, which is only found in a city. The bed, covered with a pink bedspread, seemed large and comfortable. In a corner on a table was a large enamel basin: below it a pitcher. A little mirror hung on the wall. Near one of the windows was a wooden chair. Never had Paulina seen a room so nicely arranged. It took her some time to find out how to open the sash window, but in the end she succeeded. The healthy odor of mango flowers and orange trees came into the room. "How good it must be to live here!" she thought.

It was in the evening that she made the acquaintance of her boss, the mistress of the house, and the children. She was received in the study, a vast room furnished with a big table, two cupboards, and mahogany chairs. The table had over it a crystal pendant which seemed to Paulina a marvel such as she would never even have dreamed of. The Secretary of the Interior, José Machado de Andrade, was a short stout man. His black dull eyes, underneath which were two fat pouches of flesh, frightened Paulina. His trained mustache and his hair, cut in a stubble, gave him a churlish appearance. He spoke with the severity of a judge. He told her that she would be responsible for taking care of the children. He hoped that she would acquit herself conscientiously of her task. He clapped his hands and the mother came to introduce her progeny: four boys and two girls. Paulina scrutinized her on the sly. She was a small, rather thin woman with a morbidly pale face. She seemed gentle by nature and amiable.

Paulina entered into her new life. She accompanied the children to and from school; she took them out for walks in the parks and along the avenues. The youngsters were boisterous, like all boys and girls of the tropics, but she was able to inspire them with respect for her, and show them that they were not dealing with a negress.

By the end of a month she was able to buy herself a frock. At last she was coming out of her humiliation. She was going to be able to play her game. With a new dress, a woman feels confident.

She proved it. About ten days later she made the acquaintance of Lieutenant Luis Lacerda. It happened quite simply. She was sitting on a bench in the park while the children were playing on the grass. He came to sit beside her and asked her whether she was waiting for somebody, told her that she was beautiful, that for several days he had already noticed her: he was attracted by her and he would like to meet her alone. She told him she was busy all the week but that on Sunday afternoon she was free. "Only, next Sunday," she corrected herself, "I have to go and see an uncle and a brother. I could arrange to see you in the early part of the evening."

Of course she did not tell him that she was married.

Paulina saw her dream being fulfilled. For Luis Lacerda was a white man, and, furthermore, an officer; all of which added to the attraction. He was a tall long-faced young fellow of twenty-four, with beautiful thick black hair and lively eyes. None of those coarse traits which exist in the mulatto or man of mixed breed. A delicate nose and thin lips. In short, the man she wanted.

The following Sunday, then, she made the excuse to Miguel Carlos that she had to return to the "little palace" where a reception was taking place, and she went to join the lieutenant near a rock on the beach which he had indicated to her.

At that period this beach, situated to the north of the city, served as a haven of refuge for illicit love-making. It was dangerous to go to the hotels: next day the affair was known to the whole city. Hence, the beach had many clients. The place was truly favorable: it was covered with rocks which formed excellent places of concealment; natural nests for lovers, as one might say. As the nights at Bahia are always hot, one understands why lovers chose the beach for their frolics. It must be said that the majority were Negroes or mulattoes. The white women of Society who wished to give a free run to their passions, preferred it to happen in their landau, in which they were driven to the approaches of the city on some deserted road.

Paulina didn't have a landau: so she had to be satisfied with the beach, but she so greatly desired to have a white man that this mattered little.

This was her happy period. She loved Lacerda wildly; and he returned her love. In those warm nights, when vigor works and ferments like leaven under a delightful sky sprinkled with stars, the passions become more violent.

One day Lacerda told her that he wanted her for himself only, forever, and that he was going to marry her. In spite of the exaltation into which such a declaration plunged her, she had the presence of mind to tell him that he must wait. She would rather wait until her uncle and brother were no longer at Bahia and had returned home to Ceará. It was not fitting that the lieutenant should be associated with a family of whom one member was a dock laborer and the other half mad. Moreover, she strongly hoped that Miguel Carlos would not delay long before he was on the road back to the country with Antonio. She would drop them at the last moment.

This plan would no doubt have succeeded if one of those stupid coincidences, so frequent in life, had not aroused the suspicions of Miguel Carlos. It was indeed a most unfortunate coincidence, for Paulina only very rarely met the lieutenant during the week, and Miguel Carlos never frequented the upper town.

This was a little over three months after Paulina had first made the acquaintance of Lacerda. On that particular day, a Friday, she had left the little palace at half-past three to go and meet the children at the school. She found herself face to face with the lieutenant in the *Avenida*. They had not arranged to meet. It was pure chance.

"I'll go with you as far as the school," he said to her.

He took her by the arm and told her nonsensical stories which made her laugh. They gave the impression of a happy couple.

Now, on that same day in the afternoon Miguel Carlos had been ordered by a clerk in the office of the port authority to go and pick up a parcel of documents from a bank situated in the Rua Rio de Janeiro. He had to cross the Avenida. At the moment when he was about to cross, while still on the pavement of the side street, he saw Paulina pass by a few yards away holding the lieutenant's arm. He stood there unable to move. He did not believe his eyes, but he had to admit to the reality. "Whore!" he growled to himself. He was about to rush at them and create a scandal, but he took control of himself just in time. "If I have a row with a military officer," he told himself, "I'll be put in prison, even if I'm in the right." For at that period the Army was untouchable. Hence, it was necessary to deal with Paulina by herself.

He had intended speaking to Antonio on his return home in the evening but gave up the idea. He wished first of all to have unchallengeable proof of the misconduct: this he would have on Sunday. He now realized why Paulina never spent the evening with them.

As usual on the following Sunday, Paulina came to their hut early in the afternoon. She was jubilant and as lighthearted as the sunny air. She found Miguel Carlos rather distant but did not attach much importance to that: she knew his surly moods. She gave him a little money to put in the kitty for the return journey, but this did not succeed in cheering him up.

Toward five o'clock she left them, saying that she was in a hurry to return to the little palace to rest as she was very tired. She went openly in the direction of the upper town and then, when she had gone some distance, turned off and went down toward the beach. Miguel Carlos followed her. He saw her walk slowly toward a rock beside which stood a man in uniform. Miguel entertained no further doubts: he knew that this beach was a vast hotel. Nevertheless, he was unable to resist the desire to watch them. He took up his position on another rock and saw them walk toward the sea. The sun was setting and covered the bay with great red patches. Miguel Carlos saw the lovers walk slowly along by the breakers and then, in spite of the twilight—he had good eyes—saw them disappear into the intricacies of a mass of rocks. He left his observation post and took the road back to the mocambo. His mind was made up.

For Miguel Carlos never compromised when the honor of his family was concerned. This was one of the two or three fundamental ideas on which he based his conduct of life. He could not tolerate the idea of Paulina coming to Bahia and sullying the name of the Maciels. He strongly suspected that Antonio was impotent, but this could not in his eyes justify a blow struck at the family honor. During the whole of that week he nursed his anger. He was so gloomy, his features were so drawn that Antonio, who, so to speak, lived on the margin of existence, asked him if he were ill.

"You shut up," Miguel replied. "Get on with your prayers."

On Saturday he spent a good hour sharpening his dagger.

When Paulina came to the mocambo on Sunday afternoon, Miguel was in a good mood. He told her that they would soon have enough money to undertake the journey home: he had asked the owner of a little steamer how much the fare cost. Paulina expressed her delight on hearing this.

"I'm tired of the city," she said. "It's no life for us. I wish I were back again on our fazenda. But it seems that the drought is terrible. We shall not be able to return before October. And there's another thing—it must rain first. There are people who say that droughts have been known to last for two or three years."

"That's rare," said Miguel Carlos. "In October we'll be back home."

Paulina went out at about five o'clock. Miguel Carlos followed her, but he did not keep up with her as they went to the beach. What would be the use? He knew where she nested with her lover. He made for the center of the lower town and went into a Portuguese café to have a glass of rum at the counter. He waited patiently for the sun to set. When night had fallen, he went out and walked with a firm step toward the beach. He stepped over two pairs of lovers before reaching the group of rocks where he had seen Paulina meet her officer on the previous Sunday.

He drew his dagger and went forward with the movements of a cat. His feet were bare so that he could move silently. He did not have to seek for long. The rocks formed, almost on a level with the ground, a sort of long basin, a real natural bed. There he saw a man's body stretched out beside a woman. He perceived the woman's white face but could not make out the features. For him any hesitation was not possible: it was they. He bounded forward like a wildcat and planted his dagger in the nape of the man's neck. Before the woman could cry out, he had covered her mouth with his hand. Then he thrust his knife into her side. Next he turned over the man's body, which was already limp, and drove the dagger right into his open throat. He could now take a leisurely look at the women's face. It was indeed Paulina: he had made no mistake. He cut her throat and fled.

It was a moonless night. In the weak bluish light of the stars the sparse rocks on the beach seemed like blocks of thick shadow. Miguel Carlos walked to the sea: he crouched down, washed his hands and wiped his dagger. There might be splashes of blood on his jacket. Nobody would notice them: his jacket was almost black and, at this hour, the streets were lit only here and there by miserable oil lamps. In the Negro quarter there was no lighting.

He was in a hurry, nevertheless, to get indoors in the mocambo. Not that he was uneasy: he felt a fierce joy, a sort of wild contentment. He was especially pleased that he had not mad a mistake. Had he struck down another couple, it would have been a tragedy: he would have felt a terrible remorse which no doubt would have driven him to give himself up to the police. Fortunately things had gone off well: he had executed justice. He did not even wonder whether the police would discover that he was the author of the crime. His mind was made up to deny everything. There was no proof against him. At that period inquests were rudimentary; they knew nothing about fingerprints and they proceeded only by deduction. If need be, Miguel would state that Paulina had two lovers; that it was a tragedy caused by jealousy; he would put the police on a false trail. The essential was that he had executed justice: he felt comforted, for he could not have remained with that weight of Paulina's betrayal on his conscience. Now he was at peace; his anger had abated.

Antonio had not yet returned when he went into the mocambo. Every Sunday he went to evening service in the church of St. Francis, and often remained to mumble prayers until ten o'clock at night. Miguel Carlos took advantage of this to inspect his clothing: there were only a few little spots of blood on the sleeve of the jacket: he cleaned them off with a little hot water. He drank a pint of rum and went out, as usual, to have a chat with the Negro cobbler in the mocambo opposite.

When he returned home at about eleven o'clock, Antonio had already lain down. Miguel Carlos stretched himself on his wooden bed and fell into a deep sleep like a man who had just finished a heavy task.

Next morning he was at his job in the port. There he heard them talking about the event. He was a little astonished by the speed at which news traveled and at the accuracy of the accounts. "An officer and a woman were murdered on the beach last night," they said. It was learned soon after that the woman was a refugee from

Ceará. The bodies had been taken to the police station in the lower town. A love affair. This pleased Miguel.

"You don't happen to know the woman," a mulatto asked him. "She's from your country."

"I'd have to see her," replied Miguel.

"You ought to go to the police station."

"I'll go if I'm called, but I'm not going to interfere in what doesn't concern me."

In the afternoon two policemen came to find him.

"You're Maciel, aren't you?"

"Yes."

"It seems that the woman who was murdered last night is a relative of yours."

"What?" exclaimed Miguel Carlos. "What's that you say? Is it Paulina?"

"That's right: Paulina Maciel de Souza. She was working at the Secretary of the Interior's."

"Where is she?"

"At the station. Come with us."

The station was in a one-story house with a flat roof. The two bodies were lying in the middle of the floor of the waiting room. Miguel Carlos looked at them with a cold eye. Then he drew near to Paulina, put a knee on the ground, and contemplated her for a long time. On standing up he said to the policeman: "It's her all right." He was told to wait on a bench in the vestibule. An hour later he was brought into the police superintendent's office. It was a gloomy room furnished with a table and three stools. The superintendent was a small man, fearfully thin, with prominent cheekbones, hollow cheeks, an undershot jaw and, with that, a broad forehead overhanging two keen eyes which had a disquieting look about them.

"You knew that Paulina had a lover?" he asked brusquely.

"I had been told that she had two of them," said Miguel, "but I didn't believe it."

Would the superintendent nibble at that bait thrown out in a tone of indifference? He didn't look as though he would.

"She was your nephew's wife?"

"Yes."

"And what does your nephew do?"

"Nothing. His mind's a bit weak. He suffers from a kind of religious mania: he's constantly in the churches."

Miguel felt that the superintendent's suspicions were bearing on Antonio: he reacted as best he could.

"It was a happy marriage?"

"I think so. They never used to quarrel."

The superintendent put a number of other questions: how long had Paulina and Antonio been married? Had they any children? How did it come they had left Ceará? Why didn't Paulina live with them? Why didn't her husband work? "It's not," said the superintendent, "because a man's a bit simple in the head that this gives him the right to fold his arms and settle himself in the best seat." Finally he assured Miguel that he would do everything possible to discover the criminal. Miguel thanked him and returned to the mocambo, for the sun was about to set and he was in a hurry to see Antonio. He found him sitting on the bed reading a breviary.

"You know the news?" he rapped out at him.

Antonio looked up astonished, for Miguel rarely spoke to him.

"Paulina was murdered last night."

Antonio closed the breviary and placed it on the bed. His face did not betray the slightest emotion.

"Oh!" he muttered.

Then, after a moment:

"Why?"

"She was deceiving you with an officer, perhaps with two or three, nobody knows."

Antonio showed no reaction. The disappearance of Paulina whom he had always detested, although he did not show it, must seem to him a happy event.

"You understood what I said?" resumed Miguel Carlos. "She was deceiving you with officers."

"Yes, yes, I understood. She was an unfortunate woman. I ought never to have married. On the fazenda she went with João Pio— João Pio, that was a decent man."

"You say that she deceived you with João Pio?"

"I don't know," Antonio stammered out. "I think so. I'm not certain, but I think so. Women must have a man."

"Fool!" Miguel Carlos snarled. "Slug!" and he added: "Tomorrow you'll be questioned by the police. Try not to make stupid statements or they'll make you suffer for it."

He left the hut and went over to the cobbler's. About fifteen Negroes there were discussing the beach crime and they were impatient to hear the views of Miguel Carlos. He told them about his interview with the police superintendent.

"A pity," said one of the Negroes. "She was a beautiful woman. I've sometimes spoken to her here."

"A whore!" retorted Miguel. "She slept with any officer who came along, according to what I've been told. But she kept her game very dark. I never knew anything about it."

"With hot-blooded women it's like that. They like to change men. But what I don't understand is that one of them should kill her because she'd taken another. When I hear that my girl friend has gone to bed with somebody else, I don't get angry. If she comes back to me, she just finds me better."

"With Negroes, it's not the same thing. Paulina was a white woman."

"That's true," said the Negro admitting without argument the inferiority of his race. "She was a white woman."

As Miguel Carlos had foreseen, Antonio was taken to the police superintendent's office the next morning. He still looked as absent-minded as usual when he went into the office. The superintendent gave him a nasty look.

"Where were you at the moment of the crime?" he asked him point-blank. "That is, at eight o'clock in the evening."

"In the church of St. Francis."

"Are there any people who saw you there?"

"I don't know. I was at the back of the church. I was praying."

"Were you on good terms with your wife?"

"Yes, I never used to speak to her. I let her go her own way."

"A funny arrangement. Why didn't you speak to her?"

"She likes life on the fazenda. I have a religious vocation."

"Why didn't you become a monk?"

"I should have liked to, but my parents made me stay on the fazenda and get married."

"So you got married against your better judgment?"

The little superintendent leaned forward slightly on the desk and looked him straight in the eyes like a knife penetrating. Antonio saw the hollow of the man's cheeks become accentuated, his eyebrows beetle, his lips take an evil twist as if he were about to bite. It made him feel uncomfortable, and he turned his eyes heavenward as when he besought the Virgin Mary. All of a sudden he heard the raucous voice of the superintendent saying to him:

"If you were so indifferent, why did you murder your wife?"

Antonio gave no reaction. The absurdity of such an accusation could not affect him. He felt himself far above it.

"I did not murder my wife," he said simply. "I did not even know that she was keeping company with another man."

"You're lying," the superintendent retorted violently. "Your uncle knew all about it. He must surely have spoken to you about it."

"Never once."

The superintendent became vicious.

"Don't try to defeat justice. You're the only person in the whole city of Bahia who had an interest in this murder."

Antonio did not reply direct. He clasped his hands together and, looking lost in the void, muttered:

"Virgin Mary, enlighten his mind."

"I'll teach you to make fun of me," the superintendent rapped out, getting on his feet and beginning to pace up and down the room.

"I did not kill my wife," said Antonio as unctuously as a martyr.

The superintendent had resumed his seat at the desk: he seemed to have made up his mind about something.

"Listen, my friend," he said in a hearty tone of voice, "I'm going to give you a piece of advice: don't persist in your denials. That can only lay up trouble for you. The inquest has established that you are the only possible author of this crime. So it is useless to deny it. Just admit it. The case will come up for judgment in a few days: but you will be acquitted, as the husband is allowed his revenge in the event of his wife's adultery. So you won't stay long in jail."

The word "jail" struck Antonio as if somebody had thrown a stone straight at his face.

"You're going to put me in jail?" he remarked.

"I'm absolutely obliged to, since the inquest decided that there can't be any other murderer but you."

Antonio wished to reply, but the superintendent stood up, clapped his hands and two policemen came into the office.

"Take him away," he said.

"Almighty God," muttered Antonio, "make the light enter into his mind."

They handcuffed him and the policemen led him off and put him in an old charabanc which served as a prison van. He was so flabbergasted that he did not realize how greatly he had been victimized. He took refuge in prayer.

They put him down in the courtyard of an old building with crumbling walls and pushed him into a long dark passage in which there were doors with rusty metal gratings. The handcuffs were removed and, with his closed fist, one of the policemen gave him a lusty blow in the back which sent him to the end of a narrow cell permeated with a pungent smell of excrement and rotting walls.

Very soon Antonio's eyes became accustomed to the darkness. He could make out the dimensions of his cell: three paces by two. At the far end there was a strong odor of urine; the atmosphere made his eyes smart. The floor had holes in several places. Antonio sat down near the barred door like a man who had been knocked senseless. It was not for some time that he began to think. What an amazing story, this murder of Paulina! But she had sinned. She had expiated her fault. How could Miguel Carlos have concealed from him that she had a lover? He did not understand how his uncle could have admitted this. And why should that superintendent wish to make him say that it was he, Antonio, who had murdered Paulina? He scorned her, but he would never have thought of killing her. Men imagined that he was like themselves. Poor men! They do not know where Truth is.

Antonio had no feeling of revolt against those who were inflicting on him this brutal and unmerited treatment. He was above such incidental happenings. It was enough for him to be in harmony with God.

An oppressive weariness slowly numbed him and he fell asleep. He was wakened with a start. Someone was shaking his arm violently. He got up and rubbed his eyes. The barred door opened and two men came into the cell. What did they want with him?

"Come on, quick," said one of them. "And above all don't make any noise—don't speak: we mustn't attract the attention of the guard."

It was the voice of Miguel Carlos.

As soon as he had heard of Antonio's arrest, Miguel Carlos immediately considered the possibility of getting him out of that situation. He could not suffer an innocent man to be jailed. Nor did he intend to confess either. He had punished Paulina and her lover. What did the law think it could do? Miguel knew how to arrange the escape of a prisoner. All that was necessary was to buy the night warder. He collected all his savings and the money Paulina had contributed for their return journey and then loitered about the approaches to the jail. He spoke with the men who kept guard and, in the end, singled out the night warder. He inveigled him into going for a stroll along the avenue which led to the jail, and settled the business without any difficulty. The man did not even want all the money he had brought with him.

This plan was simple: he would take Antonio out of the jail and they would both leave the city immediately, making off toward Santo Amaro, and from there they would try to reach Ceará overland. That would take a month, two months, or three; it did not matter in the least. They had to escape from the Bahia police.

"Come on, quick," Miguel Carlos repeated, taking Antonio by the arm.

But Antonio resisted.

"Where do you want to take me?" he asked.

"Never mind that. We're going to get you out of here. Afterwards we'll see."

"No," said Antonio firmly. "I'm not guilty."

"Don't start the humbug again," Miguel said. "Come now, be quick."

"Hurry up," said the warder. "You must go quickly otherwise we'll be caught."

He in turn wished to drag Antonio by the arm, but the latter shook him off roughly.

"No," said Antonio. "Truth will triumph. Nobody can go against God's Justice."

Miguel Carlos heaved a sigh of disgust.

"This is certainly the last time I'll do anything for you," he said. "You'll get out of trouble yourself. As for me, I'm going back to Ceará. Manage for yourself." Then he added: "Make up your mind: are you coming or not?"

"I'm staying."

Miguel Carlos did not like idle discussions and he had not the slightest intention of allowing himself to be caught by the police.

"Let's go," he said to the warder. "He's quite daft. There's nothing for it. You won't see him go back on his decision. He's a mule."

The barred door closed again on Antonio and the two men vanished in the darkness of the passage.

"I won't be able to give you as much as I'd promised," said Miguel Carlos, "but you can't run a risk for nothing. Come with me into the street."

They settled their account in the yellowish light of a lamp in the avenue.

Miguel Carlos had already given up thinking of Antonio. He had struck him out of his mind. He no longer thought of anything but his project to return home. His mind was made up. That evening in the mocambo he made a bundle with some old clothes and two little bags of maize and manioc. He did not take his leave of anybody. At dawn next morning he went on board a coast steamer.

12. Fortaleza

THE BAHIA JUDGE who tried criminal cases (at that time there was neither a court of assize nor a jury) was a young lawyer, son of a high official in the Ministry of Justice at Rio de Janerio. He hated vexations. Now the case of Antonio Maciel raised a problem which he felt reluctant to solve. If Antonio had contented himself with killing Paulina, he would simply have acquitted him on grounds of the irresistible impulse which drives the cuckold to take revenge. That was customary. But the murder of Lieutenant Lacerda had created a great sensation among the officers and they were demanding a severe penalty. The conviction of Antonio would have given them satisfaction but, at the same time, would have provoked lively reactions in public opinion: for, in crimes of passion, and especially in cases of adultery, acquittal was the rule. Having thought it all over, the little judge resolved to get around the difficulty. He called the police superintendent and gave him instructions to put Antonio on board a coast steamer as soon as possible, with an order for him to be delivered at the jail in Fortaleza. Meanwhile he wrote a letter to the governor of the jail setting out the case in detail. He had not deemed it to be of any use, he said, to hear the case in court—which, anyhow, must acquit—because the accused was mad. Nevertheless, there was good ground for keeping him some months in jail to calm his mind. After which he could be sent home. The prisoner was a fellow from Quixeramobim.

In the official journal of Bahia a notice was published that the criminal Antonio Maciel had been handed over to the authorities of the state of Ceará. In this way everything was covered. If the officers protested, the judge would reply that the criminal was detained in jail at Fortaleza. In a few months' time nobody would think any more about it. The matter would be as good as settled.

So it was that, a fortnight after he entered the jail in Bahia, Antonio found himself again in the bottom of a ship's hold among cases and bales. The heat there was stifling, for the vessel was an iron one and had been exposed to the sun for more than five days. As it made its way, it was constantly plunging in the sea like a duck; and then the hull was never overheated. But, when it was moored to the quay, it became scorching hot.

Two men had thrown Antonio into the hold as if he were a sack. His back was almost broken. Fortunately he had fallen on a bale of cotton. The shock was nevertheless severe. He was stiff all over as if after too much hard work and he felt shooting pains in his arms, thighs, and shoulders.

He was sitting on a case and rolling in great beads of perspiration. An oppressive dizziness overcame him: he was breathing in short breaths, the pungent odor of jute, orange, and tobacco. He felt that his lungs had become quite small and that his stomach was in his throat. What gave him heart was the beam of sunshine which reached him through the opening in the hold. He heard the men hail one another on deck. That made a change from the jail, into which no noise came. But when they shut the hold, and he was again plunged into night, a sudden apprehension overwhelmed him. He inhaled a deep breath of air and fainted.

When he regained his senses, the vessel had reached the ocean. Antonio began to feel the effects of the rolling and pitching. His stomach could not stand that infernal rocking. He soon wanted to be sick and, as he had inside him only the few worm-eaten beans which constituted the jail fare, the amount of his vomit was no more than that of a cat. But the contraction of stomach and bowels made him ill. In the end he stretched himself on his back on top of a bale: then he began to feel better. There was only the heat, which continued to be maddening. Toward evening, however, it diminished. Twice daily a man lifted one of the hatches of the hold and shouted to Antonio: "Catch!" He threw him a bowl of *fuba,* cooked maize flour, so as not to let him die of hunger. One day Antonio took a chance and asked the man where they were taking him.

"Shut up, you son of a bitch!" was the man's retort.

And he closed the hatch again.

It was in this ship's hold that Antonio decided upon a course of action which was to make him remarkably famous. Until then he had submitted with resignation to the injustices of men: he had thought it sufficient to withdraw himself into prayer. But when he had refused to follow Miguel Carlos and had said to him, "I'm staying," he cherished the hope of appearing before a court of law and there proclaiming the immortal principles of Jesus Christ. For he felt himself endowed for apostleship. Alas! instead of bringing him before the tribunal, they had flung him into a ship's hold and were no doubt taking him to one of those regions where men die of fever after a few weeks. He conceived a hatred of the authorities and swore to have his revenge.

He had a dream: he was sitting in the campo, the open farm

land, at the foot of a palm tree, when he saw coming toward him a rider clad entirely in white and wearing a golden hat. It was Saint Sebastian. "May God be with you!" said the saint. "I have come to tell you that you must begin your mission without delay. You must wrest the men of the hinterland from the oppression of all those people of the cities who have repudiated the principles of the true religion. Go, my son. May the Virgin Mary protect you!"

The mission with which he was entrusted by Saint Sebastian would be accomplished. It would serve as his vengeance. No determination upon vengeance is so firm as that of a man who is meek by nature.

When they took him out of the hold to put him ashore at Fortaleza, the moment Antonio was on the deck he assumed the proud, aggressive attitude which befits an apostle and martyr. With disdain mingled with compassion he surveyed the gang of idle Negroes and brown-skinned men who looked at him eagerly as if he were an animal from the Amazon jungles. A man clad in a dirty beige suit, and wearing a blue cap, put handcuffs on him and dragged him off brutally like a calf being taken to the slaughter-house. Some Negroes burst out laughing because he stumbled on a paving stone. *He* was the delegate of Saint Sebastian in the sertão, the vast hinterland region of Brazil.

The jail at Fortaleza had a much more wretched appearance than that of Bahia. It was a tumble-down building with mud walls swollen by the action of time and rain. The two windows, one on each side of the door, were provided with wooden bars to show that it was a jail.

The cell into which they thrust Antonio was perhaps smaller than the one at Bahia. There was no wooden floor, merely the hard beaten earth. The place was humid and hot. As he trod the ground with his naked heel Antonio felt the stickiness of the earth-worms which came up everywhere. His eyes had been blinded by the brutal tropical light while he was being taken to the jail, but now, when they became accustomed to the darkness of his cell, he made out two scorpions creeping slowly along the wall in search of prey: he could see their antennae stand out, and their pointed stings. He did not have even a bit of wood with which to crush them: moreover, he could not squash them with his naked

feet. Black ants, which exuded a characteristic odor of decomposing flesh, bit his ankles; and he felt that there were swarms of
minute and dangerous creatures everywhere about him. A rat
climbed up the barred door and he heard it walking on the sheet
of bamboo matting which served as a ceiling.

"Virgin Mary, succor me!" he muttered.

He was exhausted, utterly worn out. He would have liked to
stretch himself or at least sit down; but he dared not. Then he
hung by his hands from the bars in the door in order to rest his
legs which no longer supported the weight of his body. He was
hardly a few moments in this uncomfortable and yet restful position
when a warder struck his fingers with a riding whip shouting "Get
back!" to let him know quite clearly what the blow meant.

Antonio withdrew and stood upright in the middle of the cell.
How long could he hold out? He felt his strength gone and terribly
tired. But he had a will sustained by faith. He held out for three
hours and then collapsed on the ground.

When he awoke he called out:

"A little water, for the love of God."

The warder who was moving about in the passage outside came
to him.

"Water is distributed only during the night," he said.

And he went away.

Antonio let himself fall again and shut his eyes: he gave way.
Let anything happen which might! His right hand was giving him
pain: he held it against his chest. It was swollen from ant bites
and perhaps those of more venomous insects. And all those ants
crawling up his legs! He stood up and rubbed his hips and calves.
His nerves were completely frayed, his head ready to burst. "If I
have to remain here for a few days, I'm a dead man," he thought.
"And yet I must not die—I have to fulfill the mission with which
Saint Sebastian has charged me."

He remained five months in the jail at Fortaleza. The human
organism is resistant and becomes accustomed to the worst conditions. Antonio lived amid his excreta, with the insects, mice, and
rats. He had torn off a piece of his short jacket and made a wad
with which he crushed scorpions; he filled in the holes of the ants'
nests and in this way was able to have a few hours' respite.

His emaciation was frightening. His eyes sunken more and more under his forehead, his hollow cheeks, his protruding teeth, and long hair made him a nightmarish figure.

The thought of the mission which he had to accomplish sustained him. He was more and more convinced that he would be the apostle of the hinterland, and he lived with this dream which was stronger than the odor of the cell and could not be torn from him by any kind of insect.

They threw him into the street one afternoon in September. The warder came and opened the barred door of his cell and said to him: "Out you go!"

Completely taken aback—jail habits were now in his blood—Antonio hesitated. "Out you go!" the warder repeated, seizing him by the arm.

As they were coming to the exit door, Antonio stopped: he was blinded by the sunlight. A warder struck him a blow in the back of the neck and he found himself in the middle of a dusty and deserted street, for it was the hottest time of the day. Antonio began to amble along like a sleepwalker but soon he felt ill: he proceeded toward a long white wall and collapsed on the ground. It is hard to stand up to the sun with nothing inside one's body. He fell asleep. On awakening he perceived a man leaning over him and shaking his shoulder. He looked with lack-luster eyes at the man. He was a white with a thin face and keen eyes.

"Ill?" he asked.

"No," replied Antonio weakly. "Just worn out."

"Where do you come from?"

"From over there," Antonio pointed to the jail.

"I thought as much," said the man. "When we have the republic that will be altered. Come."

He helped Antonio to get up and led him, holding his arm. In life one sometimes meets a charitable being.

This man's name was Zarate, Eduardo Zarate. He was a Spaniard who owned a fruit and vegetable shop and took an interest in politics. He was one of the most ardent republican propagandists. He was not unaware that a considerable number of people were sent to jail for no valid reason, and Antonio's case might perhaps prove of interest.

Zarate's shop was situated almost in front of the wharf. It was a good place, as much fruit came for him on the coast steamers from Bahia and Recife. He took Antonio into a dark room behind the shop and ordered a fat negress to serve him a plate of *feijoada*. He could hardly do honor to the meal; his stomach was contracted, he was accustomed to the little bowl of jail maize gruel. When he had eaten, Zarate asked him to state his case and Antonio related the ups and downs of his adventure.

"They're a lot of blackguards," said Zarate. "They hadn't even the courage to take you before the court. But all that's going to be altered. The republic will be proclaimed; there won't be much delay about that."

He saw that Antonio did not understand anything about politics, and he asked him where he intended to go.

"I must return to Quixeramobim," said Antonio, "but I don't know whether my uncle has returned there. We fled from it because of the drought. No, I don't know . . ."

"In any case, all those hinterland people who came as refugees to Fortaleza have returned home," said Zarate. "I think you would be rash to return. It would be necessary for you to make an arrangement with a muleteer who comes down here from that part. In that way you wouldn't be alone, and from time to time you could take advantage of a horse."

"I don't know anybody here."

"I'll arrange about that. Nearly every day there are mule trains which go down toward Baturité and Quixada. I don't know whether they go as far as Quixeramobim but, once you're at Quixada, you can make your way."

"You're very kind, senhor," said Antonio.

"We're all men," said Zarate. "Go out in the garden there and have a rest under the mango tree. I'll get busy about finding you a muleteer."

It was in this way that next day Antonio was able to set out on the road homeward. He wondered what he should have done had he not met that Spaniard. A strange man, Zarate, a man who would do a good turn. It was the first time that Antonio profited by human solidarity. The muleteer also was obliging. He was a fine young man, tall and active, with a gentle face and regular features; a white

man who liked a laugh and a song. On several occasions he allowed
Antonio to ride on his horse: he certainly made half the journey
on foot. On leaving him at Quixada, Antonio told him that he
would always be welcome at the Formosa fazenda.

From Quixada onward, Antonio made the journey on foot. He
found Quixeramobim alive and animated as in good times. Mundico
had reopened his botequim. It was to it that he went. When
Mundico caught sight of him he lifted up his arms to the sky,
exclaiming:

"It's really you, Senhor Antonio? Where do you come from?
How are you? What a tragedy! Miguel Carlos has told me the
story: and they kept you such a long time? What a gang of filthy
swine! Oh, those people of the big towns!"

These exclamations got on Antonio's nerves and he did not like
the inquisitive looks of the herdsmen who were drinking their rum
at the counter.

"So Miguel Carlos is back?" he said.

"Months ago! And João Pio and all the cattle."

"Thanks, I'm going on there."

"Would you like to have a horse? . . . Yes, yes, you're tired.
Wait a moment. I'll have mine saddled. You'll send it back to me
tomorrow."

Just as the afternoon was ending, Antonio went through the gate
of the Formosa corral and at that moment he had a shock: he was
surprisingly aware of the absence of Paulina. It afflicted him and
he felt it much more deeply than the distress he had vaguely
experienced in his jail at Bahia. The fazenda seemed sad to him.
He went slowly up onto the veranda and called out. A colored
servant woman whom he did not know appeared.

"I'm Antonio Maciel," he said.

The servant opened her eyes wide.

"You're Senhor Antonio?"

"Where's Miguel Carlos?"

"He has gone back to his fazenda at Tamburil. There's nobody
here but João Pio."

"Where is he?"

"He'll be coming. He's out in the campo."

Antonio took a seat on the veranda and waited. How strange was life! He was home again: it seemed hard for him to believe. He saw again in his mind the cell at Bahia, the frightful dungeon at Fortaleza. He thought of the murder of Paulina. In recalling all that, he felt himself overcome by depression. He went to his room and found the chest again in which he had locked his personal effects and those of Paulina. In the bottom of it he found his breviaries. He took them and went back to sit on the veranda and began to read his litanies of the Virgin. It was a long time since he had last recited them: they seemed new to him. It seemed to him that he had never understood them so well.

On the stroke of five o'clock João Pio returned. When he saw Antonio he gave vent to a torrent of exclamations like those of Mundico, after which Antonio was able to relate the story of his adventure.

"They made a nice mess of you," said João. "You're nothing but skin and bone."

"One day justice will reign on the hinterland," said Antonio thoughtfully.

João Pio went to chat with the negress: he liked that better. Nevertheless, next day he sent a herdsman to Miguel Carlos to tell him of Antonio's return.

Miguel arrived the same day just as night was beginning to fall.

"Well," he said on seeing Antonio. "So you've come out of it? . . . You ought to have followed me when I went to find you in the jail at Bahia. I knew quite well that we mustn't have any confidence in those townspeople. I know them. You've seen what they're worth. A nice lesson, but it cost you dear. That'll teach you."

Antonio did not reply. Miguel Carlos continued:

"We brought back all the cattle. Everything's in order. We've had a first fall of rain. You've nothing to do but carry on, and João Pio's there to help you. I really hope that this time you've going to look after your affairs."

"No," said Antonio. "I have a mission to fulfill."

"What mission?"

"I have a mission to fulfill and fulfill it I shall," said Antonio with a firmness hitherto unknown in him.

"Where do you want to go?"

"Out into the hinterland."

"You're in the hinterland where you are."

"I know my mission. The time has come."

Miguel Carlos began to get irritated.

"All right," he said roughly, "clear out and may we never see you again. I'm beginning to be sick of it."

And he led João Pio toward the shed.

Antonio left next morning.

"*Adios!*" he said to Miguel. "May God protect you!"

"Pleasant journey," retorted Miguel.

"Good luck," said João Pio.

When he had disappeared in the direction of the river, Miguel said:

"It's better that he should clear out of here. He's absolutely crazy."

"It's better so," said João approvingly.

They remained leaning on the balustrade of the veranda. They saw him go up the slope of the line of hills on the other side of the river. When he arrived at the saddle of the sierra near the tall palm tree, he did not even look back. He vanished from sight, traveling southward.

Part II

CANUDOS

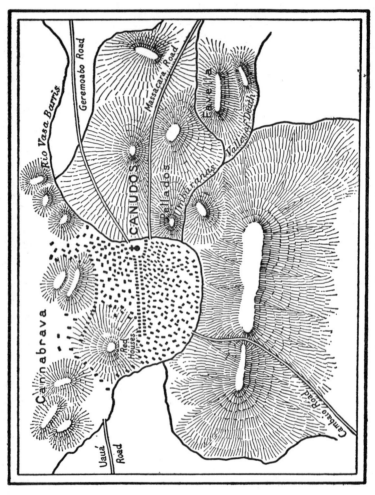

Canudos and Approaches

1. João Abbade

AT THE AGE of nineteen João Abbade was a mulatto with an Apollo's body of the kind often produced by repeated crossing of the white and black races. To his tall stature was added the litheness of a wild animal, and this gave him a distinction which provoked jealousy among the thin, bony little white students in the college. He was proud of his straight forehead, regular nose, and delicately formed lips. What drove him to distraction was his curly hair. On several occasions he had his head shaved, and massaged it patiently for days with castor oil—in the hope that this would stimulate the growth of a head of long, glossy hair like that which he admired in his companions of pure Portuguese descent. But his capillary fluid was irreparably black and never grew anything for him but a very curly short fleece. He soon enough consoled himself for this when he noticed that women were much more interested in the shape of his thighs than in the length of his hair. João Abbade had the best-shaped thighs in the College of Santo Antonio de Recife: long thighs, harmonious in repose, and sinewy with muscles which stood out when he became taut for some effort. It was to them that he was beholden for Carmela Brito's love.

At that period he was pursuing courses of study approximating those of a teacher's training college (the curriculum was very vague and courses of study were left to the judgment of the Jesuit fathers). He was not what was called a brilliant student. He showed infinitely more aptitude in organizing fetes and strumming the guitar than for teaching grammar and arithmetic. With his prolific imagination, added to an impulsive temperament, he cut a figure as a youth with initiative. He liked dawdling, daydreaming, and running. For three years now he had had experience of love, but he had never felt for any woman as he felt for Carmela Brito.

Carmela disturbed his peace of mind, unsettled him, fired him with enthusiasm, and drove him to despair. She was the daughter of the biggest exporter of cotton and cacao in Recife, a white girl with an olive complexion and big sensual eyes like those of an Andalusian woman. She came regularly to the fetes organized by the college at Christmas, New Year's, Corpus Christi, or Easter, and very properly was accompanied by her parents—whom João Abbade thought particularly forbidding. The father was a tall thin man with a deeply furrowed face and a pair of thick eyebrows veiling the two hard eyes of a former slaveowner; and he flourished one of those heavy Portuguese mustaches trained in the French fashion. The mother was an enormous sad woman adorned with gold chains and bracelets, a gold cross which hung between two great sagging breasts, and gold earrings. She was always dressed in black, and her daughter always wore a white frock with narrow flounces held in at the waist by a red sash.

João found it impossible not to admire Carmela. He had for long savored the joy of being able to contemplate her, knowing that she could never give him any other kind of pleasure. A rich white girl is inaccessible to a mulatto. He was sad and discouraged on the days following a fete: life seemed to him stupid and deceptive; he was depressed and felt a physical discomfort which made him wish to escape and go far away into the campo to his father's fazenda. Next day he recovered his calm and looked forward with anxious expectancy to another festive occasion, when he would gaze once again upon Carmela, with her eyes at one moment lively and the next languorous, her lively buttocks, the line of her arm when she arranged a stray piece of hair, and the little golden cross which spread its arms toward her small firm breasts.

He had never even spoken to her. He had, however, seen her at close hand near the exit from the hall where the fetes were held. In the crush of people at the finish of a festivity he had been able to brush against her: he had inhaled her perfume, a very strong one which reminded him of a certain dark aromatic wood called *canella preta*. But he had never dared to address a word to her nor even look her straight in the face. He was only a mulatto. He effaced himself to allow her father to pass; a stiff austere-looking man, dictatorial, and ill-natured.

It so happened that one Thursday, on the occasion of the Feast of the Ascension, the Fathers had organized a display of gymnastics in the vast playground of the college. João was winner of the foot race—as usual—and then, in one of those Brazilian "all-in" wrestling matches (known as *capoeiragem*, meaning "cutthroat"), he had defeated his opponent in twenty-six minutes after a bout which held all the spectators breathless and inspired their burning enthusiasm.

Carmela was bent on congratulating him personally. He had never pressed so soft a hand. He bowed respectfully but, as he straightened up, he was moved by an irresistible power and dared to look at her. Brief as that moment was, João felt that something penetrated him to his innermost depths. He retired awkwardly, completely bowled over. When he recovered his wits, he realized that he was sitting at the end of the playground underneath an avocado pear tree. A friend of his, Cardoso, was shaking his shoulder.

"Come, João—quick! They're waiting for you."

For the fete was to have a musical ending in which João had to sing.

When he appeared on the trestled stage, erected in the middle of the courtyard, in the reddish glimmer of the twilight, an eager acclamation greeted the winner of the all-in wrestling bout as well as the singer who had so often moved the audience with his *choros* and *fados*, those favorite songs of the people.

When João began to sing there was a religious silence. Nothing but his voice could be heard, except here and there the buzzing of the big red wasps flying back to their nests or, very high in the sky, the cawing of belated *matacas*, the local crows.

The song rose into the evening, sometimes nostalgic, sometimes sad and depressing. Like all singers from the campo, João was accustomed to improvise after the fashion of the serenaders. He improvised accordingly. He evoked the unhappy love of the poor mulatto for the scornful and distant white girl. He sang with a passion at first restrained and then released, as if he were crying out with love.

Carmela applauded so frantically that her father took her arm to restrain her.

In the confusion when people were leaving, in the great hall of the college, João suddenly found himself near her. Now he would have dared to look at her, but in terms of intimacy she whispered into his ear: "Come and see me."

She continued walking in a dignified manner, not gratifying him with a look, beside her father who was talking to the Father Superior. João was a victim of the panic of an excited male. "Come and see me!" Where? When? He was trembling slightly, gnawing his fingers with impatience. When the moment came for leave-taking, while old Brito was occupied with ceremonious congratulations, he succeeded in rejoining Carmela.

"Where?" he asked in a voice full of anguish.

"In the garden—in the evening," she said.

Then, turning toward one of the priests:

"Good evening, Father. All my congratulations. It was a magnificent fete."

At ten o'clock the following night he was in the orchard. Now, as he sat at the foot of the old mango tree, he thought that the moon was quite right that evening to miss its daily round. He was calm and had that feeling of well-being which comes with the certainty of happiness to come. He knew that she would come that evening: his presentiment would not deceive him. Even the owl there, perched on a low branch of a guava tree, which looked at him with dazed, phosphorescent eyes, could not shake his conviction. He gazed at the stars through the motionless leaves: exactly above him there was a very big one which was trying hard to shine stronger than a moon. Exactly above him. That gave him confidence.

The night began to be cold. Fortunately he had brought the cape which he used when he made a trip into the campo. He threw it over his shoulders. A beating of wings broke the silence. He looked up. The owl had flown away: now there was nothing but night and the trees.

Suddenly she was there. He saw her coming, dark and slim, dodging among the tree trunks with silent agility. He straightened up letting the cape fall. Carmela was in his arms. They gripped each other with a passion intensified by everything of the unknown in the difference of race and color. João spread out the cape and they lay down. They hardly spoke to one another; they had noth-

ing to say. She contented herself by repeating his name again and
again and caressing his head: from time to time she sighed deeply
to relieve her body charged with desire. He covered her with kisses
and then clasped her furiously. He possessed her as if they would
never see each other again, as if their passion must be sated in one
single meeting.

They were right. A little Negro boy, one of the many children
of the servant woman, had seen Carmela go out: he had observed
her and seen her throw herself into the arms of the mulatto. Concealed behind a tall avocado pear tree, he had watched them
eagerly and the following morning lost no time about telling his
mother the story. For a moment the negress was torn between religious terror and her love for Carmela, and wondered whether she
should tell the girl's father: but, on the thought that, if she did not
denounce the sin, she would burn eternally in the flames of hell-
fire, she decided to make it known to Brito. Just as he was getting
ready to mount his horse to go to his office, as he did every day,
she betrayed Carmela. Brito did not say a word, but a flash of rage
showed in his eyes and he flourished his riding whip. He remembered only in time that slavery had been abolished and that a man
no longer had the right to strike those who bore bad news. He
proceeded toward Carmela's room, which was on the right at the
end of the passage.

She had finished dressing and was putting round her neck the
little gold chain which held the cross she wore every day. When
Brito went in she gave a little start and raised her eyebrows in an
expression of astonishment, for her father never came to her room
to see her. It was not done; it was not a custom.

"Good morning, papa," she said with hesitation in her voice.

He brought his whip down on her shoulder with the force of a
blow from a bludgeon. She howled like an animal but dared not
look her father in the eyes. She hid her face in her hands and
threw herself at the foot of the bed as if for prayer. She never
uttered a word, for she surmised what it was about.

Brito was in a towering passion. Carried away by a fit of rage
which he did not attempt to restrain, he beat her until she collapsed
with her blouse torn, her hair disheveled, and her arms stained with
blood.

On hearing Carmela's cries, the negress had run to the room but remained outside; she would not have dared to face the master while his passion was let loose.

She saw him go out, tense, snarling, and looking murderous. He pushed her aside roughly. She heard his heavy shoes clatter down the stairs. Then she rushed to her young mistress, raised her in her muscular arms and stretched her on the bed. Carmela was uttering prolonged groans mingled with sobs. She did not say a word; the end of the crisis must be awaited in silence.

The gate of the corral creaked. Brito was going off toward the city.

He was a bad horseman; he disliked riding at a gallop. Nevertheless, on that day he applied his spurs to the horse's flanks, being in great haste to arrive and fulfill his intention. An hour later he rang at the door of the college. He told the young priest who came and opened to him that he wished to see João Abbade.

"The lectures have begun. This is not the visiting hour," the priest informed him.

"It's a matter of an urgent message," said Brito authoritatively. And he added casually:

"Don't tell him that it's from me."

"Very well," said the young priest, bowing with conventional respect.

He went off but he was puzzled. This visit seemed to him quite unusual. And that injunction: "Don't tell him that it's from me." Why couldn't he tell João Abbade that Senhor Brito was asking for him to give him an urgent message? He liked João Abbade. He was the most likable and most intelligent mulatto in the college. He told him that Senhor Brito was waiting for him in the entrance hall. João did not bat an eyelid. "Coming," he said in a casual manner. He did not have his revolver on him but, in this particular case, the dagger would be more serviceable. He followed the door-keeper through the long corridor which led to the entrance. The moment he went into the hall, he stopped, allowed the priest to walk ahead a few yards and then, with the agility of a cat, he bounded on Brito and planted the knife in his breast.

Brito fell backwards without a cry. The revolver which he held in his hand rolled on the tiling with a metallic noise, while João, pushing aside the panic-stricken young priest, opened the door and, rushing into the courtyard, skirting the big wooden figure of Christ with arms extended to bless the college, he fled into the street.

The young priest, dumbfounded, had not yet had time to give the alarm by the time João was already at the outskirts of the city not far distant. But he knew that flight on foot was nonsensical. The mounted police would soon catch up with him. Hence, he did not hesitate for an instant. At the end of the town, before coming to the little bridge on the road to Gravata, there was one of those big botequims—a combined general store and café bar—surrounded by corrals where the muleteers came to unload goods from the interior. In front of the arcaded façade there was a row of stakes to which the tradesmen or customers tethered their mounts. With the cold audacity which we have when saving our skin, João Abbade dashed toward one of the horses—there were five of them—cut the halter with a slash of his knife, jumped into the saddle and sped off at a gallop.

Here the alarm was quickly given. In a moment four men rose from the botequim and dashed in pursuit of the thief. Unfortunately for them—is there any justice?—they were delayed by an ox wagon which had become stuck on the bridge and completely barred the way. While they were seething with impatience, João took to the open country. He knew that he could not weaken for a moment, and he drove his heels into his horse relentlessly. But no horse, however good or of whatever race it may be, can keep up a gallop for several hours under that sun. At a point about two miles from the bridge, the road—it was, moreover, only a dusty earthen tract full of potholes—skirted a little hill. João succeeded in making the ascent at full gallop. On reaching the crest, he turned around and glanced down at the plain. There, on his side of the bridge, he caught sight of the four pursuers: they seemed to be moving quickly. Whereupon he launched his horse on the descent. From this hill, and as far as the first foothills of the Gravata Mountains, there is spread a vast region covered with natural pasture lands formed by deep layers of rich grasses known as *capim gorduar*. Bullocks, horses, and mules were grazing there in the sun. João rode down across the prairie, selected a horse, dashed in pursuit of it and

soon was holding it by the mane. In a moment he had the harness
off his mount and the new one saddled. With a well-rested horse
he was sure to outdistance the men who were after him. They had
just reached the crest of the hill and stopped there outlined against
the deep blue of the sky: they fully realized that from then on the
pursuit was hopeless. Clearly, they also could have changed mounts,
but they had no intention of abandoning their own horses in that
plain.

Feeling that he was now safe, João Abbade put his horse to the
trot. The sun was burning his back. His arms, legs, and chest were
smarting from having perspired so much. And there was not a tree
on that savanna! He found a shady place only at the foot of the
sierra where the jungle began. He would have liked to breathe in
fresh air to drive away that oppression which was squeezing his
lungs. The heated air which he was breathing made him dizzy: his
ears were buzzing and his mouth was dry. He would have given
his knife for a mouthful of water. However, the sierra was not far
away: he should reach it in an hour and there he would certainly
find some sort of well. But he was so weary that for a time he had
not the courage to gallop. The horse bore him along at an amble,
as limp as a rag. Not a thought formed in his brain: he was utterly
dominated by the burning desire to drink and to breathe some
cool air.

It took him almost two hours to reach the mountain at the foot of
which ran a little stream of clear icy-cold water. After quenching his
thirst, he sat under an enormous *gamelleira* tree and for a long
while enjoyed the coolness of its shade. Gradually the tension of
his nerves relaxed, his flesh recovered a normal temperature, the
buzzing in his ears ceased, and he began to go over in his mind the
events he had just lived through. So they had been betrayed. No
doubt by some Negro servant who had caught them by surprise.
He hated the Africans, the full Negroes with their servility. And
he hated the whites who, with their smugness and the self-
conceit in their superiority, planted animal terrors in those slave
souls. On the other hand, he felt himself in the grip of an unbounded
love for white women. Their skin was soft, smooth, not coarse and
rough like that of colored women. Carmela's hips! Satin. He, João
Abbade, had held them in his own hands. This thought awakened

in him a feeling of pride and victory. Damn it! no doubt he'd never see her again. What did that matter? He had had her: she had been his. An evening's triumph, but a positive triumph. Now he could walk among black men holding his head high: he had known a white woman. It had caused him trouble: he had had to kill Brito and now he was obliged to wander aimlessly in the campo. He paid well for it but not too much. The greatest ambition which a colored man can hope to realize in his life is to sleep with a white woman. Not with one of those broken-down whores who give themselves to Negroes for a few shillings. With a white woman who gives herself for love, like Carmela.

Besides, had Brito been killed? He might have been only wounded? João had the feeling that he had struck accurately, but it needs so little to turn a blade aside. His knife was a beauty, one specially made for him by Nico dos Santos, a young blacksmith who had recently come from Bahia. The blade was long and tapering. Made of good steel. The handle was of wrought copper. Mechanically he drew it from its sheath and gazed at it. When he cut the halter of the horse he had stolen from in front of the store, some of the blood which stained the blade had been wiped away: there still remained some below the handle and on the point. João got up and went to the brook, plunged the blade into the water, washed it with his hands, wiped it on the leg of his trousers, and put it back in its sheath. He felt strong with that blade on his hip. In the campo, the open county, you never know what you're likely to meet. But this was not the time for daydreaming: it wasn't a matter of allowing himself to drift into a dangerous softness. Darkness would soon be upon him and João had no intention of spending the night in the jungle. In spite of the numbness in all his limbs, he sprang into the saddle and went down again toward the plain with the intention of getting on the road to Gravata (providing that somebody on horseback had not given the alarm in that direction!). Skirting the first houses of the village, he rode at an amble, keeping a sharp watch to right and left for fear of an ambush. In that late burning afternoon the only street in Gravata—lined with little houses having uniform façades (a door and one window)—was calm and dusty. Two little Negro boys, quite naked, were playing knucklebones on a doorstep. A woman

passed by carrying a pitcher of water on her head. She greeted
João. A rider went past, trotting ahead of him. João reached the
church, a sort of whitewashed shed with a little square spire. An
old negress was sitting against the door. She looked like a bundle
of rags and was smoking a little pipe. At first João had thought of
asking somebody in the village for hospitality but on reflection he
abandoned the idea: he was still too near to Recife. Having passed
the last dwelling, he spurred his horse and made his way along the
red road, his mind made up to penetrate quickly and as far as
possible into the interior of the hinterland. He was hungry and his
head ached. His thighs felt soft from weariness. Maybe he would
come upon some fazenda where he could get some food and be
able to sleep? However, as far as he could see, there was not the
slightest trace of life. To the right spread a vast plain covered with
scrub but with great open spaces of a grayish color where brambles
were growing amid the stones. There was similar scrub to the left,
ending a few miles away at the forest which covered the hills.
Would he arrive at the next village before night came? He must
husband his horse's strength, for the animal was becoming nervous.
For hours he traveled across that interminable savanna which
seemed to reach to the world's end. The sun touched the crest of
the sierra, the sky became inflamed and broke into three zones—
red, green, and blue. The air was becoming cooler and João put his
mount to the trot. At the end of a quarter of an hour he arrived
at a place covered with thick brushwood—a *capoeira* they call it—in
which he became entangled. He felt that the mountain was now
not very far away, and he told himself that on the other slope
there would surely be a village. Suddenly the road branched off
southward and, in the dim twilight, João was able to discern the
white gables of dwelling houses.

He arrived in the village at nightfall. A big star was already shining above the church. He looked at it with affection, for it gave him
hope.

At the botequim, the fifth house (there were only eleven altogether in the village), he met two old Negroes who were sitting on
the threshold, while the boss, a tall thin man with a wisp of hair
which fell over his eye, was at the counter serving three cattle
drovers who seemed to be *cafuz*—offspring of Indian and Negro

parents—having prominent cheekbones like Asiatics and the slim build of Negroes.

João passed himself off as a pilgrim on the way to the sanctuaries of Bahia, and the proprietor suspiciously offered him a glass of rum.

"Where can I cross the São Francisco River?" João asked him.

"At Cabrobo," replied one of the drovers. "That's the best place: there's a good boat there."

João asked the boss if he had anything to eat. It was the drover who again replied:

"You can share our meal. We're going to the hut."

These men of cafuz breed were cheerless but obliging. They were Christians and deemed it a duty to help the pilgrim.

João ate the helping of feijoada with them and was able to sleep in their rancho, a simple little hut. Very early next morning he set out again: he must take advantage of the cool air of dawn.

It took him three days to reach Cabrobo. He ate and slept in the homes of small tenant farmers of mixed breed who gave him the welcome that is everywhere accorded to the traveler in the sertão, the hinterland. When he arrived at Cabrobo in the afternoon, a young man whom he met on entering the village pointed to the ferryman's house. A woman opened the door to him. The ferryman was busy harvesting his sugar canes. João could go and see him in his field: over yonder on the slope of the hill.

He went there. The ferryman was a white man of about sixty years of age with thick silvery hair, bushy eyebrows, a fleshy nose, and a forehead covered with wrinkles. He could not take João across that day. First he must finish cutting his canes: they were coming next day to cart them away for milling. Besides, he needed eight rowers to get across: the current was very strong just there. In spite of the force of these arguments, João insisted. He would leave his horse in payment (in any case, it was impossible to take it across), with the saddle and harness. The offer seemed to interest the old fellow. In the hinterland you don't often have the opportunity of making a deal.

"If I can find men to row us, I'll take you over," he said. "I'll go back with you to the village. But why are you in such a hurry? What have you done?"

"I'm going on a pilgrimage," João calmly replied. "I have no time to lose."

"Oh!" said the old man, looking doubtful.

Although the São Francisco River is almost a mile wide, they succeeded in crossing it before twilight.

When João set foot on Bahia territory, he felt as if he had been granted liberty, like a man coming out of prison. With that vast sheet of river water behind him, he breathed more easily: his limbs seemed more supple. A new life was opening before him. He did not know what it had in store for him, but he felt happy. With that extraordinary mental flexibility of the mulatto, he had already forgotten the incidents at Recife. He now had a completely new outlook. Carmela? Well, yes! Carmela, a white girl, a beautiful memory already dim. Brito? Who was Brito, anyhow? There was a fine college at Recife with affable priests. He knew them: he had even studied in that college.

Now he was sorry not to have his horse. From what the ferryman had told him, the first village going southward, Chorrocho, was five or six hours' journey on foot. João did not have the courage to face such a night march. He went a short way along the road in the hope of finding a house, but the place was all stony like a desert. In the end, he decided to sleep at the foot of one of the very few trees which grew in the valley. He did not succeed in falling asleep and regretted not having bought a little tobacco at the botequim in Cabrobo. He no longer thought of the past: he only wondered what he was going to do in this hinterland region, where no doubt all he would meet would be some muleteers, cowboys, a few rapacious traders, and an occasional priest. But it vexed him to think and he began looking at the stars. They're beautiful, the stars. They shine and are pleasing to see. How is it that there are so many of them? It's formidable, the number of stars in the sky.

At dawn he set out on his way.

2. Strange Encounter

CHORROCHO IS a little village like all the villages in the hinterland, and consists of fifteen to twenty little mud houses, a solitary banana tree in the offing, and around it some manioc plants and sugar canes and a little square of maize. It had a chapel to provide sustenance for the soul; and a botequim to feed the body. There was no priest. The key of the chapel was kept by the village carpenter, and the building was open only on feast days and occasions when some monk or other came to harangue the faithful. The botequim, the café bar, yes, this was open from six o'clock in the morning and did not close until late at night. It was kept by a Turk whose business at Bahia had gone badly and, by force of circumstances having had to swindle a few distinguished people, he had been driven to seek his salvation in the interior. He was a strapping fellow, with the powerful shoulders of a wrestler and a hard energetic countenance. All the same, he was very likable. He was the only man in the village with a laugh in him.

João Abbade's arrival overwhelmed him with joy. Here at last was a man who knew what a joke was. He had not seen anyone like him for years. Only muleteers ever passed through Chorrocho and they were as lugubrious as the inhabitants of the place. In João, the Turk had immediately recognized a townsman.

"Well then," asked the Turk, "what brings you into this accursed countryside?"

João told his story about the pilgrimage.

"Listen," said the Turk, giving him a wink, "you can speak frankly. There are no police here."

But João was on his guard. He maintained that he was going on a pilgrimage. "At Recife," he added, to give a semblance of truth to his statement, "there's much talk about the sanctuaries in the hinterland of Bahia." The Turk did not seem convinced but did not press him. In the hinterland, men never insist on details under pain of causing knives to be drawn. He began to speak of Recife and to ask João many questions about business there. He reckoned that sufficient time had elapsed since his flight from Bahia for him to be able to set himself up in a town without being troubled. He invited João to eat with him (in the interior of Brazil, it is the rule to invite the passing stranger). During the whole afternoon João remained sitting on the counter talking with the Turk and the customers who came to buy their piece of fat bacon or to drink a shot of rum.

They were still chatting when they heard in the distance the beating of drums and the music of guitars. Twilight was filling the valley. The villagers had returned to their homes or were in the botequim.

"That can only be the Counselor," said the Turk.

And, putting a hand on the counter, he sprang over it with an agility which nobody would have imagined in a man so stoutly built.

"The Counselor?" João asked.

"Come along," said the Turk.

They went into the street and were able to make out at the end of the village a group of men carrying bamboo torches and preceded by a big banner.

"That's just what it is," the Turk remarked.

And turning around toward two ox drovers who were inside the botequim, he said:

"Drink up, I'm going to shut my store."

When he had closed the doors, he returned to João.

"You don't know this 'Counselor'—Antonio Conseilheiro, that is? You've never heard him spoken of? That's funny. He's known as far away as Joazeiro. It's true he doesn't go Pernambuco way very much: but, for the last couple of years or so, people are talking a lot about him. Unfortunately he has with him a band of enlightened faithful who claim the right to be fed gratis wherever they go. And naturally it's the owners of botequims who get it in the neck. If we refuse them, they attack: they plunder the botequim. Real cutthroat bandits, they are. That's why I've closed my store. I'm quite willing to give my share, but I don't want to be pillaged."

The group of torchbearers had stopped in front of the chapel about two hundred yards away.

"What are they going to do?" João asked, puzzled by what he saw.

"This evening they'll say prayers: tomorrow they'll get busy with the chapel. That's their work: they repair and recondition chapels, or they build them where there aren't any. I don't say this is bad work: chapels are necessary. But they come back too often. Every six months we have to feed this gang for two or three days. It's just highway robbery!"

"Can we get close to them?" asked João.

"It's not a question of can we—we must. You'll see. They're going to mobilize the whole village for prayer, men and women."

Night had fallen with a full moon shining in the sky and casting the silhouettes of the houses on the street.

A few men left the group in front of the chapel and dispersed through the village: they knocked at every door. Soon they were seen coming out with their arms full of wood.

"It's for the bonfire," the Turk explained. "They always say their prayers around a wood fire."

João became more and more interested in the strangeness of these ceremonies. He was impatient to see this *Conseilheiro,* their so-called "Counselor," for he had never seen a prophet. He dragged the Turk toward the little square where the church was. The fire had just been lit: the wood was beginning to crackle and a thick cloud of smoke rose toward the moon. The villagers, men and women, had already arrived there and formed a little group, and the Conseilheiro's "faithful" were squatting around the fire. These for the most part were men of mixed breed; there were some mulattoes. They all had hard faces stamped with wickedness, the faces of *valentões* —roughs and toughs—quick with the knife. In short, they were bandits rather than religious types. João sought in vain among them for one who would look like a prophet. They were all alike, with the same herdsmen's appearance. Suddenly a tall Negro loomed up out of the darkness. João had not seen him coming.

"Men on one side, women on the other," the Negro called out. Those present did as they were told.

"But where on earth is the Conseilheiro?" João asked the Turk.

"No doubt he's gone to pray in the church."

It was so. A few minutes later the door of the chapel was seen

to open. Two men came out from it: the second was the carpenter,
who closed the door again. The first was undoubtedly the prophet,
the sage. He looked the part. João saw him advance into the light
of the flames which were now burning high and brightly. He had
long hair, parted in the center, which grew down over his ears and
fell on his shoulders. João had already seen Christ represented in
this fashion in the images at the college. The Conseilheiro was clad
in a long smock which went down to his knees: only the ends of
his black trousers were to be seen. He was barefooted like all the
others. João noticed that his eyes were very gentle: when he came
near to the fire, he stretched out his arms and called for the blessing
of Saint Sebastian on the village.

"Why Saint Sebastian?" João inquired.

"I don't know," said the Turk. "It appears he's the missionary of
Saint Sebastian."

The Conseilheiro had begun to recite litanies which he read out
from an old breviary, and the monotonous "Pray for us" of the
crowd mingled with the cracklings of the fire as the moon enveloped the chapel in her diaphanous light.

When he had finished, the Conseilheiro knelt down and everybody did the same. He said three *Ave Marias* and then, rising in a
solemn manner, turned toward the chapel: he went and sat down on
a little stool placed in front of the entrance. The big Negro came
forward again.

"The Conseilheiro is at the service of believers," he said. "You
can go and consult him. One by one: men first."

It was from this that he got his name: he was a man who gave
counsel. While the consultation continued, and it lasted for some
time (everybody, men and women, wanted to have the prophet's
advice), an idea was germinating in the fertile brain of João Abbade.

The bonfire was nothing but a heap of glowing cinders when the
last woman left the Conseilheiro taking his advice with her. It was
then that João Abbade went forward to speak to him. The prophet
gave him a look of indifference and asked gravely:

"You weren't able to come with the men? Who are you?"

"I am a passing stranger. I've just arrived from Recife."

"What do you wish?"

"I've heard you much spoken of," replied João. "I should like to join in your work for the welfare of the hinterland."

"Saint Sebastian accepts all who devote themselves to him," said the prophet sententiously. "You are welcome among us."

João was thinking that, by going with the prophet, it would be possible for him to live in the hinterland and not do anything. He did not look to the future: it was enough for him to have a solution of his immediate problem.

All this would be of very slight interest if that fortuitous meeting of João Abbade and Antonio Conseilheiro had not had incalculable consequences. It was, in fact, the beginning of one of the most dramatic, most baffling episodes in the history of the Brazilian Republic.

3. May 7, 1885

How WAS IT that in the space of ten years, Antonio Maciel, the thin, timid, and impotent young man, changed into Antonio Conseilheiro, prophet of the hinterland? For those who have studied the behavior of men in desert zones, there is nothing extraordinary about it. Antonio Maciel was a resultant product of the Brazilian *sertão*—the northeast hinterland region—as the prophets of Islam were a resultant of the sands of Arabia and North Africa.

At the outset, although Antonio Maciel was firmly convinced that he was the envoy of Saint Sebastian, he did not succeed in asserting himself as a prophet; and probably he had not aimed so high. It was the environment in which he evolved that made him a prophet. But, like other prophets, he had to await the growth of a legend around his name. At first he was taken for a sorcerer who went from village to village. Even then he was accorded a certain respect because of his odd appearance, his long hair and seraphic eyes. Then, thanks to certain coincidences, some astonishing cures were attributed to him: people began to relate how he had saved the life of a little girl who had been bitten by a rattlesnake (at the moment when the child was bitten, no doubt the serpent had no more poison; the Conseilheiro had arrived just in time to get credit for the cure). It was said that he had calmed an epileptic; and cured a woman who went into trances. The muleteers passed the news around. Little by little his prestige increased. When he arrived in a village people rushed to him bringing the sick and to "ask for his counsel." When they had conferred upon him the title of "Counselor" his fame had already spread over the whole hinterland region to the north of Bahia. Mystics, of whom many are to be met among the people living in the misery of those desolate parts, were so dazzled by his teaching that they did not want to leave him any more. They went with him on his peregrinations. From one week to the next and month after month the group expanded. The influence of the "Conseilheiro" became formidable because nobody understood him: in his harangues he would give voice to apocalyptic language studded with quotations from Latin, of which he himself did not understand a word; and this gave the impression that his message came from the beyond. Only a prophet could speak in that way; so thought the cattlemen and laborers who listened to him.

Antonio Maciel was aware of his prestige. He conceived an immense pride in it: his discourses became more and more flaming, more and more incoherent: he merged politics with religion, combining a disturbing mysticism with a sordid realism. He extorted supplies of provisions from villagers by threatening them with the direst punishments. Saint Sebastian had drawn his sword and the hinterland was going to pay for its sins. Only those who followed or helped the Conseilheiro would be saved. Well had he profited from the lessons of Sylvio Silveira.

Seduced by those facile pillaging operations, new elements gradually joined the group, about which there was no longer anything mystical: men sought by the police in the little towns, professional killers—*capangas*—who were unemployed, ex-bandits and cutthroats who had to leave their gang as a result of some dispute. They found in the Conseilheiro's company a way of life which nicely responded to their indolent temperaments. But the philosophy of the sage was not powerful enough to suppress their instincts, so that in many places they resorted to violence against those who refused them help—hence the Conseilheiro's troop was in the end regarded as a pack of robbers of the same ilk as those bands of wandering cutthroats known as the *cangaço*. Nevertheless, that did not affect Antonio's reputation as a prophet.

The incorporation of João Abbade in the group was to have the effect of increasing it to vast proportions; for João had a rich imagination. He easily showed the Conseilheiro that prayer in front of a bonfire was not impressive enough. A platform was needed from which he could look down on the crowd (João was thinking of the one they used to set up in the courtyard of the college at Recife on fete days).

"This is a good idea," Antonio said. "Silvio Silveira also had a platform." (He had described to João the splendors of Monte Santo.)

There was the matter of transport. Zé Venancio, the big Negro who maintained discipline at the ceremonies, took the responsibility of persuading a fazendeiro to provide him with four oxen and a wagon. This man Zé Venancio had formerly been a hired killer who, when active, had accomplished a dozen murders: he was the shock trooper, the physical spearhead of the mission. He was ably assisted in his work by Jacarandá, a mulatto who had been leader of a band but one day had fallen into the hands of the police and was imprisoned at Jacobina. After escaping he returned to the locality and killed the judge: he cut the body in pieces, sent the head to the judge at Joazeiro, the trunk to the one at Bomfim, and the legs to the one at Queimadas. He was a fearless man who had a way with him. Hence, the following week the troop had available planks, trestles, four oxen, and the wagon. The operation, declared Venancio, had not been arduous. They had not even needed to consider killing the fazendeiro, who had been most accommodating.

From that time onwards, the arrival in a village of the Conseilheiro and his faithful followers unleashed not only a mystical exaltation mingled with an unquestionable fear of pillage but, furthermore, a sort of enthusiastic excitement as if it all amounted to a fair. Men who are lost in that back-of-beyond love everything spectacular. The charlatanical fascination of the Conseilheiro's shows dazzled them.

For seven months Antonio's troop circulated indefatigably from village to village until the moment when João Abbade had *the*

Idea—that idea which in its consummation was to shake the very foundations of the Brazilian Republic.

It happened one evening in the Sierra Branca. As night was falling, the troop, on its way from Geremoabo, decided to halt at Canudos. This was not a village but a minute cluster of about fifteen little dwellings thrown up carelessly on the slopes of the mountain in a narrow valley. On the doorsteps, silent brown-skinned men were smoking little earthenware pipes with long tubes or *canos* for mouthpieces. This local custom had given or rather suggested the name of the place.

To the south, on a bare rounded hillock, rose an old fazenda, a farmhouse in a state of ruin which had been abandoned by its English owners at the time when slavery was abolished. João was thinking of lodging some of the men there but was told it was not possible: the house was infested with fleas, rats, and reptiles. Nevertheless, wishing to see for himself, he climbed to the top of the hill. From there he had a magnificent view. In the half-light, the valley, entirely surrounded by a line of hills as if by a high wall, traversed throughout its whole length by the Vasa Barris River, seemed to him the ideal site on which to build a sanctuary. He saw in his imagination a lofty white church yonder at the bend of the river and, massed before it, the multitude of pilgrims listening to the Conseilheiro's sermon. Why had he never thought of that? Why gad about from village to village? Formerly the crowds of people used to go to Sylvio Silveira. Now that Silveira had disappeared, they should come to the Conseilheiro.

He told Antonio of his idea and the prophet was perplexed but, next morning, João led him to the summit of the hill. For a long time the sage contemplated the lines of hills pointing their peaks into the sky, and the valley which formed a vast hollow in between. He admitted that, although the panorama did not equal that of Monte Santo, it was beautiful. But he added:

"I must ask the advice of Saint Sebastian. This evening I shall commune with him."

After evening prayers, as night was falling, Antonio took himself aside, knelt down (he was inspired by the methods of Christ for entering into communion with His Father, as in the Garden of Olives) and plunged into meditation. After which he came to sit near João Abbade who was on the riverbank smoking one of those long-tubed pipes which he had borrowed from a local inhabitant.

"We shall remain here," he said.

"We'll have crowds greater than at Monte Santo, you can be sure of that."

"Far greater," said the Conseilheiro. He considered himself vastly superior to Sylvio Silveira who practiced his profession of prophet only occasionally; once a year.

"We must first build some houses," continued João.

"That won't be difficult," retorted Antonio. "There's a forest on the other slope of the Sierra de Cannabrava. We have oxen and a wagon to fetch the posts and beams. The people here can lend us axes.

"We must, before anything else, mark out the site of the church," continued the Conseilheiro sententiously.

"No doubt, but we must erect a beautiful church. That will take time. What we need at once are houses to lodge the men."

Antonio was in agreement. João's imagination was working swiftly and he continued:

"We must send some messengers into the villages around here to inform the muleteers that the Conseilheiro has created a sanctuary at Canudos. The whole hinterland region must be notified, since our task is to save the whole hinterland."

João was far from suspecting the outcome of this initiative. During the whole evening they talked together, becoming excited with their idea and drunk with glory. In their minds they saw the immense crowds which would very soon invade the valley eager to listen to the good word. In spite of the embryonic molding of character received at the college, João Abbade had himself come to believe in the divine mission of the Conseilheiro: he did not doubt that it was inspired by Saint Sebastian. There is nothing extraordinary in this credulity, if we think of the environment in which he was living, and remember that in the thick of a civilized country it is not rare to find analogous instances.

Being entirely preoccupied with preaching the Gospel and the care of souls, neither Antonio nor João Abbade thought of the question of provisioning the new settlement.

Next day they went over the valley, an area of wasteland covered with thin grasses with some brushwood or clumps of brambles here and there. The inhabitants of the place went regularly to work with planters in the surrounding country and did no cultivation for themselves. They kept a small field of sugar canes along the Vasa Barris River, and a square patch of manioc at the foot of the hillock at Favella.

Antonio declared that the church should be placed on the Vasa Barris: in the bend which it formed in the middle of the plateau. It should have a big square in front, to give full significance to all its majesty. To fix the boundary, outside of which houses could be built, they had their banner brought and planted it in the soil.

And so was founded the visionary town of Canudos, the hell-town of the Brazilian hinterland.

That was on the seventh of May, 1885.

4. The Holy City

THE WORLD has seen the rise in the Far West of those mushroom towns built in a harum-scarum fashion by men in quest of gold; and in South Africa in the diamond fields; and in the West of Canada in the wheat-producing zone; and in the coffee fields of São Paulo. Nowhere have we seen a mushroom town spring up in a stony area and built by men seeking God. Certainly there are those Islamic towns, but they developed slowly in the course of centuries. But that town of Canudos was the work of a few years. It bears comparison with the gold and diamond towns.

Neither João Abbade nor the Conseilheiro had foreseen that. But, once the movement was unleashed, they were no longer masters of the situation: they were to become the heads of a large town, a city which their hybrid mystic combined with their incompetence was to make the most misshapen and anarchistic town in the world. The first stroke of the billhook was given during the misty dawn of May 8, 1885.

Obsessed by their idea of a sanctuary, they did not even think they were founding a town: they did not lay out a street; they allowed every man freedom to choose the place where he would set up his little house. A dwelling must shelter three, four, or five of the faithful. Those little houses were all the same. They were not just Negro huts but real houses constructed on the model of those of the Portuguese colonists: with solid posts of hardwood which resisted the termites, interior partitions made with a double row of logs consolidated with a mortar composed of clay and straw. They consisted of three rooms: a *sala* or main living room, a bedroom, and a kitchen. João Abbade decided that they should be roofed with tiles: he said that thatch smelled of Negro. A kiln was built on clayey ground and the manufacture of tiles began. All those men of the sertão, cattlemen as well as laborers, knew the rudimentary crafts essential to the running of fazendas: at one and the same time they were lumbermen, carpenters, blacksmiths, and tilers. They worked by rough judgment, taking measures with their hands or feet but, as their eye was very practiced, they managed to produce rough yet solid workmanship.

They did not bother about details and did not dawdle over what they built, but they worked quickly. For, if the workman of the hinterland has the bearing of a lazy fellow, spending hours listlessly stretched out in the sun, he has no equal when it comes to necessary effort. It is on such occasions that the resources and endurance of those lean yet wiry muscular bodies can be measured.

Hence, by the end of a month fourteen houses were erected. They included the "furnishing": a bench for each *sala*, a wooden bunk for each bedroom. There was no table, since they all ate with their fingers from the cooking pot.

While the building of the town continued, half-a-dozen men had set out on a mission to spread the news over the hinterland that the Conseilheiro was making a sanctuary at Canudos. This propaganda had a far deeper effect than João Abbade had ever imagined. They had just begun laying out the site of the church when, from the gap in the hills at Cambaio, a convoy arrived at the bend of the Vasa Barris. It consisted of four men and four women on horseback followed by two well-loaded pack mules and a group on foot made up of about ten children of from seven to ten years of age led by two girls of sixteen and eighteen. They were of mixed breed and came from Pombal. They had heard that the Conseilheiro had settled at Canudos; and they came to settle themselves near him.

"Good," said João Abbade to them. "You're welcome. It will be necessary for you to build your house. There are still enough tiles to roof it."

"We'll build it," said the men. "What we want is to live near the Conseilheiro."

For, after Antonio's harangues announcing that the direst catastrophes were going to beset the hinterland, many people did not feel secure unless they were near him.

Proud of the success of his propaganda, João Abbade went to find him: at that moment he was supervising the work on the church. João informed him of the intention of the new arrivals.

"Four women and some girls," said the Conseilheiro frowning. "No. Saint Sebastian does not accept women among the faithful."

Abbade had always wondered why Antonio professed such violent hostility toward women. He was not to know of Antonio's impotence and that he attributed to Paulina the responsibility for his incarcerations at Bahia and Fortaleza. This hostility could compromise everything. And so João retorted:

"Our men can't live without women."

"They have done so until now."

"You speak as if you didn't know what they used to do in all the villages we passed through," answered Abbade.

"I've never known anything about it," affirmed the Conseilheiro.

"You surely don't think I've gone without a woman for months? A man has to be relieved," said João who could no longer count the young women he had possessed over the whole hinterland since he had accompanied the prophet.

"Women represent the spirit of evil," objected Antonio.

"Women pray more than men," retorted João.

Then he launched a decisive argument:

"If you don't give authority for women, the faithful will abandon you."

The rigidity of the Conseilheiro's principles could not act as a brake on his ambition, which increased from day to day. He was not disposed to renounce his dream of lording it in a sanctuary, to the adulation of crowds of people.

"Since you are unable to impose this sacrifice on yourselves," he said resignedly, "I'm quite willing to admit women, but they must be kept separate: they must not come here to corrupt the faithful."

Even had he not given his consent, he would have been compelled to do so soon after that: for, in the days which followed, new caravans began to arrive bringing men, women, and children. They came from every corner of the sertão: from Serrinha, Pedra Alta, Inhambupe, Taracatu, and Curaça. Tenant farmers or sharecroppers who had seen the light brought their wagons and oxen. Herdsmen who came on horseback generally led a mule on which they had loaded their wives and personal effects. Humble village workers came on foot.

Soon the valley of the Vasa Barris River looked like a vast building yard. The construction of houses progressed to the rhythm of twelve a day. Three new kilns for making tiles had been installed. In the mountain by Geremoabo the axle music of ox wagons could be heard from daybreak. Mules carried bundles of logs. Standing on the tree trunks drawn there by oxen, the men trimmed them square with their axes. Others set up posts, and others did the tiling. An intense activity developed in the glare of the unrelenting sun.

The Conseilheiro's pride no longer knew any bounds. Now he wanted a church as vast as the one he had frequented at Bahia, with two spires each a hundred feet in height. Linharès, the foreman carpenter, discovered about twenty trees of this height in the forest: brauna trees, that is, of the Brazilian hardwood called by botanists *Melanoxylon brauna*. He had them felled. But the problem was to transport them over the mountain to the site. It was in the course of this labor that the accident happened. They all considered the occurrence as a bad omen; and for a moment it shook their confidence in the Conseilheiro's star.

To operate the transport of these trees, João Abbade had chosen Marcolino; all agreed in recognizing him to be the best wagoner. He was a half-breed who had come from Sergipe, a man of medium height and build but of astonishing suppleness. He possessed the art of making himself understood by the beasts, and could impose his will on them.

"To fetch timbers of such a size over the mountain," he said, "we'll need at least twenty-four head of oxen."

The operation would be difficult because brauna is a hard, heavy wood: and, even a man knowing his business well, would not easily obtain from oxen harnessed two-by-two in line a concerted effort at the same moment. If a single couple on the chain were to shift, that would utterly destroy the effort made by all the oxen pulling ahead of those two. However, Marcolino affirmed that they would manage to do the job. Like all those hinterland men, he had the soul of a pioneer and he enjoyed exercises involving strength: he loved to assert the power of man.

Marcolino wished to attack first the longest and stoutest tree trunk. It was so heavy that, in order to load it, they had to dig a trench beside the fallen tree in such a way that they could roll it with levers onto the wagon. The day before, a score of men had opened a *picada* or cutting through the forest to the summit of the mountain.

Marcolino devoted great care to the organization of his team of oxen. He knew every one of the beasts, for he used to work with them all, sometimes with this pair, sometimes with that. He distributed them in accordance with their aptitudes: the most spirited at the head of the column to spur on the others, the weakest and most recalcitrant in the middle, and the strongest near the wagon. When all was ready, he reviewed the oxen; he shook his goad which was provided with loose iron rings. The beasts knew that sound, which was like the music of cattle bells, and were aware that they must use all their strength. Mounted on a tree stump, Marcolino spoke to them as a sergeant would speak to the men of his section. "Calm, Coração! Quiet, Piano!" He observed a moment's silence and then, brusquely, he roared: *"Vamos!"*—"Come now!"—and he began to bound along the length of the chain of oxen shaking his cattle bells. You could see all the horns go down. The harness groaned. Slowly the wagon moved forward. Behind it men were placing round logs under the end of the tree trunk, which was dragging along the ground, to help it to slide forward. A young mulatto about twenty years old named Pereira threw himself body and soul into this work of placing the logs. The oxen, released from standing about, were dragging the load at a dangerous speed, yet it was not possible to modify their pace as they might not be able to get going a second time.

Suddenly one of the wheels struck a stump: it was about to get clear but the wagon overturned, being thrown out of balance and dragged over by the weight of the tree. The great tree trunk crashed on the ground with a dull noise that was cut through by a short, piercing, and terrible cry.

All the men with the convoy rushed forward. Pereira lay under the tree. He had been crushed to pulp: his head protruded from one side; an arm and leg, from the other.

Because of the twisting of the shaft, the oxen harnessed directly to the wagon were almost strangled by the yoke. Marcolino cut the harness.

It was necessary to extricate Pereira's body. He was quite dead, yet they were all in a hurry to get him free as though he were still alive, in the same manner a corpse is torn from hangmen. The men seized the logs and, using them as levers, forced them under the murderous tree trunk. It was terribly heavy, but the men's will was strong. Marcolino was in command of the work. He called out:

"*Pronto?*"—"Ready?"

"*Pronto,*" replied the men. Then:

"*Força!*"—"Heave!"

The effort was almost superhuman: the enormous piece of timber rose slowly, sufficiently for Zé Venancio with his powerful wrestler's arms to be able to grasp the body of Pereira. It was nothing but a soft mass with, at one end, a head from which a bleeding tongue protruded.

"We must take him away from here," said João Abbade, very shaken. "We'll return for the tree tomorrow."

"What are we to put the corpse on?"

"I'll take him," said Venancio.

He took it over his shoulder as he carried sacks of beans. In the good old days of his killings, he had the habit of transporting his victims thus to throw them into the jungle or some river.

When the Conseilheiro saw the funereal procession returning, when he saw at its head Zé Venancio with his macabre burden, when he saw the oxen come back without the wagon, he was overcome by an uneasy feeling. For he was always superstitious, and did not understand why Saint Sebastian or the Virgin Mary should have allowed an accident to occur at the moment when they were transporting the material for a church raised in their glory.

Zé Venancio threw the body at his feet.

"How did that happen?" Antonio asked of João Abbade.

"The wagon overturned. A wheel struck a stump."

There was a heavy silence. All felt the same uneasiness. They were all convinced that this accident was a warning from heaven, a disclaimer of the Conseilheiro's work: they were looking at the prophet with questions in their eyes. Antonio felt intuitively that they doubted him: he realized that he must speak, and that his prestige was at stake. He had become enough of an actor to get himself out of that tight corner. He knelt down near the corpse, made the sign of the benediction, muttered an *Ave Maria* and then, rising, extended his arms toward heaven and, in his sepulchral voice, said:

"He has died for the regeneration of the hinterland. Saint Sebastian has received him in the gardens of paradise."

João Abbade stood there perplexed, thoughtful and looking absent-minded as if weighed down by some dark thought.

"I didn't think," he said in a melancholy manner, "that the first visitor who should come to Canudos would be Death."

Antonio looked at him with amazement: he had never heard anybody make a statement of that nature—a philosophic one. He retorted sharply:

"Life is merely a preparation for death. *Gloria in Excelsis Deo.*"

He used many Latin quotations, knowing that they had a definite effect on the people.

Men and women had come to increase the circle around the corpse and they remained there silent in the blazing light of noon, awaiting some revelation.

João Abbade seemed to recover his spirits.

"Come along," he said, "we must mark out the cemetery. We can't bury Pereira anywhere. Besides," he added, for his sadness had not completely disappeared, "there will be others. . . ."

"That's true," said the Conseilheiro, who appeared to be somewhat thrown off his balance, "we've forgotten the cemetery. I think that the space which remains between the church and the river will be enough."

"If the graves are well aligned, we can bury many bodies in a small space," said João.

When they had marked out the boundaries of the cemetery, they returned toward the village to make arrangements for the funeral. The corpse remained where Venancio had thrown it and was already covered with flies and ants.

"We must get going," said João. "It's beginning to smell."

If Pereira had had any relatives, they would no doubt have moved him to his dwelling; but he had come alone to Canudos. He was a mulatto who had not been recognized by his father, the latter having abandoned his mother because he did not wish to live with a negress.

As they had not any boards with which to make a coffin, the Conseilheiro had a bier made with some logs. The body was placed on it and they covered the head with a dirty old shirt.

The whole community was invited to pay last respects to the victim. When they were massed on the open space where the bier lay, the Conseilheiro took out his breviary and read a few passages in Latin. Then two men took up the body and, followed by the whole crowd, went to place it in the grave. The Conseilheiro gave a final benediction. The cemetery was inaugurated.

As they were returning to their occupations the men exchanged impressions. They were all in agreement that it was a bad portent.

"That was the first pillar for the church that they were bringing. It's queer. In the Conseilheiro's place I wouldn't go on with it; the saints must not be defied."

"Strange things are happening. Simão dos Reis claims that he's seen a mule without a head in the sugar canes."

"If that's true, Canudos will be destroyed by a thunderbolt."

The uneasiness was general. . . . A feeling of despondency had overcome the faithful. In every house that evening they conjured up the strange events which they had witnessed. Some of them boiled the skins of snakes to ward off misfortune.

Next day João Abbade heard that several families had left Canudos clandestinely.

He did not mention this to the Conseilheiro, for he feared that the prophet might resume his peregrinations across the hinterland.

5. The Chief of the People

AT THE END of three months there were almost five thousand inhabitants in Canudos. The church was finished: an edifice as incoherent as the Conselheiro's doctrine. It recalled in its general lines the two-spired churches of Portuguese type. The spire on the right was not quite in alignment with the façade and, at the top, it leaned over a little as if it had been as a result of a violent wind. The entrance door was not in square, but it was very wide. The interior resembled a vast shed or hangar. An enormous wooden cross had been placed against the end wall and, in front of it, they set up the platform which was to serve as a pulpit for the prophet.

Beyond the big square in front of the temple could be discerned a swarm of little houses placed carelessly, and oriented in accordance with each man's fancy.

Nevertheless, by force of circumstances life began to be organized. The Conselheiro first established the rule about holding prayer in the morning, at noon, and in the evening: for, in his mind, Canudos was a holy city, a sanctuary, and all who came to live there could have only one object—prayer. The whole population was obliged to be present at these ceremonies, the evening one being the most important. To keep the tradition alive, they lit a big bonfire on the square and around it the crowd was grouped, men on one side, women on the other. Litanies were recited and then the assembled people crowded into the church to hear the Conselheiro's harangue.

This duty was not very onerous. However, after some time it became known that a considerable number of men and women were missing the ceremonies, notably the morning one. When he heard of the fact, Antonio flew into a violent rage.

"Let them be expelled!" he shouted. "Saint Sebastian has no truck with lukewarm people. At Canudos there can be none but true believers."

"Give them the order to leave," said Abbade.

Antonio considered that his position as prophet did not permit him to debase himself to circulate among the houses and argue with "cowboys."

"Seek them out and tell them that I expel them," he said to João.

"They won't obey me," retorted João. "And they have knives. They'll tell me that they take no orders except the master's."

This argument seemed to impress Antonio, who began to think things over and, in the end, realized that he could not continue to be the sole master. His role was the care of souls: for the rest, he allowed things to drift; yet clearly the whole population could not be allowed to behave as it pleased.

In the evening of the next day, at the end of his harangue, he announced to the faithful that he had decided to appoint João Abbade "Chief of the People." Everybody would owe him respect and obedience. He thundered against those who had not the backbone to get up in the morning to be present at prayers. "Those who become soft in the arms of women will be delivered to the eternal fire," he shouted dramatically.

A fortnight after that João Abbade, as Chief of the People, had to judge the first serious case at Canudos. He had just returned home after the prophet's daily harangue, and was engaged in warming up a gruel of black beans at the kitchen fireplace when a man came into the *sala* and clapped his hands.

"Come in here," João called out.

The man went into the kitchen. In the feeble light from the flames of the fire, João recognized a half-breed youth of about twenty years who lived down by the river.

"What's the matter?" he asked.

"Two men have just had a fight with knives. They're both wounded."

"Who are they?"

"Zé Venancio and Duilio Mangueira."

"What was the reason? Do you know it?"

"Zé Venancio raped Duilio's daughter. When Duilio heard about it, he got angry and wanted to kill Venancio."

"Rape, rape . . . Maybe she was quite willing?"

"No, it's little Anita. She's only thirteen and she was still a virgin."

"That doesn't mean anything. We must know whether she was willing."

"No, she wasn't, because Aymorès and Loureiro had to hold her."

"And where did it happen?"

"In Venancio's house. Anita was passing in front of the door. She had been to fetch water from the river. He called her, saying that he was going to give her something for her father, and she went in. Then he seized her and took her into the sleeping room and raped her, with Aymorès and Loureiro to help him. Anita wasn't able to call out, because Loureiro held his hand over her mouth. She returned home to her mother crying and didn't want to say anything. Then she told all about it and Mangueira immediately left to kill Venancio. Venancio was sitting on his doorstep. When he saw Duilio he thought he was coming to kill him, and he went for him. Venancio stabbed him in the thigh, but Duilio had time to plant his dagger in the other's arm. As the two of them were badly wounded they both went indoors again: but Duilio repeated that he would kill Zé Venancio."

João was wondering what he ought to do. He was the Chief of the People, that was understood, but he had only his title to make himself respected, and this wasn't enough to inspire respect in a man like Venancio. Why hadn't he thought of that sooner? In a town such as Canudos, a police force was needed. Meanwhile, what was to be done? Indict Venancio in front of the people? The man would be quite capable of starting a free fight, for he had some redoubtable friends who would give him a hand. The evil would be greater still.

"All right," he said to the young half-breed, "I'm going to speak to the Conseilheiro about this."

He went immediately to consult Antonio. He found him sitting on his bed with a candle in one hand and a breviary in the other. João gave him an account of the facts. Antonio roared:

"I said rightly that women would create trouble for us."

Then he expounded to João a singular line of argument which showed that he had a curious conception of the role of the sexes.

"You must haul Mangueira over the coals," he said. "Why did he get angry? Girls are made to be raped."

Somewhat taken aback, João retorted:

"If we admit that, there will constantly be free fights. There are men who don't like their daughters to be raped."

"I've said that I won't be concerned with imbroglios about women. You're the Chief of the People. Settle it yourself. It's thanks to you that the women are here. They're not my business."

"We'll have to form a police force," João remarked casually.

"Well! What are you waiting for? Create your police force. Do whatever you want to. You're the Chief of the People."

João was not a man to make decisions, but sometimes ambition helps. He fully understood that in order to establish his authority —and that title "Chief of the People" pleased him—he must act. Hence, from early next morning he set about recruiting a score of men who possessed carbines. Then he had a house evacuated and sent the three single men who lived there to lodge with friends. Over the door of the dwelling he wrote in capital letters with a piece of charcoal: CADEIA (Jail).

That was the first administrative establishment in Canudos.

The arrest of Zé Venancio, Aymorès, and Loureiro, the first police operation, took place without blows. It could have been dangerous. Venancio would certainly have defended himself with the energy of a professional killer, a capanga of his type, if his right arm had not been put out of action by the stab from Mangueira's dagger. The other two, not expecting to be molested, were taken by surprise.

João Abbade went to see them in the jail. When Venancio caught sight of the Chief of the People, he gave him a fierce look and growled:

"You'll pay for this, Abbade."

But João was miles ahead of him in diplomatic subtlety.

"Come now," he said to him cordially, "I have something to say to you."

João was fully cognizant of the danger which lay in any altercation with Venancio. He had quickly thought of a plan to smooth things over.

"I had you arrested," João said to him, "because the Conselheiro declared that he would not tolerate brawls. He made me establish a jail and create a body of police. People came and told us that Mangueira had collected about ten men and that he was going to down you. You're in a bad way: you wouldn't have been able to defend yourself. And so I had you brought here."

"I'll get that Mangueira," said Venancio savagely.

"Don't do that, we need you."

It was not easy to make a man like Venancio see reason. By dint of tact, João Abbade succeeded. All things considered, he promised the capanga, the ex-professional killer, that he would appoint him Chief of Police. Appeal to the pride of a Negro is never in vain. Venancio calmed down.

"Like that, it's all right," he said.

As he went out, João Abbade saw a crowd of several hundred men and women in front of the jail. He flared up:

"Get out of this!" he shouted. "Who told you to come here? Clear off or I'll get the police to chase you."

He felt strong now that he had a police force. He conceived a pride in it equal to the Conseilheiro's: he was becoming acquainted with the intoxication of power.

He turned his steps toward Duilio Mangueira's house.

Hitherto he had taken his pleasures with the girls whom he met here and there when he went to spend an evening with this or that inhabitant. The parents were happy to place their daughters at the disposal of the Conseilheiro's confidant. João felt surprised that he had never noticed Duilio's daughter. What was there about her so exciting that Venancio had come to rape her?

Mangueira was stretched on his bed: his wound made him suffer. Anita and her mother were in the kitchen. They welcomed João Abbade with deference, but with the suspicious looks of cats facing a stranger.

"You know that I've had Venancio put in jail?" he said, giving himself a superior air.

"We've been told so," the mother replied. "Many thanks, Chief."

João was looking eagerly at Anita who was leaning against the fireplace. She was a magnificent girl, one of those harmonious resultants from the mixture of races. Her father was a half-breed son of a Portuguese father and a Quechua Indian woman; her mother was the daughter of an Italian father and a negress of Senegalese origin. Anita had fine regular features, apart from the lips, which were rather thick and sensual, and big very black eyes in which the whole mystery of life was expressed. She thrust out her bosom like a colored girl. Her dirty torn blouse permitted the vigor of her plump firm breasts to be perceived.

João felt a lively pleasure in thinking that she was going to be his after having been possessed by Venancio.

João explained to Mangueira that the Conseilheiro did not want any brawling. Now there were police, and all those people who caused breaches of order would be expelled.

"I had to defend my daughter," Duilio asserted.

"Quite so. But you mustn't start anything new. If there's anything wrong, you must apply to me."

"I don't like fighting, but I had to defend my daughter. Why didn't Venancio ask me for her? I'd have given her to him."

"Venancio would never have a woman in his house. He's not that sort of man. . . ." said João.

After a time he added:

"I'm going to take Anita myself. In that way you'll have peace of mind."

This proposition seemed to please Manguiera very much. He felt himself honored and immediately gave his consent.

"That's it. Take her with you. Then she'll be safe. You'll be pleased with her: she's a good girl."

He felt proud and bucked up. He was to become father-in-law of the Chief of the People.

Half an hour later João returned to his home with Anita. They had spoken very little. He only asked her whether she was pleased to come and live with him, and she had replied: "Very pleased." He asked her whether Venancio had hurt her. "I hate him," she replied. And he asked how it had gone off, he wanted her to describe the rape in minute detail, but she evaded his questions. João was very excited. He led her into the sleeping room and undressed her. Her skin was whiter than his, being of a beautiful yellow, slightly brown. Her calves, shoulders, and neck were darkest in color, contrasting with the rest of her body which was much lighter, with the thighs almost white, especially on the insides.

João laid her on the bed and possessed her. He lost no time about effacing the passage of Venancio.

6. The Rum Traders

THE CONSEILHEIRO was not entirely satisfied with João Abbade's solution of the Venancio-Mangueira conflict. He approved of the creation of the police and the jail and the arrest of Venancio, Aymorès, and Loureiro, but he would have liked to see Mangueiro also arrested.

"At Canudos nobody can use a knife against his fellow man," he declared. "I won't tolerate it!"

He became more and more authoritarian, and his doctrine grew rigid in its incoherence. A few days later, when João succeeded in reconciling the adversaries, the Conseilheiro admitted that it was a good thing this time, and he approved the appointment of Venancio as Chief of Police, for, during the time when he was an itinerant prophet, Venancio had rendered him many services.

What he criticized severely was that João had taken up with Anita.

"Let the common people get on with their coupling," he said. "That's the law. But a chief must cut a figure of being chaste."

On this ground João had always opposed him.

"Anita pleases me," he replied. "I do what I like with her. I prefer to have her at home with me than to go around looking here and there for pasturage."

"Women are bad beasts," retorted Antonio. "Anita's like the others. She'll bring troubles on your head."

João refused to send her away. He seemed to be unable to separate himself from Anita. Since the arrival of Anita, he spent the afternoons with her: and this gave a fullness to his life which brought far greater satisfaction than mere luxurious idleness. Besides, the evenings had become infinitely delightful. After evening prayer they went home. João had found himself a guitar and he would sing the recitatives he had learned at Recife. In every mulatto there is a dormant poet. Was it not Gobineau who said that we owe art to the "drop of Negro blood"?

Anita was even more sentimental than he: she felt a real love for João.

But soon a grave problem was to tear the Chief of the People from his honeymoon.

During the first months at Canudos there had never been any problem of provisioning. Everyone lived on what he had brought, but those reserves could not be renewed when nothing was cultivated. Now, a town of from five to six thousand inhabitants could not consecrate itself exclusively to prayer and idleness. Men may live in the expectancy of paradise—providing they have food and drink.

And so, one day some men came to find the Chief of the People to ask him for food. He advised them to borrow a little maize from their neighbors. He said that at Canudos there must be mutual aid: that was the Conseilheiro's doctrine. The men replied that the neighbors also were short. As appeals of this nature were coming one after another, João decided to make an investigation; and he was obliged to state that they were going to lack provisions. He spoke to the Conseilheiro about it.

"Don't worry. God will come to our assistance," said Antonio with disarming calm.

While awaiting the fulfillment of this prophecy, João, being the object of these solicitations, endeavored to remedy the situation. Almost every day groups of people were still arriving at Canudos to settle in the holy city. He decided that all these new arrivals should unload their provisions at his house. He took it upon himself to distribute them. The newcomers were somewhat taken aback on seeing themselves despoiled in this way, but they told one another that it was the law of the town, and such was the prestige of the Conseilheiro that they accepted the position with a good grace.

Thus, João Abbade's house became a kind of store, a botequim without the name, but with this difference that at a botequim you paid. No money was in circulation at Canudos, since there was nothing to buy or sell. Those inhabitants who had brought some money with them left it lying in the bottom of their chests.

With the provisions of new arrivals stocked at João Abbade's, the town could hold out for a certain time, for the population was frugal. A handful of beans and half a pint of maize would feed a man for a day.

All the same, this could not last very long. The provisions brought by one or two families in the course of a day were far from sufficient for one day's consumption. João was wondering how to solve the problem. He had proposed that the Conselheiro should sally forth and pay a visit to some villages where their supplies had been adequately renewed at the time when they were itinerants, but Antonio declared that never again would he leave Canudos. Furthermore, he was certain they would get out of this trouble; but God insisted on patience. Patience was the highest virtue.

Hitherto the big open space or square in front of the church showed no animation except at the hours of prayer. Now little groups formed there in the course of the morning, and even in the afternoon, in spite of the burning sun. They became more and more numerous. At first there were none but men: then women in turn gathered together there. All the men and women who were hungry. Yet not a man or a woman among them thought of suggesting that they should take a few billhooks and rapidly clear a patch of ground to plant some maize and beans or manioc. They had given their lives to the Conselheiro; he would assure their subsistence. They were awaiting in a sort of lethargy the manna which would fall from heaven. The wait became a long one and the Conselheiro did not seem to have the magical powers of Jesus when He multiplied the loaves of bread.

They all nevertheless maintained their religious faith, but unfortunately faith does not indefinitely resist cramps in the stomach and colic in the bowels. João Abbade moved among the groups and fully realized the growing anxiety among the faithful. Certain of them—the lukewarm—allowed it to be understood that they were going to leave Canudos. This would be the end of the holy city, the collapse of the Conseilheiro's prestige, the ruination of their gigantic achievement. Women who were suckling new-born babies were shown to João. They could not live and give life with only a handful of maize as daily nourishment. João ordered two bullocks to be killed to feed the sick and the women. That was no solution. The massacre of their cattle would enable the town to hold out for another fortnight but, by then, they would have no more means of transport and no more building could be done: they would not even have the means of going to procure provisions if they found them.

João now had the preoccupations of a statesman. He began to understand that a certain amount of foresight is necessary in life. But he lacked competence and was not succeeding in solving the problems of which he nevertheless clearly grasped the facts. The only remedy he found for the situation was to send emissaries out into the hinterland to get believers to come and settle in the holy city. In this way he calculated they could obtain the newcomers' provisions, and thus hold out for some months if the immigration was on a large enough scale. After which they would see.

He told the Conseilheiro that in one of his evening sermons he must revive the courage of the faithful. Antonio became angry. What was this? Those people couldn't make even a little sacrifice? He would tell them some truths. The same evening he spoke in the crude vulgar language which he used when in anger:

"Let those people who don't know how to impose privations on themselves clear out!" he shouted. "The Church isn't a botequim. In Canudos we don't need people who think more of filling their bellies than of praying. When Saint Sebastian tells me to launch my appeal, I'll launch it, and then all believers from the São Francisco River to the Sierras de Jacobina will bring you provisions. But you must submit to the test of patience and tighten your guts!"

For he believed himself to be Master of the Hinterland and he was convinced that, on a sign from him, all its inhabitants would hasten to supply new provisions for Canudos.

This epical harangue produced the expected result. Hope returned to hearts that were appeased.

About twelve days later the Conseilheiro's prophecy seemed to be fulfilled. It was ten o'clock in the morning. Some urchins playing on the square caught sight of a loaded mule train crossing the sierra by the Cambaio cutting. They immediately scattered throughout the town shouting: *"O mantimento! O mantimento!"*—"The provisions! The provisions!" For they were among the hungriest. Soon the square was invaded by the men welcoming the train with a sort of respect.

It was not what they thought. The muleteers explained that they had been told of a new town in the hinterland. They had come to see whether they could do business: and they had twenty barrels of rum with them.

The faithful were a little disappointed. However, very soon some people remarked that, whatever might be said, this rum was a godsend. A good drink of rum puts new life into a man. But there they were, this wasn't manna from the sky: they had to pay. Then João Abbade established an interesting fact: there was money at Canudos. In a flash, some groups were formed and their members, by clubbing together, collected the amount required to buy a barrel. João himself joined with some friends and had a barrel delivered to his house. The muleteers would have finished by selling their whole load of rum if at that moment the Conseilheiro, alerted by this unusual animation on the square, had not appeared. When he heard that it was a matter of rum, he flew into a violent rage.

"Alcohol?" he roared. "Alcohol will never come into Canudos!" And turning toward his flock:

"Fetch me an ax. Immediately!"

The muleteers—two half-breeds—were dumbfounded and told him that, if it did not please him, they would take their merchandise away.

"Aren't you ashamed to hawk rum about?" growled the Conseilheiro. "I'm going to show you what's done with this demon rum, this *cachaça,* at Canudos!"

Someone had brought him an ax. He struck a barrel and the rum flowed out on the ground. It gave off a good aroma of spirit perfumed with *jatoba* wood which pleasingly tickled the nostrils of those present; but nobody dared to oppose the Conseilheiro. Excepting the muleteers.

"Hey there!" they shouted to the prophet. "We've paid for that stuff with our money."

Antonio let himself go. With his long hair, his sweeping gestures, his terrifying looks, he almost recalled Jesus driving the money-changers from the Temple. He raised his ax threateningly against the traders.

"One more word," he shouted, "and I'll strike you down."

Feeling themselves surrounded by a hostile crowd, the muleteers silently witnessed the destruction of their barrels, but this did not affect the one that had been taken away to João Abbade's house.

The muleteers were even pleased to be able to leave with their mule train intact though stripped of its cargo of rum. When they arrived at the Cambaio gap they had not yet recovered from their stupefaction.

That same evening the Conseilheiro delivered a flaming discourse against the degradation caused to man by drunkenness:

"A man who prays," he said, "doesn't drink rum. Rum is the in-vention of Satan." They had never seen him so excited, so savage. He held alcohol in greater horror than women, for his weak consti-tution did not allow him to endure it. The first time that Miguel Carlos had pressed drink on him—he always remembered it—he had such pain that he thought his intestines were in knots.

The incident of the rum traders had one unexpected result. João Abbade, having established that it was possible to harvest a little money, gave orders that they should all hand over to him what they had. With this money Canudos could be provided with food sup-plies. The operation succeeded, and a few days later a train of twenty mules bringing them maize, beans, bacon, and manioc, entered the town. They breathed freely. The specter of hunger was banished. They wondered for how long: yet, although it was the season for sowing, they did not even think of planting anything.

Hence, in a few months' time the same problems arose again, and more seriously: for the town had developed and now numbered close on 8,000 inhabitants. Neither João Abbade with his congenital weakness of character, nor the Conseilheiro with his cures for souls and counsels of patience, would have been able to provide a solu-tion of this problem of subsistence. Their whole undertaking was on the point of disintegrating, when the man appeared who was to be the infernal genius of the holy city of the hinterland: Pajehu.

7. Pajehu

ON THAT EVENING of May, 1887, the thoroughfares of the lower town at Bahia were full of animation. For the temperature was mild, the air almost cool. It was good to breathe. The spaces with tables outside bars were invaded by dockers who, having loaded sacks of cocoa or bales of tobacco for six hours in the blazing sun, came to refresh themselves with a glass of pineapple juice. Lissom negresses flitted past, heads piled high with the pottery which they had offered for sale in the market. Foreign sailors were strolling about, stopping to take long looks at the shop windows. On doorsteps Negroes were daydreaming or carving little statuettes in native wood; negresses, ugly in old age, were smoking short clay pipes.

Outside the "Amazonas," a café facing the quay alongside which transatlantic liners came, two mustached foreigners in bowler hats were arguing with a Negro who had a couple of little monkeys on his shoulders. A dozen or so other people sitting about at tables were consuming refreshments. Inside the café, seated at a table opposite the counter, four Negroes were making up accounts and exchanging moneys. At the back, three pale blond Germans gave themselves up to a consideration of Brazil sociologically, and dreamed of the splendor which could be imparted to Bahia if it were administered by the sons of the Fatherland.

Standing at the counter was a noncommissioned officer of infantry sipping a pint of rum and chatting with the owner of the café (a bulky, fat-bellied Neapolitan with a dull inexpressive face). The noncom was a man of medium height with a long massive torso posed on short legs. His brown complexion, flat face relieved by a high slightly aquiline nose, puckered eyes, and straight hair betrayed the man of mixed breed. Pajehu was in fact the son of a Guarani Indian father and a half-breed mother who was herself issue of a crossing of an Englishman with an Indian woman.

He lit a cigar and began to smoke thoughtfully, amusing himself from time to time by blowing a mouthful of smoke toward a little green latticework larder in which cakes were kept. Each puff of smoke disturbed a formidable swarm of flies.

"Have you heard this story of what happened in the Avenida?" the boss of the café asked him as he polished a glass.

"What story?"

"Four Negroes forced the door of the shop belonging to João Neves, the jeweler. They made off with a quantity of jewels, but Neves woke up and shot down two of them from his window on the first floor."

"Pity he didn't kill all four. They'll never kill enough Negroes. Negroes are the pest of Bahia. You'll never get any good out of that race. . . ."

He swallowed a mouthful of rum and was settling himself to continue his diatribe when one of the Negroes sitting at the table got up slowly and came swaying his torso to take a stand in front of him.

"A rum, boss," he ordered in a calm voice.

He was a big devil, well built and a pure African, for his hair was short and curly, his forehead receded, and he had thick lips. He did not look at Pajehu: he seemed not to be concerned with him. Pajehu stared at him and went on smoking his cigar.

The fat Neapolitan served the Negro's rum and began preparing to remove all the glasses on the zinc counter to a place inside it, for he foresaw that "something was about to happen." Pajehu turned toward him and said deliberately:

"We'll never have any peace as long as they don't send the whole gang of those lazy blacks into the interior."

"Who are you speaking about?" interrupted the Negro.

"Of the Negroes," said Pajehu in a firm tone of voice.

The colored man's fist described a quick circle, and Pajehu would have received it full in the face had he not ducked in time. He had seen the blow coming. Then his own fist, an enormous one, hard, with thick brown fingers, came up with a force to make sparks fly. The Negro toppled over and fell on the table. His three friends stood up. Pajehu withdrew to confront them but saw them make off toward the street. Doubtless they had no intention of getting into a fight with an army man. The big fellow who had attacked was already on his feet. He charged at Pajehu and tried to seize him around the waist. The half-breed, who was an expert at *capoeiragem* —Brazilian all-in wrestling—freed himself, caught hold of the Negro's wrist and tried to break his arm. Putting up an astonishing resistance, the Negro succeeded in breaking the hold. Pajehu saw him move his hand to his belt to draw his knife. Prompt as a cat he withdrew and charged. With a head blow in the stomach he sent the Negro rolling at the foot of the counter. At that moment two policemen intervened. The fat Neapolitan had gone into the street to call them. They requested Pajehu to follow them to the police station: they were afraid of a riot.

A crowd of Negroes and negresses had in fact gathered outside gesticulating and shouting: "Kill him, kill him!"

Revolver in hand, the police officers cleared a way for themselves. Pajehu looked with pride and hatred at the crowd, but he was vexed and humiliated to be under the protection of colored policemen.

"We won't go to the station," one of them said cordially. "We're going to take you direct to the barracks. *They* won't follow us into the upper town."

He was right. The crowd left them at the foot of the cliff. As they were going up the steep road which led to the barracks, the policemen asked Pajehu what had happened.

"We had an argument," he said. "He wanted to strike me: I stood up to him, and then he drew his knife."

"That'll cost him dear."

"I hope so."

He was put in the guardroom: the police declared to the sergeant of the guard that they had got him out of a brawl.

Pajehu went to his little noncom's room feeling pleased. What he had given that Negro! He was particularly pleased with his head blow: powerful, accurate, and decisive. That silly fool of a Negro who had drawn his knife! And all that riffraff waiting for him outside!

After smoking a cigarette he fell into a good sleep, with his nerves calm and relaxed.

Next morning when he was drilling his squad in the courtyard, he was called to the commanding officer's headquarters.

The commanding officer, whose name was Pinto, was a misshapen and unlikable man. His very short legs supported a narrow body with an egg-shaped belly, and his entire physique was surmounted by an enormous head out of proportion. His broad high forehead could make one think that he had a brilliant intellect. In reality he was loathsome and mediocre. Pajehu did not like his hypocritical look.

"Well, sergeant," he said in that voice of his which gave weight to each one of his words. "So you become involved in brawls?"

"Provoked," retorted Pajehu briefly.

"We're always provoked," said Pinto in a slow aggravating manner. "You know that soldiers must not get mixed up in brawls. And you, with stripes . . ."

"I'll never put up with provocation from a Negro," retorted Pajehu brusquely.

Pinto drew himself up in his chair, looked the sergeant up and down in such a scornful manner as to inspire him with respect, but Pajehu met his scrutiny and forced him to look down. Enraged, the hypocritical commanding officer muttered without raising his head:

"That will be eight days' detention."

"What?" retorted Pajehu. "Eight days under arrest because of that filthy Negro?"

Pinto pretended to be studying a file attentively. He raised his right hand slightly and said:

"Not another retort or I'll send you to the dungeon."

Pajehu's hatred of the white man went to his head like an apoplexy. He grasped his dagger and planted it in the nape of Pinto's neck as he leaned over his file. It was all over in a flash. The commanding officer's head flopped on the documents and a great jet of blood spurted over the collar of his tunic. His right arm fell, and the left remained extended over the desk.

Pajehu had calmly replaced the knife in its sheath without even taking the trouble to wipe it. Perhaps it might be used again, for Pajehu was ready to answer for his act. He went out and shut the door. In the corridor there were only two soldiers on fatigue duty sweeping the floor. Pajehu went down into the courtyard and walked toward the stables. He caught a glimpse of a man engaged in cleaning.

"Saddle me a horse, immediately," he commanded. "I have to take an urgent letter to the governor."

The man hurried to obey. Pajehu had never given a soldier justification for an order. He was surprised that he had failed to observe that rule: he regretted it, but the soldier had not noticed anything unusual.

He got past the gate of the barracks without difficulty. Once in the Avenida, he put his horse to a trot. It was a matter of disappearing before the alarm was given. When he had turned into the Rua do Maranhão, he spurred his mount and sped at a gallop toward the road to Pombal. In which direction should he go? North? South? He had no idea. All directions were good, from the moment he had got away from Bahia.

When he reached the open country he slowed down his horse to a trot. There was every reason, nevertheless, not to lose time; for his uniform would attract people's attention and his trail would quickly be picked up again. The road crossed some tobacco fields, magnificent plantations with broad-leaved plants such as are used for making cigars. What did it matter to him? He did not even see the landscape. His thoughts were now concentrated on the act he had just committed. With men of the tropics, action precedes thought; the reflexes leave no place for reasoning. Pajehu realized that he had just now shattered his career for a peccadillo. How was it he had not been able to keep himself under control? If only he had had to deal with anybody else except that foul Pinto, everything would have been different. But it was that fellow Pinto for whom he harbored a solid hatred. How had that misshapen creature been able to achieve the rank of commanding officer? Thanks to the dirty contrivings of the whites! He, Pajehu, was only a half-breed. To achieve the rank of lieutenant he would have to move heaven and earth and show exceptional capability, while as for those sons of whites . . . Having thought it over well, he was right to kill Pinto.

The road ran into a vast plain covered with sugar canes. Here and there white farmhouses could be perceived snuggling amid banana trees. Then there was a great uninhabited grassy plain spreading out as far as the foot of the sierra, which Pajehu reached at about four o'clock in the afternoon. As far away as he was able to see he could not make out anybody on the road. He felt that he was safe, and decided to have a rest before beginning the ascent of the mountain. He sat down in the shade of an aroeiro tree and allowed himself to fall into a doze. In a half an hour he took to the saddle again: he wished to cross the sierra before night came.

The road was one for muleteers and rose at first in a gentle incline, then it ran close to the flank of a peak overlooking a precipice. A moment later Pajehu reached a wooden bridge which crossed a deep ravine. The bridge was narrow and about twenty yards long; and it had no guardrail. It seemed to be abandoned and out of use. Perhaps Pajehu had taken an old trail which the muleteers no longer used? Nevertheless, he could not go back: that would have been dangerous. And, if he should be on an abandoned trail, he had all the more chance of not being overtaken. He examined the bridge carefully and decided to take his chance with it.

He himself could go across without difficulty. It lacked a few planks on its footway: some others were worm-eaten, but, for a man accustomed to the campo, such obstacles were of no importance. The problem was to get the horse across. Damn it! if only he had to deal with a mule, a wily, prudent and sure-footed animal. But a horse has too much confidence and is subject to dizziness. All the same, he must try. Pajehu tackled the problem by going backwards along the bridge, leading the horse gently by the bridle. The animal was obviously afraid; its hoofs were shaking. At times it stopped, backing on its hind feet, turning its head up toward the sky to avoid the fascination of the abyss. Then Pajehu relaxed the bridle slightly, allowing the horse some play in order that it should have time to recuperate. After which he gave a little jerk. The horse consented to take a few more steps. It was not without good will but it was afraid. They were almost reaching the middle of the bridge when the horse put its foot on a worm-eaten plank which gave way and the animal went down. There was a cracking noise. Pajehu felt that the bridge was collapsing. The traverses held. What was to be done now? The horse's right forefoot was driven up to the animal's shoulder through the opening left by the broken plank: the left was turned in under its body. Crushing down the hind legs, the crupper was leaning over slightly toward the void.

The sun had just set and darkness was slowly falling. Pajehu was still holding on to the bridle: he went close to the horse and caressed its neck and withers; and he inspected his position carefully, wondering how he was going to get out from there. He must move quickly. Pajehu squatted down, passed his shoulder under the horse's neck and tried to raise it. If the animal could regain a footing with its left leg, it would be able to recover its balance, but it did not succeed in grasping what the man wanted. Giving a vigorous heave with his back, Pajehu lifted it. Then it understood: it extended its left foot and got a foothold. It wished to get its crupper into position, unfortunately not grasping that these dangerous movements must be convulsive. The shoe slipped and the animal's whole body rolled over into the void. Pajehu jumped up immediately to avoid being dragged with it. As he had let go of the bridle, he felt nothing, but suddenly had a terrible impression of something missing, a sensation of giddiness punctuated by a dull, distant sound rising from the chasm. He turned back cautiously and, like a man knocked silly, gained the other slope of the ravine.

When he touched ground he sat down, or rather let himself flop down. His heart was beating violently because, for the first time in his life, he had felt afraid. He needed a good time to recover his calm, to get rid of that trembling of his knees and the unbearable burning in his head. Night had come: he would not dare to venture along that unknown mountain path. Better wait for the moon to rise. He stretched out on the ground and courted sleep, but the incidents of that day kept coming up in his memory with disquieting vividness. He reproached himself again for having killed the commanding officer for a mere nothing: then he congratulated himself; the officer was a man whom he would have killed some day or other, he hated him so much. And he thought himself lucky to have taken that old trail which sheltered him from pursuers. Gradually everything became blurred in his brain and he fell asleep.

When he awoke the moon was in the sky, bathing the deserted flanks of the sierra in its gentle light. Pajehu was hungry. When would he find a village? This region seemed to be uninhabited. He set out on his way. The path followed the bare flank of the mountain. At the end of half an hour Pajehu reached a pass, from which point the path plunged downward toward a valley at that moment shrouded by a thick mist. Perhaps in that depth there might be a fazenda or a hamlet. He went down. Soon before reaching the bottom of the incline he went through a plantation of sugar canes. He cut a stalk with his knife and began sucking it. It appeased his hunger. He stopped suddenly. "It would be better," he thought, "for me not to show myself before daybreak. In this uniform I'll be taken for a police officer and that'll cause the devil of an alarm." He sat on a stone at the side of the trail and waited for morning.

He was very patient, yet the wait in the mist seemed very long to him. When dawn came he was worn out: his head was heavy, his ears were buzzing. The sun plunged its rays into the dense haze, broke it up and dispersed it in little clouds which began creeping up the hillsides. The village appeared, a fairly important one, overlooked by the two white spires of the church. Pajehu reached it in about ten minutes.

Some Negroes were busy yoking oxen to a wagon. He went up to them. They looked at him suspiciously.

"Don't worry about my uniform," said Pajehu. "I'm merely a noncommissioned officer who's got lost in the mountain. I followed an old trail and lost my horse trying to cross the bridge."

"Did you try to cross that bridge?" one of the colored men asked, opening his eyes wide with stupefaction and admiration.

"Yes, but it didn't work."

"The bridge is rotten," said another.

"I saw that," said Pajehu.

They offered him a cup of coffee and a few biscuits made of manioc flour. Then they left with the wagon, while Pajehu made his way toward the church square where a gathering of people could be discerned. A half-a-dozen mules laden with big bales were tied to stakes under a great avocado pear tree. Some men were sitting in a row against the façade of the church. A few stood about chatting in the middle of the square.

Once again he told the story of his adventure in the mountain. At that moment a priest came out of the church and spoke to the men who were sitting about. They got up, gathered together, and seemed to be in consultation.

"What's happening?" Pajehu asked.

"Those are the people who are leaving for Canudos," replied a tubby little Negro.

"Where's that?"

"You don't know Canudos? The Conseilheiro's town?"

Pajehu expressed surprise:

"Who's the Conseilheiro? I've never heard him spoken of in Bahia."

The Negroes looked at one another as if they were accomplices. Pajehu repeated to them that he wasn't a police officer, and that they could speak freely.

"The Conseilheiro," said the tubby little man with a sort of timid respect, "why, he's the prophet of the hinterland."

"Ah! Ah! And these people are going on pilgrimage?"

"No. They're going to live in the holy city at Canudos. The curate is taking them there."

"I understand," said Pajehu, "the Conseilheiro is a monk."

"No," said the Negro, "a prophet."

Pajehu seemed to be very interested in this news. He asked for details.

"The Conseilheiro came only once to Tucano," said the Negro. "That's a long time ago. Now he doesn't leave Canudos any more. He's a great prophet."

"I'd like very much to know him," said Pajehu.

"Go with them," said the Negro. "Speak to the curate."

The curate made no difficulty about admitting him into the party. "All believers are invited to follow us," he said, adding under his breath: "If you're a spy, look out."

"Put your mind at ease," was all Pajehu said, for he had his plan.

At ten o'clock the party set out on the march.

8. Raids

THE TUCANO PARTY arrived at Canudos on the fifth day of the novena which had been ordered by the Conseilheiro to ask heaven for the dispatch of a few convoys of provisions to the holy city. Hence, even before the end of the novena, heaven had responded to the prophet's appeal. It was high time, for the situation had become tragic: many men were leaving the town on the pretense of going out to look for supplies and did not return. João Abbade was again having nightmares: he was in a state of nerves and no longer made love; and he thought that they would never solve the problem.

The party from Tucano brought enough food for a few days, but then what? By the blessing of heaven the next days saw the arrival of six new groups of faithful. A formidable enthusiasm seized the population and the Conseilheiro was frantically acclaimed. The religious faith of the followers had become unshakable.

"I knew that Saint Sebastian would not refuse me his support," said the prophet to João Abbade.

Abbade was now convinced of this. You cannot dispute facts.

Unfortunately Saint Sebastian's help was only momentary. During the next month there was not one more arrival of immigrants, supplies ran out, and once again the specter of hunger arose over the town.

"We shall make another novena," was all the Conseilheiro said.

They said fervent prayers which were repeated by men, women, and children animated by a burning faith. These, however, were without effect. Abbade wondered what really could be Saint Sebastian's point of view in this matter, what criticism he could formulate against this novena, which was organized with the utmost care.

He told Pajehu of his uneasiness of mind, for he had quickly become the half-breed's friend. A noncommissioned officer's uniform could not pass unnoticed at Canudos. Abbade reckoned that a soldier with stripes must be a man of some education and could be useful. Every afternoon they met in one or the other's house, and they would talk of the days when they lived in cities. Pajehu had not yet told his story: he had said simply that he left the army because he loathed it.

"Just like me," said João. "I couldn't bear city life. You can't help it, when you come from the campo."

Each of them suspected that the other was lying but did not press matters.

When the question of supplies came up, João Abbade asked Pajehu what he thought of it.

"The Conseilheiro says that the whole hinterland will respond to his appeal. Let him launch it!"

"But who is to make it known? If we send a few men into a village, they won't be believed. The Conseilheiro ought to go himself; and he doesn't want to. He even declared the other day that he would never again go out of Canudos. Maybe you, with your uniform?"

"As for me, I'm very willing to go, but not with three or four men. I want twenty men on horseback with firearms. In that way we can make an impression. We must inspire traders with respect or otherwise they won't collaborate. They're too stingy."

That same evening after prayer they told the Conseilheiro of their project.

Antonio declared that he was certain of success.

"I know the hinterland," he said proudly. "It's mine. It will be enough for you to present yourselves in my name, and they'll give you everything you ask for."

He turned his eyes heavenward as if to ask for one more inspiration and then, brusquely, as if a revelation had just come to him:

"Listen," he said, "if you go to Sitio you'll be received in a worthy manner as messengers of God. Sitio has always welcomed us. Isn't that so, Abbade?"

"It is, in fact, one of the good places. The Conseilheiro has many partisans there and it has three botequims."

"Good," said Pajehu. "I shall communicate your appeal to them. Is there a political chief—a mayor—in this place? We might as well apply direct to the political chief so that he can invite the population to collaborate."

"That's Soarès, the man who has the dry goods shop. Deliver my blessing to him, and tell him that Sitio has been placed under the protection of Saint Sebastian."

Pajehu was happy to have been put at the head of this mission. He was bored since he had arrived at Canudos, although in the first days there the strange life of the town interested him. That evening prayer around the bonfire especially had impressed him. It had become fascinating: every evening there were women who went into trances, and they ran throwing themselves at the Conseilheiro's feet, uncovering their bosoms and crying out that they offered themselves wholely to Saint Sebastian. Sometimes a Negro would execute a frenzied dance in honor of the Virgin Mary. At other times there would be a singer accompanying himself on the guitar to improvise a chant in homage to the sage of the hinterland. But, as these scenes were repeated every day, and the harangues of the Conseilheiro were always so apocalyptic, Pajehu in the end grew tired of it. Accustomed to the ardent life of Bahia, to the exciting atmosphere of the cafés in the lower town, he did not succeed in getting used to the mysticism of Canudos. Fortunately he was able from time to time to drink a pint of rum with Abbade, who had carefully concealed the barrel purchased from the muleteers. Abbade had told him that the Conseilheiro was a fierce opponent of alcohol. They could drink only on the sly. That was no life. Hence, Pajehu was pleased to go on an excursion outside the town, to get out of the oppressive atmosphere of this holy city in which there was never any laughter. Furthermore, in barracks he had acquired the mania of command: he loved to line up men and give them orders, to march at their head and to have the role of chief.

Consequently, the little troup of twenty horsemen which he had mustered on the big square looked well when it set out on the road for Sitio. Pajehu rode at the head of the column: the riders followed two by two. They were clad in dirty, torn shirts and patched trousers and had all kinds of headgear: one was wearing the broad-brimmed Bahian straw hat, another the leather cap of the *jagunços* or hinterland plainsmen, another the silk kerchief of the Gaucho. But they marched in order and gave an impression of strength and will.

They did not return until the day after the next, in the forenoon.

About ten o'clock they appeared in the Cambaio gap. Pajehu was easily recognized by his uniform. The horses were well laden. In addition to the rider, each one carried two sacks which hung one on each side of the saddle. The Conseilheiro's appeal had been heard. The town was saved.

In a moment the church square was thronged with an excited crowd which suppressed its jubilation, for the Conseilheiro forbade joy as a manifestation of the devil.

Nevertheless, the women could not restrain themselves entirely and on its arrival the troop was greeted with some rousing hurrahs. Pajehu made immediately for João Abbade's house, where the load was deposited, pending distribution.

"So everything went off well?" said João to him jubilantly.

Pajehu looked him straight in the eye for a moment and then said casually:

"Very well. Only two were killed."

"*What?*" said João, his eyes opening widely. "Two killed . . . Come into the next room. All those people hanging about on the doorstep have no need to know that."

"In any case the men will tell about it. Give me a pint of *cachaça*. I'm tired. And take a look in the *sala:* there are two barrels of that rum wrapped up in sacks. Put them aside. The Conseilheiro has no right to imagine that we're going to remain without having a drink."

Abbade rolled the barrels into the sleeping room and then sat on the edge of the bed with Pajehu. Eager for information, he said with slight emotion in his voice:

"Those casualties, they're not our men? These have all returned."

"Naturally," said Pajehu scornfully. "You don't know me yet. I know how to command a troop."

"And how did it happen?"

"Very simply. We arrive in the village and I ask an old boy sitting on his doorstep where's the shop kept by Soarès. He points it out to me, in front of the church. We advance along the street. Everybody was shutting their doors, thinking that we were *cangaceiros,* cutthroat bandits. The botequims hadn't time to close. In the first one we came to, all the customers were still in front of the counter: they looked terror-stricken as they saw us pass by. I shout

out to them: 'No need to get frightened, we're sent by the Conseilheiro.' That doesn't appear to reassure them. And here we were,
outside Soarès's store. I halt the troop, jump from my horse and go
in. I don't know whether you know that fellow Soarès. He's one of
those fat Portuguese merchants you meet everywhere. He's already
old, and he's bald, with big white mustaches. 'Are you the political
chief of Sitio?' I say. 'Yes,' he replies, looking at me suspiciously. I
don't care for people who look at me like that. Had I been there on
my own account I'd have given him one in the face with my fist. 'I
bring you the Conseilheiro's blessing,' says I. He continues to look
at me distrustfully, then makes up his mind to speak. 'The Conseilheiro's blessing doesn't concern me. That fellow has come to cause
trouble in the whole hinterland. He'd do better to retire and not
have himself spoken of any longer. Let him stay hidden in Canudos
and leave us in peace!' I could have downed him on the spot, that
dirty Portuguese, but I restrained myself: it wouldn't help in any
way. 'The Conseilheiro has sent us to find supplies at Sitio,' I say.
'Do you refuse to give us any?' 'Make your own arrangements with
the botequims,' was what he then said to me. Now I don't like things
which drag. So I go out of the shop, get into the saddle again and
turn with the troop toward the botequim a little further down the
street. The boss was a young, tall thin man with thick long hair. He
had a forelock which fell down into his mouth: a negress would give
a lot to have one like it. 'Now then,' I say to him, 'the political
chief says that you can supply six horseloads. What have you in
your shop?' 'The political chief said that?' he asks me, looking
doubtful. 'Get a move on,' I retorted. He hesitated. 'Who's going
to pay?' he asked. 'Settle that with Soarès. Come now! Load me up
those six horses, immediately. Maize, beans, manioc, a bit of bacon,
and some *bacalhao*, dried salt fish.' He glanced at my men, who
had got off their horses, and began to fulfill the order. Once the
horses were loaded, we went down the street looking for another
botequim. Suddenly three shots rang out. They were firing at us.
It's dangerous to play that game with Pajehu. I lead the troop back
on the square and take cover near the church; I leave six men with
the horses already laden and, with the other ten, I swoop into the
street at a gallop toward the place where the shots came from.
Naturally, the sharpshooters had decamped, thinking rightly that if

they fired once more we should dash at them and we shouldn't have missed them. Then five of us patrolled the street while the other five loaded the horses at the botequim. There was nobody in this store: our men could take what they wished. When all was ready, I sent a man to fetch those who had remained near the church, and it was then I caught sight at the end of the street of a few individuals who were spying on us. They were reckoning to get us as we passed by. I pretended not to notice anything: I gave a sign to my four men and all of a sudden we attacked. Frightened, the enemy fled toward a house on a height from which they could easily have held us under their fire. But they all hadn't time to reach it. We fired into them and two were shot down. Meanwhile, all my men had rallied together; and we left the village at a gallop. They fired a few shots at our backs but the bullets didn't carry. That's the story. Now you know how we're received when we come on behalf of the Conselheiro."

João Abbade scratched his chin and then scratched his head. This story left him perplexed.

"A bad business," he said, "they'll send the police after us."

"Pooh!" said Pajehu. "The police? Have you ever seen the police pursue bandits?"

"No, but bandits take refuge in the sierra. You never know where they are. As for us, they know we're to be found at Canudos."

"They daren't come to Canudos. Moreover, they'd be well received here."

Abbade was not reassured. He retained from his colored forefathers that fear of blows, that lack of reaction, the fatalism and resignation which characterize Negroes. He was impressed by the half-breed's pluck, but he could not share his quiet contempt for the possible consequences of this bloody expedition.

"We'll go and have a talk with the Conselheiro about it," he said.

By candlelight that evening, Pajehu retold his story. Contrary to what Abbade had thought, Antonio declared that Pajehu had done good work, done well to castigate those unbelievers in Sitio. It was, moreover, only the beginning of their punishment.

"All those who deny me," he said, "will be chastised. They don't want to support Canudos: Canudos will support itself. Henceforth nothing can stand up against Canudos, against the capital of the hinterland. All will be made to yield. Those who refuse shall perish!" He was in a fury, unable to swallow the affront which had just been done to him: he was ready to put the whole hinterland to fire and sword if the hinterland dared to rise against him.

"That gang of scoundrels," he growled, "they want to ruin my work, the work of ten years, to set up their foul republic. From today onward, no more mercy for the exploiters of the believers. Those who don't wish to give supplies freely must be executed without mercy. We'll sweep the hinterland clean of all who aren't with us. These merchants are all republicans, tools of a godless administration, exploiters of the people. There's not a botequim at Canudos; there never shall be. The botequims are Satan's taverns: it's the botequims which have corrupted the men of the hinterland. Commerce must be destroyed and souls brought to God—by force if need be. Besides, a few examples will be sufficient. Pajehu, I charge you with the execution of my orders."

Pajehu did not ask for more. The Sitio expedition had revealed to him that he had the soul of a bandit leader. He passionately loved operations of that kind. Not only did they procure for him all the satisfactions of command, but they gave him the opportunity to make use of weapons, to fire at men. They gave him all the joys of battle, pillage, and killing.

"Where shall we go next time?" he asked.

"As soon as João Abbade reports that supplies are getting low, I'll indicate the place to you," replied the Conseilheiro who was beginning to like organization.

Pajehu would have wished to undertake a new raid immediately. He was disappointed. Once again he was going to have to put up with the mystical boredom of Canudos. Fortunately the night brought him an inspiration. Next morning after the distribution of provisions he rejoined Abbade. He led him out on the square and pointing to the church said:

"That church is not bad, but I've never seen a real church without a bell."

"Quite so," Abbade admitted. "It's needed, but we haven't the wherewithal to make one."

"There's no question of making one. We must go and find one in some village or other."

"If you do that, you'll have the whole hinterland up against us. They'll say it's sacrilege."

"Those who are partisans of the Conselheiro will approve. There's nothing to prevent our being given one. There are parish priests who approve of the Conselheiro, for I came here with a curate."

"No priest will ever despoil his church of its bell. What would he call his flock with? There would be a fight and the whole village would be up against you."

João Abbade was a weak man: he knew that in the end he would yield to the half-breed's arguments.

"If the Conselheiro agrees," he said, "get on with it, but it can lead to trouble."

Little did that matter to Pajehu. Little also to the Conselheiro, who was roused to enthusiasm by the idea. "It's true," he said, "we need a bell. We ought to have thought of it long ago."

What astonished João Abbade was that the entire population became most excited with this idea. As soon as the project was known, it aroused general enthusiasm. Women went around with the news: "We're going to have a bell!" Men came to find Pajehu asking to be allowed to take part in the expedition. According to information provided by former muleteers who knew the sertão well, there was a magnificent bell at Pombal. It was rather far away, and in that part the Conselheiro did not have many followers, but the game was worth the candle: for, in short, the bell is the essential element of a church. An Angelus unaccompanied by the tolling of a bell lacks power of flight and remains earthbound.

Pajehu intended to succeed and he engaged in his team only tough men, men who had shown their mettle: ex-hired killers like Zé Venancio and Tranca-Pés; cold-blooded criminals such as Quimquim de Coïqui who had stabbed his mother and hung her by a leg to an avocado pear tree; Pedrão who had liquidated an entire family—father, mother, and three children; Pacheco, who had stabbed a woman and two men in the course of an affray from which he came out unscathed. With a team like that, Pajehu felt easy in his mind. The wagon with ten oxen yoked to it was driven by Marcolino. In short, all the elements for success were mustered.

The troop set out on the march at break of day to the frenzied cheering of the whole population massed in the main square.

The days which followed were passed in a state of anxiety such as Canudos had never known. The Conseilheiro had ordered special prayers to assure the success of the enterprise. Throughout the whole day and during the whole evening, in every house they talked of nothing but the bell. There were some who said that the men of Canudos would have a stiff job. Pombal, they said, was a considerable village; the inhabitants were proud of their church, and the priest had much power.

When the fifth day passed without a word of news of the expedition, they began to wonder whether their *jagunços** had been massacred. The Conseilheiro put new life into the people, declaring that he had seen a vision. Saint Sebastian had shown him the bell on its way to Canudos.

The sixth day was spent with them waiting anxiously. A few men went and took up their position at the cutting in the sierra at Cambaio, from which point they could see as far as Rosario. They returned at sundown and declared that they could not catch sight of anything on the horizon.

In spite of the Conseilheiro's efforts, a vague feeling of discouragement spread throughout Canudos. The rumor went from house to house that Pajehu's entire convoy had been wiped out.

"João Abbade knows it," said the defeatists, "but doesn't want to say anything." The fanatics retorted that, if such an enterprise failed—a holy enterprise, since it was a matter of procuring a bell for religious purposes—the Conseilheiro wouldn't be himself any longer. But the majority began to be tormented with doubt.

João Abbade was troubled and sent two men on horseback in the direction of Pombal with instructions to bring back news at any cost.

On the morning of the eighth day, these two emissaries had not returned but, at about ten o'clock, the men posted at the Cambaio gap galloped back to announce that a convoy was making its way toward the town. In a few minutes the square was covered with an excited multitude wishing to go out to meet Pajehu. João Abbade prevented them.

* See Translator's Note, page 7.

"Line yourselves up on the sides of the square," he shouted. "Don't congest the road. The wagon must come right up to the church."

Wild cries intended as hurrahs greeted Pajehu when he emerged on the square followed by his men and the wagon, whose axles were creaking under the weight of the bell. When the vehicle stopped in front of the church door, half-a-dozen Negroes began to prance in one of those crazy dances imported from Africa; others lit an enormous bonfire. Yet the midday sun was harsh and glaring, but everyone thought that such an event could be celebrated only with fire.

At that moment the Conselheiro came out of the church into which he had gone to commune with himself. He climbed on the wagon and, with one hand on the bell, the other raised toward heaven, he cried out:

"God be praised for this new victory of Canudos."

"Long live Pajehu!" roared the more realistic crowd, which no doubt considered that Pajehu had done at least as much as God in the conquest of the bell.

The Conselheiro decided that the bell should be blessed that evening and installed next day. Then he retired into his house with Pajehu and João Abbade.

"We feared at one moment that you had met with some misfortune," he said to Pajehu.

"It's been a tough business," said the half-breed, "but that's not what delayed us. We had an accident with the wagon: one of the wheels broke just as we were arriving at Bom Conselho. It had to be repaired, and that took us two days."

"Some people said that you had been massacred," said Abbade. Pajehu shrugged his shoulders scornfully.

"If they knew who I am, they wouldn't talk like that. It wasn't easy, but I defeated the Pombal people, I did."

"Was anybody killed?" asked Abbade.

"A few. I don't know how many. On our side three or four men have been wounded."

"You didn't kill the priest?" inquired the Conselheiro.

"No. Neither the priest nor the political chief. I'm a strong believer in avoiding trouble but, in every business, there's always a few roughnecks who show up to cause disorder. I'm going to tell you how it went off. After two days' march, there we are at Pombal. I have the political chief's house pointed out to me and go there at a gallop with my men. I tell him that we are charged with a mission by the Conselheiro, and that we'll need him but that we'll also need the priest. I don't tell him any more about it: I leave two men to keep him in sight and run off to the priest's house. I tell him that we must have a meeting in the church, with the political chief and the notables of the place to inform them of a proposition on the part of the Conselheiro. He was suspicious but I tell him I'm charged with a mission which I intended to fulfill and that I had no time to lose. I left him guarded by two men. Then I had the seven notables of the town brought: three fazendeiros and four merchants. I assemble them in the church and declared that we needed a bell at Canudos; and that we thought of the one at Pombal, which would suit us very nicely. Whereupon the priest said: 'You're in force, I can't prevent you from taking my bell, but it's sacrilege and you'll answer for it before God's tribunal.' 'You ought to be ashamed,' upheld the political chief with his big head and pouched eyes. 'It's banditry.' 'It'll be banditry if you drive us to it,' I say to him. 'You ought to make a present of your bell to Canudos. All men of the hinterland ought to help the Conselheiro, who's sacrificing himself for them.'

"The political chief began laughing. I struck him in the face with my hand to remind him to behave properly. Then I gave my men the order to get the bell out. They had procured chains and ropes at the house of one of the fazendeiros whom I had arrested. It was a difficult operation: that bell's heavy, it is. It had to be lowered from outside. Little by little the villagers began to arrive on the square. Naturally they were furious and said among themselves that they couldn't allow that to be done. I didn't hear them, but I strongly suspected that they were going to try to attack us. I wasn't afraid, but my opinion is that, as far as possible, fights are to be avoided. I called out to them:

" 'The priest, the political chief, and seven notables are in the church. If you budge, I execute them.'

"That impressed them and we were able to continue with our work in peace. When the bell was loaded on the wagon, we set out immediately and I took the hostages to the end of the road leading out of Pombal. There I released them, thanking them. So everything went off well so far. We were already two hours' march away from the village when we were attacked. They had prepared an ambush in the sierra. Fortunately we have some good marksmen: the fight hardly lasted half an hour. They daren't risk it hand to hand, and we got through. Three of our men were killed; I don't know who, but Pedrão knows them. We also lost five horses: it was necessary to finish them off as we couldn't take them with us. We were in sight of Bom Conselho when the wheel broke in two. That's what set us back. The wheelwright in Bom Conselho is a good craftsman, but he's slow. The main thing is that the bell's arrived here."

"Quite so," the Conselheiro wound up. "As it is, the bell will toll the evening Angelus. No need to say that an Angelus accompanied by a bell tolling will be far more alluring."

9. Major Sariema

WITH THE BELL, life became more rhythmical at Canudos, even more ordered. Also more animated, because, morning, noon, and night the bell broke the mortal silence which enveloped the town. Its reverberations filled the birdless sky. Without being heavy, the resonance nevertheless had a masculine accent, with none of those childish tinklings of the bells of a women's convent. This especially pleased the Conselheiro.

In the houses people did not cease speaking highly of Pajehu's initiative and energy. "That's the man we wanted at Canudos." As for the three men killed on the expedition, they were quickly forgotten. Next day their wives were assigned to three men of mixed breed who had arrived recently from Alagoas; and no more was said about it.

The choice of Antonio Paes as bell ringer was also much commented upon. Certainly nobody suspected the Conselheiro of practicing the vulgar vices of other men. It was nonetheless noted in some houses that this Antonio Paes had often submitted himself to the fancies of Tranca-Pés. People hardly thought that, having become toller of the Angelus, he could continue to frequent the house of Tranca-Pés.

Antonio Paes was a white Negro (an *aço* or "streaky" Negro, as they say in Brazil), son of a mulatto and a negress. He was sixteen years of age, a well-proportioned boy with soft flesh. His face was mat white and only slightly rosy on the cheekbones. His eyes were very soft and he had a shifty look when dealing with men, a seraphic one when it was fixed on heaven.

Although unaware of the special relations existing between Paes and Tranca-Pés, the Conseilheiro put an end to them without willing it by attaching the youth to himself in person. Hitherto he had always prepared his own food. Henceforward Paes would be entrusted with looking after him. He would in like manner be the prophet's assistant throughout the ceremonies, handing him his breviaries, the cross which he brandished during some of his discourses, and his rosary. The boy was at the same time responsible for keeping the church clean—which, as it happened, was reduced to giving it a few whisks with the besom.

Thereafter the Conseilheiro was constantly to be seen accompanied by Paes, like a priest followed by a choir boy, and those people who like nicknames no longer referred to Paes by any other name than that of Antonio Beatinho, the last word meaning "little beatific one."

A short time after these events—they were important events at Canudos—the population of the holy city was able to witness the arrival on horseback of the most improbable figure they had ever seen. He appeared one afternoon at about four o'clock just as the sun was beginning to go down. Numerous groups had already formed on the square to wait for evening prayer. When the horseman arrived, there was astonishment for a minute, after which the crowd pressed around him. The *jagunços*, the hinterlanders, had never seen a rider in such a getup and in such an attitude. He looked like a toad on horseback, he was bent so far forward on the neck and withers of his mount. He was a stout little man with the aquiline nose of the Indian but the thick lips of a Negro. His skin was of a dirty black color and he had a thick excrescence at the base of his nose. He wore a black shirt and trousers, a white collar and red necktie; on his head was a straw hat of the type known in England as a "boater."

On catching sight of this phenomenon, João Abbade came up: "Where are you going?" he asked.

"I think I've arrived," replied the rider, who seemed out of breath. "This is Canudos here, isn't it?"

"Yes, it's Canudos. What do you want?"

"Nothing. I'll explain, but first I'm going to get down from my horse."

He tried to lift himself from his mount but, as his legs were very short, his foot struck the horse's crupper and he would have fallen backwards if Abbade had not received him in his arms.

"Excuse me," said the new arrival, "I'm not used to horses."

João Abbade wanted to know whom he had to deal with, although the fellow seemed inoffensive, so he took him to his house.

"Are you on the way through here?" he asked the stranger. "Who told you of this route?"

"I'm not on the way through. I come to settle in Canudos."

"Oh, really!" exclaimed Abbade, taken aback. "What's your name?"

"Major Sariema."

"Where do you come from?"

"From Bahia; and that hasn't been easy. You understand, I've never before traveled in the hinterland. I took the train as far as Joazeiro, from which point I've had to make the journey on horseback. I've been three days on the way, and I'm just about worn out."

"Would you like a glass of spirits?"

"I wouldn't refuse it."

Abbade poured him out a pint of white rum and continued.

"How did you get the idea of coming to settle here? What have you done?"

"It's very simple," retorted Sariema, whom the question did not disturb. "I'm a barber by trade. I had a *mocambo,* a cabin, on the fringe of Bahia, and I must tell you that I had a good business, especially for shaving on Saturdays and Sundays. Nothing but Negroes. They pay badly. I had to shave for a matter of centavos.

For a long time I had been hoping to save enough money to settle in the lower town. I'd have done very well there, as I know by business. My razor's like velvet. I'm not afraid of competition with any white man. But, there you are, my outgoings were too heavy. You understand, when you're a hairdresser in the city, you must dress properly. That costs dear. You have to trim a lot of beards to buy a suit in the upper town! But one fine day a customer spoke to me about Canudos and the Conseilheiro. He told me that a prophet had created a big town in the hinterland and that there was golden business to be done there. I didn't hesitate: I came. A man must make up his mind in life."

Abbade who had listened with lively interest, immediately disillusioned him.

"My poor friend, I think it'll be difficult for you to make any fat profits here. There's no money used in Canudos. We've no need of it. Canudos is a holy city: it's not a commercial and moneyed place."

"How strange!" said Sariema.

He thought for a moment and added:

"What do you live on?"

"The whole hinterland helps the Conseilheiro and his faithful followers."

"So you don't do anything? You don't work?"

"We pray. I've told you: Canudos is a holy city."

"And what has to be done to become one of the community?"

"Nothing. Approve of the Conseilheiro."

"Hence, if I wish to stay among you, I can?"

"All believers are welcome."

The bell began to toll for the evening Angelus.

"Come," said Abbade. "I have to lead the praying. Mix among the people and come and see me after the ceremony. You can sleep in my house and tomorrow we'll look for one for you."

João had always had a weakness for city Negroes. He thought to himself that Sariema might perhaps be useful in some way or other. Townsfolk must never be overlooked.

A few days later he installed Major in the house of a man named Leitão, a half-breed from Pernambuco who suffered from liver trouble, did not speak to anybody, and remained stretched on his mat for whole days on end: a man who took up little room and so could have somebody to live in his house.

It did not take Sariema long to transform the sala or principal living room into a hairdresser's establishment, and the customers— if they can thus be described—flowed in. All the jagunços wanted to have their hair cut by the "hairdresser from Bahia." Major was anxious to justify his presence in Canudos.

He often went to see Abbade, who loved to hear him relate incidents of life in Bahia. Pajehu came to join them in order to while away time. The trio had long conversations together in the evening. They were all three of city origin and, as Sariema knew Bahia as well as Pajehu, they were not lacking in subjects to talk about. And so it was that an intimacy was established among them which was to lead to forming a triumvirate that, little by little, took over governing the town. Nevertheless, at first Pajehu did not conceal his suspicion of the barber. "He's a *cafuz*, a mixture of Indian and Negro," he said to João Abbade. This was true. Sariema was the issue of an Indian and negress. "What does it matter?" Abbade had replied, not having the racial pride of the half-breeds. "He's intelligent; and he can be of service to us."

As a consequence, Pajehu became more friendly and even spent his forenoons teaching the *cafuz* how to ride a horse.

About that period there was a recrudescence in the arrival of new disciples. After heavy rains the São Francisco River overflowed its banks, several villages were wiped out, and the rumor went around that this was the beginning of the fulfillment of the Conseilheiro's prophecy to the effect that one day the hinterland region, the whole sertão, would be invaded by the waters. Many people were coming to settle in the holy city to escape the catastrophe.

Once again Canudos became a building yard. There had never been such activity. The town expanded into a capital city. Intoxicated with pride, the Conseilheiro announced in his harangues that soon he would overthrow the republic, that the whole hinterland would rise to put an end to the regime of Antichrist. Galvanized by the flaming eloquence of the prophet, the jagunços worked tirelessly under the heat of the sun, while Pajehu and his band operated their forays in almost every direction to provision a population which was becoming more and more numerous. All this took on such magnitude that João Abbade became frightened by it. He was wondering whether, one day soon, they would not have a visit by the mounted police.

"Let them come!" replied the Conseilheiro. "We're stronger than they are."

He was convinced more than ever of the reality of his mission and of his power. More than ever before he considered himself the harbinger of new times, the regenerator of the hinterland.

10. Anita

IT IS PROBABLE that vice originated as a pastime, from which no doubt we have the maxim: "Satan finds some mischief still for idle hands to do." In the spring of 1896 Canudos comprised nearly 12,000 inhabitants—12,000 men and women whose only occupation was to recite a few litanies thrice daily. In the early days of the town, the men were busy building houses or the church. Now that everything was set up, there was nothing more to do. Life had become monotonous, even for those who were little inclined to work. In other towns, men conceived all sorts of ways of killing time: in the cafés, where the hours pass so quickly when a man is slightly inebriated; the organized dances which excite and make one forget even sleep; the concerts which transport you into a universe where there are no annoyances; the circus which arouses strong emotions. Even in the villages there are distractions: the botequim and its rum; the processions; an occasional *batuque;* a *reinado*, which is a colorful procession with dancing; or an *encamisada*, a display of horsemanship. At Canudos the Conseilheiro had forbidden fermented liquors, dances, music, and batuques; and they had not the wherewithal to organize proper processions. He had gone so far as to say that displays of horsemanship were the festivities of brutes. For the jagunços there remained nothing but sexual vice from which to draw a little pleasure.

Hence it was that the town gradually lost every moral sense and wallowed in debauchery. The men lost all reserve; the women, every sense of decency.

Perhaps Anita alone in the whole town proved refractory in this. When she heard that João Abbade had deceived her with the Madeiros girl, she reproached him and declared that, if he didn't want her any more, she would go home to her father's. João dissuaded her: he argued that, if she returned to her father's house, she would be given to any Negro who might call there on a visit, whereas he would never give her up. She dared not tell João that she wanted him exclusively for herself, and that she reserved herself exclusively for him; which was not in conformity with the views then current in Canudos. But she had her own idea of things.

Sometimes, though rarely, the sexual act gave place to an argument. One day a young Pernambucan went to the Conseilheiro to complain that a young man had abused his twelve-year-old daughter. "She's too young yet," he said. But the Conseilheiro had no intention of taking up the defense of women. "They must all pass beneath the tree of good and evil," was his reply. This retort was immediately made known throughout the town. Now they knew that they could give themselves up to the joys of the flesh without restraint.

The jagunços were not lacking in opportunities. This was the only pleasure they had. Debauchery, until then practiced behind closed doors, was flaunted in broad daylight.

João Abbade wanted to liven up the town somewhat, and decided to organize a monster orgy on the big square. It just missed becoming tragic.

At the moment when the festivity was in full swing, Tranca-Pés ran up to João Abbade and, taking him a little to one side, spoke to him under his breath. The two men went quickly away and reached the house of the Chief of the People. João was up the two flights of stairs with a vigorous bound and stopped suddenly. On the floor of the main living room Anita was lying on her back. Her wet garments were clinging to her body showing all its curves. Her head was leaning slightly to one side and her hair hung disheveled. Major Sariema was squatting beside her. When João came in, he stood up.

"We've been waiting for you," he said. "You must act quickly. Take her clothes off. At Bahia, when somebody was drowned, they worked his arms. Hurry up."

With remarkable scruples Sariema had not wished to lay hands on the Chief of the People's girl. Can anyone ever know what passes in the mind of a man of mixed breed? João seemed to be all at sea. He was like a man whose blood had curdled.

"Make haste," repeated Sariema.

João tore off the blouse and the dress. He did not speak: he panted as he breathed. After a moment, Anita half-opened her eyes and turned her head.

"She's coming around," said Sariema.

João eagerly followed the return of life on his girl's face. He was on his knees beside her, and at heart terrified by the thought that she might die. At last she uttered a moan.

"Supposing we moved her over on the bed?" said João.

"Tear the sleeves of her blouse," said Sariema. "We must make her comfortable now."

They carried her over to the bed. She began to heave little sighs and to make efforts as if to recover her breathing. Then she held out her arms and said, "João!"

João drew near her and caressed her face with his cheek. "Anita!" he whispered. "João!" she repeated softly, grasping his arm.

"Wait. I'll return immediately," he said in her ear.

Now that she was alive, he was anxious to know what had happened. He went back into the sala with Tranca-Pés.

"Where did you find her?" he asked.

"In the river," said Tranca-Pés. "You mustn't bear me ill will, Chief, if I didn't attend your fete, for just at that hour it's cool on the riverbank: it's the best time of the day. I was lying on the sand when, suddenly, I heard something heavy falling into the water. I sat up and saw a woman being carried away by the current. Naturally I didn't hesitate: I pulled off my jacket and threw myself into the water. In a few strokes I caught her, lifted her and brought her to the bank. It wasn't without some trouble: she struggled like a cat. Once on the sand, she seemed to be dead, but I felt her heart and it was still beating. I saw immediately that it was

Anita, so I took her in my arms and brought her here. As I went into the lane I met Sariema and said to him: 'Come quickly.' I left Anita in the sala and went to let you know."

"And what was Anita doing at the river during the fete?"

"Don't know."

"Where did she fall from?"

"She must have fallen from the top of the little rock just where the beach begins."

"Good for you, Tranca-Pés, and thanks. Would you like a drink of rum?"

"It would go down nicely."

João poured out a pint of spirits, which Tranca-Pés drank in one swallow, then he returned to the bedroom.

"Leave me with her, Sariema," he said.

"She's safe now," said the cafuz as he went out.

Anita seemed to have fallen asleep. João heard her regular breathing as he squatted at the foot of the bed. He was still all upset, but already he was being overcome by remorse. Anita had wanted to commit suicide because of him, because of that fete. It was suddenly revealed to him what that woman felt for him; and what he felt for her. He had not believed it was so deep.

Night had come and João felt sad: he was not thinking, he was just sad.

Anita woke up.

"Where are you, João?" she asked in a distressed tone of voice.

"Here I am," he replied. And he took her hand. "I'm going to get a light."

He lit a candle of palm wax, and put it in the middle of the room. By the yellow light of the candle he saw that Anita was sitting on the bed.

"You feel better?"

"Yes, I'm all right. I'd like to get dressed."

He took out a dress which lay in a little packing case at the end of the room and held it out to her. When she had put it on, she sat down again on the bed.

João sat down beside her.

"Tell me quickly how it happened," he said, taking hold of her knee. "What did you go to the river to do?"

"Don't ask me anything about it. What happened had to happen."

"What do you mean? Come now, tell me all about it."

"I just can't tell you. It wouldn't serve any purpose."

"I want you to tell me what happened. I have a right to know."

Anita put her elbows on her knees and held her head in her hands. She made no reply and sat there as if absorbed in her thoughts. At any other time João would have shaken her, but now there was something within which restrained him: he dared not be abrupt with her. He put his arms around her waist and said:

"Do tell me what happened, Anita. Why did you do that?"

"You won't hold it against me?"

"No. Tell me everything."

"I wanted to die," she said in a toneless voice.

"I know that. But tell me why. Was it because of me?"

"Don't ask me anything more. It's too sad, and you wouldn't understand."

"Don't say that. I knew that you were disgusted with the fete. Isn't that true?"

"It is true."

"Why didn't you speak to me about it? Why go and throw yourself in the river without saying a word to me?"

"You wouldn't have listened to me. There's nothing to be done about that. It would have been all the same for you to give me to your friends . . . but it's useless for me to explain to you since you don't care."

"What do you mean?"

"Leave me. I'll die one of these days and it'll all be ended, quite ended."

He thought that she was weeping. He stood up, lifted her in both arms. They were face to face: the yellow light of the candle accentuated the features of their bronzed countenances.

"Why do you speak to me in that way? What have I done to you?"

"When you went with the Madeiros girl, I wanted to go home to my father's. You didn't want me to. You were keeping me for your fetes but, as for me, you see, I can't lend myself to such things. I just can't."

João drew back a pace.

"You can go ahead, but I'll return home to my father's house. I should like to leave, to go back to my own village."

João felt his pride brought down: he felt for this girl something he had never felt, even for Carmela Brito—something inconceivable in Canudos and conventionally called love. The thought that she could escape from him made him feel ill at ease.

He went up to Anita again as she turned her head away and put his hand on her shoulder:

"Listen," he said in a gentle voice. "There shall be no more of those fetes, and I won't go with other girls any more."

She bowed her head and did not reply. Yet she thought that there was sincerity in João's voice; and she felt the secret satisfaction of victory. Now he could come to her: she felt that he would come. And she took him to her.

11. The Mission of the Capuchin Monk

ON A BEAUTIFUL MORNING in August of 1895 a sumptuous coach drew up in front of the governor's palace in Bahia. Two flunkies bespangled with gold dashed toward the entrance. Monsignor Ferreira drew out his stout body, whose proportions were nicely set off by his violet soutane, and climbed the monumental stairway at the foot of which two sentries presented arms.

The governor received him in the vast office which he occupied on the first floor; it had been the viceroy's study during the period when Bahia was the capital of Brazil.

The governor was an enormous man with a fat face and pendulous cheeks which made it almost square. Under his very black eyes with their shaggy eyebrows two heavy pouches set off a fleshy nose of reddish brown. A very full collar of flesh supported his face, which seemed pained and sad, but to which a head of close-cropped hair imparted a sort of energy. Across his large paunch was a gold watch chain and his thick short and tight-skinned fingers were loaded with rings, including one embellished with a ruby, which meant that the governor was a Doctor of Law. He was fifty-two years of age, liked good living, and had a horror of political complications. He was an old friend of Deodoro da Fonseca who, when he proclaimed the republic, had entrusted him with the government of the state of Bahia. The governor had been to Europe on two occasions, visiting Paris and Rome, and professed a deep admiration for Auguste Comte. He would have liked to build a great Temple of Humanity in the city of Bahia, but the power of the Catholic Church was such, in this city of two hundred churches, that he had to abandon his project. He took life easily from the time when he saw his dream fade away.

The bishop was almost as stout as the governor, but his paunch was more rotund and kept in better shape by his silk soutane. His face was rounder and fuller and his cheeks were pink and chubby. A nose as round as a billiard ball, no pouches under the eyes, not a roll of flesh under the chin. His head was completely shaven and gold-rimmed spectacles gave to his countenance an aristocratic distinction.

"Well now, dear friend," said the governor, who had a horror of ecclesiastics, "to what do I owe the honor of Your Eminence's visit?"

"I should like," said the bishop unctuously as he folded his hands, "to speak to you about this extraordinary matter of Canudos."

"Canudos? Yes, I've heard some talk of it. Pooh! The usual tale of jagunços."

"You take things lightly, sir. This fellow Antonio Conseilheiro is causing enormous harm to religion."

"I don't see in what way he's dangerous."

"He's a false prophet and you know the credulity of those hinterland people."

"This is at least the twentieth tale of prophets I've been told. They are common phenomena in the hinterland region. You know this as well as I. They will disappear in accordance as civilization penetrates further into the interior. In the meantime, I think that we have something else to do besides bothering about the tomfooleries of a man such as this Antonio Conseilheiro."

The bishop had no intention of allowing himself to be outmaneuvered. He was aware of the impious indifference of this functionary of the republic. Hence, he replied calmly but firmly:

"The question is more serious than that. I have just received a report from the parish priest of Joazeiro. He informs me that several curates in the region—and even two priests—have rallied to the Conseilheiro. Furthermore, it has been reported to me that a padre in Ceará—Padre Cicero—a man of very great influence, also propagates these monstrous heresies. The plague is threatening to spread. This is a fact which you cannot overlook. In such a case as this, the State has a duty to give all its support to the Church. The free development of a heresy would end by creating a rebellious class which would endanger the security of the State."

The governor, whose face remained expressionless, opened a drawer, took a little box from it, emptied some white powder into a glass which he filled with cold water. (A small Negro boy brought a fresh carafe every half hour to replace the one on the desk.)

"You are ill?" asked the bishop in a deeply sympathetic tone of voice.

"No. I take a little bicarbonate of soda to ease my stomach."

He drank it and wiped his lips with a handkerchief.

"Eminence," he resumed, "from your point of view, that is to say from the religious point of view, you are certainly right. But you will admit that the government cannot intervene in these matters except in case of absolute necessity. The republic has inscribed liberty of conscience in its program. Antonio Conseilheiro has therefore the right to defend whatever theories he likes. But you have equally the right to fight them. You have a numerous staff at your disposal. Bahia is full of monks. What are they doing here? I often wonder how they spend their time. Why don't you send them to preach the Gospel in the hinterland? It's by persuasion that you will bring the straying sheep back to the fold, not by force."

The bishop was not put out of countenance. He obstinately kept his hands folded, but from time to time there was a slight nervous twitching of his right nostril.

"I think that you are making a mistake," he said solemnly and, looking the governor up and down haughtily, he came out with his crushing argument: "A town such as Canudos is a standing shame for the state of Bahia. Those people do not recognize your authority. They do not pay any taxes. They are rebels. It is your duty to bring them back under your authority."

"I'm very willing, Eminence," the stout functionary cried out, lifting up his arms. "But why employ the police when I have the railway. At this moment we are building railways in the north. As soon as this program is achieved, order will be restored—from the administrative point of view, in any case. Prophets are powerless against locomotives."

This time the bishop became animated. He unfolded his hands, leaned forward over the desk and, darting a severe look at the governor, he said:

"When the population has been led astray, when hearts have been corrupted, it will be difficult to lead the hinterland back into the way of the Lord. Think of your responsibilities; you are allowing a nest of anarchists to develop in Canudos."

The prelate's obstinacy began to get on the governor's nerves so that he could not restrain an outburst.

"I've told you that it was a matter for monks, and from that I'm not budging. What are all those monks doing in Bahia, men as fat as eunuchs at thirty years of age? If the Conselheiro has been able to acquire such influence in the hinterland, it's their fault. Let them go and evangelize the population instead of pillaging every garden to adorn their altars to the Virgin Mary."

"Do not blaspheme, sir," retorted the bishop in a haughty manner. "The fact of the proclamation of the republic does not give you a right to deny your support to the Church. The republic is Christian. As for our monks, they have always been at the breach and are ready to render their service."

"Let them do so! Get rid of this Conselheiro fellow for me. Reduce him to silence or send him to the devil in the depths of the sertão, and I'll stand you a bottle of champagne!"

"Thank you very much. I know what remains for me to do," said the bishop getting up with dignity and shaking out his soutane which was inconveniencing him. (It was almost noon and the heat was becoming intense.)

The two portly men shook hands in a hostile manner.

About a month after this interview, João Abbade, Pajehu, and Sariema were squatting in the shade against the frontage of the church. It was four o'clock in the afternoon and the heat was torrid. The square, swept by the burning sun, was deserted. All the jagunços were asleep indoors, except those who mounted guard in the passes of the sierra through which the roads to Canudos came. This guard system was one of Pajehu's innovations. At first he had strongly affirmed to João Abbade that the police would not concern themselves with Canudos, but, with what followed, he thought it over. The banditry which he practiced on a grand scale in order to provision the town would end by attracting the attention of the authorities. There was, consequently, a need to avoid being in any way surprised.

The three men were engaged in discussing a new project. Sariema had suggested building a big house, one as big as three ordinary houses: in fact, a palace. They would install the Conseilheiro in it; and a big room would be reserved for the "Council." Abbade had spoken to the prophet about it, but Antonio declared that he did not want his house to be any different from the others.

"All men are brothers," he said. "Here I'm the shepherd, but the shepherd must remain among his flock."

"In that case, let us put up a building for ourselves," said Sariema, who dreamed of living in a palace.

"That wouldn't serve any purpose," said Pajehu.

"We mustn't aim at putting ourselves above the Conseilheiro," said João Abbade.

At that moment two men appeared at the other end of the square escorting a monk clad in a brown homespun habit and wearing a broad sombrero. They walked toward the three "chiefs."

"Who can that be?" said Abbade.

"It's a monk," said Sariema.

"Don't bother your head about him," Pajehu rapped at him.

They did not get up when the monk was brought before them.

"There you are," said one of the men escorting him. "He came by way of Monte Santo and says he wants to speak to the Conseilheiro."

Pajehu gazed at him with his wicked eyes like those of a panther observing its prey.

"Take your hat off. You're in the shade here," he said in a hard voice, remembering the rules of politeness which he was taught in the army.

The Capuchin—for he was a Capuchin monk—did so.

"Who are you?" João Abbade asked in a self-important manner.

"I am delegate to Antonio Conseilheiro from His Eminence Monsignor the Bishop of Bahia."

"What does the Bishop of Bahia want of the Conseilheiro?"

"I should like to speak to the Conseilheiro himself."

"Go easy, my friend," interrupted Pajehu. "The Conseilheiro doesn't speak to everybody who comes along. We must know first what your business with him is."

The Capuchin did not reply.

"Come now, speak up," João Abbade ordered. "Otherwise I'll have you taken away from here."

The Capuchin hesitated for a moment and then drew from his habit an envelope which he held out. João took it, tore it open and read:

Diocese of Bahia
To the Most Excellent Antonio Conseilheiro.
CANUDOS.

Most Excellent Sir,

We have learned with the deepest satisfaction that for a long time you have devoted yourself to propagating the word of truth in the hinterland. We congratulate you and thank you for so doing. Hitherto we have not been able to give you our help, but now that the railway reaches Joazeiro, we shall be able to send you as many preachers as you wish.

We should be grateful if you would facilitate their task and allow them to expound to the peoples whom you are evangelizing the latest instructions from Our Holy Father the Pope.

Wishing you the greatest success in your apostolate,
I remain,
Your brother in Our Lord,
THEOPHILO
BISHOP

"Read that," said João, holding out the letter to Pajehu.

When the half-breed had finished reading, João stood up and

went to the Conseilheiro's house. Little Beatinho came almost immediately to bring the Capuchin. Pajehu and Sariema went with him.

The Conseilheiro had been agreeably impressed by the tone of the bishop's letter. This missive flattered his pride. Hence, he offered a particularly polite welcome to the young Capuchin.

"So you'd like to hold a meeting in our church?" he asked the visitor.

"Quite so."

"What will you speak about?"

"I should not be able to say everything at one meeting. I shall deal particularly with the recent instructions from Our Holy Father the Pope relating to communion and the worship of the Virgin Mary."

"Good. You'll speak this evening, after prayer."

The Capuchin thanked him warmly. He had thought that this would not be easy. He found the jagunços rather brutal and rough, yet understanding. They were not the bandits described to him at Joazeiro and Monte Santo.

João Abbade led him into the house with Pajehu and Sariema. They asked him how he had reached Canudos, for he had come on foot. He had taken six days from the railway station at Queimadas.

They were still engaged in discussing the difficulties of the route when the bell tolled, calling to prayer.

"You have a bell, too," the Capuchin remarked.

"Have you ever seen a church without a bell?" Pajehu rapped out.

They went to the big square. The monk's presence had been reported everywhere throughout the town and the people thronged to see him. As it had been announced that he would preach a sermon, they were all waiting impatiently to go into the church. The litanies were hurried through more quickly than usual and there had never been such a scuffle at the entrance to the temple.

Inside the church the men were placed on one side, the women on the other. They were separated by a passage which some of Sariema's men, to whom the policing of the ceremonies had been entrusted, made them keep clear.

The Conseilheiro went up on the platform erected at the end of the church in front of the huge wooden cross. He invited the Capuchin to come up there also, and then he addressed the people:

"Today we have the honor to have among us the Delegate of Monsignor the Bishop of Bahia. He is going to tell you the latest instructions sent by Our Holy Father the Pope. God be with him."

The young Capuchin, although a professional preacher, was a little nervous. He had before this addressed only crowds that were sympathetic to his thought. Here, he had to win over the people— there and then: for it seemed to him that the Conseilheiro might be difficult about authorizing another meeting.

His improvised discourse opened brilliantly to everybody's satisfaction. He congratulated himself on finding, in the depths of the hinterland, a city in which men dedicated themselves to prayer and were absorbed in the idea of God. When he found that the sympathy of the crowd had been gained, he went on to the delicate points. The work achieved had been very fine. It was not enough. Unfortunately the people of Canudos could not have the benefits of the Mass, of confession and communion. It was absolutely necessary to return to traditional worship. . . .

At that moment there were various movements in the crowd. The men were looking at each other; and the women were glancing over at the men's side.

"You think that you live in the bosom of the Church," shouted the Capuchin, allowing himself to be carried away by his own eloquence, "yet you are living on the fringe of the community of the faithful. . . ."

"Long live the Conseilheiro!" roared Pajehu who was stationed near the entrance door.

As if only awaiting the signal, the crowd in turn roared: "Viva! Long live the Conseilheiro!"

Somewhat thrown out of countenance, the Capuchin raised his arm to restore calm. But the jagunços were unleashed. In the tropics passions flare up quickly. On a gesture from the Conseilheiro, the intruder would have been murdered. It was then that Pajehu advanced along the passage, jumped on the platform and, seizing the Capuchin by the collar, threw him down. The monk regained his feet and took out from underneath his habit a little cross which he brandished to make the crowd withdraw. Pajehu was already on him and seized hold of him again.

"Death to him!" shouted the jagunços.

"Let us pass," commanded Pajehu. "I'm going to settle his account."

The crowd opened and Pajehu pushed the Capuchin out of the church.

At the door he turned around and called out:

"Zé! Gidiö! Theo! Augusto! Come with me."

These were his constant companions, his henchmen. They went out. As they went away, João Abbade shut the door, restored calm among the crowd so that they could hear the Conseilheiro's harangue as he strode from one side of the platform to the other.

Outside on the square, which was bathed in the feeble starlight, two men held the Capuchin by the wrists.

"Aha, you scum!" Pajehu said to him. "You wanted to preach the Gospel in the hinterland. You'll see what that's going to cost you."

"Where must we take him, chief?" one of the men asked.

"To my place."

The Capuchin was not trembling: he had drawn himself up proudly. He was not afraid. He had offered himself as a volunteer when the bishop had asked for a preacher for Canudos. He had, nevertheless, been told that it was a haunt of bandits. He was ready to sacrifice himself, for he was a young man with the soul of a martyr. But he had never expected the torture that was inflicted on him.

There were seven of them in the dark living room of Pajehu's house. One of them lit a candle and placed it on a stool in the corner of the room. The Capuchin was wondering what they were going to do but he was not yet trembling: he was silently praying.

"Take his clothes off," said Pajehu.

They removed them, his habit, trousers, and shirt, stripping him naked. The Capuchin offered no resistance. But he was deeply puzzled.

"Hold him well," Pajehu said to his men.

The Capuchin wondered what was going to happen. When he realized what it was, he uttered a cry of horror.

"Get him dressed again," commanded Pajehu. "We'll put him back on the road."

He stood before the monk and, with a sardonic laugh, said:

"You can make a nice report to your bishop. Give him plenty of details. That'll amuse him."

The young Capuchin met his look and remained silent.

"Take him back to the road for Monte Santo."

Zé and Gidiö led the bishop's delegate toward the Cambaio pass while Pajehu and the others returned to the main square which was now invaded by a dense crowd. The Conseilheiro's harangue had been short. He had been satisfied with thanking the jagunços for their loyalty, and he had thundered against the myrmidons of the republic.

12. Major Sariema's Investigation

WHEN Pajehu told João Abbade how he had settled accounts with the Capuchin, João gave a start.

"And you sent him on his way?"

"Why not?"

"I thought you'd killed him."

"That wouldn't be any use. Better to send him back so that his bishop may know how useless it is sending us preachers."

They were on the square with Sariema, among the crowd which continued to discuss the incident. Gradually the square cleared of people: the jagunços returned to their houses. The night was turning cool, and the stars were twinkling as in a northern sky.

"Don't you think," said João Abbade, "that this time the police will get busy about us?"

"Possibly so," said Pajehu. "Anyhow, the day's coming when they'll do so."

"All the same, it would be interesting to know what effect this business will have produced in Bahia. I think myself that the bishop will excommunicate us."

"But what difference will that make to us?"

"None. Yet the government might then take a hand and send troops here. Bishops are very powerful."

"They'd have to have fine troops to beat Canudos!"

The square was empty. The moon was casting her light above the sierra. They were walking in front of the church, whose recently whitewashed façade stood out strongly against the dark background of the mountain. They stopped for a moment without speaking and then João Abbade, by way of conclusion to his thoughts, said:

"I have a proposition to make."

"Speak out."

"To send Sariema to Bahia so as to know what they're saying about Canudos."

"That's an idea."

"Sariema has never had trouble with the police and he won't be noticed. He could spy out quietly on our account."

"It's a long journey. It costs a lot of money and we haven't any," interrupted Sariema.

"That'll do," said Pajehu. "I'll take charge of the money problem. And if you're too lazy to go there, say so."

"I'm not frightened of it," said the half-breed. "There's only the question of money."

"If you go there," replied Pajehu, "don't try to play any tricks on us and not come back. You'll suffer for it if you do. I should go after you and get you. You know me."

He had the right way with him of speaking to the half-breed: he knew how to make himself respected.

"We'll go and speak to the Conseilheiro about this," said Abbade.

Antonio was in agreement. He was restless to know what was being said about him in the capital.

Next morning Pajehu, at the head of about fifty mounted men, set out in quest of the money. As the sun rose his troop was climbing the slopes of Cannabrava at a time when the morning mist was not yet dispersed. They did not return until the afternoon of the following day. Pajehu immediately went to Abbade's house. João was asleep in Anita's arms. Pajehu shook him by the shoulder.

"What? What's the matter?" João grumbled as he sat up.

"It's only me," said Pajehu. "Here you are."

He held out a roll of filthy bank notes.

"How much is it?"

"Four contos."

"That's too much. If we give four contos to Sariema, he'll never come back."

"Say rather that he might intend not to return. But he won't dare to break his pledge with us. You'll see the way I talk to him. A cafuz—a half-breed of Indian and black blood—must be battered into shape. Those people are more panicky than the Negroes."

Anita had awakened and looked at them with interest. Men are up to all sorts of extraordinary things. . . . João put on his trousers and tightened his belt.

"Now where did you find that money?" he asked Pajehu.

"At the fazenda of Coqueiros. I knew it was a big fazenda but I'd never been there—it's a bit far away. There's a still for rum-making, a mill for sugar canes, a factory for manioc flour, and a storehouse for flour. It's a big place."

"And the fazendeiro gave in straightway?"

"Right away. I told him we had to send a couple of men to Bahia to make indispensable purchases. We needed four cantos of reis. They'd be paid back in a month or so. I invited him to come and see the Conseilheiro. He's a very affable young man, about thirty years of age."

"I thought it would have been harder than that."

"Me too. To be sure, I had fifty men with me, but I think that even if I had only two, he'd have given me the money for the sake of peace. He must be very rich."

They went out to give their instructions to Sariema. They found the cafuz in his sleeping room, in gallant conversation with two negresses.

"Get your clothes on and come into the sala," Pajehu ordered. "We have something to talk about."

Sariema sent the negresses away and came to sit beside them, for there were only two seats in his living room.

"You're going to go to Bahia," said Abbade. "Here you are, four contos."

"Four contos!"

The cafuz opened his eyes wide. He had never had so much money in his hands. He looked greedily at the dirty notes.

"Don't squander them," said Pajehu, "and try to keep well in mind what we're going to say to you."

João Abbade gave him his instructions. For Sariema it was a matter of talking to as many people as possible, to find out what was being said about Canudos, and of bringing back every newspaper that should have mentioned the subject. As he would have a surplus of money, he must also bring back certain things. João wanted an alarm clock, one of those little clocks with a bell, he explained. Pajehu ordered a Spanish pistol.

"You understand?" he said to the half-breed. "A Spanish one and no other mark."

"If you find any nice dresses for women, you can bring two or three," João added.

"You've nothing else to order?" Pajehu said scornfully. "That girl's turning your head."

"It's my business," retorted João who had become touchy on this point.

"And what else?" asked Sariema.

Apart from the alarm clock, the pistol, and the dresses, they did not see what they could require. Life in Canudos was simple.

"Choose them yourself," said João. "You'll easily see what's interesting. It's on seeing goods that you want to buy."

Sariema's departure was as picturesque as one could expect. He had thoroughly shaken out his clothes: he had put on his collar and tie again and once more was wearing his "boater." Although he had made great progress in horsemanship, he did not succeed in sitting upright on his mount and retained his toadish appearance. João Abbade made Chico Ema, a wily young Negro, accompany him as far as the railway station at Queimadas, where he would await Sariema's return.

Only three days later Sariema stepped out of the train in the Northern Station at Bahia. He felt very tired, for he had not dared to sleep in the train for fear of being robbed of his money. His eyes were dry, the rims of his eyelids smarted, he had gnawing pains in his stomach, and his knees were stiff. On finding himself once again in Bahia, he felt a great solace, like a man who might be returning home after a nightmare adventure. He wondered whether it was really the Sariema from Canudos who was walking down the street of São Bento among all those well-dressed men and

women. It seemed to him that he was returning from the end of
the earth. Mechanically his steps led him to Giuseppe's café,
Giuseppe being an old friend of his who had a bar-restaurant near
the docks.

Giuseppe was no longer there: he had given over his café to
another Italian called Raymundo. Major Sariema was disappointed.
Now that Giuseppe had vanished, he felt as if he were in a strange
city. Fortunately the feeling did not last long; the new owner was
a likable man. He had a long face with regular features and a magnificent mop of black hair through which he was constantly passing
his hand in a somewhat voluptuous way. He spoke quickly and
with much gesticulation. His Portuguese was generously mixed
with Italian words, but he had business instincts and he took a
seat at Major Sariema's table. New customers must be treated in a
friendly manner. Major told him that he was an old friend of
Giuseppe and that, on coming to Bahia, this was the first place he
called at. He regretted his friend's departure but, as the new proprietor was very amiable, he was not sorry for having come. To
seal this new friendship, Major offered to stand a bottle of Italian
wine. He had never been able to treat himself to such a luxury in
the course of his life, but today he was rich to the tune of several
contos of reis. He could testify that wine contributes powerfully
toward the furtherance of good relations. Raymundo showed as
much friendship toward him as if he were a white man. Major felt
confident of himself. He asked Raymundo whether he knew of a
good hotel. "Not one of those places for Negroes," he said. "I want
a hotel for respectable people." Raymundo informed him of an
establishment kept by another Italian.

"He's a friend of mine," he added. "He's near here. I'll go with
you and recommend you."

With wine to help, Major began to realize his own importance.
In former times, when he was a simple barber, he had never been
accorded such consideration on the part of café proprietors, not
even by Giuseppe. Today it was different: he was wealthy. He put
up a second bottle of wine.

It seemed to him that the café was more frequented than in
Giuseppe's time. There were now dockers, money-changers (who

dealt in lottery tickets), foreign sailors, and even some passengers from steamers for Europe. The service was managed by two Negroes.

A second bottle of Chianti was brought to them and the conversation became more intimate.

"You don't happen to know of a good 'house'?" Major asked under his breath. "Not a hole where dockers go but a house with white girls. You understand? I've been ten days traveling."

"There's Aristides' house, my friend. You'll be well served. There's a tiptop selection. Nothing but European women. But that costs dear."

"It doesn't matter," retorted Major grandiosely, "so long as they're whites, but not those flabby whites you sometimes find in Negro dens."

"You can put your mind at ease. In Aristides' house they're nice fresh women. He has it well organized. New ones arrive every two months."

"Good, I'll go there this evening. Now, if you wish, we'll call at the hotel. I'd like to have a little rest."

He slept all the afternoon. When he went out, night had come. He had a nip of rum in a café on the Rua de Portugal, to put himself in good trim, and turned his steps toward the Aristides establishment.

One would have said that it was a private house. The outside shutters were closed, but the wide entrance door was open on a long vestibule lighted by a smoky lamp which hung from the ceiling. Major wondered if that was really the place. Two doors opened on the vestibule. Which should he open? He was not used to such establishments. He pushed the first door and found himself in a drawing room lit by a big paraffin lamp placed on a little table surrounded by four chairs in Arabian sackcloth. A deep silence permeated the house. After a moment which seemed very long to Sariema, a big fat woman appeared. Her white fleshy face was surrounded by thick, disheveled hair. She was dressed in a pale blue low-cut frock open almost down to her navel.

"Would you be so kind as to come in?" she said with great affability, darting a scrutinizing and suspicious glance at Major.

Major went into the next room. It was furnished with a long

table surrounded by upholstered chairs. Two paraffin lamps with pink shades ornamented with fancy paper provided a pleasing light. Major made out five women, all of them whites, as Raymundo had said. Two were playing dominoes at the end of the table. Another was reading an illustrated magazine; another was working at crochet. The last one, who was doing nothing, no doubt kept the proprietress in conversation while awaiting the client. Major was not at his ease but the fat woman came to his help and invited him to be seated.

He took a seat and looked the women over. They all smiled at him; they did not say anything.

"Make your choice in your own time, my boy," said the fat woman.

"I've already made it," said Major, who was beginning to get excited.

And he indicated the woman who was crocheting.

"Good," said madame. "That will be a hundred milreis. And don't forget to give her a present." (She realized very well that he did not know the customs.)

The girl chosen pushed her crochet on the table and got up. She was clad only in a garment of transparent gauze. Major looked at her. All he had ever seen of white women were their faces. This one was tall and well-proportioned except for her breasts, which seemed to be rather too flat. Major had a feeling of dizziness and his heart was beating violently. He held out a hundred milreis note to madame and followed the girl to the staircase which led to the floor upstairs.

What happened then? How did it come that next morning just before daybreak, Major Sariema awoke on the pavement with a strange feeling of numbness?—so much so that he had the impression of having his bones broken. He has never known.

At first he wondered where he was: it was dark and there was no street lamp at that place. Then, as dawn came, he ascertained that he was in dockland. How had he arrived there? He did not succeed in remembering. He recalled only that he had taken his pleasure with the girl; and then there was a gap in his memory. Little by little he became conscious of things: he succeeded in standing up and then, rummaging mechanically in his pockets,

established the fact that his money had disappeared. A cold perspiration broke out on his forehead and he became overwhelmed
with terror. He had been cleaned out by that tart. In a flash he had
an inkling of all the consequences which that could bring in its
wake. He would not be able to go back again to Canudos: Pajehu
would come to kill him. Carried away by a mad rage which deprived him of all control, he rushed toward the brothel, determined
to recover his money at any cost. Daylight had not yet come and a
thick mist filled the streets. All of a sudden he found himself in
front of the door of the Aristides establishment. He was preparing
to go in when a colossal Negro rose up in front of him.

"Where are you going?" asked the Negro. "The house is closed."

It was as if Major had been poleaxed. He looked at the tall
stature of the African and his courage left him.

"All right," he said, "I'll have to come some other time."

And he went off. He was on his uppers. He began to wander
haphazardly in the fog like a waif. When the sun rose he found
himself in the upper town. After long reflection, he resolved to go
and tell Raymundo of his misadventure.

Raymundo listened to him compassionately and advised him to
apply to the police. Major asked him if he couldn't at all events
have a cup of coffee.

"You understand, my friend," Raymundo said to him, "if you can't
pay, I can't provide any more. I've got to pay for my goods. You're
not the only one those things happen to. If I were to come to the
assistance of everybody . . . You understand, don't you?"

Major Sariema left the café without a thank-you. He was in a
rage bordering on apoplexy. To calm himself, he went and lay on
the beach. His prowess of the night before had left a void in his
stomach but, stretched on the sand, he could bear that. He began
to consider a plan to recover his money. Like all his racial brethren,
he had an inexhaustible capacity for patience. He went over it in
his mind throughout the whole day, lying or sitting in the sun whose
dazzling light gave him comfort. By evening his plan was formed
and his decision taken. He was now calm.

Late at night he went back again toward the upper town and
began to walk along the street of São Bento, one of the wealthiest
arteries of Bahia: it was lit only at long intervals by poor lamps

giving a yellow light. The passers-by were becoming fewer and fewer.

Presently, Major ran across a well-dressed man wearing a straw hat and walking with a cane in the fashion of distinguished people of that time. He shadowed him but, as Major drew near to him, the gentleman took out a latchkey and went into a house. Major resumed his walk. It was very late when the opportunity came which could be his salvation. The gentleman appeared to be getting on in years, for his mustache was partly gray—from what Major had been able to make out by the light of a street lamp. He must be a man of the upper class, as he was wearing a Panama hat. No doubt he had remained late in some club, since a man of his rank rarely goes about on foot at night. Major did not hesitate. The street was deserted. He hastened his pace and, when he was abreast of the man, Sariema planted his knife in the back of his neck. Rapidly he emptied the man's pockets and fled without even looking at what he took with him.

He walked briskly down again toward the lower town and made for the docks. It was indeed there that one would be least troubled at night. He was still very unbalanced by what he had just done; his hands were trembling. He was afraid. Now everything was black but, tomorrow in the full light of day, people would perhaps read the crime in his face. And wasn't there some blood on his clothes? When he had recovered a little from his emotion, he got up and made for the beach. There he could inspect himself at his ease and recover his calm.

Only at dawn was he able to count the result of his robbery. What a miracle! He was in possession of more than *six* contos of reis! A feeling of pride flowed through his veins. Somebody had struck him a bad blow; he had given another one. He had been robbed of four contos: he had recouped six. Major Sariema was not to be squashed like a fly. Yet he wondered how he could have possessed that energy which so filled him with pride. He was astonished at himself. The feeling of vengeance achieved made him cool and collected and he began to examine his clothes very carefully. There was only a tiny splash of blood on his right sleeve. The sheath of his dagger was clean, for he had had the presence of mind to wipe his weapon on the victim's jacket.

He felt himself light and full of energy. Nevertheless, he told himself that it would be better to leave without delay for Canudos. He returned to Raymundo's just to show the Italian that a man of mixed breed, a *cafuz,* had no need of his charity.

"I've been to see my friends again," he said to the Italian. "They've advanced me a bit of money. Give us a bottle of Chianti, as I'm returning to the hinterland this evening."

There could be no more question of the mission with which he had been entrusted: and yet he could not go back to Canudos without bringing something in the way of information. He asked the cafékeeper whether he could obtain for him the last fortnight's newspapers. Raymundo, who was quick to act when there was money in it, sent one of his Negro waiters to make a round of the newspaper offices. They were situated in that part of the city, so that, half an hour later, Sariema had what he needed. He settled his account and said that he would call and take the newspapers in the afternoon.

For he still had to make the purchases. He bought an alarm clock for João, a watch for himself. Pajehu had ordered a pistol: he bought two of them. The Syrian in whose shop he bought five frocks asked him whether he had a harem. He also obtained for himself a new straw "boater" and a pair of black-and-white check trousers. After having done this, he still had plenty of money but did not know what to do with it. He looked in vain at the shop-windows, not seeing anything which could be of some use to the jagunços. Had he known of another resort with white girls, he would have gone there to pass the afternoon: he thought of asking Raymundo for another address. Nevertheless, all things considered, he abandoned the idea; he did not wish to be skinned again.

He was satisfied with returning again to Raymundo's to collect the newspapers and drink a few glasses of rum.

At six o'clock in the evening he took his ticket at the Northern Station.

He slept for a long time in the train. The nervous release had made him drowsy. As he had not spoken to anybody about Canudos, he would have liked at the very least to read the newspapers to see if he could find some article relating to the holy city: but, as the carriages were not lighted, there could be no question of reading.

After a few hours he awoke, and, with his forehead against the windowpane, he looked out into the night. There was nothing he could make out except a blackness with a starry sky overhead and, in the background, the golden crescent of the moon. He began to turn things over. He experienced a lively satisfaction to think that in Bahia the police were now in quest of the author of the crime in the street of São Bento. The Bahians had cleaned him out, but *he* had played *them* a damnable trick! In short, a murder's a simple enough thing. A man's easily killed. All that's needed is to have no hesitation. He was proud to have made that decision, to have struck with such precision. Right in the nape of the neck: it was well calculated. At Canudos, Major Sariema had always been impressed by that fellow Zé Venancio who had downed fourteen men. Now he found nothing so extraordinary about that. It was very much easier than he had ever believed.

He regretted not having made more purchases. But damn it! Really, he hadn't seen anything that could be useful. What was to be done with all that money?

On getting out at Queimadas, at eight o'clock next morning, he immediately caught sight of Chico Ema who was sitting at the foot of a wall opposite the railway station with half-a-dozen other idlers in rags and tatters. Chico thought that he had returned very quickly: he was not expecting him for three or four days. But he preferred it so. He was becoming bored at Queimadas.

They mounted their horses and plunged into the hinterland toward Canudos. The sun was scorching hot.

13. The Ambush

MAJOR SARIEMA's arrival could not fail to impart a comic note to the monotonous existence at Canudos, as happened every time he mounted a horse. Chico Ema, who rode ahead of him, spurred his horse on coming to the square, and made it gallop so that he could draw up brusquely in front of the Chief of the People's house—as every good horseman ought to. But, without being asked, Major's horse inspired by the example in turn began to gallop. Not expecting this, Sariema fell back on the crupper, and his straw boater— the new one, that is—began to describe circles on the square. Vigorously pressing the horse with his little legs, the half-breed succeeded in righting himself, and he arrived at João Abbade's house clinging to the animal's mane.

João helped him to put his feet on the ground and to carry the parcels hanging on the saddle.

"Has everything gone well?" João asked him, for he was impatient to know what was being said about Canudos in the state capital.

"Very well. The city hasn't changed."

"That's not what I'm asking. What are they saying about us?"

"Nothing much. You'll see it in the newspapers. I'll explain to you. Just now I'm very tired: I'm going to rest for an hour." If there's anything in the newspapers, he thought, they'll speak to me about it and, if there's nothing, I can tell them any old story.

João let him go, and fell on the packet of newspapers. He had already scanned a dozen without having found a single allusion to Canudos when, in an issue of *O Imparcial* he read a flamboyant heading spread over four columns: "When will the government decide to put an end to the Canudos scandal?" Before reading the text of this article, which must nevertheless have been thrilling, he opened the other papers. *A Liberdade* (a sheet for intellectuals) came out with a long study under the title: "A singular phenomenon of collective hallucination: the case of Antonio Conseilheiro." Finally, on a more vulgar level, *O Globo* wrote: "Loony defies the Bahia government: an intolerable situation."

João sent Chico Ema to Pajehu's house.

"Tell him to come here immediately."

The half-breed did not delay. João showed him the press. Pajehu skimmed it with scorn in his face. These articles were made up out of nothing: they represented Canudos as simply a den of brigands. Only *A Liberdade* seemed to understand that it was a question of a mystical movement. All the newspapers were, moreover, in agreement about demanding a police operation to destroy this "nest of bandits."

"It's just as I thought," said Abbade. "They're going to get busy about us."

"And what then?" retorted Pajehu in a crushing manner. "We'll get busy with them. They're a gang of cowards. They haven't even the courage to say what happened to their Capuchin monk. Have you read this? 'The delegate of Monsignor the Bishop has been ignominiously outraged.' What outrages? Eh? They daren't write it?"

"You're right about that, but you can be certain that they're going to send their police after us."

Abbade was haunted by this fear of the police. He was afraid of being arrested and thrown into jail. As for Pajehu, *he* wasn't a man to allow himself to be intimidated.

"We'll give them a good welcome," he said sarcastically. "I still have a barrel of rum. And where's that mutt Sariema?"

"He's gone to have a rest: he was worn out."

"Lazy devil! Chico!" he shouted at Chico Ema who was sitting on the doorstep. "Go and find Sariema. Tell him that Pajehu wants to see him."

The cafuz did not need to be told twice. He was no longer frightened by it, he had his plan: he could reply to all their questions. There was no need to. The minds of Abbade and Pajehu were made up from their reading of the newspapers. But there was something else besides the news.

"My pistol?" Pajehu asked.

"Everything's in that parcel, in the corner over there."

They opened the package.

"Aha!" said Pajehu, taking up the pistols. "You were intelligent enough, all the same to buy two of them."

They were pistols of Spanish-Basque manufacture, the butts covered with arabesques. Pajehu held one out to Abbade.

"Take that one." Then, addressing the half-breed: "You've been careful not to buy one for youself. . . . The day you're to be seen in a fight hasn't yet come."

Sariema was on the point of relating his affair in the street of São Bento to show that he, too, knew how to kill a man, but then he would have had to tell that he had been to the brothel and that he had been cleaned out. No, better not say a word.

The conversation was already bearing on another subject. Pajehu was talking about the measures he was going to take to avoid any sort of surprise. After that they decided to go and communicate the news to the Conseilheiro.

When he had perused the newspapers, Antonio went into one of those rages which came to him whenever a blow was struck at his prestige.

"The rabble! Let them come! I'll show them how the Conseilheiro receives the republicans. They want to make me out as a bandit, a half-dafty. I'll teach them to respect the interests of Truth. What do they take me for?"

He seized one of the newspapers, crumpled it in his hands and then began tearing it into little pieces.

"That's what we'll do with them if they dare come and face us. But they won't come: they're too cowardly."

He thought himself so strong and so high in the world that he could not imagine anybody might come to defy him. He considered himself as untouchable.

He was making a mistake. A fortnight later Bahia police appeared at the sentry post installed at the Cambaio gap. There were seven men of the mounted police: a lieutenant, a sergeant, a corporal, and four men.

The sentry post was commanded by Quimquim de Coïqui. He was precisely the man needed in such circumstances. Quimquim knew how to keep cool and collected; he was prompt to act, but he could keep his impulsiveness under control.

"Get down!" he calmly ordered the policemen.

"Where are we?" asked the officer. "Are we at Canudos?"

"*Dismount!*" Quimquim repeated coolly.

He was standing upright, legs apart, his hands resting on the barrel of his gun. Behind him were his men, each with his weapon under his arm, holding themselves ready to intervene.

On an order from the lieutenant the policemen got off and tied their horses to the stunted shrubs growing on the embankment.

"Your weapons," said Quimquim.

"See here," said the lieutenant, "we belong to the police: we

don't have to give up our arms to you. That means you're in rebellion against the state."

"That's nothing to do with me. *Your weapons.*"

On a sign from the lieutenant the police took off their carbines—
they carried them slung across their backs—and handed them to
the jagunços.

"Now the knives and pistols," continued Quimquim.

"I'm the only one who has a pistol," said the lieutenant. "But officers, even when they're prisoners, always have the right to keep
their arms."

"Not here," Quimquim spoke decisively.

The lieutenant did as he was bidden. However he did it, he must
fulfill his mission and see the Conseilheiro. Quimquim turned to
his men and said:

"Take them to Abbade's house."

The jagunços took their places on each side of the policemen
and they went down toward Canudos.

As the sentry post of Quimquim de Coïqui was set on the slope of
the sierra, the police had not yet caught sight of the town. After
they had crossed the saddle of the hill at Cambaio, it loomed up in
front of their eyes. When they saw all those houses scattered over
the plain, that sea of red roofs overlooked by the spires of the
church, the lieutenant said to himself that they had entrusted him
with a peculiar mission. After the description which had been given
to him, he had imagined that Canudos was a little village. Yet, at
all events by its appearance, it had the importance of a large town.
If it was wholly populated by jagunços, it wasn't easy to see how
seven police officers could impose order. The instructions they had
been given him—to arrest the Conseilheiro—were ridiculous. Now,
to get out of this pitfall, he would need to use much diplomacy.
These plainsmen did not seem to be accommodating.

The officer was still turning over in his mind how he was going
to get himself out of this trap when the little party stopped in
front of the Chief of the People's house.

João immediately appeared on the threshold, followed by Pajehu
and Sariema. They had already been warned. For a moment they
looked the envoys from Bahia up and down and then João Abbade
asked:

"Who are you?"

"Lieutenant Loureiro, of the Bahia police."

"What do you want?"

"I should like to speak to Antonio Conseilheiro," replied the officer diplomatically, "in order to regularize the situation of your locality with him."

"You have to be seven men to do that?" remarked Pajehu.

"You know quite well that a man does not travel alone in the hinterland, especially when he doesn't know it."

Loureiro was thinking about Pajehu's uniform and wondered whether it was stolen or whether the wearer was really a soldier.

"I don't see why there should have to be seven of you," Pajehu insisted in the deliberate manner of somebody who is looking for a quarrel.

"We obey orders," retorted Loureiro.

"Fortunately," said Pajehu enigmatically.

While this was happening, João Abbade sent a Negro to the Conseilheiro's. The prophet came to them clad in his long smock, with his long hair flowing over his ears and shoulders.

"I am Antonio Conseilheiro," he said arrogantly. "What do you want with me?"

The officer looked at the hinterland agitator with stupefaction.

"The government of Bahia has charged me to inquire of you how you reckoned to organize your locality from the administrative point of view. Canudos has now become a city. You must appoint a political chief and nominate a municipal council."

The Conseilheiro turned his eyes heavenward as if he were asking the divinity for inspiration, and then said:

"Canudos is a holy city, above all other cities. It is not in any way concerned with the Bahia government. It depends only on Jerusalem. Tell your government that Canudos has been founded by Saint Sebastian and that the only orders it takes are those from Saint Sebastian."

The lieutenant did not understand much of this rigmarole except that it was the utterance of a crack-brained person. He would have liked to speak about Pajehu's pillagings and the matter of the bell, but it was enough for him to look at the types of faces among the jagunços who were all around him to realize that it was wise to say nothing.

"Good," he said, "I shall inform the government accordingly."

It was a matter of getting out of that hornet's nest as quickly as possible. The officer felt that he was surrounded by a fierce hostility which might break loose any moment. The interview seemed to be ended. It only remained for the envoys from Bahia to get to the Monte Santo road, when Pajehu intervened:

"Not so quickly."

And looking intensely into the officer's eyes, he said slowly:

"I want to know why there are seven of you."

"An officer is always accompanied by a troop. That's the regulation."

"That's all I wanted to know," said Pajehu. And he went off.

When the Conselheiro had returned to his house, João Abbade, fearing complications, said to Lieutenant Loureiro almost cordially:

"Tell the government not to concern itself with Canudos for the time being. It will create a vast agitation in the hinterland."

"Thank you," said Loureiro.

He would have liked to continue the conversation with João Abbade, who seemed to him to be the only reasonable man in the place, but one of the jagunços shouted:

"Get a move on!" and they had to set out on their way.

They climbed the slopes of the Favella. When they drew near to the Cambaio gap, the jagunços pushed Loureiro and his men ahead, and, at the moment when they were struggling through the gap, a volley from a dozen guns laid them out on the ground. Quimquim then appeared, to make sure that they were all dead. Four were still alive: he finished them off with a bullet in the head. Pajehu then appeared.

"Have all those uniforms stripped off and brought to my house with all their weapons," he ordered.

At last they were going to have some good weapons, Mauser carbines, as well as some uniforms in which to dress those who would be appointed to some position of command. Pajehu had his plan. It was clear that they had not finished with the police and that there was need to prepare to receive further visits; and no

doubt more important ones. He was certain that they would not
settle this by negotiations and words. They would have to fight.

The naked bodies of the Bahian officers lay in the dust of the
road: there were two white men and five Negroes or mulattoes.

"You'll have them taken a bit further off, on the Monte Santo
road," said Pajehu to Quimquim. "The black vultures will soon get
rid of them for us. They don't often have the chance of such a
repast in this part."

While Quimquim de Coïqui was busy clearing away the corpses,
Pajehu went down toward Canudos. The sun was shining in a
spotless sky the color of washing blue. The air was light and
warm. Pajehu had a feeling of exaltation rising within him; he
experienced a sense of power, of strength. It seemed to him that he
would be able to checkmate anybody who should wish to challenge
Canudos.

14. The Black Battalion

BAHIA HEARD of the assassination of the police delegation a month
later. They were surprised in the city not to see it return by the end
of a fortnight. The governor had telephoned Colonel Azevedo, com-
mandant of the garrison, to report his uneasiness. The colonel had
reassured him, telling him that, in the sertão region, things were
never hurried; that the stages of the journey were hard going; and
that it was a matter of being patient. But, after twenty days, the
governor considered that it was absolutely essential to make an
inquiry and find out what had been the fate of the delegation. He
sent instructions to this effect to the chiefs of police in Queimadas
and Joazeiro. It was a muleteer from Joazeiro who, having gone to
Canudos on the pretext of selling four sacks of beans (for which
João Abbade had furthermore paid him with the money brought
back by Sariema), returned with the news of the massacre. Some
Negroes had spoken to him about it: "The police," they said, "had
wanted to meddle in the Conseilheiro's affairs, and their account

had been settled. Canudos could not be touched. Whoever rose against the Conseilheiro would receive his punishment immediately." On returning by the Monte Santo road, the muleteer was able to see the skeletons of the police officers scattered in the brambles.

The governor would have liked the whole thing to be kept dark from the public, but the muleteer had talked about it in the botequims in Joazeiro and, a few days later, *O Imparcial* published a special edition announcing the sensational news. Public reaction was immediate and violent for, at that time, the repression of banditry was the major question in the order of the day. No government could hold power which did not inscribe in its program the campaign against cutthroat banditry known as the *cangaço*. The state could make no progress if order was not maintained in the interior. People considered that the first duty of the government was to assure the safety of the population.

Hence, at about five o'clock in the evening a considerable crowd had massed in front of the palace. The governor, having spent the afternoon in his villa at Cachoeira, had just returned. He had drunk his glass of bicarbonate and was walking to and fro in his office. He was agitated: he had a horror of those upsets. If those fiends of journalists had not published the story, everything would have passed off quietly. For a moment he hoped to be able to calm the crowd by having it announced that severe measures were being taken against the hinterlanders but, in the oppressive heat of the evening, this crowd was getting excited and beginning to bawl: "Death to the Conseilheiro!" "Down with Canudos!" "Long live the Republic!" He must resign himself to intervention by the military.

The governor sat down at his desk and telephoned to Colonel Azevedo.

"I'm taking the necessary steps," replied the latter. "In half an hour the square will be swept clean."

"Not so quickly," said the governor. "Just place a curtain of troops in front of the palace and wait. I don't want any trouble."

The colonel only partly respected these instructions. Arriving at a gallop by the Avenida da Liberdade, his mounted troops swooped into the square. The crowd divided to make way for them. There was a terrible scuffle: the piercing cries of the women mingled with the furious oaths of the men. Fortunately there was no mishap and the horsemen drew up in line with sabers drawn in front of the palace. The crowd again began to roar with renewed energy as the colonel made his way into the governor's office.

"It's done," he said, "when you want me to disperse them . . ."

"Let us keep calm," said the stout functionary. "We don't want this to have repercussions reaching as far as Rio."

He was in fear for his post. The new president of the republic, Prudente de Moraes, was a levelheaded man, an opponent of violent methods, whose program was to restore peace and tranquillity throughout the country, which had been violently shaken by the revolt in Rio Grande.

"I agree: it's necessary to act prudently," said Azevedo. "But don't forget that crowds are impulsive and that they must be controlled in time."

The governor who held to his idea said, "I should like you to announce that a military expedition against Canudos is organized. I think that would have the desired effect."

"Perhaps so. We'll have it settled at once. If that doesn't work, would you like me to clear away the crowd?"

"No. Come and see me. We'll see about that."

The colonel went downstairs. He thought at first of speaking from the top of the entrance stairway, but he was too far away there; his voice would not carry. He sprang on his horse and advanced toward the demonstrators, raising his arm to impose silence. He was not under any illusion regarding the efficacy of his gesture, but it was enough for him to obtain comparative silence on the part of those who were near him. He announced in a strong voice that Canudos was going to be destroyed, that a military expedition was going to sack that nest of bandits. Contrary to what he had expected, the effect was immediate. The news spread like a prairie fire and soon shouts of "Long live the governor!" mingled with those of "Down with Canudos!" and "Death to the Conseilheiro!"

Azevedo went to see the governor again in his study. From the window they could see the demonstrators who were beginning to disperse.

"You were right," said the colonel. "They've understood. I'm astonished that it is so: it doesn't happen once in a hundred times."

"Had you asked them for moderation, you'd have failed. But you promised them vengeance. So you ought to have succeeded."

The colonel had always had much respect for the governor whose philosophical theories greatly appealed to him, since he was himself an adept of Comte, but he found that the governor had gone far more deeply than himself into the ideas of the French sociologist.

"Now," said the governor, resuming his place at his desk and inviting the colonel to be seated, "we have made a promise: it must be kept. Unfortunately I'm lacking in precise data on Canudos. If Loureiro had returned, he could have provided us with a report. How many men do you think we'll need to clean up this lair?"

"According to the information published in the newspapers when that affair of the Capuchin happened, it seems that Canudos is a fairly important locality, but it's clear that those people aren't armed, that is to say, they haven't any modern weapons of war. Their guns are old blunderbusses and stone weapons made as best they can by blacksmiths lacking tools and having a crude way of working. In these conditions, they're hardly in a position to offer much resistance. I think that with a company of 250 men we'll settle the whole business."

"That seems reasonable to me. . . . Would you like a cigar? . . . Help yourself. Two hundred and fifty well-armed men should be able to disperse that band of jagunços. When it comes to it, they're not redoubtable except when they act by surprise. If the villagers were well armed, there wouldn't be all those pillagings. So, 250 men. But you'll need a mule train for supply. It seems that the country up there is absolutely like a desert."

"Put your mind at ease. We'll take every precaution."

They lit their cigars.

"And who are you thinking of putting at the head of this expedition?"

"Captain Braz Barroso. He's the best man. He knows that hinterland."

"Is he a white man?"

"His father is Brazilian but his mother is Austrian."

"Does he know his business, and is he energetic?"

"I tell you he's the best man."

"All right. Organize this expedition as soon as possible. I want to finish with this Canudos matter. Those jagunços are a permanent nuisance."

"We'll liquidate the whole lot, sir."

While this conversation was going on between the two principal authorities of Bahia, a council was being held at Canudos in the Conselheiro's house. As the moon was directly opposite the window, lighting up the whole room, the candle had not been lit. Apart from the Conselheiro there were: João Abbade, Pajehu, Sariema, and, in a corner, Antonio Beatinho.

Abbade had begun by taking Pajehu to task in a lively manner for having had the police officers killed.

"It served no purpose," he said. "Now they'll send the military to massacre us. They're stronger than we are."

"We'll see about that," said Pajehu. "We couldn't let those police-men get away: they'd have made a report"—he was right, as we have seen—"and they would have throttled us without difficulty. In any case, they'd have sent strong bodies of police. In these circumstances it was better not to provide them with intelligence about ourselves."

"Let them leave us in peace," interrupted the Conselheiro. "What are they coming to Canudos to do? What goes on here is no con-cern of theirs."

"*They* don't think so," remarked Sariema.

"I don't care what they think," said the prophet. "Who is there who has been able to do what I've done in this hinterland? We have been capable of setting up this holy city. We shall be capable of defending it. You surely don't believe that we could build a city like this without the help of God?"

"In any case, if we're attacked," said Pajehu, who believed more in Mauser carbines than in God, "we'll be ready. I'm going to organize a battalion like they have in the Army, with none but toughs."

"You're right, Pajehu," said the Conselheiro sententiously. "Get your men together as quickly as possible: I shall bless them. That will be the holy battalion. It will be placed under the protection of Saint Sebastian and, you can believe me, nobody has ever been able to strike the sword from Saint Sebastian's hands."

Pajehu immediately set about constituting his little army. He

recruited it with scrupulous care. The news having got around that
he was forming a battalion for the defense of the town, many came
forward asking to be enlisted in it, but Pajehu took only men of
strapping build. All those who were chosen boasted of it to their
neighbors. Before being formed, the battalion already seemed a formidable body of men. It consisted of a majority of colored men. In
spite of the contempt which he secretly professed for Negroes, he
was compelled to acknowledge that they were fine stout fellows.
Some puny half-breed Indians who had been rejected went about
everywhere telling that this Pajehu gang was a battalion of Negroes
—"*um batalhão de negroes.*" When he heard of this malevolent
gossip, Pajehu shrugged his shoulders and said:

"Damn it! Yes, it is a black battalion and it will be talked about."

The name remained. It was all the more justified in that Pajehu
had chosen a pure Negro to be its lieutenant: Pedrão—a giant who
could overturn the ox wagon with a heave of his shoulders. Pedrão
was certainly the strongest man in Canudos. With his chest muscles
standing out, his sinewy arms, his powerful shoulders, his broad
back, and neck like a bull's, he was the incarnation of physical
strength. Nor did he lack tact or cunning: although he might seem
dull, he had a mind which, if not shrewd, was quick on the uptake.
Pajehu had been able to witness for himself in the course of various
pillaging expeditions that he was a man whose brutality was of
sterling quality. He much preferred him to Zé Venancio, who was
too egotistic. Pajehu needed a man who would execute his orders
without arguing.

A few days later the black battalion was blessed in the church
during a short ceremony. In a brief but flaming harangue the
Conseilheiro declared that it would put a check on the republic and
be the glory of the hinterland. This prophecy was soon to be fulfilled.

Pajehu was only a noncommissioned officer in the Brazilian Army
but he had a profound sense of military matters. He knew straightway the prestige of uniform. Hence, he made Pedrão put on that
of Lieutenant Loureiro. The trousers were too short and Pedrão
could not button the tunic across that wrestler's chest of his. What
did it matter? Canudos was not a stylish city and its army was not
one for show purposes. The main thing was to display an officer's

uniform. The uniforms of the sergeant, corporal, and soldiers murdered by Quimquim de Coïqui were distributed among the six best marksmen who were also given the Mauser carbines.

Once these steps were taken, Pajehu gave orders to begin making gunpowder. All the jagunços knew how to make powder. Some were sent into the Cannabrava forest to make charcoal. Others went out to obtain saltpeter from the mineral veins to be found in the direction of Geremoabo. In this way they would not run short of ammunition.

By the end of a few days, all was ready for a worthy reception to be accorded to the republic's representatives of order. There was nothing more to do but wait.

The population was a little nervous. People were wondering what was going to happen, and a vague threat could be felt hanging over the town: but they had confidence in the Conseilheiro who every day informed them that very soon the hour of triumph would ring out for the hinterland.

Nevertheless João Abbade was anxious. From the time that Anita had wished to commit suicide, he had fallen completely under her sway. She had bewitched him and put him under her spell. Pajehu had endeavored to shake him out of this state, telling him that the Chief of the People in Canudos ought not to allow himself to be led by a woman. João bridled: he asserted that he did not allow himself to be influenced, that, furthermore, he didn't have to take orders from anybody and that it was his own business if he thought highly of Anita.

In reality he nearly always yielded to the half-caste girl's reasoning.

"Pajehu will lead us to disaster," she said. "With all his bravado, he'll end by attracting so many police here that we'll all be killed."

"Don't you believe that," replied João to reassure her. "That black battalion will never be any use for anything. Maybe the police will come in force, but they will only ask us to set up an administration. That's all the government wants of us."

"You're wrong: you'll see that Pajehu will instigate a fight. He thinks of nothing but battles. He's an army man. If I were you I'd picket a couple of horses ready saddled at the entrance to the

Cannabrava forest so as to be able to clear off if the police should come into Canudos again."

João was sitting on the edge of the bed beside her. He heaved a sigh and then said:

"If they heard about it," he said, "they'd take me for a coward."

"I'll get the horses placed by my father," she said. "Nobody will know they're for us."

João did not reply. He was the victim of conflicting feelings. He felt himself a coward, but he did not wish it to show.

"No," he said. "I don't want to do that. I'm the Chief of the People. They'd say I was a traitor and they'd kill me."

Anita put her arm around his neck.

"João, listen to me. They won't know that those horses are for us. I'll arrange things with my father. You can be sure that the police will come, and you'll be the first to be arrested. They'll take you off to jail."

Unsettled in mind, João said nothing. Then Anita kissed him on the lips and said:

"Tomorrow I'll go to my father's place."

"All right," he said in a hollow voice.

He was humiliated and felt a mental discomfort which would not allow him to remain still in one place, and he said that he was going out to have a breath of air.

"Don't stay too long," said Anita. "I'm going to bed."

The night was cool, the moon was high in the starry sky. João walked around haphazardly among the houses and across the lanes, some of which were dark and some bathed in the clear moonlight. He chatted for a moment with a jagunço sitting on his doorstep who asked him whether he thought there'd be a battle with the police. When he reached the square in front of the church, which now seemed very much bigger in the pale light of the moon, he caught sight of Pajehu's silhouette. He saw the half-breed contemplating, one after another, the sierra de Cannabrava, the peak of Cambaio, the Red Hills: no doubt he was saturating his mind with the contour of the mountains in case of battle. . . .

João felt that he ought to have spoken to him in order to regain his self-assurance, but he turned aside and went into a dark lane.

15. The Massacre

Braz Barroso's company detrained at Queimadas on a Saturday morning. For that place a considerable crowd of men and women had come to welcome them at the railway station, as the newspaper which arrived from Bahia the day before said that the operation directed against Canudos was of capital importance for the future of the state. The inhabitants of Queimadas had no need of this piece of information. They knew that the raids by the bands of pillagers from Canudos were spreading more and more and that they themselves risked being the victims in the near future. The arrival of the troops brought them comfort.

The municipal authorities (the political chief and four counselers), the town's two lawyers, the magistrates, the three doctors, and the two collectors of taxes were on the platform when the train arrived. Captain Braz Barroso was received by the political chief who gave him the *abraço*—an embrace in which they slap each other's back—and forthwith invited him to have a cup of coffee.

The mayor lived in the only two-story house in the town. The ground floor was taken up by his shops—fabrics and groceries. The reception room was on the first floor, a spacious but simple sala with whitewashed walls and furnished with a little round wooden table and wicker armchairs.

The town's personalities took their stand around Braz Barroso, on whom was lavished all their attention and looks. He was a fine looking young fellow of twenty-seven with a swinging stride. His very slightly bronzed face indicated a dominance of purely white blood. His features were very regular, his nose sharp, he had a fine head of black hair and his eyes were equally black, shining and lively. Of slightly above medium height, he was somewhat thin. By his quick gestures and rapid manner of speech, one realized that here was a man who did not have much time for the softness and usual nonchalance of those who live in the tropics. He presented a striking contrast to the political chief, fleshy Flores da Silva, a paunchy short-legged man with a full face and heavy chaps, a fat shiny nose, altogether a man whose slow-measured and almost precious gestures, as well as a singsong lackadaisical way of speaking, exuded lassitude and despondency.

As there were not enough chairs, a negress brought some stools and then served coffee in little cups, a glass of water with each. Livers are sluggish in the tropics, and it is advisable to neutralize the action of coffee.

"Excuse me," said Flores addressing the captain, "this coffee is sweetened with *rapadoura,* unrefined brown sugar. We haven't any nice white sugar here."

"Excellent," said Barroso, "the crude sugar has more flavor."

One of the magistrates, a man of about thirty, with an insipid inexpressive unnaturally white face, said:

"Well, captain, and so you're going to rid us of this Canudos rabble?"

"I don't think it'll take long," replied the captain, lighting a cigar which a doctor had just offered him. "The greatest difficulty is to get to Canudos. We haven't a map: we must rely on a guide. Have you one here who knows the region well?"

"Our muleteers know the road. There's no difficulty in that," said one of the doctors. "But do you think you'll come out of it successfully with one company?"

"I think so."

They all raised their eyebrows expressing doubt.

"They'll put up resistance," said one of the tax collectors. "Those men are jagunços—tough hinterlanders—and there's a good number of them."

"What's the population of Canudos?" asked Barroso. "I haven't been able to obtain any precise details on that point."

"According to the accounts we have received from some muleteers who have passed through there, it must now amount to nine or ten thousand inhabitants."

Barroso seemed surprised.

"You're certain of what you say?"

"Certain, no. It's merely an estimate, but we have good reason to believe that it's accurate, for several muleteers have given us more or less the same figure."

"Ten thousand," said Barroso stroking his chin, "but there are
the women: that makes from four to five thousand men armed with
old-fashioned firearms. Supposing they should wish to put up opposition to our mission, it would cost them dearly and they'd risk
disaster."

"All the same," one of the judges said, "if they attack you in mass,
you'd have your work cut out: you might perhaps be outflanked."

"No. You seem to me to overlook the power of repeating rifles.
The more assailants there are, the greater the havoc caused by
the Mausers. This is not my first experience: I took part in the
repression of the revolt of the Gauchos in Rio Grande. With a
single company we broke up and then annihilated a force of three
thousand men. I don't think that the jagunços are more formidable
than the Gauchos."

Some of those present raised their hands in a gesture of doubt.
Barroso continued:

"Moreover, we must be quite clear about the object of our mission. We are not going there to put down a rebellion. So far there's
no rebellion. I'm charged by the government simply to request the
people of Canudos to regularize their position with the administration. I'll have that communicated to them when I arrive in front of
the town."

"I doubt whether they'll accept," commented a doctor, blowing a great puff of smoke toward the ceiling.

"In that case we'll fight it out. If they seem to me too many, I'll
withdraw to await reinforcements but, before that, I'll inflict a
hard lesson on them."

"I hope you do," sighed Flores. "We've had enough of these forays
and incursions. For months now we've been living under the threat
of being plundered. If the jagunços were to attack Queimadas, I'd
be obliged to let them go ahead: I haven't an armed force big
enough to hold them off. This is no longer a life for anybody."

"It's going to end. The government is firmly decided to extirpate
this canker; and that's why I'm here."

They returned to the station square where the troops had piled
arms. Men were sitting about in groups of four or five playing
cards. Others were chatting with the civilians.

"I say, chief," said Barroso to Flores, "you'll have to give us a

dozen mules to transport the men's equipment and the ammunition. I don't want to arrive in front of the objective with exhausted
units."

"When are you setting out?"

"This evening. You don't really think I'm going to kill my company
with marches in the sun."

"Look out for ambushes."

"They're no danger. I know this kind of hill warfare."

The company set out on the march at five o'clock in the evening
followed by the train of mules on which the men's equipment,
medical supplies, and victuals had been loaded. The soldiers carried
only their rifles and a few rounds of ammunition. Flores had provided the guide: he was one of the muleteers who one day had
wished to sell rum in Canudos. The moon, he said, wouldn't rise
until about nine o'clock, but as long as they hadn't got beyond
Monte Santo there was no danger.

The town notables warmly shook hands with Captain Barroso
and wished him good luck.

"See you soon," he called out cheerfully to them.

On the fourth day the company arrived at Uauá, a little hamlet
less than two miles from Canudos.

"The town's over there," the guide told the captain, "on the other
side of this mountain, in the valley of the Vasa Barris River."

Uauá had only about ten dwellings. The company did not find a
single inhabitant there. The houses must have been abandoned a
very short time ago, for in many of the kitchen stoves they found
cinders still hot.

"A bad sign," thought Barroso, "they have wind of our arrival
and they're getting ready to fight."

He must act quickly. He immediately ordered one of his noncommissioned officers to go and propose a parley. While the men
were engaged in unloading the mules, and settling themselves in
the houses, he watched his delegate make his way toward Canudos
until he had disappeared behind the sierra. What would be the
response of the jagunços? The fact that Uauá had been evacuated
had strongly shaken his confidence in a peaceful settlement. It was
advisable to study the lay of the land in expectation of attack. The
place was not a favorable one. Uauá was situated in a narrow

valley surrounded on all sides by hills: it communicated with
Canudos only through that mountain pass which was just wide
enough to allow a horse to pass through. Should the jagunços' reply
be negative, it would be necessary to approach the town from another
side. This would not be easy; Captain Barroso knew nothing about
the relative position of these places. He must grope his way. It was
dangerous: they could fall into some trap. But the fact could not
make him withdraw; he had known similar difficulties before now.
In the Rio Grande, he had skirted towns and villages to strike a
good place. They could certainly have access to Canudos by routes
easier and more strategically favorable than that of Uauá. The guide
had no doubt taken the only route he knew, but from the military
point of view it was bad. Hence, Captain Barroso immediately
made up his mind to seek another, whatever the difficulties of the
operation might be, for he intended to fulfill his mission.

He took his position in the shade of a house in which the principal
living room had been reserved for him. He asked a noncommissioned officer to bring him a cup of cold water, but the sergeant
replied that they had searched in vain and it had not been possible
to find any water.

"It's just as I thought," said the captain. "We can't stay here: the
place is badly chosen. We must approach Canudos by another
side."

The men slept in all the houses, for, although they had been
relieved of their equipment, the four night marches on this stony
uneven ground had exhausted them.

The sun was already high in the pitilessly blue sky of the sertão,
and the truce bearer had not yet returned. Nevertheless, there wasn't
much in what he had to communicate: perhaps the jagunços were
forming a delegation?

The sierras were wrapped in a menacing silence. The wait became prolonged: it was almost noon. The captain became nervous:
he went out into the street and shaded his eyes with his hand to
look toward Canudos.

It was just at that moment that the first shot rang out. The captain heard the bullet whistle past. He bounded toward the sala in
which the noncommissioned officers had gathered.

"To arms!" he said to them. "Distribute ammunition to the men

and deploy them in skirmishing order here and there in the village.
Quick!"

The three sergeants rushed into the street to alert the men. They
were hardly outside when there was a burst of fire. One of them
collapsed in the dust with a stifled cry. His companions dashed toward him to take him away, but a second burst of gunfire swept
the street. The second noncommissioned officer rolled on the
ground.

"Pedro! Get back in here," shouted the captain to the third.

For he realized that, suddenly, the situation was beginning to
take a bad turn. Three of his noncoms lost in the twinkling of an
eye: the one who had been held at Canudos and two others either
killed or wounded.

One of the wounded men writhing in the dust was moaning with
a rattle in his throat: "Oh, mother dear . . ."

"All the same, we must get them away," the captain thought.

But the jagunços kept the street under fire: they were sheltered
behind a bulge of terrain on the way into the village. First, they
must be dislodged from that place, Braz Barroso decided. From the
doorstep he shouted:

"Get out of the houses, deploy in skirmishing order here and
there in the village."

Some soldiers went out into the street. The jagunços' fusillade
started again, well-sustained and accurate. Some men fell.

"Not in the open street, good Lord!" roared the captain. "On the
other side of the houses and advance in the direction of the hill
where the shots come from."

What a misfortune to have lost those noncommissioned officers:
now he had to do everything himself. He felt himself involved in a
very strange adventure. He could not deny that he was the victim
of a surprise attack: only a daring maneuver would get him out of
it.

"Pedro," he ordered the only noncommissioned officer who was left,
"try to get to the first house over yonder. There must be twenty or
twenty-five men in it. Get up in one of the beams, take away some
tiles from the roof and no doubt you'll have these devils of jagunços under your fire. Riddle them with bullets."

At the moment when the noncommissioned officer was going out by the kitchen door, a burst of fire spent itself against the wall. He was not hit, but it was becoming clear that the village was surrounded.

"Oh! Oh!" said Barroso. "That changes the situation. Pedro, go as far as the first house and give the order to beat a retreat. In order. One man at a time. We must withdraw to that gorge where the road forks toward Rosario. It's not an easy operation. There's well over a mile of open ground, but I'll cover the retreat while extricating the troops from this side."

While Pedro was crawling forward, Barroso got out the fifteen men in his house and deployed them. The coppice from which the last volley had come was just over five hundred yards away. "The jagunços have picked a bad position," he thought. "The coppice doesn't allow any mobility. We're going to be able to wedge them in."

"Open fire," he commanded.

The fusillade crackled. There was no reply: the coppice was abandoned.

"Advance," commanded Barroso. "Not too far. Enough to establish a passage wide enough to permit the others to beat a retreat."

The men advanced. The coppice remained silent.

Pedro had reached the last house and, on his instructions, the soldiers began to fall back, slinking along by the houses in Indian file. Barroso ordered them to regroup at the way out from the village.

The operations were going on for a quarter of an hour and Braz Barroso had hardly got his troops in hand when a band of jagunços on horseback loomed up from the gorge toward which the captain thought to withdraw. Barroso tried to form his company in line to receive the charge. If those jagunços should succeed in disuniting his troops, he was lost. A first burst of musketry made some of the jagunços bite the dust: it did not break their impetus and they reached the approaches of the village. A savage combat took place. The riders were all armed with long knives with a broad blade such as is used by most of the *cangaceiros*, the hinterland cutthroats: they wielded them with the strength of demons. The soldiers had fixed bayonets and were driving them into the horses' bodies. The affray became an imbroglio. The captain tried to form a solid square with its back against the houses: that would give the defense a solid base. He had succeeded in forming a line which would shoot almost point-blank at the riders over those who were fighting with their bayonets. Fine weapons, those Mauser repeaters. They wrought such havoc that the jagunços began to give way.

"Forward! Charge!" roared Barroso.

The soldiers hurled themselves into the attack. They were fine big Negroes and mulattoes, strong and stout material. An intimation of victory put them in a sort of delirium.

This was of short duration, for hardly had they cleared about five hundred yards, when a veritable cloud of jagunços, those on foot, fell on them. The battle was resumed without mercy. Every man realized that this must be decisive. Better armed, the soldiers held their own against the mass of assailants. Barroso directed the battle with the coolness and dynamism of a true leader.

The sun was frightful. The dust raised by the combatants parched their throats. A heavy animal odor rose from their bodies, filling the air as if it were a battle of wild beasts.

Pistol in hand, Captain Barroso was shooting down jagunços one after another as if automatically. The perspiration, standing out on his forehead in great drops, saturating his eyebrows, ran into his eyes and blinded him. He was now hardly conscious of what was happening. The glaring light made him dizzy, the dust suffocated him. He was no longer seeing anything but jagunços—in thousands —when suddenly an enormous Negro loomed up in front of him, after which—nothing.

Captain Barroso had just fallen victim to Pedrão's knife. The black battalion had annihilated the company of volunteers from Bahia: not a man escaped. Pedrão strolled among the bodies strewn on the ground. With his big knife he cut the throats of the wounded who were still alive.

Upright on his little black horse in the middle of the street, Pajehu was enjoying the flavor of his victory.

"Pedrão," he shouted, "have all those uniforms stripped off them. Collect all the rifles and ammunition. Put them all in a heap: we'll come with the wagon and fetch them. Let nothing be lost!"

It was four o'clock in the afternoon. The jagunços set about robbing the corpses and, as they were many, the task was quickly fulfilled. At five o'clock everything was finished. Pajehu had got down from his horse and was sitting in the shade on a doorstep. When Pedrão came to announce to him that everything had been done, Pajehu asked him to bring the objects which had been found on the captain. There was a pistol, a dagger with a gold handle, a gold ring with a big emerald, a Venetian leather pocketbook which he opened: he drew from it a sheet of paper with instructions from Colonel Azevedo—this he put into his pocket—two letters from women, which he threw away without reading, and the photograph of a young girl. "She'll never see him again," he thought proudly. He threw the photo in the dust, slipped the pocketbook into one of his trousers pockets, and jumped on his horse. He gave a last quick look around the place of the massacre which was covered with naked corpses: they were all black or dark brown bodies, in contrast to the whiteness of the despoiled remains of the captain. Pajehu seemed to think for a moment, and then he called Pedrão:

"Cut his sex off," he said, pointing to Barroso's body. "We'll make a present of it to João Abbade."

He took the road for Canudos.

When he arrived, the sun had just gone down.

The news of the massacre of the column from Bahia had reached the town and the whole population was massed on the church square where João Abbade had had the platform set up. When Pajehu appeared, a frenzied ovation rent the silence of the twilight. Without a gesture, impassive, the victor of the day pressed his horse toward João Abbade, to whom he delivered his "present." Enraptured, the Chief of the People fastened it to the end of a stick, jumped on the platform and brandished it in front of the crowd, shouting:

"That's what's left of the leader of the expedition. Down with the republic!"

They were delirious. The appearance of the Conseilheiro was greeted with wild roars. Four bonfires were lit at the four corners of the square. The Conseilheiro spoke in the apocalyptic language which he made his own on great occasions. He declared that, without being present at the battle, he had taken part in it, for Saint Sebastian had given him a vision of what was happening at Uauá;

he spoke of the Antichrist and of the president of the republic, and wound up crying out:

"There you have the punishment which awaits all those who dare to set Canudos at defiance."

Whereupon the bell began to ring out a loud peal announcing to the hinterland the victory of the jagunços.

16. Dr. Quadrado

NOT ONLY at Canudos has the world witnessed mysticism allied to cruelty, crime, and vice. History, even recent history provides us with many examples of this natural association, it seems, of idealism and bestiality. It is, moreover, interesting to note that certain mystics degenerate into sadists, as if the excess of spirituality is capable of reverting to beastliness. A vicious circle: borderlines of the human domain. Man who is made of flesh can hardly succeed in behaving with purity of spirit.

Canudos was an astonishing example of the eternal struggle of men of every race to free themselves from their animal origin. With their crimes, vices, and cruelties, they exerted a desperate effort toward the realization of an ideal. A degenerate ideal, but an ideal even so. The Christian principles sown in those arid souls grew there like rickety, tortured plants. They grew differently in accordance with the races involved.

If Antonio Maciel was able to rally to a lame, incoherent, and often absurd doctrine, that fortuitously anomalous population, it was because those people responded to an instinctive aspiration toward spirituality. It was because he incarnated the spiritual principle—the need of which is found in the most primitive peoples— that the population remained grouped around him. Had he disappeared, Canudos would have collapsed. Neither Pajehu nor João Abbade, whatever prestige they might acquire, would have been able to hold it up.

This they fully realized when the Conseilheiro all but died on the day after the victory celebrations.

These festivities had been magnificent. On the proposal of João Abbade, the Conseilheiro had suspended all his interdicts for two days. Pajehu had set out immediately on a pillaging operation with his mounted raiders but he did not have to engage in battle. The news of the victory at Uauá had spread everywhere and the jagunços were received with open arms, so that there was no shortage of maize, beans, manioc flour, fat bacon, suckling pigs, fowl, or rum. The jagunços gave themselves over to a formidable orgy, one that was all the more frenzied because they had been deprived of these pleasures for so long. Everywhere, in the lanes, on the church square, along the Vasa Barris River and as far as the Red Hills, fires burned brightly in the night and on them quarters of meat were roasted. The guitars were brought out, and the mandolins and accordions. Under the vast starry sky nostalgic *choros,* those sad old folk songs of the Negroes, mingled with the exciting sambas of the half-castes. During the daytime the Negroes organized a *reinado*—a sort of procession or file-past in which they performed old war dances they had brought from Africa: then on the square there was a kind of collective dance to the monotonous rhythm of *modinhas,* popular songs from the cities. At night there were several *batuques* (the nature of which has been described earlier). Pajehu organized a monster orgy with about thirty young men, but João Abbade refused to take part in Sariema's *batuque* in which fifty men and fifty women were brought together. He contented himself with proposing to the Conseilheiro that for once the rules of conduct which had been imposed should be relaxed and that the sage should participate in a ceremonial banquet.

Drunk with pride since the Uauá victory, the Conseilheiro agreed; and that was the cause of all the evil.

The meal, prepared by Anita, was lavish: chicken, suckling pig, black beans, maize, manioc biscuits, and creamed cocoanut.

The Conseilheiro's conscience was at ease.

"After Uauá," he kept saying, "they won't dare to attack us again."

He grew excited as he spoke and ate with the appetite of a dock laborer. The carousal ended late in the night.

Next day the Conseilheiro renewed his acquaintance with the

fierce dysentery he had succeeded in curing, or at least in keeping dormant, thanks to the regime of an anchorite which he had imposed on himself, but with another object.

João had Lourival Pinto attend him. This man was a quack healer acquainted with the art of using medicinal herbs. He was a half-breed of medium height with the strong shoulders of the Indian, and a shifty though intelligent face. He prepared an infusion or tea, and said that the cure would be a matter of days.

A week passed without improvement. The Conselheiro became visibly thinner. The bones of his face became even more conspicuous: his eyes sank deeper into his head, his hands assumed a skeletal appearance. He grew more feeble from one day to the next. He dared not get up because of dizziness.

João Abbade had forbidden access to his house, into which nobody except himself, Pajehu, and Sariema could go.

The jagunços and the women came in increasing numbers to take their place for hours on end in front of the prophet's dwelling. João reckoned that this could create a bad frame of mind and had the approaches to the house guarded by Venancio's "police."

Far from curing the evil, this measure contributed to make it worse. People were saying that the Conselheiro was at very low ebb, and that he was going to pass away from one moment to the next. Some of them were already insinuating that he was perhaps dead, but that the chiefs did not wish to admit it. However, the true believers affirmed that it was a trial sent by God to the master of Canudos: but that he would come out of it victoriously, as from other trials through which he had passed for the salvation of the hinterland.

Every evening the chiefs held council in João Abbade's house.

"If he dies," said Pajehu, "it's all up with everything. The people will abandon us."

João wracked his imagination to find some way of keeping the population in Canudos, but he had to yield to the evidence: all who were living in Canudos had come there only in the hope of making sure of a better life in the beyond. They had come because they had faith in the Conselheiro's promises, because they felt themselves in security near him. Neither Abbade, nor Pajehu and still less Sariema would be able to inspire them with a faith strong enough to hold them firmly to the unproductive soil of the Vasa Barris valley.

"We must save him at any cost," said João Abbade.

"There's nothing more to be done," replied Pajehu. "The drugs have no effect any more, and he's hardly eating anything. It's the end."

"There ought to be a doctor," retorted Sariema.

Pajehu shrugged his shoulders.

"What doctor would want to come to Canudos? All those white people would let us croak. They wouldn't ask for anything better."

"I'm not speaking of the whites," retorted Sariema.

Pajehu looked him up and down scornfully.

"Have you ever seen a Negro doctor? Why, you won't find even a half-breed."

"I know a mulatto doctor," Sariema asserted.

"A bonesetter of your Negro quarter in Bahia?"

"Not a bonesetter, a medical doctor, one who knows how to mix drugs. He cured many people in my district."

"If he was as good as you say he is, he'd have set himself up in town."

"No, the white people don't like to let themselves be treated by the blacks."

"They're quite right," Pajehu snapped back.

"For me," said Abbade, "I don't see why a mulatto shouldn't be as well acquainted with medicine as a white man."

"I'd like very much to go and find him," said Sariema. "In six days he could be here."

"The Conseilheiro won't hold out for six more days," said Pajehu.

"We could try, just the same," João Abbade broke in, "since there's no hope otherwise."

In the end they were in agreement. The same day Pajehu went out to "borrow" some money from the Geremoabo fazendeiro and, on the next day, Sariema went off to Queimadas accompanied by Chico Ema.

The morning, noon, and evening ritual prayers continued in the anxious town. João Abbade announced supplementary prayers in the form of a novena. According to a vision which the prophet had just had, the novena would bring about his cure. This news revived their courage and it was with intense fervor that the crowd began to recite interminable litanies, for all the jagunços had faith in the efficacy of prayer.

The Conseilheiro was sinking dangerously. Pajehu maintained that his mind was wandering, but João Abbade said that he had always had ideas that were difficult to understand. "You don't understand religious matters," he said to the half-breed. What became frightening was the patient's emaciation. His eyes had sunk in so deeply under his forehead that he had the look of a man beyond the grave, and his fleshless hands made them think of a witch's. He was now refusing to take the infusions prepared by Lourival Pinto.

"I ought not have taken those drugs," he would say. "We can't go against God's will. The Lord has sent me this dysentery because I've been unfaithful to my mission. I allowed myself to go and eat that suckling pig. I have sinned and have suffered the punishment of my error. May God forgive me!"

João Abbade and Pajehu anxiously awaited Sariema's return. They were so desperate that they no longer doubted the mulatto doctor's knowledge. They were convinced that, if he arrived in time, all would be saved—their future as well as the Conseilheiro's life. They did not even wonder whether Sariema would succeed in inveigling his friend to Canudos. They waited.

For once, the half-breed kept his word. On the sixth day toward the end of the afternoon, João Abbade and Pajehu, who had gone to sit in a corner of the square from which they had a view of the Cambaio gap, saw three horsemen loom up from the pass.

"Saved!" Abbade shouted enthusiastically.

"We'll see," said Pajehu who had become pessimistic again.

The three riders got down in front of the Conseilheiro's house. Chico Ema led the horses away. Sariema took off his straw boater and mopped his forehead with a pale blue handkerchief.

"Is he still alive?" he asked.

"Yes," said Abbade, "but he's very low."

"Here's Dr. Manuel Quadrado," said Sariema glibly, introducing the new arrival.

He was a man of about forty years of age, of medium build and acquiring a corporation. He had a round face and, although his complexion was very dark, his forehead was straight and his slightly curly hair quite long. He had a vague, absent-minded look as if he were constantly absorbed in some besetting thought.

"You know what's the matter," said Pajehu whose mind was practical. "Have you brought your remedies?"

"They're in my valise," said the doctor, pointing to a little black attaché case.

"You must go quickly," said João Abbade. "We'll show him to you."

They entered the house. Manuel Quadrado went to the bed on which the prophet lay.

"This is a doctor who's come from Bahia: he's going to cure you," said João Abbade.

Contrary to what might have been feared, the Conselheiro made no objection. He allowed Quadrado to draw up his smock, take down his trousers and knead his belly.

"Pity I didn't come sooner," said Quadrado. "Now it will be difficult. He's very far gone."

"Do you think that he won't recover?" Abbade asked apprehensively.

"Don't know. We'll see."

Quadrado opened his valise and took from it a small phial, asking for a cup of water. He poured a little of the contents of the phial into the cup and held it out to the Conselheiro. The prophet drank it without hesitation as if certain that the draught was going to relieve him.

"What is it?" Pajehu asked.

"Tincture of opium," said the doctor. "There's no other remedy and, if that doesn't give any result, then it's all up."

"Do we have to wait long to see the result?" asked João.

"No, the effect is immediate. The day after tomorrow we'll know definitely."

That suits, thought João, since the novena will not be finished before three days; all those prayers won't have been said in vain.

For forty-eight hours they lived in a state of deep anxiety, going constantly to see the patient as if it were possible to read the effects of the medicine on his face. João Abbade had cleared a house to give it to the doctor, and in the evening the four of them gathered together there: the doctor, Pajehu, Sariema, and himself. They conversed in the light from candles.

Manuel Quadrado was a mild likable man without any pretensions, which is rare in Negroes and mulattoes with some education.

"I'm not a medical doctor, as Sariema told you," he said. "I have never been to the higher schools, but I know many things about medicine. At seventeen years of age I was employed as a messenger boy in a pharmacy, and I gradually learned about the chemical products which were being sold. The proprietor, a Portuguese, found that I was not lacking in intelligence and got me to work with him; and so, in about ten years' time, I became more or less his assistant. I made up powders in capsules, and pills: and thus I became acquainted with the drugs administered for the principal maladies. Later, the Portuguese handed over his business to a German who didn't want to keep me on as his assistant. The Germans don't like Negroes. It was then that I went and set myself up in the Negro quarter. I've always done quite well out of it, but Sariema told me that I'd make much more here. It seems that you haven't a doctor? How many of you are there?"

"You've been able to see that we're numerous," said João Abbade. "I think that we're at least twelve thousand."

"And you've never had a doctor?"

"We have a few healers who know about medicinal plants."

"That's better than nothing," said Quadrado. "But many of you must die?"

"There are between six and seven hundred crosses in the cemetery. The children die easily."

"And the women, do they look after themselves in childbirth?"

"No, there are many men here who know how to deliver a child and there are some women who take it on."

"All the same, you need a doctor."

"If the Conseilheiro recovers, you'll stay with us."

"I'll see. If I can live here better than in Bahia, I'll remain in Canudos. I don't like big cities very much. The white people treat you badly, and the Negroes don't want you because they think that you can mix in white society. Hence, you haven't friends any more and you're spurned on all sides."

On the day before the end of the novena the Conseilheiro's health began to improve. Manuel Quadrado declared that he would recover.

In the evening after prayers next day, João Abbade went on the platform and announced to the people that God had answered their prayer: the Conseilheiro was on the way to being cured and soon could resume his sermons. On the announcement of this miracle, three women went into a trance: they came forward like sleepwalkers and threw themselves at the foot of the platform. It generally happened on such occasions that they offered their bosoms to the Virgin Mary: this time they offered them to Saint Sebastian, to whom the cure was due.

Moved by the Chief of the People's declarations, the jagunços left the church commenting on the event. Most of them were convinced that the Conseilheiro had just come to life again. His death had been concealed from them: the novena had brought about his resurrection. For it was astonishing nevertheless that the miracle had occurred on the exact day on which the novena ended. There could be no possible doubt: it was the prayers which had brought the Conseilheiro back to life.

It was not, however, until twelve days later that the prophet was able to resume his harangues. João Abbade had arranged things well for his reappearance on the scene. On the platform at the end of the church he had placed a little table covered with a white cloth: on each side he had put six candles fixed in bottles.

And the Conseilheiro loomed up in a yellowish halo like an apparition in a nightmare. When he stood up in front of the little white table, a cry went up from all:

"Long live our Conseilheiro! Long live the good Jesus!"

He raised his skeletal arm to impose silence and spoke in a low sepulchral voice. He said that the time was near when the hinterland would fulfill its destiny. God had called him back to life so that he should not abandon those who had faith, for a formidable cataclysm was going to sweep down on the world, and the waters of the sea would once again cover the entire hinterland, submerging the republic and all those who had become its myrmidons.

He excused himself for not speaking longer, because he still felt very weak.

After the ceremony he returned to his house accompanied by Abbade, Pajehu, Sariema, and Manuel Quadrado.

"So, doctor," he said, "you think that I'll get completely well again?"

"Certainly. You're sound in body. You've had this attack only because you ate too much when you've been accustomed to eat very little."

"It was that suckling pig," said Abbade.

The prophet began walking about the room excitedly, and then stopped suddenly:

"Never again," he said in the abrupt manner of speaking which he assumed when angry. "Never again will I permit those carousals. Such things are against nature. Never again!"

Manuel Quadrado was observing him narrowly. He was convinced that the man was crazy.

17. The Tocsin

To HAVE so narrowly escaped death gave the Conseilheiro food for thought. The state of rapture in which he had been living since the foundation of Canudos had faded away: he returned to his old self and once again found Antonio Maciel, Paulina's husband, the nephew of Miguel Carlos. In his mind he relived his youth in Ceará, the drought, the exodus, the dungeons in Bahia and Fortaleza. All that was so remote and yet so near. He recalled with surprising clarity the last salutation of Miguel Carlos. What had become of Miguel? He had never troubled himself on that score, and now he felt some anxiety in not knowing whether he was dead or alive. This thought became fixed in his head, became an obsession which he could not turn aside. After a few days he could not bear it any longer and he called João Abbade.

"Abbade," he said, "I need a man who has a good horse, to go to Ceará. It takes twelve days: at least, I took twelve days to go from Quixeramobim to Monte Santo; but I'm a bad rider."

"We're not short of men accustomed to traveling in the hinter-land."

"I want one who can be trusted: it's to take a letter to my family."

"You have the letter?"

"No, I'm going to write it. But first I want to know who's going to take it."

"I'm going to send you Domingos dos Reis. He's young, but you can put your trust in him."

"You'll send him to me tomorrow. Tell him to take a good saddle —a Mexican—for it's a long ride."

Antonio Maciel set to writing his letter, the first for fourteen years. He possessed only a piece of wrapping paper and a bit of pencil lent by Pajehu. This was enough to transmit what he was thinking. He formed his words with difficulty: his fingers no longer responded, and they became contracted after writing a few lines. Antonio was a strong-willed man: he took some hours to do this piece of work, but he did it. In his missive he explained to Miguel Carlos how, once he had set out southward, he had begun to preach the Gospel in order to fulfill the mission which, as he had told Miguel, had been entrusted to him by Saint Sebastian, explaining how the people had gradually rallied to him, and how he had founded Canudos, which had become the capital town of the hinter-land and of which he was the master. He asked for news of him, and invited him to come and see him.

When the messenger had left, Antonio felt more at ease: he was relieved of that burden which weighed so heavily on his conscience. As his health had greatly improved, he became again the flaming apostle who galvanized the jagunços.

It was at that time—a few days after the dispatch of the letter— that Chico Ema who, on instructions from Abbade constantly prowled around Queimadas and Joazeiro, returned with some seri-ous news. Bahia was preparing a formidable military expedition to raze Canudos to the ground. According to the talk going the rounds of the botequims in the villages along the railway, the town was going to be reduced to ashes and the jagunços would be deported to the Amazon region. They knew what that meant. Deportation to the Amazon meant forced labor clearing the jungle in malarial regions where men died like flies.

The same evening the chiefs—Abbade, Pajehu, and Sariema—met in the Conseilheiro's house. They invited Manuel Quadrado, who had their utmost respect, and to whose advice they attached great importance.

The Conseilheiro was beside himself. He strode to and fro in the room, a sign of anger.

"That republican rabble," he muttered, "they're after our skins. But we shall fight. We'll fight like *onças*—like jaguars. Whatever happens, they won't take me alive."

"It might be better to try to come to some agreement," Abbade suggested. "They'll crush us. Chico Ema talks of three thousand men with cannons."

"They'll overwhelm us, but it will cost them dear," roared the Conseilheiro, shaking his fist.

Pajehu was rolling a cigarette. With his right index finger he was patiently arranging the tobacco in the maize straw.

"They haven't won yet," he said calmly.

"You'll never be able to stand up to three thousand soldiers," said Abbade sharply. "It would be a massacre."

"It remains to be seen who'll be massacred," retorted the half-breed. "The last time they came . . ."

"They were only three hundred. This time they'll be three thousand, ten times more."

The Conseilheiro stopped short, spread his arms as if he were going to preach.

"I'm going to proclaim holy war," he said angrily. "I'm sure that the hinterland will back us: the sertão against the republic. We'll see who'll be strongest."

"It's a good idea," said Pajehu. "Abbade ought to send out emissaries everywhere asking for men to be sent to us, and with supplies and powder."

"I'll take charge of that," said Abbade, "since opinion is in favor of fighting."

"The Conseilheiro doesn't bend to anybody," shouted Antonio.

"I'm starting straightway to form new battalions," said Pajehu. "To stand up to them, we must be organized like an army."

"You can advise your emissaries," said Manuel Quadrado, "to have medical supplies sent to us. They'll be needed."

"I never thought of that," said Abbade. "We've been living for so many years without drugs."

The Conseilheiro posed himself dramatically in front of them and, raising his arm, said:

"Go, and may God be with you."

Next day more than a hundred men on horseback took their departure for all points of the hinterland, going toward São Francisco, Pombal, Joazeiro, and Sergipe, to proclaim the holy war.

The results of this initiative were decisive. It was soon evident that the Conseilheiro had many partisans in the hinterland region. Canudos had a widespread influence which, in spite of all their pride, his chiefs underestimated. A few days had hardly elapsed after the departure of the emissaries when groups of horsemen began to show themselves on the slopes of Cannabrava, at the saddle of the hill at Uauá, at the Cambaio gap, and on the Geremoabo road. They were preceded by men carrying long poles with a cross at the top, as if it were a matter of a crusade. There were men only. Soon they found it difficult to lodge them in Canudos and Abbade decided that new houses should be built. To avoid offending the old inhabitants, who considered it an honor to have been the first to come and live in the holy town, it was arranged that the new houses should be erected on the red hills and that they should be limewashed in red: this quarter was known as the "Red Houses."

Canudos was in the grip of a new fever for building. The ox wagons again began to haul tree trunks, the kilns for tile-making began to smoke, and once more the noise of hammers and hatchets filled the valley.

While one part of the population was busy with the construction of a new quarter, another, under the stimulus of Pajehu, was engaged in overhauling the firearms and making powder and cartridges.

Notwithstanding all this activity, their souls were not neglected. Morning, midday, and evening Angelus were followed more fervently than ever. The Conseilheiro in his harangues told the jagunços again and again that the republic wanted them to die in the swamps, but that Saint Sebastian was on their side and they were certain of victory.

Every day Pajehu, accompanied by Venancio, Pedrão, and Tranca-Pés, went out on the Monte Santo and Rosario roads to find out the position of the places where they could await the government forces.

The jagunços got worked up among themselves. It would be worse than at Uauá, they were saying. They felt themselves ready for the most terrible atrocities, and glutted themselves with their rage. On their doorsteps in the evening they put a very sharp edge on their knives.

Reinforcements and provisions continued to arrive. Abbade had even received two cases of medical supplies. The sertão was not leaving the Conseilheiro in the lurch: it was accepting the government's challenge. To this must be added that many of the fazendeiros who had not the slightest regard for the prophet, but were hostile to the republic, sent their men and sharecroppers to defend Canudos.

The church square was no longer big enough to hold all that throng, which overflowed into a kind of long avenue extending to the foot of the sierra de Cannabrava, this being the road used by the ox wagons.

In the afternoon of May 24th, Chico Ema came down the slopes of the Favella at full gallop and drew up in front of Abbade's house. He came to announce that the government troops had detrained at Queimadas. This was a severe shock to João; it took his breath away. He dragged Chico to Pajehu's house. The half-breed was sitting on the doorstep smoking a cigar which he seemed to enjoy voluptuously.

"What now?" he asked seeing João Abbade's drawn face.

"They've arrived," said Chico Ema.

Pajehu shook the ash from his cigar.

"How many of them are there?"

"Thousands and thousands. Queimadas is full of them."

"Have they any cannons?"

"Two. They're on the station square. Everybody's looking at them. They say it's going to be terrible."

"It will be," said Pajehu.

That same evening the bell rang out noisily for half an hour to announce to the people that the battle was about to begin.

Part III

THE BATTLE

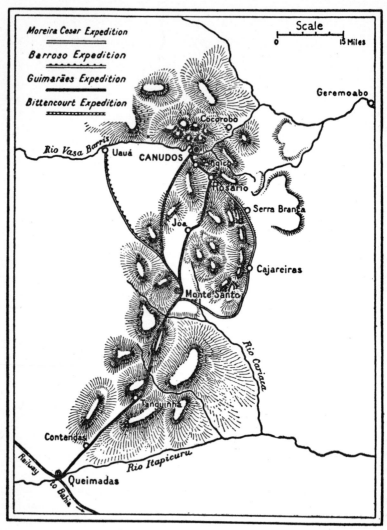

The Campaigns against Canudos

1. Moreira Cesar

THE REPUBLIC of Brazil was six years old at the time when the decisive struggle between the jagunços and the federal authorities was about to begin. The young republic made slow progress in the undergrowth of discords and revolts. Nevertheless, the change from an authoritarian to a democratic regime had never been achieved so smoothly. The Emperor Dom Pedro II, a philosopher enamored of progressive theories, had realized that an imperial regime did not harmonize with social conditions in America. He would often say to his friends that he was the first republican in Brazil. Hence, on November 15, 1889, when General Deodoro da Fonseca proclaimed the republic, there was no opposition on the part of the Emperor, who consented to the *pronunciamento* and simply embarked on board the liner *Alagoas* to join the Empress Theresa Christina already in Lisbon.

The people on the whole gave the new regime a warm reception, at least in the cities. In the interior the population was too scattered to create any change of opinion. The Constituent Assembly of 1890 succeeded in endowing the country with a flexible constitution inspired by a lofty ideal.

Unfortunately, although Deodoro da Fonseca had proclaimed the republic, he had not the soul of a republican. He had heard democracy spoken of, but he did not know very well what the term signified. Like a good soldier he set up a dictatorial regime and took a series of steps which made the loss of the empire regrettable. After the brutal dissolution of the Constituent Assembly, Admiral Custodio de Mello rose against him. Whereupon Deodoro had the happy inspiration to resign and give place to the vice-president, Floriano Peixoto. This did not at all suit Custodio de Mello, whose only object in rebelling was to seize power and who, failing in this, put himself at the head of a revolutionary movement. Peixoto did not allow himself to be intimidated and organized the repression of the revolt with such energy that the republic was saved: and for this he was called the "Iron Marshal."

The rebels were concentrated in the state of Santa Catharina, and to Colonel Moreira Cesar was given the responsibility of subduing them.

Moreira Cesar was a man of short stature. His head was very small and baldness accentuated its triangular shape. His regular features were of a pallor strange in a man accustomed to living in the sun. Under a bulging forehead his chestnut eyes remained inexpressive and dull even in moments when his nerves were on edge. From the time of his youth Moreira Cesar concentrated on making himself more inflexible, more obstinate, and more impassive. He succeeded in achieving an absolute control over his gestures which, through will power, had become slower and colder. For he knew how to disguise most effectively the disease from which he suffered. Moreira Cesar was an epileptic. He was incensed by this disability. His vindictive nature and cruelty were merely the manifestation of his resentment against the human race of which he was merely an abortive product.

Consciousness of his ailment had developed in him an inordinate ambition, which was served by a lively intelligence and a rare tenacity. His violent behavior was forgiven because his genius for organization as well as his energy and courage were admired. He was extremely touchy and, when people spoke to him, they had to weigh their words. Once, in the course of a banquet, he had raised his dagger against an Argentine officer for some misunderstood remark. The incident was smoothed over with the plea that he was an epileptic. Soon afterwards he took part in the chastisement of a journalist who had been engaged in revolutionary propaganda. He had planted his knife in the victim's back when he found that the whipping was not enough. After this exploit he was sent into the Matto Grosso by Marshal Peixoto, who nevertheless held him in high esteem. But when the revolt fomented by Custodio de Mello spread over the whole of Santa Catharina, and threatened to reach the states of Paraná and Rio Grande do Sul, the Marshal did not hesitate to recall the strong-minded man who could assure the government victory and re-establish order. As was to be expected, the repression was savage. Colonel Moreira Cesar ranged over the state at the head of a flying column executing with the firing squad everybody who had come to terms with the rebels. Terror reigned in the south for two months. Deprived of the support of the terri-fied inhabitants, the rebels took to flight and dispersed. Custodio de Mello sought refuge in Argentina.

Moreira Cesar returned to Rio covered with blood and glory, but a nervous wreck. On the boat which brought him and his troops from Paranaguá, he had the captain put in irons for having made some remarks in his presence which were displeasing to the colonel. When Marshal Peixoto was taking him to task about the matter Moreira cut in frigidly:

"Good-by, Marshal. I'm leaving for France."

But his services were retained and he organized the best dis-ciplined regiment in the Rio garrison, the one which won all the cheers of the multitude: the crack regiment it was, the iron regi-ment.

On November 15, 1894, Marshal Peixoto gave place to the new president-elect, Prudente de Moraes. Passions had cooled and the government was able to devote all its activity to the economic organization of the country.

For two years everything was going well when the news came of the massacre of Braz Barroso's company at Canudos.

At that period nobody in Rio could have said where exactly Canu-dos was; nobody had ever heard the Conselheiro mentioned. The public was aware that the *cangaço*—cutthroat banditry—was the scourge of the northern states, but supposed that those bandits, the *cangaceiros,* existed in bands of fifty, one hundred, or two hun-dred men. Nobody could conceive that one of those bands could over-whelm and massacre, down to the last man, a company of infantry. The conclusion drawn was that, in this instance, it was not merely a matter of simple bandits but of rebels hostile to the republic. This conclusion seemed very natural when it was known that the bands of cangaceiros were often solicited by politicians, whether to put pressure on the population in time of an election, or maybe in sup-port of some revolutionary movement. Hence, the press and public opinion called for extremely energetic action on the part of the federal government, all the more so because such incidents were giving the country a deplorable reputation abroad. What foreign government would grant credits to a country in which bandits could vanquish the army?

In the presidential palace they were conscious of the danger inherent in such a situation. Nevertheless, they did not conceive it to be as grave as it was represented in the report of the governor of Bahia which reached them only eight days after the news of the massacre. According to this report more than ten thousand bandits had taken refuge at Canudos, to which the approach was extremely difficult. Such a band could not be suppressed by a simple police operation. It demanded a thoroughgoing military expedition. All the ministers were of opinion that the repression must be ruthless; and all considered that the only man who could bring it to a successful issue was Colonel Moreira Cesar.

When it became known that the man charged with suppressing the rebellion in the north was the one who had crushed the rebellion in the south, people's feelings became calm as if under the effect of some magic potion. The prestige of Moreira Cesar was such that the matter was regarded as settled. The jagunços were going to be exterminated. The *cangaço*—brigandage with violence —was going to be ended. They had had enough of that anarchy in the northeast.

When the commander of the expedition embarked for Bahia on board the *Paraná* a vast crowd covered the quays: a turbulent motley crowd of Negroes, whites, and people of mixed breed yelling hurrahs for Moreira Cesar. The anger of the people of Rio against the jagunços who were defiling the good name of the hardly born republic was let loose like a Matto Grosso hurricane.

Leaning on the ship's rail, Moreira Cesar looked coldly and with impassive features at all this agitation. When the propellers began turning and the boat slowly drew away from the quay, he stood to attention, gave a quick salute, and escaped to the saloon.

At Bahia they received a frenzied welcome. The carriage in which the colonel took his place advanced slowly between two thickly packed lines of inquisitive people and was preceded by a picket of cavalry. Here the yells of the crowd were more to the point. The shouts of "Long Live Moreira Cesar" were mingled with "Down with Canudos!" and "Death to the Conseilheiro!"

The governor was awaiting the colonel at the entrance to the

palace. He gave his guest the *abraço*—the welcoming embrace—
to the acclamations of the multitude which covered the entire square,
and then led him indoors to his office.

Although he did not mean to meddle any more than this in a
matter which he regarded as exclusively within the province of the
military—and of which he was happy to be relieved—he had nevertheless done his utmost to collect as much information as possible
about Canudos in order to facilitate the colonel's task. He had summoned the chief of police from Joazeiro, an enterprising and intelligent young officer, whom he had ordered to make an exact
report on the lay of the land and the resources as well as the
armament of the jagunços. The colonel would not fail to appreciate
this initiative at its just value.

Seated in one of the low armchairs in the office, Moreira Cesar
finished mopping his forehead. The governor offered him a cigar
and they began the conference by smoking. After a few puffs, the
colonel cleared his throat, spat into his handkerchief, and said:

"I don't think that you know all about the plan, sir. You couldn't
yet have received it, since I'm the one who made it and I've come
by the first boat. I'll expound it to you briefly. The expedition will
consist of two battalions and a brigade of cavalry. One thousand
men from Bahia, 1,000 Pernambucans, and 1,000 Gauchos from Rio
Grande. I also count on taking with me two .75 field guns. Cannon
are cumbersome in this kind of operation but in this case as it's a
matter, not of subduing a band, but of attacking a locality, I think
they'll be useful to me."

"Certainly, colonel, but you'll have some difficulty in getting guns
up in front of Canudos: those trails in the hinterland are so bad."

"Fiddlesticks! If the guns arc too awkward I'll abandon them.
Don't you realize that with 3,000 men I'm in a position to exterminate this vermin without the help of artillery: after all, the cannon
would only serve me to create panic."

"There's no doubt whatever that with 3,000 men well armed,
well trained, and well commanded, you'll have no difficulty in over-
coming a few thousand men without any practical experience of
war and equipped with old-fashioned firearms. The massacre of
Barroso's company was a mishap and we have to admit that 300
men, well armed but not knowing the country, found themselves in

a state of inferiority. It's the terrain, you see, that's dangerous. The route is strewn with ambushes. In regard to this I should like to introduce to you our police officer from Joazeiro who knows the region well and will be able to provide you with useful particulars. . . ."

He shook a little bell.

"Call Mattos," he said to the Negro usher, who made a cringing bow to him.

The young officer came in carrying in his right hand a file with a green cardboard cover. He saluted the colonel military fashion, clicking his heels. The governor puffed his cigar.

"Mattos," he said with an air of importance, "would you read your report to us?"

Moreira made an abrupt gesture with his hand.

"No, no. No report," he rapped out. "I don't work on reports but on the terrain. In Santa Catharina I never needed reports."

"But," ventured the governor, "this report refers precisely to the terrain."

"I don't want it," snapped the colonel. And, addressing Mattos: "You may go, young man."

The young officer withdrew crestfallen and embarrassed. The governor prepared for himself a glass of bicarbonate.

"You see, sir," said Moreira whose face was sullen, "you must leave to the military what comes within their capacity. I have nothing to do with police reports."

"I was hoping to be useful to you, but do believe me that I shall not interfere in this matter. It is entirely in your hands and I'm certain you'll make a success of it."

He knew that the colonel must not be crossed.

The day after next the coastal steamer *Aracajú* brought the battalion of Pernambucans. In general they were men of short stature with bony faces, very black eyes and straight hair: men of mixed breed, with at least seventy per cent of Indian blood. They marched past badly, nonchalantly, and all out of line. "A week of intensive drill," Moreira gave the order to Major Valladarès who was in command of the battalion. "And I shall be present at it."

He had spoken in a loud voice in order to be heard by the

soldiers, and he then jumped down from his horse and requested Valladarès to follow him.

"Bad troops, major," he said to him. "They don't even know how to march abreast. That's a lack of discipline. And yet I asked Recife to send me crack troops."

Major Valladarès was a small lean man with eyes that were very soft and very big like those of a woman. But a straight wrinkle like an exclamation mark between his eyebrows indicated a downright, tough, and strong-willed man. His aquiline nose betrayed his Semitic origin; his mouth was small but thick-lipped. His skin was of a nondescript color, brown and at the same time grayish. Valladarès was the son of a Portuguese father and a Syrian mother.

"The value of a body of men, colonel, is not measured by its capacity for marching in line but by its capacity for courage: and, on that level, the Pernambucans don't yield to anybody."

Moreira was not accustomed to such retorts. He looked the thin little man up and down.

"You're not lacking in cheek, major," he said putting on an air. "We'll see how you shape up at work."

"May I remind you of the campaign against the Dutch, colonel?"

"That's enough," snapped Moreira Cesar who did not tolerate arguments.

Although he reacted with brutal violence against those who dared to criticize him, or who gave voice to displeasing allusions, he did not dislike men who knew how to defend their point of view firmly. Valladarès pleased him, because he would not stand any disparagement of his men. Later, Moreira was to take him as adviser and confidant.

He insisted on nothing less than having the Pernambucans put through a stiff course of training. He took a hand in it himself, as he said he would, for he liked this business of training soldiers. In reality he had the soul of a sergeant.

On the third day he was diverted from this task by the arrival of the Gauchos, the "cowboys" and plainsmen recruited from the southern state of Rio Grande do Sul. As soon as it was announced to him that the steamer had docked, he went to the quay, for he meant to receive them personally and lead them through the city to the barracks. He himself wished to show to the people of Bahia the most brilliant horsemen of the republic. The Gauchos arrived preceded by a formidable reputation for their handsome appearance and bravery. All Bahia was there to welcome them. The crowd massed along the pavements was with difficulty held back by the police, with infantry called in as reinforcement. And in truth they were fine men, those Gauchos, with their blue shirts, their big red silk neckerchiefs and their heads well set off in green kerchiefs. Riding bolt upright on their magnificent horses from Rio Grande, they had a fine bearing. All that created confidence.

They marched in file amid unceasing acclamations, with Moreira Cesar at the head of the column, the colonel enjoying one of his favorite pleasures.

He was so enthusiastic that he decided to hold a parade next day on the Residency Square. In this way he would have the opportunity for a second time of basking in the applause of the multitude—the only thing capable of intoxicating him.

The show was a success. Moreira Cesar made the Gauchos do some exercises in horsemanship which produced rapturous excitement. Women threw flowers at them in expectation of having them in bed. Men stood enraptured before the horses: beautiful animals, well set up, high-steppers, and spirited.

Supported by the band of the third infantry battalion, the crowd's enthusiasm became frenzied, as it always did under that sky of dazzling light.

That same evening in the café bars of the lower town the Gauchos had to submit to the negresses' onslaught. Drink was poured out for them: the improvisers sang in their honor. Until well into the night the streets near the port were permeated with the music of guitars and accordions.

The women were firmly counting on seeing those likable cavaliers next evening. Innumerable trysts had been arranged. In the forenoon they were terribly disappointed to hear that in the course of the night the troops had been embarked on special trains for Canudos.

This was well in keeping with Moreira Cesar's way of doing things.

2. Canudos under the Threat

ON HEARING of the detrainment of federal troops at Queimadas, the Canudos chiefs were unable to deny feeling somewhat deeply concerned. Although the Conseilheiro felt certain of Saint Sebastian's co-operation, and Pajehu was sure of his battalions, they found it hard to overcome their uneasiness. As for João Abbade, his mind drifted amid conflicting feelings; and Sariema was fatalistic.

The news was having a disastrous effect among the people. Chico Ema had told frightening stories about the head of the expedition, gossip which he had picked up in the botequims at Bomfim, Riuba, and Bom Conselho. This Colonel Moreira Cesar was depicted as a bloodthirsty brute who had crushed the rebellion in Santa Catharina. He had, in fact, put the whole population to fire and sword. He had burned down the towns, plundered the villages, and sacked private dwellings. He was a formidable man; and he had asserted that he was going to raze Canudos to the ground.

Among the jagunços, there were, certainly, the hired killers now at loose ends; and the *valentões*, the tough outlaws, who were not afraid of free fights or battles: but there were also people who had come to Canudos in the hope of living there quietly without effort and with peace in their hearts. These were not disposed to fight: still less to die. When they saw that things were taking a bad turn, they began to desert. They were sending their women and children to find wood in the Cannabrava forest, and joining them by night to escape into the hinterland.

João Abbade did not become aware of this subterfuge until some days had passed. He informed Pajehu of it.

"Things are going badly," he said. "They're beginning to leave us in the lurch. They're scared."

Abbade himself was afraid, but when he was in Pajehu's company he felt full of fire and courage.

"It won't last long," retorted the half-breed with a knowing look.

That same day he organized cavalry pickets responsible for watching the roads day and night. This measure had a double advantage: no spy could penetrate into the town; and the deserters were stopped.

What was most astonishing was that, while some were abandoning the Conseilheiro, a new flux of reinforcements was coming up from the hinterland. On the news that the government was sending against Canudos an expedition commanded by that brute Moreira Cesar, the sertão reared up and ranged itself behind the Conseilheiro who incarnated its spirit and mysticism.

A great disappointment, however, awaited the volunteers on their arrival in the town. There they found people in a panic, demoralized and troubled, with women in tears begging to be taken back to their villages. Pajehu comforted the newcomers, telling them that fainthearted and cowardly people were to be found everywhere. In Canudos, at all events, there were sufficient stouthearted men to assure the defense of the town.

Fear is contagious: it continued to gain ground. There were desertions even from the pickets sent out to keep watch.

"Gang of cowards," growled Pajehu. "The first one I catch I'll down like an ox."

"You won't bring them around by force," said João Abbade. "I know them better than you. Leave it to me."

In his mind it was a question of striking their imagination. He conceived a stage production capable of mystifying the jagunços. He had the platform erected on the square in front of the church door and on it placed a table covered with a white cloth.

When twilight came he had two fires lit, one on each side. At the moment when the bell began to toll the Angelus, he bounded onto the trestles and in a powerful voice commanded the whole crowd to assemble for prayer: "On your knees!" Men and women knelt down wondering why there was this alteration in the daily ceremony.

João himself began to recite the litanies, articulating with unaccustomed vigor the holy words:

"Morning star . . . Tower of ivory . . ." To which in response came the deep murmur of "Pray for us."

When he ended, he jumped down from the platform as the door

of the church was slowly opening and, in the yellow halo of the fires, the Conselheiro appeared like a phantom. He was not wearing his blue smock but was clad in a long red robe: he was not now brandishing his little cross, but a long dagger.

The bell ceased ringing. Silence came over the kneeling crowd, a silence broken only by the crackling of the twigs in the fires. And the solemn voice of the prophet rose into the night:

"Verily I say unto you, when in the beginning of the world Don Sebastian was on the point of vanishing with his army, he buried his sword in the stone and said: 'God be with you, World! Until the year one thousand and so much . . .' And on the day when he shall come out with his army he shall with the edge of his sword tear all men from this comedy of a republic.

"Already I have told you in 1896: herds of cattle shall rush from the coast to the hinterland. Then the hinterland shall become seashore and the seashore shall become hinterland, and the waters shall be bloody, and a planet shall appear in the East with the first ray of sunshine and it shall face the earth as the earth faces the sky.

"But, in 1897, the pasture lands shall be beautiful. There shall be one shepherd and one herd of livestock."

The jagunços did not understand this language in the least, but the rapid succession of images which the Conselheiro called up bewildered them leaving the impression that he was a magician.

"At the ninth hour," continued the prophet, "when Our Lord was resting on the Mount of Olives, one of his apostles asked him: 'Lord, what signs do you leave us for the end of this epoch?' He replied: 'Many signs: in the sun, moon, and stars. There shall appear an angel sent by my Father who shall go out preaching from door to door, building churches and chapels, giving counsels and creating communities in the desert . . .'"

Thrown off their balance, carried away by an uncontrollable enthusiasm, the jagunços rose up and began to shout: "Long live the Conselheiro! Down with the Antichrist! Down with the republic!"

Late in the cold night when the people had returned to their houses in a state of dread though somewhat comforted, Abbade, Pajehu, and Sariema met in the Conselheiro's house.

"What do you think of it?" asked João Abbade, proud of his success.

"They have regained their faith," said the Conseilheiro. "They needed a lesson. They don't pray enough."

"It can have some effect," conceded Pajehu.

"It was thrilling." Sariema thought he must say something.

"What's that got to do with it?" Pajehu snapped at him contemptuously.

And, turning to Abbade:

"There's no more time to be lost. Tomorrow we must collect all the picks, hoes, billhooks, and axes and form two or three working parties. It's time I prepared a reception for Moreira Cesar."

Next day at dawn Pajehu went to the roads for Monte Santo and Rosario at the head of working parties. In many places these roads sink between little chalky hills. On all the heights overlooking the trails, Pajehu made them dig holes capable of providing cover for three men. For he did not possess sufficient weapons. There was one firearm for every three men according to his calculations. With three sharpshooters in each hole, should the first be killed, wounded, or tired, he would give place to the second; and the second eventually to the third.

They took three days to do this work. The Conseilheiro then said that the defenses must be blessed and he proposed organizing a procession around the town with the whole population taking part.

This took place in the afternoon next day. It must have been a curious spectacle: ten or twelve thousand men and women going around their town in a long file extending to the hollows in the sierras to make a rampart of their faith. For this ceremony the banner on which the Conseilheiro was shown crushing the Antichrist had been taken out of the church. A somber fervor animated the whole crowd as it recited the *Ave Maria*.

Just as the procession was going down the slopes of Cannabrava to re-enter the town, a man on horseback appeared at the summit of the Flavella. He waved his arms and swooped down toward the church. It was Chico Ema. João and Pajehu dashed forward to meet him.

"They've set out from Queimadas," said Chico Ema. "They're advancing toward Monte Santo."

"You've seen them?" Pajehu questioned him.

"Yes, there's horsemen and men on foot."

"How many of them are there?"

"A great number. When you're at the head of the column, you can't see the end of it."

"Go and get me my horse," said Pajehu. "I'll look into this myself."

3. The Hinterland Sun

MOREIRA CESAR did not want to delay at Queimadas, for he was burning to get into action: he wished to fall on Canudos like a thunderbolt. He himself was present at the detrainment of the troops and refused the political chief's invitation to dinner.

"I haven't come here on a picnic," he said to the latter.

He agreed, however, to receive local personalities in the rustic hall of the little station hotel where he was staying. But he had put an end to the interview after half an hour, saying that he had no time to lose. He hated the lack of determination, the dillydally and chitchat of these people of the interior.

"We leave tomorrow," he said to the portly Flores, taking leave of him and his friends. "It's fully understood, then: you're to get me twenty bullocks."

The effort he was going to ask of his men would be a hard one: they would need fresh meat to sustain themselves.

The troops were mustered at dawn in the morning haze on the piece of open ground near the station. The column set out on the march to a flourish of bugles. The Pernambucans were at the head, most of them being used to the hinterland. They were followed by the Bahians and the Gauchos. Behind came a troop of twenty pack mules transporting the rations and munitions, then the bullocks requisitioned at Queimadas, the medical service vehicle and, finally, the two .75 guns. Moreira had put them in the rear to avoid holding up the column at difficult parts of the route.

It was nearly forty miles from Queimadas to Monte Santo. Moreira Cesar reckoned to cover them in two days. Colonel Tamarindo, who was in command of the Bahians, remarked to him that twenty miles a day under the hinterland sun would exhaust the infantry.

"The men are much tougher than you think," he retorted. "I guarantee you that troops under my orders give their maximum effort. In the Matto Grosso I made them march up to twenty-five miles in a day and the next day I put them on maneuvers."

All the officers from the state of Pernambuco, accustomed to the climate of that region, and even those from Bahia, considered that this march in broad daylight was a mistake, but none of them dared to contradict the chief.

During the forenoon all went well. The trail, which was quite broad, followed the valley of the Itapicuru River. From time to time it ran through little woods or tall coppices where they enjoyed a cool restful shade. But, after Contendas—a muleteers' shack —it rises on the flank of the bare hill under a little chalky plateau. It was nearly 10 A.M. when the column approached the acclivity. The sun was already burning: from minute to minute the heat was increasing in intensity. The men, who until then had been conversing and singing cheerfully, became silent. The sweat was rolling off them in great drops: a man no longer dared to put his hand on his rifle, for the barrel was burning hot as if it had been in a fire. The reflection of the sun's rays from the trail, covered with a thick bed of white dust, was blinding. Their shirts were clinging to sticky backs.

And the bare unsheltered trail mounted toward the cloudless sky.

It was nearly one o'clock in the afternoon when the column reached the plateau. Moreira Cesar ordered a halt.

It was a plateau of chalk and loose stones, grayish in color, without trees, shrubs, or grass. The men—apart from those who rode, they nearly all suffered from dizziness—flopped on the baking soil. But they were not able to remain outstretched for long: they wriggled like worms swept by the flame of a blowpipe. Some stood wafting their handkerchiefs to fan a little air from a fearful stillness.

Moreira was sitting, his back against the wheel of a cannon, with Colonel Tamarindo and Major Valladarès.

"I think, colonel," said the latter, "that if we reach Tanguinha today, we should do well to wait there until tomorrow night before resuming the march. No man will stand up to this infernal sun."

"At what o'clock does the moon rise?" Moreira asked.

"I don't know," said Valladarès.

Moreira Cesar shrugged his shoulders and said scornfully:

"You propose a night march in a dangerous zone to me and you don't even know if there's moonlight!"

"The zone isn't dangerous as far as Monte Santo," Valladarès asserted. "At least according to the information given to me."

"And supposing this information is wrong? Rely only on yourself. I don't rely on information provided by the local inhabitants. These jagunços can have accomplices."

"In any case, for my part I should risk the night march."

For once Moreira Cesar allowed himself to be convinced. The sun justified his decision. Under the brutal action of the heat his heart was beating violently: he had a feeling as if his legs and arms were shaking and on the top of his head he felt a sort of burning which was demoralizing him.

It was three o'clock in the afternoon when he gave the order to resume the march. The heat was reaching its height. It came down from the sky with such intensity that it could almost be touched: it rose from the ground in waves which interrupted the breathing. The men got up painfully, dazed, reeling, drunk with the heat and the glare. Ranks were re-formed: the Gauchos sprang into the saddle, excepting one man who remained laid out near his horse. A corporal went up, seized him by the shoulder, and shook him.

"Are you ill?"

The man did not reply. His body was limp and his head wobbled as if it were almost detached from the trunk. Major da Rocha went to him and put his hand on the man's heart.

"He's dead," he said, standing up.

He went off to inform Moreira Cesar.

"Put him over his horse," said the colonel. "We'll bury him at Tanguinha."

The column began to go downhill. In the ground at the bottom there was a well of cool water where the men could quench their thirst, but, as the yield from it was poor and formed only a small pool, this took much time. The men went to it three at a time, knelt down and drank direct from the pool like dogs.

"Make haste," commanded Moreira Cesar. "At that rate we won't be at Tanguinha before midnight."

The men obeyed: they did not drink their fill, contenting themselves with refreshing their mouths slightly. They were very frightened in the presence of the chief.

The Gauchos' horses also wanted to drink but were prevented from doing so.

"They can wait until we get to Tanguinha," Moreira decided.

It was 4:30 P.M. The sun's violence did not seem to have abated. The column was now following a stony road in the valley, one covered with little round pebbles like shingle and as hot as the inside of a stove. In the distance they could make out the trail mounting straight toward the summit of a sierra which the native Indian and *caboclos*, half-breed laborers, called *morro acima*, "top peak." There were still no trees, shrubs, or grass; and not a single house.

One would have said that the men had lost their habit of speech. Even the officers were no longer saying anything. Moreira Cesar, who had taken his place between the Pernambucans and Bahians, sat on his horse stiff and silent.

When the column began the ascent of the mountain, the sun was going down toward the horizon. The men took courage again. They were heard encouraging each other: "*Vamos gente!*"—"Come on, fellows!" Nevertheless they continued to breathe in gasps, for a heavy heat was still rising from the ground and deep wafts of hot air contracted the chest.

They reached the summit of the sierra about six o'clock. From there they could make out, at the bottom of the valley which extends to the foot of the other slope, a little fazenda and half-a-dozen small houses surrounded by a few palms and banana trees. That was Tanguinha. They could reach there in two hours' march. Fortunately the trail led downward, and the flaming sky in the west indicated that the sun was at the end of its course.

The air became suddenly cooler the moment the column reached the valley. The men rebuttoned their short jackets and began to breathe more deeply. Flesh which had become flabby under the action of the heat became consistent again, like those leaves which go limp under the hot sun and stiffen up vigorously in the evening mist. Some half-breeds began to sing a nostalgic *choro* and the Negroes gave rhythm to a samba.

"Well," said Moreira Cesar to Tamarindo and Valladarès who were trudging along at each side of him. "What did I tell you? The men are much tougher than you think."

For all that, the Gauchos remained silent. Although they were on horseback, they had felt the bite of the sun more severely than the Pernambucans and Bahians, who were more adapted to the climate. They had lost their proud and easy bearing and sat listlessly on mounts which were beginning to totter at each step.

They arrived at Tanguinha at about 8:30 P.M. without incident except for the Gaucho who had died on the plateau of Serra Branco from a clot of blood.

Moreira ordered two bullocks to be slaughtered. They were roasted in quarters on two wood fires while the inhabitants of the place gave a hand in preparing some maize flour in camp kettles. Well into the night the soldiers could be seen sitting in the corral of the fazenda and around the houses, heartily devouring great pieces of tough meat and rolling little balls of cooked maize flour in the palms of their hands.

The whole of the next day was spent in complete relaxation. The men lay still in the fazenda, in the big shed and in the houses, or in the shade of the trees, hardly stirring except to eat at eleven o'clock in the forenoon and five in the evening.

At seven o'clock, the moment the moon appeared above the sierra, Moreira gave the signal for leaving. The men were alert, rollicking and happy not to have in front of them the prospect of another march under that sun. Under the stars they were prepared to go to the end of the earth.

"Yours was a good idea, Valladarès," conceded Moreira Cesar. "I'm glad I decided on this night march."

He himself felt more sprightly and not so prostrate.

The journey of about eighteen miles to Monte Santo was achieved without difficulty and at a normal pace. It was five o'clock in the morning when the head of the column entered the village.

Monte Santo is known not only as the "Road to Paradise" which enjoyed its fame in the days of Sylvio Silveira. It is also known as "Watering Point" in the event of drought. All the muleteers halt there, for it is a sort of oasis in the middle of an arid desolate zone. Within a radius of less than three miles around the village, the hills are covered with forests, the valleys offer natural verdant pasture lands which are well watered by the Cariaca River. Plantations of sugar cane, manioc, and bananas surround the cluster of houses concealed amid thickly wooded orchards.

Since this village was quite important, there was no difficulty about billeting the soldiers in the sheds, huts, and houses. Moreira Cesar and Valladarès were lodged with the political chief who put at their disposal two rooms, each with a wooden bed and a stool.

"We haven't apartments like those in Rio. You understand, we're in the campo, right in the country," the political chief—a thin bald little man of forty with side whiskers—thought it necessary to explain in order to excuse the simplicity of his lodging.

"We're soldiers," retorted Moreira Cesar. "But there's a service I'm going to ask of you. We need a guide to lead us to Canudos. Can you get one for us? I suppose you have men here who know the roads well?"

"I shouldn't like to pledge my word on that, colonel," replied the political chief reservedly. "Nobody goes to Canudos. People no longer dare to venture in that direction."

"I must have a guide," snapped Moreira. "Find one. You won't delude me into believing that there's nobody here who knows the road to Canudos."

"Very well, colonel, I'll take the matter in hand," the thin little man replied obsequiously.

At noon he had not yet found a trace of one.

"This is a white-livered lot," growled Moreira. "They know the road but they don't want to go with the army. They're scared stiff. All right! I'll do without a guide; I don't need one. I've never needed one. Get out of my sight!"

4. The Guide

MAJOR VALLADARÈS was not on his first expedition. He had already taken part in quelling several riotings and even in the suppression of a minor rebellion in the direction of Ilheos. But he did not like to dash headlong into an adventure. Besides, he did not altogether like Moreira Cesar's way of sending everybody to blazes on the pretence that he did not need anybody. In his opinion it was a serious mistake to go without a guide into this unknown, dangerous, and even mysterious region which lay between Monte Santo and Canudos.

While the colonel was lolling in his armchair having his siesta, Valladarès went down to the village square (the commercial square, common to all villages), directing his steps toward the botequim: for, as a man experienced in the ways of the interior, he knew that if there was a guide to be found, it was in the botequim he would find him. The botequim in Monte Santo was a store with only four arcades: the counter was only about ten yards long. In the corner, to the right, half-a-dozen men in leather trousers, and wearing the leather hats usual in the hinterland, were having quite a lively discussion as they made play with their riding whips. A few yards away, to the left, there was one who stood by himself drinking rum. Still further to the left some women were making purchases.

Valladarès approached the men:

"Good morning, senhores . . . May I ask you for a little information? You're from this region, I suppose?"

"We're from Bom Conselho."

"Where's that?"

"About eighteen miles north of here."

"You know the parts around Canudos?"

"We don't go in that direction since the Conseilheiro settled there: it's too dangerous."

"But before that you used to go, didn't you? You know the road?"

The muleteers gave him an almost mocking look as if to say: "We see what you're up to, but that won't take us in."

"As a matter of fact, we used to know it," a long thin fellow admitted, "but we don't know it any more. All the trails are obliterated. Some of them for sure are obstructed by brambles."

"Several of them are," said a voice behind them. "You can't any longer even go to Canudos by Rosario."

This was the solitary individual who, drinking rum by himself, was now joining in the conversation.

"Do you yourself know the region?" Valladarès was quick to ask.

"I went through it recently."

"Where are you from?"

"Geremoabo. It's a bit further away than Canudos."

Valladarès scrutinized him closely. He was a half-breed of medium height, thick-set, broad-shouldered, and clad in a pair of old blue linen trousers, a dirty shirt, and wearing an ancient felt hat with holes in it.

"Are you a muleteer?" asked the major.

"No, I'm a *caboclo*, a farm laborer. But I have a horse."

He pointed to his horse tied to a stake outside.

"Could you guide us to Canudos?"

"Guide who?"

"The Army."

The half-breed thought for a moment, drank his rum and replied:

"It's a dangerous business. The jagunços will attack you. If someday they get to know that I'm the man who guided you, they'll down me. You understand: I live in this region. I've got to keep on my guard."

Valladarès did not wish to drop him.

"You have nothing to be afraid of," he retorted. "After we have passed that way there will be no more jagunços: they're going to be exterminated and Canudos will be reduced to ashes."

The half-breed drank another glass of rum and, after a moment's reflection, seemed to have made up his mind:

"I'd greatly like to guide you," he said, "but not as far as Canudos. A mile and a half or so before getting there I'll leave you. I'll willingly show you the direction, but I don't want to get mixed up in battles: I'm no soldier."

"That's all right. Come with me."

He dragged him to the political chief's house where Moreira Cesar who had just waked up was stretching himself to loosen his slightly stiffened muscles.

"I've got a guide, colonel," he said, going in and presenting the half-breed.

"Ah!" said Moreira Cesar looking the recruit up and down. "You know the route?"

"There are several of them. I know the one I always take when I'm returning home."

"Is it a good track?"

"There's no longer any good track in that direction; there's not one wide enough to get through. This one's the best."

"Good. We'll leave tomorrow morning. Hold yourself in readiness."

Valladarès handed over the half-breed to some Pernambucans billeted in the next house, enjoining them to keep an eye on him.

Moreira Cesar wanted their departure to be spectacular. It was necessary to give the population the impression that the hour of their deliverance had struck. The Federal Army was marching on Canudos.

At five o'clock in the morning the troops were lined up on the square, Bahians to the left, Pernambucans to the right and, in the rear, the Gauchos.

"Where's the guide?" asked the colonel who was curvetting on his horse in front of the troops.

"Over there, beside the Pernambucans: the man holding his horse by the bridle," replied Valladarès.

"What's that bouncer's name?"

"Domingos Texeira."

"Texeira!" yelled Moreira. "Take the head of the column."

Then, facing the troops:

"Shoulder—arms! Move to the right in fours— Forward!"

The bugles blared, beating out the time of the "Rio Grande March," rending the silence of the little town. The column moved off.

And the sun rose above the sierra.

During the first hour they went over cultivated fields, then through some thickets and next through a little wood. It was cool and the soldiers were full of zest.

Having crossed a hill covered with coarse grasses, they suddenly entered the arid zone. One would have said that a cataclysm had laid the region waste, sweeping away every trace of life. The landscape had become mineral. As far as one could see there was no vegetation.

Under the devastating sun the column trailed uphill and down, extending in valleys narrowly enclosed between cliffs of white quartz which reflected the light fiendishly. The men, saturated with perspiration, did not sing; they advanced wilting under the severity of the heat.

With the exception of Moreira Cesar, the officers could not help feeling dismayed as they saw themselves penetrating so far into a hostile inhuman country that was formidably mysterious. They had the feeling that they were advancing by guesswork, for no trace of any track could be perceived. The three thousand men of the Federal Army were delivered over to the whim of that guide who rode at their head sitting upright on his horse like a drover at the head of a herd of cattle and leading them to the slaughterhouse. It made Valladarès shudder.

Moreira Cesar had decided that they would break off the march at midday. But he changed his mind. After a brief halt, during which the soldiers were asked to eat some iron ration biscuits, the column set out again under that terrifying sun.

Although he would not admit it, Moreira Cesar was very ill at ease to find himself in these lonely places: the desert set his nerves on edge. He was eager to find himself in the presence of the jagunços. He remembered the remark made by the governor of Bahia: the main thing is to get to Canudos. He regretted not having listened to the report of that young police officer from Joazeiro. But with him regrets were short-lived. He was a man of action.

At about two o'clock in the afternoon they went down into a little plain entirely covered with brambles—lianas as thick as the handle of a hoe, without leaves but having enormous thorns as hard as spurs, whose prick was extremely painful. The Pernambucan said that these scrub brambles were called *cunanans*—botanists name them *Euphorbia phosphorus*—and that they were very dangerous: their pricks were poisonous and caused big abscesses. The brambles were all hung with great webs to which fat black spiders were clinging. It was necessary to go right across this plain but the track which, as the guide had said, had not been kept in use, hardly gave passage for one man. The column had to extend in Indian file.

Moreira was biting his lips in rage. He was very well aware that, if he were attacked during the crossing of this plain, his troops would be crushed. He hailed the guide. Texeira, who was by this time involved among the brambles, had difficulty in getting back to him.

"You couldn't have found any other way?" roared Moreira. "This is a death trap. We could have gone around that hill on the right."

"No, colonel. That side of the road is barred by a precipice. There's a falling of land and only this trail is left."

Moreira resigned himself: he would rely on good luck. Meanwhile he held his Gauchos in reserve in the event of a flank attack.

It all went off without incident. By the end of two hours the army had crossed the sea of brambles. It was four o'clock: the men were worn out, completely tired out. Several had been pricked and had drawn blood with scratching; others were rolling on the ground, victims of violent colics. Some twenty horses were lacerated by the brambles. Affonso Amaral, the young medical officer attached to the expedition, came to find Moreira Cesar and declared that it was not possible to go any further. The men were at the end of their strength and the number of ailing was going to increase in such proportions that the Medical Service would be overwhelmed.

"Mind your own business," Moreira Cesar replied to him. "I don't have to take orders or advice from a greenhorn like you. You see quite well that there's no means of camping here: it's bare land."

And, turning to Valladarès:

"Call the guide. In spite of everything there must be a muleteers' rancho somewhere, a resting place near a well where we could make a halt."

Valladarès sent a Bahian noncommissioned officer to look for Texeira. In a quarter of an hour he returned alone.

"The guide's not to be found," he said. "He's disappeared."

"What!" shrieked Moreira. "They've allowed him to get away? That beats everything! And he's been able to clear off in this way without being seen or detained by anybody!"

"The men are so exhausted that they've not bothered about the guide."

"Shut up! Get out of here! Let me not see you again! You all deserve to be shot!"

He was as red as a turkey cock and gesticulating violently with his short arms. Had he been able to fix responsibility on a few men for the guide's escape, he would have killed them there and then.

"Calm yourself, colonel," Valladarès said to him. "We can't now be so very far from Canudos. We'll get out of this. I'm going to make arrangements for the encampment."

"Place a cordon of sentries. I wonder if that guide has drawn us into a trap. Perhaps he has directed us on a false trail."

"I don't think so. He's sheered off because he's afraid of being dragged into the battle."

"We'll soon see."

That evening the men had again to be content with an iron ration biscuit. They could have killed a couple of bullocks but they had no firewood to roast them with.

The night seemed to justify Valladarès: it passed without incident and at dawn the march was resumed on a trail which, by a miracle, was fairly easy to see. At about eleven o'clock they came to a valley covered with brambles, but here the track was a little wider. The army went into it. It was at that moment that the first shot rang out. A Bahian collapsed with a short dull cry. The shot came from a hillock to the left, beyond the brambles. Moreira Cesar gave the order to halt and sent two Gauchos to inspect the terrain to the right. They soon returned saying that there must have been a landslide on that side, as great blocks of rock obstructed the passage.

"Forward!" commanded Moreira who decided to go through at any cost.

Another shot cracked from the same place and a Gaucho collapsed on his saddle.

"Pick a few good marksmen, Valladarès, and let that fellow have a volley of bullets."

Valladarès lined up a dozen men who peppered the hillock with bullets. But a shot came from a cliff on the right near the end of the valley. A Pernambucan fell beside Moreira Cesar.

"Take your place in the rear, colonel," advised the major. "It wouldn't do for anything whatever to happen to you at a time when we need you."

The colonel drew himself up proudly on his horse.

"What do you take me for?" he retorted arrogantly. "Moreira Cesar doesn't know fear. He knows only what his duty is. Moreira Cesar always marches in front."

However, as the guide's disappearance worried him, he decided to send ahead of the column a patrol of scouts selected from the best of the Pernambucans who were used to the sierra.

This patrol, made up of a dozen men, went ahead and began to explore the terrain actively, for nothing sets the soldier's nerve on edge like invisible pressure in guerrilla warfare.

The army had come out of the brambles, but, in the closed-in valley which it was following, shots succeeded one another in an increasingly rapid rhythm. Meanwhile the enemy never once appeared. The ground was bare, deserted. One might well wonder whence those jagunços popped up, and in what direction they made themselves scarce. On several occasions Valladarès launched sudden sharp attacks with cavalry on the places from which the shots came. The Gauchos swooped at full gallop and, when they reached the point in mind, the phantom sharpshooters had vanished.

Demoralization was beginning to affect the troops, weakened by the unbearable heat and a march in the hot sand in which they sank up to their ankles. The colonel resolved to call a halt at the first rancho or fazenda they should come to.

The trail left the sandy terrain: it became stony again and led into a gorge. The patrol had thoroughly scouted over the two hills between which the trail ran, and the column entered the gorge. It had moved almost entirely into the defile and outside in the open nothing remained but the guns and bullocks when the attack against them was launched.

The artillerymen who were asleep on their ammunition wagons, and the cattle drovers, walking with eyes half-closed to save them from the reflection of the sunlight, would not have been able to tell where the jagunços came from. The enemy had risen up suddenly in front of them. The soldiers hardly had time to take to their heels and dash toward the gorge when they heard the war cry: "Long live the Conseilheiro! Long live the good Jesus!" This time it was not a matter of isolated marksmen.

With impetuous verve some jagunços had thrown themselves on the guns and overturned them, while others were shooting point-blank at the Gauchos caught in the gorge. Colonel Tamarindo, who was on the spot, tried to make the horsemen half-turn to get them to charge the enemy, but the trail was completely shut in: and this attempt ended only in creating an indescribable chaos of bucking horses and men hanging onto their horses like acrobats. Moreira Cesar, warned of what was happening, rushed there.

"On foot! On foot!" he yelled. "And attack with the knife."

In a moment the Gauchos had sprung from their saddles and hurled themselves into the attack. Corporal Claudio Barbosa, a veteran from the Chaco War, with experience of battles of this nature on the frontier of Paraguay, encouraged his troops shouting: "At them, men!"

The jagunços seemed to be under the command of a huge Negro naked to the waist belt. He was yelling and brandishing his big *jacaré*—alligator knife, a weapon with a stout broad blade—and he threw himself like a mass into the free fight. Barbosa knew that in such cases one must aim to get the chief. Pushing aside two Gauchos, he forced his way in the direction of the Negro. A jagunço rose up in front of him: the corporal struck him down with a knife thrust right in the belly and then hurled himself on the Negro. But the giant was supple. He dodged the blow and his jacaré would have been driven into Barbosa's back when the latter, throwing himself on the ground, seized the Negro's right leg and toppled him over. Barbosa was already on him and raising his knife. The Negro quickly grasped him by the wrist and twisted it relentlessly and then, straightening himself up with a powerful effort of his back muscles, planted his hooked fingers in the Gaucho's throat. The Negro picked up his jacaré and cut his throat.

Meanwhile the Gauchos were gradually gaining the upper hand and the jagunços suddenly gave way and began to flee toward a fold in the ground about fifty yards distant.

"Fire!" yelled Moreira Cesar. "Let them have it!" There was a crackle of firing which was kept up. With the exception of two, the

men in flight did not succeed in reaching cover. The huge Negro
was seen to beat the air with his enormous arms and fall on the
ground.

The action had been hot. There were dead and wounded; some
horses had broken the bones of their feet and the bullocks were
scattered. They had to be got together again, the guns righted, and
the horses that were no longer fit for use had to be killed.

"Leave the dead on the side of the road, we'll recover them tomorrow," ordered Moreira Cesar. "And put the wounded on the
ammunition wagons."

The sky became flaming red announcing the setting of the sun.
The march was resumed. Notwithstanding the "victory" the men
were weary and made their way in silence. All who had taken part
in the battle were consumed by the burning thirst which is caused
by any effort under that sun.

It was only after a march of an hour and a half that they discovered two little huts beside a well in the depth of a narrow valley. This was the place called Rosario.

That evening the troops camped in the open air and they did not
eat, for the reserve biscuits were exhausted and there was no wood
to cook food. This did not really matter very much to the men: they
bore hunger well, and it was not the first time that they lived "on
the breeze," as they said in their slang to indicate the days on which
they did not eat.

Fortunately they could quench their thirst. The water was sweet
and cool.

5. The Crisis

Moreira Cesar had installed himself with Valladarès in one of the
two ranchos or little huts, the other being occupied by Colonel
Tamarindo and Captain Vieira. These ranchos had two rooms
separated by a partition of woven bamboo. There was neither bed,
stool, nor straw, so that the colonel would have had to lie down

on the beaten earth had they not discovered a few small planks which served to make what looked like a bunk for him.

As they were then in the danger zone, Valladarès had organized a guard of sentries and patrols. At about one o'clock in the morning, when the colonel was snoring and snorting strongly, Valladarès went out to make an inspection, because, exhausted as the men were, it was to be feared that they would fall asleep at their posts. Valladarès ascertained that they were wide awake. They were sturdy men. As soon as the sun went down they no longer remembered the fatigue of the day.

Satisfied, the major turned back toward the ranchos and was looking at the stars when he heard a cry like that of a man struck down by a knife wound; and it seemed to him that this cry came from his rancho where he had left the colonel. He quickened his pace, stepping over men sleeping here and there on the ground.

Four Gauchos were standing in front of the rancho. Their attitude was uneasy like that of people wondering whether or not to go in.

"The colonel cried out," one of them said . . . "We didn't know what we ought to do. Two men have gone in to see . . ."

Valladarès then went in. At first he could not perceive anything. Everything was in impenetrable darkness.

"What's the matter, colonel?" he asked.

One of the Gauchos whom he could not see replied:

"He cried out. We came and asked him what was the matter, but he doesn't answer. It was a strange cry. He doesn't budge. He's as if he was dead."

"Light a candle," said Valladarès.

"We haven't one."

"Find some. There are men who have them. Come now! Make haste."

A few moments later a Pernambucan brought two ends of a carnauba candle.

Valladarès lit one and stuck it in the ground in the middle of the room. Then he lit the other and moved it to and fro above Moreira Cesar's face. The colonel's countenance was contracted in a grin in which laughter and pain were mingled. The lips on the right corner of his mouth were twisted downward; the nostrils were dilated. His

wide open eyes under the yellow light of the candle gave a strange
reflection like that of still water.

"I'll go and call the doctor," said a Gaucho.

"No," Valladarès ordered. "Remain here. Don't move. I know
what it is."

On the eve—it might be—of the attack on Canudos, the troops
must not be disconcerted by spreading the rumor that their leader
was having an epileptic fit. To call the doctor would be to give the
alarm.

Valladarès was aware that the colonel was subject to fits of this
nature. This was one of them. Moreira Cesar held his hands clenched
on his stomach as if he would tear out his intestines, and one of his
legs was folded underneath him.

"We could stretch out that leg for him," one of the Gauchos
advised timidly.

"Don't touch him," interrupted Valladarès who knew that an
epileptic must not be disturbed during a fit.

They all three moved back against the bamboo partition and
waited in silence, looking at Moreira Cesar's motionless rigid body.

The piece of candle which Valladarès had fixed in the ground had
burned out. The wick was floating in the molten wax. The flame
gave a few flickers and died out. But the other piece which the
major was still holding in his hand could give them light for a
little longer.

"Shut the door," said Valladarès. "The night's getting cold."

He was impatient to see the colonel return to himself. He wondered what they would do if he were to disappear. Tamarindo did
not strike him as the man to lead in the battle against the jagunços.
Then he suddenly thought that, if the colonel were to pass out, he
would be reproached for not having called the doctor: he suddenly
grasped the seriousness of his responsibility. What was to be done?
He wiped away the cold sweat that was forming in drops on his
forehead.

At that moment a shot rang out in the far distance, its echo
reverberating for a long time through the sierras. Valladarès gave
a start. "If only he regains consciousness before the attack!" He
looked fixedly at the colonel's face: it still presented the same grin,

and the eyes remained in a state of immobility which froze one.

The candle was getting less in the major's hand. He was thinking of sending one of the men to find another and then gave up the idea: the man would talk. For the men must not know of this. . . .

Moreira Cesar made a move as if to turn himself on his side. He freed his leg and Valladarès saw him stretch himself as if he were being controlled by a tired spring.

The candle was about to go out when the colonel sat up.

"It's finished. You may go," said Valladarès to the two Gauchos. "You see, he was just slightly out of sorts."

And he let the candle fall. In the black darkness Moreira Cesar's voice rose:

"Is that you, Valladarès?"

"Yes, colonel."

"No incidents in the course of the night?"

"Nothing so far."

"Good. Warn the officers: muster before dawn. We're going to set out. Yesterday's attack indicates that we're not far from Canudos. I should like to reach there today."

"You're not thinking of that, colonel? The men are not in a state to sustain this effort and, if we do arrive at Canudos, they'll have to fight. They haven't eaten anything and they've had only a few hours' sleep."

"It's an order," the colonel rapped out.

About an hour before sunrise the vibrant and cheerful notes of the bugles and trumpets sounded in the little valley. One would have said they were setting out for a fete or a grand parade. Passing along in front of the troops, Moreira Cesar called out to them: "We're going to have our morning meal in Canudos!"

The soldiers were in a state of enthusiasm. They had had enough of marches under the hot sun. Now they were almost at their goal. They were ready to make this last effort to reach it rapidly. The battle? They were not even thinking of it: they felt themselves strong, and under the command of a leader who was unconquered and unconquerable. And then those jagunços had only old-fashioned firearms and they had no guns: the danger was not great.

The column advanced recklessly, preceded by a patrol of Gauchos, through closed-in valleys and, when passing a watering point named

Angico, six Bahians were laid on the ground by a volley from at least twenty rifles. With a promptness which astonished even Moreira Cesar, Captain Vieira launched a lightning attack on the hill. The jagunços had vanished.

These sudden disappearances, inexplicable on such naked terrain, struck home on the soldiers' spirits and gave them the idea that the jagunços were bewitched, elusive beings, and still further intensified their desire to arrive at Canudos. Canudos, at least, would be visible. And they would fight face to face.

"If they imagine that they can escape punishment with a few guerrilla actions they're very much mistaken," said Moreira Cesar to galvanize the troops.

The column skirted a rounded hillock and then began to climb a hill above which was a little plateau. They had hardly reached the top when the Gauchos, who led the march, turned right about and went down again at a gallop, raising their arms and shouting: "Canudos! Canudos!"

Moreira did not feel like believing them. He could not understand why the jagunços had allowed the army to approach so close to their town without attempting to bar the way. But, when he himself had reached the plateau, and he was able to perceive in the valley the sea of red roofs of a mass of houses which in that desert seemed enormous, he knew that he was in front of the holy city of the hinterland.

It was eleven o'clock in the morning.

Valladarès would have liked to give the troops an hour or two of respite. In the course of previous expeditions he had been able to see for himself that men who are tired out by marches in the sun would not be capable of stopping the impetus of well-rested bandits. But the colonel was not of this opinion, and he decided to open the attack immediately.

With the aid of binoculars he began by taking a good look at the town. To the right rose the tall spires of the church glittering white in the midday sunshine. The main square was deserted. On the terrain enclosed in the bend of the river there was the dense agglomeration of red-roofed houses around the church square; then, to the left, they were more scattered as far as a hill on the which rose houses of the same type but with red frontages. A single street could be made out: it began at the main square and ran in the direction of the Cannabrava sierra.

Before deploying his troops, Moreira Cesar had the two .75 guns placed in position and gave the order for two shells to be fired on the town.

At twelve-thirty two violent explosions such as had never been heard in the valley of the Vasa Barris rent the silence. Turning proudly to the group of officers around him, Moreira Cesar remarked:

"Those are two visiting cards for Antonio Conseilheiro!"

6. The Attack

AFTER Pajehu's departure, the Canudos chiefs lived in a state of feverish anticipation. Every evening João Abbade, Sariema, and Dr. Quadrado met in the Conseilheiro's house. There was nothing for them to say to each other and they sat for hours without speaking, or even thinking. They were waiting for Pajehu because Pajehu represented the sum of all their hopes.

"If he gets caught," Abbade said one day, "it's all up with us."

"Never!" roared the Conseilheiro. "We'll fight to the last man."

"All the same, we'd have a better chance if we had Pajehu here," said Abbade, who realized that, apart from the half-breed, nobody was capable of taking command at Canudos.

They held their patience for three days, expecting from one moment to the next to see Moreira Cesar's troops loom up on the sierra.

In the early part of the morning of the fourth day a horseman was seen coming down the slopes of the Favella at full gallop. Every one of them recognized Pajehu by his bearing and style of riding.

When he arrived on the square a crowd was already forming there and the people greeted him with enthusiastic cheers. He thanked them with a sharp gesture and went into the Conseilheiro's house with Abbade and Sariema.

"Well then?" said the Conseilheiro in his sepulchral voice.

"They're arriving. They'll be here tomorrow afternoon or the day after tomorrow. I left them a little this side of Cajareiras. From that place onward they couldn't take any trail other than the one which passes through Rosario. Hence we're certain not to be surprised from the rear."

"And how did you manage to be able to follow them?"

"I didn't follow them. I guided them," retorted Pajehu proudly.

"*Guided* them?"

"Yes. I passed myself off as a certain Texeira of Geremoabo and they asked me to guide them to Canudos. I agreed but warned them that I'd follow the route I usually take, and that I'd leave them a little before reaching here, because I didn't want to have trouble with the jagunços. They understood my point of view and said they agreed."

"And they allowed you to go off after Cajareiras?"

"No. I just cleared off. They were worn out after getting into those poisonous brambles, the *cunanans*. I found myself with some Pernambucans. I told the troops that I was going to see whether there was water in a well that I knew of. Naturally they thought that a very fine idea. And I cleared out. It's a pity I can't be on both sides at the same time! If I'd only had Pedrão's battalion at my disposal I should have wiped out Moreira Cesar's whole gang while they were stuck in the brambles."

"Pedrão sent some men with João Grande. They overturned the guns but only two of them returned and João Grande was killed."

"That didn't serve any purpose. When we attack, we must attack in strength."

"Why didn't you kill Moreira Cesar?" Sariema asked.

"You fathead. I wanted to see you down a leader at the head of his troops."

"And now what?" asked the Conseilheiro. "What are we to do? Shall we attack them on the Favella when they get there?"

"No," said Pajehu. "Leave it to me. It's going to be a hard job."

João Abbade was looking with admiration at the man who had the audacity to propose himself as guide to Moreira Cesar. This exploit revived his vacillating confidence.

As Pajehu had announced, the federal troops appeared on the

Favella height the day after next a little before noon; and at twelve-thirty Antonio received Moreira Cesar's two visiting cards. They did not produce the effect which the colonel expected. As those shells did not kill anybody, the jagunços reckoned that artillery was not as dangerous as it was said to be.

Pajehu had his reasons for guiding the government troops on to the Favella. It is in fact on that side that the contours of the terrain render the approaches to Canudos very difficult. The troops would have to go down into narrow valleys and then cross the Vasa Barris River at the place where most of the houses were, and these houses would be small fortresses. If the federals should succeed in forcing their way so far, they would then have to fight with the river and the mountain in their rear.

Moreira Cesar was somewhat astonished to see that the jagunços made no attempt to hinder the deployment of the troops. He had expected a lively resistance and he was wondering whether the town had not been abandoned, for he could not discover any sign of life.

Taking the Valley of Death, the Pernambucans proceeded to the right toward the mouth of the Umburanas River, while the Bahians, descending by the Massacara road, went on to occupy the slopes of the Pellados, a bluff which stood facing the church. The Gauchos took up their position on the Geremoabo road.

On the colonel's command the bugles sounded the charge. Negroes from Bahia and men of mixed breed from Pernambuco dashed to the assault. They had first to cross the Vasa Barris. The bed of the river was about thirty yards wide but at this period it was almost dry and formed only a little brook two or three yards in width and not deep: the water did not come up to the knees. It hardly constituted an obstacle and here was an exposed area in which the soldiers were subjected to the murderous fire of jagunços sheltered in the houses. Nevertheless, well-spattered with bullets, the Bahians and Pernambucans advanced intrepidly and, in spite of quite heavy losses, succeeded in getting a foothold on the other bank. They penetrated into the town.

Elated, Moreira Cesar drafted the text of a telegram which he entrusted to a Gaucho to take to Queimadas at full gallop, for the colonel kept to his reputation as a man of quick action. This text read:

> *In front of Canudos. Punishment near. Federal troops have entered the town. —Moreira Cesar.*

The same day the telegraphs transmitted the news to all the state capitals in the republic.

Meanwhile the battle was assuming very strange features. The troops which had penetrated into Canudos had to sneak along the narrow little streets of the town: they were advancing only very slowly, for it was necessary to lay siege to each dwelling. The jagunços were defending themselves fiercely. From doors and windows, from the roof tops of houses they shot down the assailants. The battle disintegrated into a multitude of minor fights. If half-a-dozen soldiers attacked a house, two or three immediately went down under the bullets of the better-covered jagunços. The door gave way under the blows of rifle butts of others; but then one or two jagunços, or alternatively one or two women armed with long jacarés—alligator knives—hurled themselves on the attackers with aggravated fury and knifed them before they had time to use their weapons.

By the end of an hour, wounded Pernambucans and Bahians were to be seen going back across the river. Then others rose into view: they seemed to be demented as if coming out of a fiery furnace. The movement became more pronounced from minute to minute. It became clear that the army was beating a retreat.

Moreira Cesar went forward in a terrible rage.

"What the blazes are they doing backing out there? And they're well supported too."

In fact, on the Favella height the guns thundered unceasingly. The shells were bursting in every corner of the town. More than ten fires had sprung up, their flames rising in sheets toward the intensely blue sky. One had the impression that the whole town was about to go up in flames.

Valladarès who, from the Pellados rising, was following the battle at the colonel's side, said:

"It would perhaps be a good thing to sound the retreat and regroup the men . . ."

Moreira Cesar jumped.

"Is it the word 'retreat' that you said, major? You don't know me. I'm inside the town. There I remain. We're going to settle this business. Get the Gauchos going."

"On foot?"

"Are you crazy? On horseback, major. Make them occupy the church square. From there they'll spread out in the town. We're going to break up the resistance of these bandits."

Valladarès communicated the chief's order. Nevertheless he thought the idea preposterous. On the church square the Gauchos were going to become an easy target for jagunços ensconced in every house. And how could men on horseback penetrate into little narrow streets where the infantrymen could hardly get through?

From the beginning the operation, clearly, was even more catastrophic than they supposed it to be. The Gauchos began to cross the Vasa Barris opposite the church. Now Pajehu had placed in the spires his best marksmen armed with the Mauser carbines collected at the time of the massacre of Braz Barroso's company; so that, before coming to the square, the Gauchos were already thoroughly decimated. Once on the open space the situation became worse. From all the houses came a sustained fusillade, a veritable raking fire, point-blank. Disconcerted and without an objective to attack, the horsemen turned about and went back again at a gallop across the Vasa Barris.

When he saw this movement, Moreira Cesar made a gesture of irritation.

"Bring me my horse. Immediately," he said. "I'm going to put some zest into those fellows."

He sprang into the saddle and went down the slope of the Pellados toward the Geremoabo road followed by Lieutenant Avila. He had hardly covered two hundred yards when he sank on his horse. Lieutenant Avila hurried to him.

"What's the matter, colonel?"

"It's nothing. A stray bullet . . . In the thigh . . . Take me to Valladarès."

"Can you keep in your saddle?"

"Yes. Lead me back."

The lieutenant seized the horse's bridle and went up the slope again. Suddenly the colonel uttered a hoarse cry, as if it came from the stomach.

"Colonel!" said Avila.

"It's all up," said Moreira Cesar. "This time they've got me properly."

He had just received a bullet in the back.

With the help of Valladarès they took him down from his horse. They laid him out on the ground.

"Quick, the doctor," said Valladarès.

"Where is he?"

"I don't know. Find him. No doubt he remained with the artillery on the Favella."

While Avila set off at a gallop, Valladarès knelt beside the colonel. Moreira Cesar had for so many years given himself an impassive mask that not a feature of his face moved: he merely closed his eyes as if he wished to concentrate all the pain within himself.

"Are you suffering, colonel?" Valladarès asked.

Moreira Cesar did not reply to the question but said:

"Send for Tamarindo. It's he who must take over command."

"Very well, colonel. I'll go and call him . . . Are you in pain?"

"There," said Moreira, pointing to his belly with a listless gesture.

Valladarès loosened his trousers and pulled up the bloodstained shirt. On the right side of his belly there was a dark stream of blood. The bullet had not entered the thigh but had perforated the intestines. Valladarès tried to staunch the wound with his handkerchief, but in a moment it was sticky with blood. He was perspiring in great beads which dropped on the colonel's chest.

When he got up from his knees, Valladarès had a feeling of emptiness as if he were the victim of an attack of vertigo. Gradually his vision became clearer. On his right the Pernambucans were recrossing the Vasa Barris in disorder: in front of him at the foot of the Pellados the Bahians were surging back toward the Massacara road, while the Gauchos, massed on the Geremoabo road, seemed to be awaiting orders. In Canudos itself the fusillade was cracking but on the Favella height the artillery had become silent. The seventy-one shells given to them—and deemed to be sufficient to kill the jagunços—had all been fired.

The situation was becoming tragic. Valladarès was in a state of nerves. He hailed the Bahians who were going up again toward the Favella.

"Tell Colonel Tamarindo to come here, urgently," he shouted to them.

"Where is he?"

"Find him. I'm giving you the order to send him here urgently."

Avila returned with the doctor and two stretcher-bearers. Amaral quickly examined the colonel's wounds in the stomach and back.

"We'll carry him to our ambulance," he said. "He can't be treated here."

When they had gone off carrying the chief, perhaps mortally wounded, Valladarès experienced a feeling of isolation. He was awaiting Colonel Tamarindo impatiently, for decisions had to be made. The army had been driven back to the right bank of the Vasa Barris. Would they resume the attack or decide to beat a retreat?

He caught sight of a man on horseback coming from the Geremoabo road and making his way at a gallop toward the Pellados. "That must be Tamarindo," he thought, dreading that it would not be he. It was the colonel. He sprang lightly from his horse although he was a tall solidly built man. He had a big head with close-cropped hair—this was the fashion at the time—and small blue eyes between fleshy eyelids hidden under thick eyebrows.

"You know the news?" asked Valladarès.

"I've just heard. It's a disaster."

"He said that the command reverts to you. What do you mean to do? We must act quickly."

"There's nothing to be done but order the retreat. This business is a failure. What do you think of it?"

"I think we ought to have beaten a retreat before now."

"We'll regroup the troops on the Favella and meet together by Monte Santo. There we'll see what's to be done. I'll send a report to the government."

But neither Tamarindo nor Valladarès had any idea of Pajehu's infernal genius.

7. The Rout

OFFICERS—captains, lieutenants, second-lieutenants—and even non-commissioned officers were running in increasing numbers to the command headquarters to receive instructions. They then received the order to regroup around the artillery on the plateau. Soon afterwards the whole army could be seen straggling in confusion up the slopes of the Favella. The jagunços did not take advantage of the opportunity: they made no attempt to impede the movement. When Tamarindo and Valladarès in their turn decided to regain the plateau, they were able to do so without being troubled, and there was the feeling among them that they could camp that evening at Rosario, so as to take the road for Monte Santo next day.

It was 5:30 P.M. The sun was approaching the crest of the Aracaty sierras. The fusillade in Canudos had ceased and nothing could be heard but the shouts of the soldiers hailing one another, or wounded men calling out for help.

At that moment the bell in Canudos began to toll the Angelus. The silence became so deep that even on the plateau could be heard the dull droning of the litanies.

The soldiers were all amazed. Apart from the Gauchos, they all —Bahians and Pernambucans—belonged to the same race as the jagunços. There were mysterious similarities between the temperaments of the men on both sides of this struggle. Astonished by the inexplicable reverse they had sustained, and the death of a leader whom they believed to be as invulnerable as he was invincible, the soldiers all but accepted the legend of the Conseilheiro's sacred personality. In their turn they also fell under the hoodoo of the prophet's mysticism. They were experiencing the sensation of having been repulsed by an invisible and invincible force, and they had only one aim: to flee, to flee as far away as possible! The pulsations of the bell in Canudos re-echoed within them like a knell.

The sun blazed on the horizon and then went down behind the mountain. The sky became covered with stars but the heat did not

diminish. It was one of those very hot nights which are not rare in
the hinterland, and in which every star gives the impression of being a source of heat. Behind the sierra of Cannabrava short flashes
of lightning began to flutter. Utterly exhausted, the men had thrown
themselves in confusion on the soil. They had not eaten for thirty-
six hours and they were burning with a fiery thirst. But they could
hope for a little water only on the way back, toward Angico.

On the right of the plateau there was a little shelter covered with
thatch from which in times past the Conseilheiro harangued the
multitude on certain feast days. It was there they had deposited
Moreira Cesar. The medical officer had dressed his wounds but
declared to Valladarès that the colonel would not recover from
them.

Tamarindo held council surrounded by some ten officers. It was
unanimously decided that the retreat must begin immediately:
they must take advantage of night. Tamarindo went in under the
shelter, knelt down and informed Moreira of the decision. The
wounded man clenched his fists, tried to raise himself on his elbows,
and then fell back with a groan. He shot a fierce glance at
Tamarindo:

"You're not ashamed, colonel?" he said. "Retreat, when you are
dominating the situation, when your artillery is intact, when you
still have at least two thousand men? One doesn't always succeed
in the first assault. Attack again at dawn."

"No," replied Tamarindo. "It was with unanimity that we decided
on retreat. We have no more shells and the men have reached the
limit of their strength."

Moreira Cesar raised his arm as if in a threat.

"You're not going to be guilty of this monstrous act of coward-
ice? . . . Not in my name . . . Not in my . . ."

He could not finish speaking. Blood came to his mouth, his arm
dropped. He was dead, taking with him to his grave the bitter-
ness and despair of his first defeat.

Tamarindo got up, made the sign of the cross and quickly rejoined the other officers as though he had just committed a crime.
He announced the death of their leader, but it went without comment. The officers had only one purpose—flight.

"So the order to leave is to be given, colonel?" a captain asked.

"Immediately . . . I think," he added, "that we must take Moreira Cesar's body."

They approved wholeheartedly.

"And the wounded?" asked Valladarès.

"The wounded," said Tamarindo with a vague gesture. "Those who can follow on . . . The others . . ."

"Let us get moving," said Captain Vieira. "We have no time to lose."

The orders went around and the army set out on the march in formidable disorder, for not one company had been re-formed. Cavalry was mixed with the infantry. Sentimental Negroes had loaded on their shoulders wounded comrades; they were jostled by brutish half-breeds trying to advance more quickly. The others had lost all authority. It was a rout. The troops were soon drawn out over the best part of a mile.

It was then that Pajehu launched his attack.

He had posted the black battalion on the slopes of the hills between which the road to Angico winds its way. When the troops were well into the gorge they were subjected point-blank to a volley from more than a thousand rifles. This was tragic. All those who had not been hit dashed in a mad race toward Angico, throwing away haversacks, belts, weapons, and ammunition. The mounted men hurled themselves through the mob crushing the wounded under the horses' hoofs. The fusillade from the jagunços continued, unrelenting. The men who were not yet caught in the gorge wanted to climb up again toward the Favella: but, from that direction, they were driven back by enemy pressure toward the road for Angico, for a tide of jagunços was coming up from the Umburanas River and the Valley of Death. There was nothing to do but to fight. Colonel Tamarindo, at that moment giving proof of vigor which he had hardly shown hitherto, ordered the bugles to sound the charge. The Pernambucans, who were ahead, charged resolutely at Pajehu's black battalion. A savage struggle took place; a fight with knives which both sides handled with equal dexterity, for they were all sons of the sierra. The battle developed in the intense heat of the night and amid deafening yells which prevented them from recognizing one another—for Pernambucans and jagunços were speaking the same language and uttering the same cries.

The jagunços were beginning to gain the upper hand when the Bahians, driven back from the plateau, came into line. The battle went on again, the men fighting tooth and nail. A hundred or so jagunços rose up on the Angico road, barring the way and firing on the Negroes.

While this fight to the death was proceeding in the gorge, the plateau was assailed by thousands of jagunços to the battle cries of: "Long live the good Jesus!"—"Long live the Conseilheiro!" Encircling the guns, the Negroes and Gauchos—the latter had abandoned their horses—fought like trapped panthers. Colonel Tamarindo himself animated the battle. A little half-breed gave him a stab with a *jacaré* knife which went right through his belly.

Gradually the fusillade died down and the yelling subsided; a great stillness again covered the battlefield from which arose only the feeble moans of the wounded.

The stars were shining without a twinkle in the clear sky. The heat reached a frightful intensity, as if nature was about to asphyxiate the living. A human odor which was at the same time insipid and musky—a mixed odor of whites and blacks—hung about in the air.

Sitting astride one of the Krupp guns, Pajehu lit a cigarette.

Pedrão was the first to join him again, then João Abbade. They did not speak to one another immediately. They were too tired to exchange impressions. At last Pajehu said:

"Good work, Pedrão."

"I'm going now to move the wounded, chief."

"That's it. Have them carried into the church, or leave them on the square if they're too many."

Exhausted by the battle and nauseated by the heat, the jagunços worked all night carrying off their wounded in their arms or over their shoulders. They were not only jagunços but men.

João Abbade could not find words to speak to Pajehu. The success had so flabbergasted him that he kept silent.

"Let's go and see the Conseilheiro," said Pajehu. . . . "My back's broken. I had a fall over there in the sierra of the Cambaio when I was leading Pedrão's men."

"The Conseilheiro's in the church; he's looking after the wounded with Quadrado."

"We'll have to see what we're to do with the dead. We could leave them for the vultures, but I think it's too copious a meal for their stomachs."

"We'll have to burn them," said Abbade. "A trench stinks. It's easy to burn them. You make a pile: one layer of wood, a layer of men, a layer of wood, a layer of men. With a few such piles, the job will be done. I'll send for some loads of wood in Cannabrava."

"I think that's the best thing we can do. . . . A battle's a bit of a nuisance because of the corpses. It's like when you've eaten: you don't like the smell of cooking any more."

They found the Conseilheiro in the church, as Abbade had said. The wounded had been laid out in disorder all over the place. Some fifty candles threw a dirty yellow light, creating a sort of hallucinating chiaroscuro.

The indefatigable Quadrado was going from one wounded man to the next. His medical treatment was rudimentary but efficacious: tincture of iodine on slight wounds so that they would not become septic. For the others who were in too much pain, a little tincture of opium in warm water.

João submitted to the prophet his proposal concerning the dead.

"Burn the federals," said Antonio sententiously. "As for our own men, they must be buried in the cemetery."

They went out. The square was covered with jagunços whose black silhouettes were moving about in the bright bluish starlight. Some women were sitting along by the church walls weeping quietly.

The heat was terrible, but the flashes of lightning had ceased. It would not be long before dawn would break over the sierra.

"I'm going to take a rest for an hour or two," said Pajehu. "We'll have plenty of work to do presently."

8. Up Canudos!

THE HALF-BREED slept on his thoughts. The hatred which fermented within him had produced emanations which were becoming reabsorbed in ideas. As he was going out of his house he had formed his plan. He turned his steps toward João Abbade's dwelling. The mulatto was still asleep, but Anita was up getting water to boil on the stove.

"Wake him," said Pajehu. "We have work to do."

She looked at the half-breed timorously. Nevertheless, in the depth of her heart she felt an undoubted admiration for him. Abbade, who had thrown himself on his bed, appeared rubbing his eyes.

"I've thought over the matter of the dead," said Pajehu. "Here's how we're going to arrange it. Tell Venancio to have all our men brought to the cemetery, and have two or three big graves dug. In regard to the federals, I'll take charge of that with Pedrão. But you'll have to fetch me about fifty bundles of firewood to the Favella. Where are the mules?"

"Not far away. Over in the direction of Varzea da Ema. In two or three hours they'll be here. Before you've finished gathering the corpses together."

"Good. Besides, I'm going to strip off their uniforms. That'll take a little time."

Throughout the whole of the day the valley of the Vasa Barris showed the same animation as during the great periods of building. Droves of mules were moving about on the slopes of Cannabrava and the Favella. Gangs were engaged in stripping the soldiers of their clothes; others were collecting weapons and ammunition and carrying them to the square. The women were massed in front of the cemetery: they were trying to identify the bodies being taken there. When one of them recognized her man or brother or relation, she went up silently and gave him the farewell kiss. Some went off weeping; others proudly held up their heads crying: "Long live the good Jesus!"

On the Favella the naked corpses were piled up in several heaps: stacks of heads, legs, black, white or brown thighs. Pajehu was gazing at them with sadistic joy. Toward the end of the afternoon he made up the funeral pyres—a layer of wood, a layer of men—but they could not be lit until shortly before sundown. When the flames began to rise high, Pajehu went down to the town to be present at the evening Angelus, for he wanted to hear the Conseilheiro's declamation.

As it was the occasion of an important event, and the church would not have held the whole crowd, João Abbade had the platform erected outside in the open. When Pajehu reached the square it was covered with a multitude awaiting in silent fervor the appearance of the prophet. For, now more than ever, the Conseilheiro was for them all the man sent by God, the mysterious and marvelous delegate of Saint Sebastian. The victory was a miracle, the greatest ever achieved by the prophet. Men and women felt themselves secure under his protection: they were ready to worship him, to give themselves to him body and soul.

Gently the bell began to toll and the Conseilheiro to recite the litanies in a reverential voice, speaking slowly to render them more solemn. The "Pray for us" given in response was firmer, more animated than usual: it had lost its resemblance to a refrain.

Evening had come and, on the height of the Favella, seven huge pyres were burning under the stars.

The bell ceased tolling and the Conseilheiro preached to them. This time he had something to say and his style was clear. The jagunços had been unjustly attacked. God, who is Justice itself, had not permitted the tools of the Antichrist to achieve their goal. Moreira Cesar had announced that he was going to raze Canudos to the ground. He had never known anything but victories. At Canudos he had known defeat and death. Thus would God punish all those who rose up against the Conseilheiro. The republic was an invention of Satan, but all its efforts would be shattered against the ramparts of the holy city of the hinterland. However long the struggle might last, the jagunços would emerge from it victors, for Saint Sebastian was at their side.

Who would still have refused to believe him? The facts showed that he was right.

He had not spoken of Pajehu because he could not, for all that, attribute to Pajehu a miracle which was due to the intervention of Saint Sebastian; and it is quite possible that he was beginning to be a little jealous of the half-breed's prestige.

The latter had his revenge next day. He had made Pedrão keep aside the corpses of Moreira Cesar and Tamarindo, easily recognizable by their uniforms of higher officers. In the forenoon he had Moreira's head cut off and exhibited, fixed on a long stake in the middle of the square, wearing his colonel's peaked cap. At noon when the whole population assembled to recite the *Ave Maria,* Pajehu put in an appearance on his black horse. He knew that he would be the object of an ovation. This he was, and an infernal dance was organized around the sinister trophy which the jagunços continued to threaten with their fists, yelling: "Scum!" and "Long live Pajehu!" Then the head was given over to urchins who amused themselves during the afternoon, rolling it about like a ball in a game of skittles.

For Tamarindo's corpse, Pajehu had reserved another fate. Accompanied by a little party he went to Angico. There, at the watering point, rose one of the rare trees of the region—an old *umbuseiro.* He had the corpse hung from a branch by a leather thong. Underneath he placed the colonel's effects, neatly folded and surmounted by the peaked cap.

"That will serve as a warning to those who might think of paying us a visit," he said.

On the Favella the pyres were burning out. In the dry air, in which not the lightest breeze was stirring, the pungent odor of burned flesh hung about. While looking at the town Pajehu noticed that, from a number of little fires, smoke was rising in thin straight lines toward the sky. He wondered what it could mean. When he arrived on the square he heard that it was simply the women, whose sense of smell is more delicate than that of men, burning bits of bark of an aromatic tree to overcome the intolerable stench with their incenselike perfume.

Pajehu went into Abbade's house. He found him sprawling on

his bed in the arms of Anita. The half-breed took a stool, sat beside the bed, and began to roll himself a cigarette.

"As soon as you feel disposed," he said, "we'll go and distribute the weapons."

"You really have a moment to spare?"

"Just as you like."

As he stretched himself and was yawning, João Abbade continued to converse.

"You've collected a lot in the way of weapons?"

"They make a good pile. We must sort them out; there are Mauser carbines, Comblains, and Mannlichers. The cartridges must be sorted so as not to give Mannlicher bullets to those who have Comblains. This work we must do ourselves if we want it well done. Venancio can give us a hand: he's well up in this. Perhaps Sariema, too. Where *is* Sariema? I haven't seen anything of him for three days. As soon as the rumpus started he vanished."

"I ran into him not long ago. I believe that during the battle he went off to hide himself in Cannabrava."

"It's now we ought to send him to Bahia. Will he dare? He's a coward."

João did not reply. He continued to stretch his limbs. Pajehu was becoming impatient.

"Are you ready? We've got to work."

The distribution of arms took on the atmosphere of a fete, like a distribution of prizes. To each *cabecilha,* or chief of a group, rifles of the same type were given with cartridges to correspond. Thus, Pedrão had Mausers, Venancio had Mannlichers; and Quimquim de Coïqui, Comblains. Massed on the square, the jagunços were waiting impatiently to be put in possession of the beautiful instruments of death. With such weapons they would be invulnerable; and secretly they were hoping for a new governmental expedition in order to try them out.

After the distribution there was a meeting of the chiefs at the Conseilheiro's house: the triumvirate, plus Dr. Quadrado.

The prophet was intoxicated with pride, but it was an internal intoxication which he did his utmost to avoid showing: a prophet must maintain an impassive mask, in joy as in grief. He was turning over in his mind grandiose projects, trying to raise his spirit to the high level of events. He took the floor immediately:

"God," he said, "wishes that we should commemorate this victory which he has granted to us. He has sent me an idea: we're going to build a new church, one much bigger than the old one; and we shall build it in stone to render it immortal."

Everyone showed his enthusiasm.

"We have good masons," said Abbade. "Some of them have worked at Joazeiro, Aracajú, Maceio, and even at Recife."

"Where shall we put it?" asked Sariema. "A beautiful site must be found. It ought to be placed on a height."

"No," said the Conseilheiro. "On the other side of the square, facing the old one. It's the will of Saint Sebastian."

Sariema's idea was the better one, but he would never have been able to impose it from the moment that Saint Sebastian was of a contrary opinion.

"In that case," said Sariema, "it must be made at least the same size as the church of St. Francis in Bahia."

"Exactly," replied the Conseilheiro, "that's what I want. We shall show all those people on the coast what we are capable of making at Canudos."

He was convinced that under the impetus of Saint Sebastian the jagunços could demonstrate their ability to those architects and stonecutters in Bahia. He had become so elated that he believed himself capable of achieving anything. His claims were contagious. They were all convinced that they would build a bigger and more beautiful temple than any in the world.

"Even in Jerusalem such a temple as ours won't be found," said the Conseilheiro.

"We'll form the gangs this evening and the works will begin tomorrow," said Abbade in exaltation.

Canudos resumed its appearance of a builders' yard. Stimulated by the faith reborn from their victory, the jagunços worked with a fierce ardor. Those men have no equals for the "sudden spurt." After all, many of them had known slavery and, in that period, they had been made to do inhuman labors thus enabling them to measure how far their efforts could be sustained. Today they were doing similar work for the glory of Saint Sebastian and the Conseilheiro.

More and more emaciated, his liver ailing and his dysentery latent, the prophet did not leave the building yard and remained for twelve hours in the sun at a stretch. João Abbade directed the transportation. Sariema as usual contented himself with running from one group to another giving advice.

As for Pajehu, he had vanished. After being inebriated for two days, he was in his house sleeping off the effects of the drink.

A week after the beginning of the labors, the messenger sent by Antonio to Ceará returned. The Conseilheiro, who was in the building yard, made him sit beside him on a stone.

"What news do you bring to me?" he asked unconcernedly—for recent events had been so extraordinary that family matters were relegated to a second place.

"Bad, senho'" (Domingos could not pronounce his *r*'s and say "senhor.")

"Is Miguel Carlos dead?"

"Yes, senho'. He was killed in a brawl in Quixada."

"As all strong men in the hinterland die," said the Conseilheiro pensively.

"In an argument on your account."

"On *my* account? He knew about me?"

"Yes. A fazendeiro in the botequim said that you ought to be killed because you stirred up the hinterland. Up yonder in Ceará there's much talk about Canudos. Padre Cicero says that it's the holy city of America and that you have been sent by God. But they say that He supports you because He is against the republic. And then there were arguments and brawls. When the fazendeiro suggested that you should be annihilated, Miguel Carlos said that you were his nephew and that the man must have it out with him. The fazendeiro gave him a blow in the face with his fist. Miguel got up and planted his knife full in the man's chest, but a foreman who was there, a *capataz* of the fazendeiro, stabbed Miguel in the back."

"And so," said the Conseilheiro, disillusioned, "he knew that I was the Conseilheiro and that I was at Canudos; and he never came to see me."

He held his head in his hands and began to think. If Miguel had not come to see him, it was from pride, so as not to have to acknowledge that he, Antonio, really had a mission to fulfill. Miguel Carlos had never believed in his mission.

Nevertheless, the prophet said to himself, he was a man of decent feelings: he was killed because of me, while defending me. I ought perhaps to have invited him sooner. He was the older: it was for me to make a sign to him. This evening we'll say six *Ave Marias* for the repose of his soul.

9. The Riot

MOREIRA CESAR's telegram—publicized throughout Brazil—aroused formidable enthusiasm, so that, at the moment when the government troops were being defeated by the jagunços in the fiery hinterland night, the evening newspapers in Bahia, Rio de Janeiro, and São Paulo, and every town connected by telegraph, came out with special editions carrying a headline across the page: DESTRUCTION OF CANUDOS: UNDER MOREIRA CESAR's FIST.

All that night and the forenoon of next day the journalists awaited the details which the telegraph must transmit to them. The directors of the great organs had prepared leading articles explaining exactly the scope of the event. Some editors had written articles in an elevated sociological tone on the "development of collective hallucinations in desert zones." One of them had established a parallel between the Conseilheiro's heresy and Manichaeism. Another, which had subscribed to French and German medical magazines, had written long articles on "the paranoiac." A third, which devoted special attention to racial problems, had conceived an original article on "a mixed-race religion." Everything was ready to document a public, eager to get to the bottom of this Canudos affair: for, with the fragmentary information which the press had been content to give until then, the affair resembled a Chinese puzzle. It was not known whether they had to deal with a common brigand or a mystic. Was it a case of the bullet or of a St. Ignatius? Was it a hinterland revolution, a schism, or was it rather a mere matter of suppressing banditry?

The newspapers were waiting. They had already had to abandon the idea of special midday editions and were preparing to launch the evening editions. At 4 P.M. they were still without news of the operations in the hinterland. Certain newspapers telegraphed to Bahia. The governor replied that he also was without news, but that this was not surprising on the part of Moreira Cesar, who no doubt considered that his telegram sufficed. It was really necessary to announce to the public that they did not have a single detail of what had happened. The distances, said the journalists, are great; and it is difficult to get about in the hinterland. "We hope to be able to give you precise information any moment now. We shall publish a special edition in due course."

But the next day they were still without news. Once again it was necessary to placate the public. They were beginning to get worried in the newspaper offices. Something out of the ordinary was happening. This man Moreira Cesar was a strange person: "Pooh!" people said. "He wants to finish the job so as to be able to telegraph: 'I have razed Canudos to the ground!' He loves sensational news."

At last, on the third day at noon, a humorous periodical called *A Espingarda*—"The Carbine"—brought out a special issue. In it one read in enormous print: JAGUNÇOS WIPE OUT EXPEDITIONARY FORCE. MOREIRA CESAR KILLED AT THE HEAD OF HIS TROOPS.

A Espingarda gave an account of the battle. It showed how the Gauchos had gone into a charge against the houses in the manner of Don Quixote's charge against the windmills. It described the attack made by the Pernambucans and Bahians, the death of Moreira Cesar, the retreat to the Favella, and finally the massacre.

Nobody gave credence to this account because it was a very well-known procedure on the part of *A Espingarda* to relate events "the other way about": to find beauty in what others declared to be ugly, to present losers as winners, and so forth. Hence, people considered that this description of the battle of Canudos was a hoax to make fun of the other newspapers which were not able to obtain precise details. All the same, the paper sold many thousands

of copies. Everybody agreed in admitting that there was an astonishing note of truth in this imaginary account.

When it was known twenty-four hours later that the statement in
A Espingarda was true, there was an explosion of popular anger
such as is seen only in those volcanic cities of tropical regions. Mobs
gathered immediately in the principal thoroughfares of Rio and the
mounted police began to circulate.

In the Rua Ouvidor some tradesmen were expressing their feelings
to one another:

"Pay taxes for such an army? No! Let them go to the devil with
their Moreira Cesars!"

"Fancy putting an epileptic brute at the head of so important an
expedition!"

"It seems that he didn't even know where Canudos was!"

"You can be certain that this is a blow struck by the monarchists.
You well understand that on his own this Conseilheiro wasn't capable
of fighting an army. He received help. He has certainly been sent
arms, munitions, and military instructors."

"Certainly. And every expedition will fail if Bahia is not put
under military occupation."

Bahia was, in fact, regarded as the citadel of partisans of the
empire. People implied that the state authorities had been conniving
with the Conseilheiro. Even in Rio de Janeiro the number of empire
partisans remained considerable. The situation was delicate.

As usual, the press did not fail to throw oil on the fire. *O Paiz*
wrote: "The tragedy of March 3rd, in the course of which, together
with Moreira Cesar, the distinguished Colonel Tamarindo and other
brilliant officers of our army lost their lives, is confirmation that the
monarchist party, thanks to the tolerance of the powers that be, or
even with their involuntary encouragement, has grown in audacity
and strength." The São Paulo *Daily* on its part said: "It is a matter
of a Restoration; there is a conspiracy; an imperialist army is in
course of formation. The evil is great. Let the remedy be in proportion to the gravity of the evil. Is the monarchy arming? Let the
President call the republicans to arms!"

In the evening twilight Rio de Janeiro was in a ferment in spite
of the police patrols which had not ceased circulating during the
whole afternoon. A dense and excited crowd had invaded the

Avenida, the Rua Ouvidor, and the Rua Primeiro de Março: in various places it moved in eddies, in others it remained still while awaiting the ringleaders who would channel it in one direction. Suddenly a shout went up, was repeated and passed through the streets by thousands of voices:

"To Lapa! To Lapa!"

As if this were the awaited word of command, the multitude began to march toward the Largo da Lapa, but not knowing why it was going in that direction. The pressure was powerful. When the square was completely covered with this human tide, a man was seen climbing a street lamp. Addressing the crowd, he yelled that he was proposing for its approval a resolution which he was going to read. He had quickly scribbled on a scrap of paper:

The people of Rio de Janeiro—
assembled in a meeting—
having become acquainted with the painful reverse
suffered by the government forces in the hinterlands
of Bahia, which are in the hands of monarchist
leaders
grouped around the government—
applaud all actions of civic energy which must be
taken to wipe out the insult to the army and country and
anxiously await the suppression of the revolt.

A vast acclamation rewarded the orator for having so well interpreted the people's feeling.

While he was speaking, the police had surrounded the square and the mounted police, massed in the street of Mem de Sá, were ready to intervene. Rising nobody knew from where, shouts then reverberated across the square: "To the newspapers! To the newspapers!"

This was a definite objective for popular anger which was going to be sated at last. There were at that time in Rio three monarchist newspapers: A Gaceta da Tarde, A Liberdade, and Apostolo. Their editorial offices and printing works were in the Rua Ouvidor. The moment the shouts resounded, like one man the multitude surged back toward that thoroughfare. The police attempted to bar the way, but what could a few police do against the raging mass? They were overwhelmed, and the people hurled themselves into the onslaught on the buildings of the newspapers held responsible for the defeat of Moreira Cesar. Doors and windows were smashed. Soon the tables and chairs and shelves were thrown into the street; then the cases of type and reams of paper. A bonfire was lit whose flames went up in the narrow street as high as the roofs of the houses.

All of a sudden, from the direction of the Avenida the piercing shrieks of women and the raucous shouts of men were heard. The mounted police were charging. The crowd flowed back, hemmed in by the police on foot. It was cut in two: one part was driven back toward the Rua Primeiro de Março, the other toward the Rua Uruguayana. A detachment of infantry, brought up urgently, occupied the Rua Ouvidor.

While the soldiers were exerting themselves to extinguish the fires lit by popular fury, a volley crackled from the direction of the Primeiro de Março. Feeling themselves overwhelmed, the police had fired. There were dead and wounded. This time there was great confusion.

The next day Rio awoke in an atmosphere of martial law. Cavalry pickets cantered along the principal thoroughfares, while the foot police guarded crossroads. The shops remained closed and, only here and there were seen audacious passers-by who had dared to risk their lives to reach their posts. The life of the city was paralyzed: Rio de Janeiro was dead.

From ten o'clock in the forenoon all the ministers were in conference at the presidential palace. It seemed evident to all of them that by themselves the jagunços could not have been capable of inflicting such a defeat on an army commanded by a man with Moreira Cesar's experience. They were certainly backed up. By whom? It could only have been by the monarchists. A minister declared that he had heard from a "most reliable source" that the defense of Canudos had been organized by an Italian engineer. Another asserted that the monarchy had chosen, as "restorer" of the monarchy, the jagunço leader João Abbade, Chief of the People in Canudos.

Convinced, the president delivered a speech in which he stigmatized the politicians who were not afraid of using those bandits of the northeast to achieve their ends.

"We know," he said, "that politics is at work behind the Canudos fanatics. But we are prepared. We have the means of winning, no matter how, and against no matter whom."

And so the new crusade against the Conseilheiro was to begin under the slogan of suppressing the monarchist rebellion.

10. Long Live the Republic!

IN CANUDOS—where saying their litanies and *Ave Marias* had been resumed—they had no suspicion of the agitation set in motion by the defeat of Moreira Cesar. Never had the jagunços enjoyed such peace: never had their faith been so ardent. After those hard battles which they had fought, after all the atrocities they had committed, they had fallen back again into a mystical dreamland in which they were now certain they could live, since all the tools of the Antichrist had been annihilated.

Even the leaders like João Abbade and Pajehu, who previously were elated by the success, no longer drew any vanity from the victory. They, too, were in the grip of that vague mysticism, and convinced that the Conseilheiro possessed a mysterious driving power against which all assaults would be shattered. They felt no need to know what was happening outside the community. The internal life of Canudos sufficed for their barren souls.

It was only when José Brandão brought his three hundred horsemen that they heard of the exaltation aroused in the whole hinterland—from Bahia to Fortaleza and from Recife to Pirapora—by the jagunços' victory.

This José Brandão was a half-breed from Minas Geraes, a former professional killer who had contracted leprosy in a Negro den in Tremendal. He was thirty-six and had the build of a wrestler. In him the disease was only in its first stage: his face was breaking out in spots and there were some patches of a dirty brown color on his chest.

When the malady had become apparent, he had to give up his "profession," as the fazendeiros for whom he had "worked" no longer wanted to have him. He had then taken refuge in Ibrahy, a small leper village which—in order to get rid of the diseased as quickly as possible—had been established in a place rotten with malaria on the banks of the São Francisco River.

Brandão had the soul of a rebel. As the village was badly supplied with victuals, he persuaded all the men to follow him in a demonstration of protest in Pirapora, the nearest town. When the lepers went into the little city, the population, seized with fear, closed doors and windows and isolated themselves. The lepers went to the town hall where, following Brandão's example, they rubbed their hands on the walls until these were covered with blood, since it is by blood that leprosy is most easily transmitted. This tragic protest resulted in the abandonment of the town by the whole panic-stricken population. The government announced that it was going to deal most rigorously with the lepers. Brandão thought it prudent to decamp and, accompanied by about three hundred men, he withdrew further northward into the sertão. His band soon became the terror of the region. When he heard of the jagunços' victory, the idea struck him that perhaps Canudos would be a good place for him and his companions, and he decided to go and join the Conseilheiro.

When João Abbade and Pajehu saw him coming down the slopes of the Favella with his cavalry, they wondered what it could be.

"One more bringing reinforcements," they said to one another. They were used to it: some used to come nearly every day. This particular contingent was important. Brandão directed his men to the square where many jagunços had run to welcome him. He asked who was the chief. João Abbade made his way toward him and held out his hand, but Brandão refused to take it.

"We are lepers," he said.

Abbade was not frightened for he knew that leprosy is not easily contagious: this had been explained to him at the college in Recife long ago. It was advisable, nevertheless, to take precautions, for, once contaminated, a person is lost and sees himself fall to pieces.

"You reckon to remain with us?" he asked.

"If you agree."

"Even if you do, you'll have to settle yourselves away from the center."

"That's just what I think. Show us the place."

João glanced around the outskirts.

"Not on the right bank," said Pajehu, always preoccupied with his strategic considerations. "Over yonder, in the direction of Cannabrava."

While the chiefs were in discussion, the jagunços gazed with interest mingled with compassion, fear, and disgust at the motionless lepers on their horses. They were horrible to see. Some who had lost their nostrils had nothing but two holes in place of a nose. Others had eyes tinged with blood under eyelids covered with scabs: others had only two fingers on their hands; and the faces of others were covered with excrescences.

"Forward!" said Brandão.

The troop went off by the main street leading to the sierra.

João Abbade took Pajehu into his house. They were both perplexed.

"What do you think of this?" said Abbade.

"I don't like having contact with those people," replied Pajehu, "but . . . they can be useful if we're attacked again. A leper is accustomed to looking death in the face."

In the course of the weeks which followed, the lepers built a vast shed which they covered with a roof of baked clay. They lived there in a community. They did not mix with the jagunços for the recital of prayers and were not present at the sermons but, as the Conselheiro considered that disintegrating flesh could not defile their souls, he used to go and deliver discourses and recite litanies to them. At Canudos the religion of Christ was practiced; the disinherited were not abandoned.

For two and a half months, until the day when what was called the "Grand Council" met, the town lived in the mystical fervor of a monastery. After sundown during the torrid nights the jagunços, squatting in circles out in the little streets, would go over the exploits which they had accomplished in the course of the battle. These conversations always ended with the same thoughts on the victory and the same haunting sentence:

"Nao faz duvida. E um milagre!" ("There's no doubt about it. It's a miracle!")

Never had the people of Canudos fallen so greatly under the Conseilheiro's spell. Even the bandits had become mystics to the point that they had more faith in prayer than in their weapons. Tranca-Pés, who had always been an unbeliever and had the habit of missing evening prayer, was now present at it regularly. He was afraid of being killed in a future fight if he did not fulfill his religious duties.

The walls of the new church, made of great blocks of stone, were going up rapidly. All day long the Conseilheiro walked about pensively where the work went on, pursuing his dream of building the biggest church in the world.

Twice monthly Major Sariema accompanied by Chico Ema went to Queimadas or Joazeiro to get a newspaper in order to know what was being said of Canudos. But he had not been able to obtain the issues which gave accounts of the riotings in Rio. They thought too late about organizing this service of buying newspapers, and so all the interesting issues were not to be found. All Major Sariema heard was that Moreira Cesar's defeat had provoked troubles in the capital. The papers which he brought back to Canudos dealt with the jagunços, but only to say that they ought to be exterminated.

"They talk a lot," said Pajehu. "Let us wait. We're strong and we have plenty of weapons."

It was on May 17th that Sariema brought the news. It was published in *A Liberdade*. The federal government was organizing a monster expedition against Canudos: it would be under the command of General Arthur Oscar de Andrade Guimerães. If reliance could be placed on the newspaper accounts, it would be "formidable." It would consist of the:

1st, 5th, 30th, 31st, and 3rd battalions from Rio Grande do Sul;
27th from Parahyba;
34th from Rio Grande do Norte;
33rd and 35th from Piauhy;
5th from Maranhão;
4th from Pará;
26th from Sergipe;
14th and 5th from Pernambuco;

2nd from Ceará;
7th, 9th, and 16th from Bahia;
5th and 9th cavalry.
—and finally, the artillery regiment from the federal capital.

After reading this catalogue, João Abbade let his arms fall by his sides.

"This time we're done for," he said to Pajehu.

"Let me see the newspaper."

Abbade held it out to him. Pajehu studied it closely and then threw it on the bed.

"Don't forget that we have 3,000 army rifles," he said. "When we took on Moreira Cesar, we had 300."

They went to the Conseilheiro's house. Antonio was not impressed by the list of the battalions they were going to send against him. Nothing could impress him any more. Nevertheless, he began to stride about in the room more from anger than fear.

"Nobody," he asserted, "is capable of overthrowing Canudos. Do you hear me? Nobody. They can come in their 5,000 or 10,000 or 20,000. We'll smash them."

Pajehu considered that in the meantime there were practical measures to be taken.

"It's going to get hot," he said. "We must be sure of all the men. I propose to assemble the chiefs here. You must speak to them and tell them that you are relying on them."

Influenced by Abbade, Pajehu gradually became aware of a certain role that psychology played in these matters: it was not only a question of strength and technique.

And so it was that, for the first time, the Grand Council of Canudos met in the Conseilheiro's house. It consisted (apart from João Abbade, Pajehu, and Sariema) of: "Doctor" Quadrado, Norberto, Zé Venancio, Tranca-Pés, Quimquim de Coïqui, Pedrão, and the two brothers Macambira.

"God is calling us to battle," the Conseilheiro said to them. "The republicans are sending another army against Canudos. We shall wipe it out, as we wiped out the first, with Saint Sebastian's permission. This will be your last battle for, after that, the hinterland will be independent."

Then, looking haughtily at all the leaders, he said:

"All of you swear loyalty to Canudos and to Saint Sebastian."

Each of the chiefs raised his hand and then made the sign of the cross.

"Good," said the Conseilheiro. "Now make arrangements with Pajehu. It's to him that I have delegated my powers."

Although this session of the Grand Council had been very brief, it had impressed itself very strongly on the minds of the group leaders. It was the first time they had been summoned to meet at the Conseilheiro's house. This agreeably tickled their vanity. Hence, the appeal which they launched to their men was particularly energetic. The ground was well prepared: after the miracle of the victory over Moreira Cesar, all the jagunços were certain that another miracle would shatter the new expedition which the reckless republicans were daring to launch against the holy city. Not only was there no weakening noticeable, but a wild excitement took possession of the town.

A thousand miles from there an equally violent excitement drove the people of Rio de Janeiro into the streets to applaud the arrival of the contingents which were to take part in the great operation of mopping up the Bahian hinterlands. The surging, seething, and impatient crowd, obsessed by the idea that the rebellion in the northeast was a supreme effort of the dying monarchism, did not tire of shouting hurrahs for the republic. When they heard that the .320 Whitworth cannon, the biggest piece of artillery that the country possessed, was to be turned on Canudos to reduce that haunt of the jagunços to ruins, there was an outburst of jubilation throughout the city. In the Rua Ouvidor the usual comments were to be heard:

"This time those jagunços are going to be cleaned up. In three shots that big gun will reduce their filthy hovels to dust."

"Have you seen that cannon yet? It's a colossus!"

"The shell weighs more than 1,200 pounds. Do you realize what that means? 1,200 pounds of case shot and dynamite in Canudos? The Conseilheiro's going to strike something!"

Nobody wondered how they were going to get that mass weighing over a ton and a half into position in the hinterland.

A vast crowd swarmed along the quays on the day the Whitworth

was shipped on board the *Amazonas* for Bahia. When the cranes began slowly to lower this monster—the symbol of force—into the hold of the vessel, a single yell went up from the whole multitude:
"Long live the republic!"
People felt that the regime was saved.

11. A Hard Blow

DEMOLISH CANUDOS. Annihilate the jagunços. Pulverize the Conseilheiro's den. Avenge Moreira Cesar. Such were the main purposes of the expedition. In order to be sure of achieving them, and to avoid setbacks, the military staff conceived a grand style offensive in the best manner of Von der Goltz, one which seemed quite out of proportion with the objective. According to the plan adopted, a column commanded by General Guimerães should set out from Queimadas, and another, under the command of General Savaget, would leave Aracajú. They would come together in front of Canudos and then carry out the decisive assault.

By launching two columns against the town, it was hoped to compel the jagunços to divide their forces. For it was strongly suspected that, being armed with the whole arsenal left to them by Moreira Cesar's expedition, they would do their utmost to bar the way and would not quietly allow the troops to occupy the heights overlooking the town. They would have to face two simultaneous attacks; and they would have to deal with men who had a profound knowledge of military science.

The column leaving Queimadas was entrusted with bringing up the .320 gun which was going to show the hinterland the strength of the republic.

"A nice piece of nonsense," said General Guimerães—he had been settled for three weeks now in his general headquarters at Monte Santo—to Captain de Queiroz of the Artillery. "I wonder who the individual was who had the preposterous idea of having such a piece of artillery transported into the hinterland."

For the Whitworth cannon was giving them great trouble. At Queimadas it had been loaded comparatively easily on an ox wagon with strengthened wheels. But no track leading in the direction of Canudos allowed a wagon to pass, so that it had been necessary to build a road. For three weeks the battalion of engineers had been working at it. They had reached Joa. As for the cannon, it had not yet arrived at Monte Santo. As it was moving out of Queimadas one of the wheels of the wagon went into a hole and the gun had overturned. They had to set about getting it back on the wagon without the means available at the railway station in Queimadas. Under the burning sun of the hinterland a piece of artillery weighing over a ton and a half is not handled easily or quickly with manual labor. In the end they got it up into position using cables drawn by gangs of fifteen or twenty men—as in the days of slavery —and then they had to dig a trench to bring the apron of the wagon to the base of the piece which they then slid onto the wagon with levers.

Then again, as they were arriving in Tanguinha, the oxen had taken fright: they had made a formidable swerve and the cannon was upset for a second time.

"This is a real Way of the Cross," General Guimerães said.

During this time all the troops were immobilized at Monte Santo, for they could not advance without the cannon and the whole country was feverishly awaiting its first roar.

General Guimerães became irritable. He was a spare little elderly man with the fleshless hands of a poorhouse inmate, a small very bony head, too broad a forehead, an aquiline nose, a wide mouth, black eyes and thick eyebrows: in short, a typical product of the tropics. He wore big spectacles which gave him the look of a scholarly bookworm.

"Without that fiendish cannon," he said, "we'd have reached Canudos by now." The Conselheiro was no longer mentioned.

"Take care, general," replied Captain de Queiroz. "Take care. These jagunços have more than one trick up their sleeves. You'll perhaps need all your material to win out."

De Queiroz was an officer thirty years of age, one of the most brilliant products of the Military School. Of medium height, his face was quite round, he had a bulbous nose, chubby cheeks, and he was prematurely bald. The general thought highly of his opinions. However, he retorted:

"You don't understand the position, captain. The disaster suffered by the first expedition belies your judgment. You fancy that it's due to the jagunços' strategy only that Moreira Cesar's death was caused. Let us see. You knew Moreira Cesar. You can't possibly believe that he let himself be beaten by a few badly armed bandits?"

"Possibly so, general, but we have only jumbled accounts regarding the setback to the first expedition, and I consider that two precautions are better than one."

"So you really believe that we have an absolute need of this devil of a .320 cannon in order to defeat Canudos? You don't think that we shall do it with our .75s?"

"We may, but it's not a bad idea to be equipped to meet every eventuality."

At last, after three weeks the big gun arrived in position at Monte Santo. There was rapturous jubilation. The whole population —men, women, children, and old people—flocked to admire the monster which was to pulverize Canudos. The enthusiasm, however, was of short duration. This engine seemed satanic to the hinterland people. It frightened and at the same time humiliated them. It was, once more, one of those inventions of the whites for crushing the colored men. No doubt they would have liked to be rid of Canudos and the threat of pillage but, at heart, they felt a solidarity with the jagunços. The destruction of the holy city would be a defeat for the hinterland. There were some who, obsessed by this idea, went to the Conseilheiro to give him intelligence of the government troops.

When the pioneers of the engineers attacked the last lap of the new road between Joa and Rosario, General Guimerães prudently decided to bring forward four battalions, for he had every reason to fear a surprise attack by the jagunços.

Contrary to all that had been foreseen by the strategists, these troops did not meet with any resistance and were able to occupy the two ranchos at Rosario without firing a shot.

"Really," said the general, "this hinterland war is very strange. These jagunços must surely know that, if we occupy the heights

overlooking the town, we'll be able to raze it with our artillery. . . .
In the time we are dragging along here, they have been able to
inform themselves of our war material and soldiers fit for duty."

"I must admit that I don't any longer understand their strategy,"
replied de Queiroz.

"If they've decided to wait for us in the town, then the .320 could
be really useful to us," the general admitted. "All the more reason
why it should arrive in good condition. Where is it at this moment?"

"Approaching Rosario. But, yesterday, the wagon was stuck in
the sand."

"Try to make them get a move on. Let them finish with the
delays."

The general was now impatient to see the huge piece of artillery
installed on the heights dominating the city of the jagunços. He was
all the more anxious to see it in position and to begin operations,
for, as a result of long immobilization in the sun, the troops were
becoming demoralized. More and more men were falling sick.
Many livers, especially among whites, do not resist the hinterland
heat. Cases of dysentery were becoming more and more frequent
and several cases of sun blindness had already been notified.

Every day convoys of ailing men were sent to the rear loaded on
the backs of mules or horses. The general saw his troops melting
like grease in the sun and there had not been even a skirmish. The
situation was becoming disquieting: it was time to act.

On August 3rd, the general sent out patrols to reconnoiter the
immediate approaches to Canudos. They returned without having
encountered a single jagunço. They had observed the town closely,
yet they had not caught sight of a living soul, just as if it were
abandoned.

Somewhat bewildered, the general began to pare his nails. What
ridicule he would suffer if the jagunços had left the town!

Obviously he could not know that Moreira Cesar had had the
same impression.

Spurred on by this apprehension, the general immediately gave
orders for all the troops to be concentrated on Rosario. That took
three days: for one had to reckon with the sun.

At dawn on August 11th, the army set out on the march toward
the Favella height. It met with no resistance and appeared on the

plateau at eleven o'clock in the morning, as had Moreira Cesar's troops. When General Guimerães arrived there himself and was able to take in with a glance the panorama of Canudos spread out on the plain, he became concerned: it was clear that an area, so extensively built-up, so dispersed, could not be destroyed by cannon fire, especially as the .320 could fire only about ten shells. Hence, he must join battle.

He dispatched two runners to General Savaget, whose column must be in the vicinity somewhere on the Geremoabo road. He proposed to launch the attack without delay.

The runners had hardly left when a fusillade crackled. It came from the Cambaio. The general drove his horse on the slope toward the Angico gorge. The Favella plateau was swept by bursts of fire. Men were falling by the dozen. Among the artillerymen there was a veritable panic.

Guimerães was not lacking in coolness. He ordered the retreat to be sounded by the bugles of the 7th Pernambuco battalion, regrouped the troops in the valley, and put into position two .75 guns which he ordered to shell Canudos. At the same time he gave the order to attack the town. He did not intend to have the same worries as Moreira Cesar.

Under cover of artillery fire the troops advanced by the Valley of Death and the Massacara road to reach the Vasa Barris, in front of which they deployed. At this period the river was completely dry.

It was one o'clock when the bugles sounded the charge. The assault was carried out with dash. Soldiers from Pará, Maranhão, São Paulo, Bahia, or Rio Grande hurled themselves into the attack with the ferocity of wild beasts.

The jagunços withstood the clash. As soon as the federal troops reached the first houses, the Conseilheiro's men enforced their own method of fighting and it had to become a fight with knives. . . . The relentlessness of the struggle was even more terrible than on the occasion of the first expedition. Two soldiers of Pará had smashed in the door of a house: with a bayonet thrust the first one killed the jagunço who opposed him face to face, but imme- diately a woman planted her long *jacaré* knife in his stomach. Struck down by the second soldier's rifle butt, she fell to earth with a death rattle. As the man was leaning forward to see whether she was killed, she spat in his face shouting: "Long live the good Jesus!"

In all the little streets there was the same ferocity. Jagunços would cut off a head and from the roof top throw it at the soldiers sprinkling them with blood.

The federal troops were, however, making progress—like those of Moreira Cesar—at the cost of losses out of proportion to the result.

After forty-eight hours of this merciless struggle, General Guimerães suspended the battle. He in turn had the feeling of having become engulfed in a dead end. He had just as much energy, as much pluck and courage as Moreira Cesar: he had gone down on the field of battle and had established his advanced headquarters in one of the conquered houses bordering the Vasa Barris, believing that his presence would stimulate the troops. He himself directed the battle with a few officers around him: he wished to win it, whatever the cost and whatever the sacrifices might be. Little by little, however, with the piling up of corpses and the cries and death rattles of the wounded, his will began to weaken. He flopped on a stool with his head between his hands. After a moment of reflection, he said:

"Order the cease fire. But let them all remain where they are. We can't withdraw."

He took out a writing pad and wrote a few words for General Savaget: he asked him to launch an attack behind the old church in such a way as to take the jagunços from the rear.

"See that this gets to him immediately. If Savaget can attack tomorrow, the matter is resolved."

In the meantime he had to consolidate his position and assure communications with the rear. Troops were spread out in echelon between Canudos and the Favella to establish the liaison.

The general had stood up and was walking up and down the room in the manner of the Conseilheiro. He lit a cigar. That helped him with ideas.

"Have the corpses taken away," he ordered. "Let them be brought over yonder behind that hill and send a working party to dig a trench."

He had a horror of the smell of death.

The sun had almost disappeared behind the sierra: the fusillade and shouts had completely ceased. A strange disturbing silence had fallen on the valley. The bell in Canudos began to toll the Angelus. The general and officers looked at one another and a blush of shame rose to their foreheads, for they felt powerless to take up the challenge of the jagunços. The general clenched his fists: he felt like giving the order to attack. But, through the window, he could perceive in the red twilight the long procession of wounded limping along toward the Favella and, to his right, the file of men carrying corpses.

Suddenly he had an inspiration.

"Give me a piece of plank."

He began to write a report to the government to ask for a reinforcement of 5,000 men.

He had just suddenly realized that the destruction of Canudos demanded other means than those with which he had been provided. He read the text to his officers.

"There's nothing else to be done," he said. "Even if Savaget attacks, it doesn't follow that we shall clean up this riffraff which defends itself step by step. One ought to be able to surround the town completely."

The night was calm but, as soon as the sun rose, the battle began again in all its fury. The jagunços counterattacked. On the first clash, the government troops yielded and at ten o'clock, at the moment when the fight was abating, they were in possession of only a thin row of houses along the river.

General Guimerães was considering the launching of an attack to regain the lost positions when, at about two o'clock in the afternoon, a vigorous fusillade crackled on the heights in the direction of Cocorobó.

"That's Savaget," he said rubbing his hands. "As soon as his troops reach the approaches to the town, we shall attack."

12. The Charge of the Leper Cavalry

SAVAGET'S COLUMN, coming from Geremoabo, had in fact reached Cocorobó, but had just fallen into the ambush laid by Pajehu.

The name Cocorobó is given to a place consisting of half a dozen ranchos or huts, situated in the middle of a plateau of less than half a square mile and surrounded by hills. Pajehu had spread his men in the windings of the crags all around the plateau leaving free the pass through which the road runs to Geremoabo.

Until then the Savaget column had not met with any resistance, it had not even caught sight of a jagunço: it had not had occasion to fire a shot. It advanced in complete quiet, preceded by a cavalry patrol. As the Cocorobó plateau seemed to be completely uninhabited, the column proceeded on to it unsuspectingly. Six battalions had gone through the pass and advanced on the plateau when Pajehu joined battle. He opened with an intense fusillade from the hills all around. There was the beginning of panic among the soldiers: some threw themselves flat on their stomachs, others tried to get under cover in the ranchos. Finding himself on open ground, General Savaget spurred his horse vigorously to get to a sheltered place. Too late: a bullet went right through his chest. The horse was at that moment in full gallop. The general fell headfirst on the rocky soil: he was lifted up by two soldiers who carried him into one of the ranchos where Colonel Medeiros had already taken cover.

Savaget was not dead. His head was covered with bloodstains and dirtied by the dust. He half-opened his eyes and wanted to speak but did not succeed.

His eyelids fell and the fingers of his right hand curled in a clench as if to close on the handle of a saber.

Outside the fusillade continued. Some officers tried to deploy the men in extended order, but they did not know in what direction to direct their effort. Several of them hurried up to Colonel Medeiros. What was to be done?

"Beat a retreat. Relieve the Geremoabo pass at any cost."

They first had to face an attack by the black battalion which had hurled itself into the assault. Those who received the shock were men from São Paulo. The Paulists had been recruited from among the farm laborers and herdsmen of the São Paulo plateaus. They were accustomed to a mild climate and to a heat tempered by the altitude. The sun in the northeast enervated them. After a hand-to-hand fight in which the men cut one another into shreds with knife slashes and bayonet strokes, the superior physique of the jagunços asserted itself. Staggering, their faces drawn, overwhelmed by the heat, the Paulists sought cover behind the ranchos.

Meanwhile Colonel Medeiros had launched into the attack the battalions from Bahia and Maranhão to open the Geremoabo road. Although they had to pass over about three hundred yards of open ground, the soldiers had gone bravely ahead. Colonel Medeiros and his officers observed their progress: they were astonished that the jagunços did not receive them with a fusillade.

"They're going to let them have a salvo point-blank," he gave as his opinion. "It's dangerous. Our men may pull it off so long as there's no panic."

Things happened differently. The soldiers still had to cross a hundred yards when the jagunços, rising from their shelters in the mountain, fell upon them.

"They prefer hand-to-hand fighting," one of the officers commented. "It's more in their line."

"The men of Bahia and Maranhão aren't afraid of them at that exercise," said Medeiros.

He looked through his binoculars to follow better the development of the battle. All of a sudden he seized one of the officers feverishly by the arm:

"Look," he said. "Do look! What on earth's happening?"

Bahians and Maranhanses were surging back in disorder, in an incomprehensible panic: they were throwing away their weapons and raising their arms in gestures of despair, yelling like madmen.

"What are they saying? Do you understand them?"

"No, there's too much confusion."

The men in flight were drawing near and soon their cries could be made out.

It was in fact to Zé Brandão's three hundred men that Pajehu had given the order to bar the way of retreat. They were let loose. Colonel Medeiros could not make them out through his binoculars, with their noseless faces, their stumps of limbs, and their scaly heads.

Long before bacterial warfare was ever spoken of, Pajehu had measured the horror which fear of contamination could provoke. He had judged accurately. This charge of the lepers had the effect of a cataclysm on the soldiers: they fled before Brandão's men as if in front of a prairie fire.

"We're done for," said Colonel Medeiros resignedly.

He knew that with the jagunços there could be no question of surrender. The fight was to the finish, to the death. Calmly he drew his pistol; the officers followed his example. Outside the men went past yelling. An officer shut the door of the rancho. He had hardly pushed the lift of the latch when this was smashed in by a forceful blow from a rifle butt. The colonel received a splinter of wood in his forehead. He had no time to shoot. A Negro's jacaré knife entered his stomach. The other officers suffered the same fate: the scuffle was so sudden that they did not even succeed in downing a single one of their assailants. It was more like a case of murder.

Out on the plain the flight took place in utter bewilderment, for the men did not know which way they were fleeing: they were running to right and left and were falling one after another under the blows of the jagunços.

Under the immutable blue of the sky the sun threw a dazzling light on this scene of horror. Some jagunços went over the ground strewn with soldiers. All those who were not dead they mutilated horribly, leaving them in the sun with their death rattles.

At that moment, under the azure sky in the direction of Canudos, the silhouette of Pajehu on his horse stood out. Rolling a cigarette, he was ambling over the plain to take account of the work. He hailed Pedrão and Zé Brandão.

"Pick up all those rifles and cartridges," he told them. "Don't lose any time. The government rabble is regrouping at Taxandril. We've only had part of it."

Turning to Zé Brandão he added:

"In the part where the lepers worked, see that the weapons are picked up by your men. They could be stained with blood. That's dangerous for the others."

Pajehu missed nothing. He was a leader.

It was five o'clock in the evening. A formidable explosion shook the sierra with a crack like a tree shattered by a storm. At last in position, the Whitworth cannon had just fired its first shell on Canudos. Pajehu spurred his horse and galloped to the edge of the plateau from which he could take in the panorama of the town. A thick cloud of black smoke overhung the Red Houses. Some flames shot up. Pajehu saw a group of men running across the main road to Cannabrava. That was João Abbade's party responsible for putting out fires.

With the aid of Moreira Cesar's binoculars, which he always carried on him, he began to study minutely the system adopted by General Guimerães to assure liaison between the troops in Canudos and those on the Favella plateau.

When he had mastered it, and thought out his plan, he went down again to the town looking quite unconcerned. Evening was falling. From the Red Houses only a few streaks of white smoke were rising: João Abbade had fulfilled his task well. Gradually night covered the red sky, the first star appeared in the dark blue firmament, and the Canudos bell began to toll the Angelus.

In the house in which General Guimerães was billeted, an officer had just lit a candle. Half-a-dozen captains and lieutenants were gathered around the general. From a man who escaped they had just heard of the disaster suffered by Savaget's column. Nobody had the courage to comment on it.

Seated on his stool, the general was trying to recover from his stupefaction.

"It's a remarkably strange situation," he said at last. "I'll end by believing that this hinterland is really bewitched. I tell you quite frankly I'd like to throw my hand in. We're in a dead end. We'll never defeat Canudos unless we surround it. To do that, we need at least 20,000 men; and Rio won't give them. It's not possible for those people in the capital to understand the problem. They'll say: "What? You're not capable of putting an end to a handful of bandits? I'd just like to see those gentlemen of the ministry here on the spot."

"Perhaps in a few days the situation will clarify itself, general," said a young captain of the Gauchos. "The .320 has begun bombardment. As soon as it has produced its effect, we can resume the attack. I'm convinced that if we take the old church we shall be masters of the terrain. One must strike these jagunços in their faith."

The young captain was not lacking in shrewdness, but Guimerães was also right when he replied:

"That's quite possible, only they'll defend this church to the death. It would be slaughter."

"The .320 would be able to destroy it," retorted the captain.

"We can try. Demolish the church and then start a bombardment with the .75s at the same time as we launch the attack here."

They would have put this project into execution if Pajehu had not put his plan into execution during the night. At four o'clock in the morning he launched the jagunços in a mass attack against the liaison troops.

It was no doubt expected that the liaison troops would have to repel some skirmishes by the enemy: they had not expected an offensive of this scope which, after all, had been made possible only by the defeat of the Savaget column.

The battle was soon over. In the face of the crushing numerical superiority of the jagunços, the soldiers gave way on the first clash and fled in disorder through the valley of the Umburanas River. The jagunços occupied the Pellados. General Guimerães with five battalions was a prisoner in Canudos!

If, that same day, Pajehu had attacked in numbers, it would have been the end of the expeditionary force which, after Cocorobó, had lost half its fit soldiers. No doubt Saint Sebastian was nodding. In any case he did not send the inspiration of which the effect would have been decisive. Whether he judged his men to be too exhausted, or overestimated the capacity for resistance of the encircled troops, Pajehu did not attempt any movement.

13. The "Killer"

JOÃO ABBADE would not have been capable of directing military operations as Pajehu did; nor even a simple action like Tranca-Pés. He was too impressionable and he lacked coolness. But he was a man with the imagination to think of audacious measures and to bring them off. He was not without courage in spite of certain appearances: his courage, like his temperament, was mercurial. Capable at certain moments of running any kind of risk, he experienced sudden fits of demoralization. He had been terribly upset by the effects of the .320 shells. Among the Red Houses he had seen women and children blown to bits: arms, heads, and legs blown all over the place; he had been present in the panic and was able to read on every face a terror with which he had himself been affected.

Anita never ceased repeating to him that they would all be massacred: she insisted on fleeing. He was on the point of giving in to her, but succeeded in pulling himself together in time. Whereupon he decided to finish with that "Killer" which was creating panic.

That evening he told Anita that he was going to a meeting of the "Council."

There was no Council meeting, but he summoned one of his own in Tranca-Pés' house. He had called only reliable friends: the two Macambira brothers, Zé Venancio, and Norberto.

"Now then," he said to them, "we must destroy the *Matadeira*, the 'Killer.'" (This was the name given to the .320 cannon.) "I have a plan. Are you ready to follow me?"

"We'll follow you wherever you wish," said Venancio. "Speak up."

"I want twelve *giraos* of powder. Two for each man."

The *girao* is a leather bucket which is part of the equipment of every jagunço household.

One of the Macambiras said that he had enough powder at home to fill the twelve buckets.

"Good," said João. "We'll set out from your place."

"When?" asked Norberto.

"About halfway through the night."

They remained silent, half-asleep, squatting in the darkness of Tranca-Pés' living room. Only Venancio asked at a given moment: "Pajehu knows about this?"

"No. He wouldn't agree. He means to follow only his own idea. Now I say that if we don't blow up the *Matadeira*, there will be panic."

They relapsed into silence until the moment when João Abbade said: "It's time. We're going."

They went to the Macambiras' house to fill the *giraos* and, passing around by the church, made their way toward the Cocorobó road. As they advanced, the stench of decomposing corpses on the plateau became more nauseating. Following the slopes of Cocorobó and Taxandril, they reached the Favella.

"Let's rest here for a while," said Abbade.

They sat down facing the Favella. Against the starry background of the sky they could see the long menacing tube of the big gun jut up, and they could perceive two sentries moving about like shadows.

"We have to succeed in downing those two men without making a sound," said João.

"Let us go, my brother and I," said one of the Macambiras.

"All right, but we must first arrive together halfway up the Favella hill. From there you'll go ahead."

Slowly and silently they went down toward the Massacara road and began to climb the slope of the Favella. Now they had to crawl: they advanced on hands and knees pushing the buckets of powder in front of them.

João Abbade, who was leading, stopped and gave a signal to the Macambiras.

"Get on with it."

"What about our giraos?"

"Leave them: we'll carry them."

The Macambira brothers went off like snakes. João Abbade's

attention was fixed on the sentries. They were moving about unsuspecting with their rifles slung. João inspected the bucket that was provided with a fuse. His eyes became tired from looking at the sentries going to and fro against the background of stars, and he felt himself in the grip of an attack of nervousness. He had never been capable of maintaining his composure for long. He stretched his arms and legs and took a deep breath. The night was hot, and he felt the perspiration stand out on his forehead. Suddenly the two shadows were erased from his horizon. There was not a cry, not the faintest sound.

"Go ahead," said João under his breath to his companions.

With nerves strained for a supreme effort, the jagunços climbed the ground which lay between them and the cannon. In a twinkling the giraos were heaped under the enormous piece of artillery and the fuse lighted.

"Quick! Stand to arms!" shouted a soldier who had caught sight of this unusual flash of light.

A number of shadows rose up on the plateau. João and his men fired their pistols into the middle of them to cause confusion. Then, taking to their heels, they raced down the slope.

An enormous column of fire shot into the night, followed by an explosion which seemed to shake the plateau. The big gun rocked and turned over on its side.

Yells arose from the plateau and then, suddenly the Massacara road toward which the jagunços were retreating was spattered with bullets. They threw themselves flat on their stomachs to escape this burst of fire. João was not quick enough and a bullet hit him in the nape of the neck.

"Oh, mother dear!" he moaned.

He collapsed near Tranca-Pés.

"What's the matter, chief?"

As he did not reply, Tranca-Pés turned him over on his back; he took his head in his hands.

"Chief!"

The bullets continued to rain all around them.

"Venancio!" Tranca-Pés called out. "Come here! The chief's hit."

Venancio crawled up to them. He felt João Abbade's body and placed his heavy hand over the heart: it had ceased beating.

"We can't leave him here," he said. "Let's wait until they've stopped this heavy fire."

Gradually the fusillade diminished in intensity and it was turned in another direction. Venancio lifted the chief's body over his shoulders and, followed by the others in great distress, took the road for Canudos.

"Is he dead?" asked Tranca-Pés, who could not believe it.

"Killed stone dead," said Venancio who knew all about killings.

They continued on their way in silence, crossing the Vasa Barris, then the cemetery behind the church and reached the square.

"Where must we take him?"

"To the Conseilheiro's house," said Tranca-Pés.

Awakened by the explosion, the Conseilheiro was at his window and seemed to be absorbed in contemplation of the sky. When he saw the little party of men arriving he asked:

"Where are you coming from?"

"From the Favella. We've blown up the 'Killer.' "

"You have a wounded man?"

"A dead one."

Venancio had gone into the living room and laid down his burden. The Conseilheiro lit a candle and looked. The body was stretched out on its back. The yellow light of the candle which the Conseilheiro held in his hand fell on the face. When he recognized it, Antonio stood rooted and his features took on a fixed expression. He did not say a word. After a moment he held out the candle to Venancio, knelt near the corpse and, staring at it intensely, as if he could bring it back to life with the power of his look, he called in a whisper: "João!"

He got up slowly and, clasping his hands, began to recite the *Ave Maria*.

While he was praying a man loomed up in the framework of the door: Pajehu. He had been notified by one of the Macambira brothers. He pushed Venancio and Tranca-Pés aside roughly and stood in front of the corpse which he contemplated for some time. Turning toward Tranca-Pés, he asked sternly:

"How did this happen?"

"It was he who wanted to blow up the *Matadeira*. It did blow up and we were already at the bottom of the Favella slope when he was hit."

"Why wasn't I told anything about it?"

"He didn't want you to know."

Pajehu went and sat on a stool at the end of the room. Venancio fixed the candle on the floor and they remained around the corpse to watch over it in silence.

It was an hour before Anita arrived. She stood on the threshold hesitating for a moment, for never had a woman crossed the Conseilheiro's doorstep. Then, carried away by her womanly instinct which she had never been able to control, she threw herself on the corpse, clasped it to her, lifted the head between her hands, covered it with kisses, and sought in it for that look which used to transfix her. All of a sudden she straightened up, uttered a cry, the cry of an animal; and, turning about with a violent movement of her back, she rushed out of the house.

The jagunços had remained impassive during the scene. The Conseilheiro had retired into the other room. When he reappeared Tranca-Pés asked:

"Shall we bury him tomorrow?"

"Tomorrow morning, after the Angelus. Are there any open graves?"

"A dozen."

The Chief of the People's funeral was the first witnessed at Canudos. Until then they had been content to put the dead into the ground without any ceremony. Wrapped in a red covering, the body of João Abbade was carried on a rough bier into the old church. In spite of the proximity of the enemy, in spite of bullets whistling here and there all over the place the jagunços—men and women—felt obliged to render a last homage to the man whom they had always regarded as the Conseilheiro's lieutenant.

Inside the church Pajehu found himself at the head of the men; Anita was at the head of the women.

The Conseilheiro approached the body and uncovered it so that everybody could look on it for the last time. And, while the prophet was reading the prayers for the dead in his old breviary, the jagunços filed past before the man who had been Chief of the People.

Pajehu went first. He bent over the corpse, took the hand and shook it for the last time. When he straightened himself, one could see that he was contracting his features; he would have liked to hold back a tear which ran gently down his right cheek, the first he had shed since manhood.

When it was the women's turn, Anita stopped in front of the last remains of her man and looked long as if she was still hoping that he would open his eyes. Then, very slowly, she placed on his chest a stalk of dried maize. For there were no flowers in Canudos.

The Conseilheiro did not make a speech. He did not feel his courage up to it. But he said solemnly that João Abbade was in the Kingdom of Saint Sebastian.

Two men took the covering from the corpse, which they carried away to throw it into the trench.

Some black vultures were still wheeling around in the limpid sky over Cocorobó.

14. A Setback

PAJEHU returned to his house with a heavy heart after the funeral. For the first time he was overcome with despondency. He felt himself terribly alone. Never would he have thought that João Abbade had such a place in his life. He had always believed that he was self-sufficient. Now, the death of Abbade gave him the feeling of an enormous void. It was to Abbade that he was attached in Canudos; not to the Conseilheiro. With Abbade gone, it seemed to him that there was no longer any sense in defending the town.

Often he had found that Abbade was lacking in energy: at certain moments he had even taken him for a coward. He had been mistaken. Abbade had blown up the *Matadeira*, the huge "Killer."

As he continued thinking, he gradually overcame his lapse into despair. No, he could not abandon the cause for which João Abbade had just died. He owed it to the memory of his friend to continue the struggle implacably. He must avenge him.

In short, he had the upper hand of himself: Savaget's column was done for; five battalions were prisoners in Canudos; the "Killer" was rendered useless.

He tightened his belt, examined his pistols, and took up the riding whip which he never went without. He sent a young Negro to find Tranca-Pés, Venancio, and Norberto. They held council together in the afternoon. Pajehu expounded his plan to them. Tranca-Pés must remain in the town itself to assure the service previously directed by João Abbade: extinguishing fires and dealing with panics among the women. The other minor chiefs, the *cabecilhas,* with their men would accompany Pajehu on the Pellados where Pedrão with his black battalion were already stationed.

Pajehu wished to take the Favella and the .75 artillery which was installed there. If he should succeed, the encircled enemy battalions would be doomed to rapid extermination and the government expedition could be considered as annihilated.

He would probably have succeeded, and perhaps without any great difficulties, had he not come up against a man of his own stamp on the government side.

Captain Luis Campista belonged to one of the oldest families in Bahia. He was a man of about thirty years of age, of medium height and build. As one must when from Bahia, he had a thick head of hair; his eyes were black but his complexion was only slightly brown. In him the blood of the pioneers had not degenerated: he was endowed with an astonishing dynamism and the physical toughness of a *bandeirante,* as those original Portuguese pioneers were called. He was well acquainted with the sertão from having gone over it on several occasions, but no doubt he was considered too young to be put in command of an expedition: he was only a subordinate. And, as his family was not on the best of terms with that of General Guimerães, he had not been summoned to join the leader's circle of confidants. That was a stroke of luck, for all the officers who accompanied the chief into Canudos were now prisoners of the jagunços. Captain Campista had nevertheless one satisfaction: he had been entrusted with the command of the 5th Bahia battalion. This unit was made up exclusively of men recruited on the banks of the São Francisco River and in the sierras of Itiuba who were, all of them, of the same race, from the same environment,

and had the same customs and habits as the Conseilheiro's jagunços. General Guimerães, believing that he would be able to take
Canudos by assault, had not wished to give the 5th Bahia battalion
the opporunity to distinguish itself, and so had left it behind on the
plateau to guard the artillery, with the Amazon battalion and two or
three others recruited in São Paulo, Pará, and Piauhy.

That is why, when Pajehu launched his attack, he came up against
the 5th Bahia battalion. The fight immediately became fierce and
desperate. It was a case of jagunços fighting against jagunços. Both
sides handled the knife with the same versatility, they had the same
very formidable nervous releases, the same contempt for death.

Luis Campista was a man of decision and initiative. When he saw
the battle well clinched, he took it on himself to follow up. He gave
the order for more than he expected of Captain Barreto, that his
Amazon battalion be put into the fight. These Amazonians were also
good soldiers. Working in the cultivation of rubber, they were accustomed to a hard life and the struggle without respite against all
the perils of the jungle. They were men of short stature, short on
the legs with great strapping bodies, and they did not retreat. Not
having been able to get a footing on the plateau, Pajehu's jagunços
were on the slope, which was very much to their disadvantage. The
onslaught by the Amazonians made them lose ground.

Campista immediately took advantage of this. Calling the troops
from Piauhy and Pará to come to the rescue, he threw all his cards
into the game.

Campista gave no respite to the jagunços as they fell back toward
the Pellados: he launched his men into the assault. The other
officers were not in agreement with this, but he imposed his will
on them.

"I'll take every responsibility," he shouted.

"We're going to fall into a trap," said Captain Varela.

"Let me get on with it," yelled Campista. "We're going to liberate
the general."

One could have believed for a moment that this counterattack
would fail. Rallied by Pedrão, the black battalion put up so vigorous
a resistance on the Pellados that it seemed impossible to beat down.
On both sides the men's wills were indomitable, their physical endurance equal. At that moment Pedrão, who had advanced too

deeply among the Amazonians, was twice bayoneted. The death of their chief shook the confidence of the jagunços; they began to yield ground.

When Pajehu, who was on the Cocorobó plateau, saw the movement and heard at the same time of Pedrão's death, he gave the order to withdraw toward the church.

In spite of the half-darkness, Luis Campista quickly appreciated his advantage. Instead of pursuing the jagunços, he directed his men toward the quarter of Canudos occupied by the troops of Guimerães. They met with no resistance: the jagunços had abandoned their positions. Liaison was re-established between the government troops.

The arrival of the Amazonians was greeted with the hurrahs which may be imagined. Captain Campista rushed to the house where the general was. Guimerães was with his officers, sitting in a circle around the candle fixed in the soil as is customary in ranchos with a floor of beaten earth. When Campista appeared, the general held out his hand to the captain with all the lofty manner and haughtiness of a superior officer.

"I congratulate you," he said. "I shall recommend you for promotion."

For General Guimerães had a very administrative mind.

"Thank you, general," replied Campista, "but meanwhile there are some urgent steps to be taken."

"Tell me. Of course I haven't any idea of the situation."

"I believe," said Campista, "that we must withdraw immediately to the Favella. We're not sufficiently strong to continue the attack. If we remain stubbornly in Canudos, we risk being surrounded a second time."

"I'm far from wishing to remain stubbornly in Canudos, my friend," said the general. "All I want is to get out of it at once. The attack on Canudos must be based on another plan. What they've asked us to put into practice was conceived in the offices of the Ministry of War. It's on the terrain that a plan is made. Besides," he added, complacently, "I've already drafted my report."

The retreat began in the torrid night. The fusillade had completely ceased in the direction of the old church and the valley was wrapped in deep silence. In spite of their exhaustion, the sol-

diers who had been held in Canudos hurried toward the top of the
Favella where they hoped to appease their hunger and thirst.

When all his men had withdrawn behind the Vasa Barris, Pajehu
returned to his house and flopped on the ground. He was almost
at the end of his strength. His head was buzzing: for some hours a
decayed tooth was plaguing him with nagging pains. His nerves were
on edge.

Toward morning Tranca-Pés came to see him with Norberto.

"Hello Pajehu!" Tranca-Pés called out from the doorstep.

The sala was plunged in complete darkness and he could not
see the half-breed stretched out in the middle of the room.

"What is it?" said Pajehu.

"They're gone."

"Who?"

"The troops. They've gone up toward the Favella."

Pajehu got up. The news astonished him. After their success, the
government troops withdrawing? What did that mean?

"You're certain?" he asked.

"Come and see."

"I'll go . . . But do you know where that loafer Sariema is?"

"I think he's in a house over Cannabrava way with some women."

"Bring him to me immediately, if need be by force. I want him
to pull out a tooth. This tooth's going to drive me crazy."

For Sariema not only made a speciality of cutting hair and shaving beards: he had become the town dentist. He had a remarkable
trick for extracting a tooth with a shoemaker's awl which he had
brought back from Bahia.

While the two mulattoes went off to look for him, Pajehu went to
inspect the quarter which had been retaken.

"I wonder what they're up to," he said. "We'll have to keep our
eyes open."

He sat down on a doorstep and held his head in his hand.

"This toothache is unbearable. And that ne'er-do-well Sariema
is never where he ought to be."

He returned to his own house. The throbbing of the tooth was
depriving him of his senses.

The sun had already risen when the mulattoes brought Sariema.

"Lazy lout!" shouted Pajehu who was in a very bad mood. "You went on messing about with women while the others were fighting. Come now, show that you're of some use. Take out this tooth for me."

"Let me see it," said Sariema calmly.

Pajehu opened his mouth and showed the aching tooth.

"Sit down on the doorstep, I'll see clearer," said the half-breed.

Pajehu sat down. Sariema took out his awl and, using it as a lever with another tooth as prop, he succeeded in the operation at the first attempt. Pajehu shot out the tooth in a great spit of blood.

"That's all right," he said. "I don't need you further. You can go back to the women."

Insensitive to the scorn with which these words were loaded, the half-breed held out his hand to Pajehu.

"If you need me, I'll be there. Always at your service . . ."

Pajehu felt like giving him a clout. He restrained himself: he might still require him; he still had two decayed teeth.

Once relieved of his pain, Pajehu felt himself a different man. He was ready again to take up the defense of the town. The withdrawal of the government troops disconcerted him: had they remained in Canudos, he would have turned on Zé Brandão's lepers to attack them. He regretted not having done this sooner. He had hesitated because lepers' blood spattered about could infect the whole town. Now he no longer hesitated; he saw clearly that he must fight with every available means.

It was ten o'clock in the morning. The sun was shining. The government side had not yet sent a shrapnel shell into the town. What could they be up to?

15. The Will of God

CANUDOS had not known so calm a day for a long time. Not a shot from a rifle; not a shell from a cannon. It was as if hostilities had been suspended.

In the afternoon Pajehu went to the Conseilheiro's house to consider the situation with him. He found him laid out on his bed.

"I'm not disturbing you?" he asked.

The prophet did not reply. Stretched on his back with his eyes closed and his hands folded on his chest, one would have thought him dead. Pajehu approached and pressed his arm.

"Conseilheiro!"

Antonio opened his lack-luster eyes.

"Is that you, Pajehu?" he said in a weary voice.

"What's the matter?"

"Call Quadrado. I'm ill. I think I'm going."

"What do you feel?"

"Cramps in the stomach and a lump which rises in my throat."

"Since when?"

"It took me about noon. I thought I was done for."

"Why didn't you call out?"

"I was waiting for Beatinho, but he didn't come and I fell into a doze."

"All right, I'll go to find Quadrado."

The "doctor" was in the church sleeping among the wounded. He was utterly exhausted: for days he had not closed an eye. Some women were helping him to dress the wounds, but all the wounded men wanted to be examined by him; they had confidence in him only. Quadrado was a man devoted to his work. He did his best, but a moment comes when the will weakens under nervous strain. He was sleeping with his fists clenched and his mouth open. Pajehu had to shake him energetically to awaken him. He opened his eyes but remained lying on his side.

"Let me be," he said. "I can't do anything more."

"It's me, Pajehu," said the half-breed. "The Conseilheiro's dying."

Laboriously and heaving a deep sigh, Quadrado got up.

"What's happening to him?" he asked, pulling up his trousers.

"I don't know, but I think it's going badly with him."

"Still his dysentery no doubt. His intestines are weak."

"That's it, cramps in the stomach."

They found the Conseilheiro in the position in which Pajehu had left him. On hearing Quadrado's voice he opened his eyes.

"Where's the pain?" asked the "doctor."

"In the belly, there," said the Conseilheiro indicating the pit of his stomach.

Quadrado pulled up the smock, opened the trousers and pressed on different parts of the stomach with his fingers.

"Stop, you're hurting me," said Antonio.

"How long is it since you've not eaten anything?"

"Not since yesterday evening: I ate a little dumpling of maize flour."

"All right," said Quadrado, "I'm going to bring you a dose of medicine."

He dragged Pajehu away. When they were outside, he said:

"There's not much hope. I have no more tincture of opium. I've used it all up. I'm going to give him a glass of *jatoba* juice, but I don't think that's strong enough."

"In any case," said Pajehu, "if he passes out, don't say anything. The men mustn't hear that he's dead, otherwise I'll get nothing more out of them."

"Put your mind at ease, I'll not talk."

Pajehu went out to find Tranca-Pés, Venancio, Norberto, and the Macambira brothers who were all together in a house on the bank of the river facing the Pellados. The astonishing calm of that day was also causing uneasiness to the group leaders who were wondering what the republicans were preparing.

"We must send a patrol to see what they're doing," said Norberto. "Maybe they've gone?"

Pajehu shrugged his shoulders.

"Gone? Expect a forceful attack at any moment."

"As for me," said Venancio, "I'd try once more to reach the Favella height. At any cost. Let us have a thousand men and I'll get there."

Venancio believed that will and daring sufficed to win victories.

"You wouldn't get there," said Pajehu coldly, "and you'd have a few hundred men killed. Soon we'll have too few. The losses are heavy. There's nothing to be done but wait. Each time they've attacked us in the town they've been beaten."

After the evening Angelus Pajehu returned to the Conseilheiro's house. Quadrado was there. The prophet was now lying flat on his stomach on the bed.

"Well?" Pajehu asked.

"It's going badly," Quadrado replied in a low voice. "I've made him take half a cupful of jatoba juice, but he's had a violent cramp in the stomach and he brought it all up in mucus tinged with blood. He's very ill."

"What does he say?"

"He says that he doesn't want to take anything more and that we mustn't bother about him any longer."

Night filled the room. Quadrado lit a candle and fixed it in the earthen floor. Pajehu sat down on a stool and began to roll a cigarette.

The Conseilheiro uttered a deep groan and turned on his side. Quadrado wished to take his hand to feel his pulse, but the prophet pushed him away with an ill-natured gesture.

"Clear out," he said in a raucous voice.

He lay on his back again.

"The fever's rising," whispered Quadrado.

They remained silent, looking at the flame of the candle flickering. After a time the Conseilheiro began to mutter:

"Sylvio Silveira didn't know Saint Sebastian. If he'd known him, Canudos would never have existed. . . . It's those who suffer who shall enter heaven. . . . Not João Abbade . . ."

He uttered a cry: "João!" and then became silent as if expecting a reply.

"It's the fever," Quadrado whispered.

The Conseilheiro again began to mutter.

"It's the good Jesus who'll save the hinterland. Saint Sebastian told me so that day on the boat, but Miguel Carlos didn't want me to go with the good Jesus. . . ."

For a long time he continued to wander in his mind, mixing all his recollections, and then suddenly he doubled up with his head touching his knees, yelling with pain.

Quadrado and Pajehu looked at him but could do nothing to relieve him.

Antonio's throat gave a deep rattle and he again fell on his back. Quadrado put his hand on his forehead. It was hot.

"Conseilheiro," he said, "I'm going to give you an infusion of *mulungú:* that will give you relief."

"Get out of it! I don't want anything more. The will of God must be fulfilled. Saint Sebastian is going to come and rescue me. . . ."

He retched and leaned over the edge of the bed to vomit. . . .

A shot rang out. In the deep silence of the night the report acquired great resonance.

"I'll come back," said Pajehu. "I'm going to see what's happening."

He returned in half an hour.

"What was it?" asked Quadrado.

"Nothing. That was a watcher on the church spire who thought he saw some movements on the Pellados. . . . How is he?"

"I don't think he'll last until dawn."

"It would be better if he died straightway. The night is quiet. He could be buried easily. Tomorrow there may be ructions."

Quadrado looked at the half-breed with questioning eyes.

"One can't kill him all the same."

"Why not?"

"No, Pajehu," said Quadrado persuasively. "Don't do that. The punishment would be terrible."

Quadrado, a mulatto, believed in mysterious powers, in the justice of God. He was horrified by the cold-blooded skepticism of the half-breed.

"Very well," said Pajehu, "but if the jagunços hear that the Conseilheiro's dead, the punishment will be even more terrible. All will be lost. Look," he said drawing his dagger, "with that blade I'd finish him at one go."

Appalled, Quadrado straightened up in front of him and seized his arm, looking him in the eyes:

"Pajehu!" he gasped.

The Conseilheiro stirred and began to writhe slowly on the bed moaning softly: "Oh, mother dear! Mother dear!"

Pajehu put the dagger back into its sheath. The Conseilheiro's breath began to come in a death rattle.

This lasted for some time. Quadrado was perspiring steadily, as much from the state of his jangled nerves as because of the enervating heat which was coming into the room by the window. In the distance there were incessant flashes of tropical lightning.

All of a sudden the Conseilheiro's death rattle stopped. Quadrado went to the bed, placed his hand on the forehead and then over the heart. He turned to Pajehu.

"I think it's all over," he said. "Give me the candle."

Pajehu held it out to him. He went to the Conseilheiro's face and lifted the eyelids.

"He's dead," he said rather solemnly.

Pajehu went to the bed.

"Let me see to this," he said. "I'm going to roll him up in this bedspread. I'll take him straight away to the trench."

With haggard eyes Quadrado watched him wrapping the corpse. He could not understand this indifference in the face of death.

"And now," said Pajehu, "silence! The Conseilheiro is ill. Nobody can see him, nobody can speak to him. If you say one word too many, I'll kill you."

Quadrado could not find the strength to reply. Pajehu lifted the body on his shoulder to go and throw it into the trench.

16. The Armistice

A WEEK LATER when Pajehu was quite satisfied that there was no activity on the part of the government forces, that they were no longer even sending a shell on Canudos, he realized that they were waiting for reinforcements and that they did not wish to waste their munitions. Had he at that moment decided on a mass sortie, he would certainly have defeated the Guimerães army: but ever since the setback on the Favella, he no longer had confidence in himself and was content to organize surprise sallies. He had a weakness for guerrilla tactics: this was more in keeping with his temperament. Every night a dozen jagunços made a raid on this or that point in the government positions: they managed to kill three, four, six, and up to ten soldiers. In this way the enemy troops were kept on edge. In the daytime they were struck down by the sun; at night by the jagunços.

Inside Canudos the position was getting worse. In order to avoid a panic, Pajehu declared that the Conselheiro had had a vision and that he would not leave his house until the victory which was certain.

Unfortunately the victuals became scarce. Until then the neighboring villages had sent convoys of beans and maize. With the prolongation of the war, lassitude set in and the consignments of provisions became rarer and rarer. Water was becoming short. The Vasa Barris being dry, the town now had only two little wells at the foot of the Cannabrava sierra. They yielded hardly enough water for drinking and cooking. The men and women, having no longer the wherewithal to wash themselves, were covered with vermin. Every day some of them could be seen on a piece of waste ground by the Red Houses taking off their clothes and rubbing their shirts, trousers, and dresses in the hot sand to get rid of the fleas.

The jagunços would have been able to abandon the town, since the roads to Varzea de Ema, Uauá, and Cannabrava were open to them. Not one of them, however, suggested such a thing. They preferred to be killed rather than abandon Canudos.

During this period the "Jagunços' War" became the nightmare of the population in Rio. The most exaggerated rumors were in circulation about the holy city. The story of the Italian engineer who was organizing the defense still had a great vogue, and the reputation of João Abbade as monarchist leader seemed to be solidly established. It was asserted that shiploads of arms coming from Germany had been landed on the Sergipe coast and taken by road to Canudos. It was no longer a matter of talking of the "repression of a revolt" but of a veritable war.

There were constant demonstrations in the streets calling for energetic action on the part of the government.

At last, after three months, it was learned that another brigade consisting of 3,000 men was being sent against the Conselheiro's haunt. It was placed under the command of General Girard. Hopes rose again. This time one could be sure that the jagunços would be crushed.

Hope was of short duration, for people soon heard that a new phenomenon had appeared: all the officers designated to accompany the new expeditionary corps were falling ill one after another. There were some who felt the attacks of illness as soon as they reached Bahia; others did not notice them until their arrival at Quiemadas; others again only at Monte Santo. But not one of them arrived in the theater of operations. The Canudos war seemed like something so atrocious and inhuman that nobody had any wish to take part in in it. In the overexcited imaginations the jagunço had become an invulnerable, mysterious, and formidable individual. Even in official circles this idea began to assert itself. They were living in a sort of illusion. And, when it was seen that the Girard brigade arrived on the terrain only in bits and pieces, deprived of its establishment of officers, people asked whether the efforts of the government had not been frustrated by some occult power.

Under the influence of these ideas the cabinet at last decided on a far-reaching measure: one more corps would be sent to Canudos and the operations would be placed under the command of the highest-ranking officer in the Army: Marshal Bittencourt.

The battle was going to become unequal. Bittencourt, profiting by the experience of his predecessors, and having available plenty of troops, had left with a plan for the encirclement of the town. Pajehu would not have been able to repeat against him the blow he had struck at Cocorobó. The fit fighting men of the jagunços, moreover, were greatly reduced.

On December 4th, some men who had been out getting supplies at Varzea da Ema came to tell Pajehu that the military were in occupation of all the crests of the Cannabrava line of hills. Without replying the half-breed ran to the old church, climbed up into the spire and, using Moreira Cesar's binoculars, began to spy out all the hills surrounding Canudos. The men had told the truth: all the crests were covered with soldiers.

He came down and went to find his group leaders, the *cabecilhas*.

"We're surrounded," he said. "I was expecting that. They think they've got us, but inside Canudos nobody can beat us. We're going to divide the work among us, for we'll have to face several sides at the same time. I'll hold the Vasa Barris, Norberto will take command of the Cannabrava side, Tranca-Pés in the direction of Uauá, and Venancio the Varzea da Ema side. To defend the ground step by step."

"Let them come!" growled Tranca-Pés. "We're waiting for them."

"Make your arrangements immediately. They may attack."

There was no attack that day but next morning a new section of artillery installed at Cannabrava began to bombard the center of the town. It was at ten-thirty that a shell burst right in one of the spires of the old church. It shook slightly and then collapsed whole, dragged down by the weight of the bell which crashed in the middle of the square.

Pajehu felt a pang. Would the destruction of the bell perhaps shake the courage of the jagunços? Under the haphazard shellfire he went to see Norberto, Tranca-Pés, and Venancio. No, the fall of the spire had not scared the men; they were ready, they wanted to fight, they had a wish to kill.

Pajehu ran into Quadrado in a little street.

"What are you going to do?" asked the "doctor."

"Fight. What else do you want to do?"

"There's a vast number of them. I don't think we can hold out."

"They won't re-enter Canudos," asserted Pajehu.

Quadrado scratched his head. . . . Just as Pajehu was about to leave him, he held him back by the arm.

"Listen," he said. "In your place I'd send the women away. We mustn't mix women in fights to the death like this. And besides, they're going to be in your way and there's not much in the way of food supplies."

"What do you want to do with them?"

"Send them away."

"Send them away where?"

"To the other side of the lines. We'll ask for an armistice."

"Well I never!" said Pajehu derisively. "You're simple-minded enough to think that those people would agree to an armistice? That's done in wars, not in a knife fight like this."

"I'm not of your opinion," retorted Quadrado. "Would you like me to try?"

"You'll get killed."

"No. I think they'll agree."

"If you want to risk it, go ahead. I don't ask better than to be rid of the women."

They considered that the best place for a parley would be the exit from the town toward Cannabrava, where Norberto's men were stationed. They went there. Quadrado tied a white handkerchief to the end of a stick and, brandishing and shaking it above his head, he advanced toward the government lines.

Pajehu had very slight confidence in the effectiveness of that little white handkerchief and he was expecting to see Quadrado laid out in the dust by a volley of bullets.

Had he, Pajehu, been in command of the government troops, he would not have parleyed. He looked at the "doctor" advancing calmly on the bare stony ground, keeping his finger on the trigger of his Mannlicher rifle, ready to reply if the federals murdered Quadrado.

The federals did not fire a shot. Quadrado vanished into their lines. Pajehu placed his rifle against the wall. So then there could be discussion with those people? It seemed to him, all the same, that the jagunços had committed so many atrocities that nobody would agree to speak to them. He recalled Uauá, the corpses hung from trees at Angico, the Capuchin's mission.

Who knows? The government side had received Quadrado: perhaps this was only a maneuver. They must stand on their guard.

He remained for a considerable time in the house on the lookout for the doctor's return. Finally, at the end of his patience, he went to find Norberto who was further away.

"I think they've killed him," he said. "Otherwise they're holding him to tap him for information about the situation here."

"It's possible," said Norberto. "But we'll have to wait. If the negotiation isn't finished and we break the truce, they'll certainly kill Quadrado. He doesn't deserve that."

"All right," said Pajehu. "We'll wait until sundown."

About half an hour later the doctor reappeared. He was no longer carrying his white flag. He was walking simply as a man walks in the street. Pajehu could not get over it. He hailed him from the doorstep.

"What did they say to you?"

"They agree. I'll explain."

Quadrado went into the room and they squatted down.

"It took a long time," said the doctor, "because they led me to the marshal's headquarters. It's Marshal Bittencourt, the commander in chief of all the armies in the country, who's directing operations. He's a decent man who wouldn't ask better than to come to an arrangement with us. He explained to me that we're surrounded and that he has 20,000 men at his disposal. Resistance is impossible. I proposed to give up the women. He agreed at once, but added immediately that we should do better to surrender. To fight is crazy, we're beaten in advance."

"Halt!" said Pajehu. "I don't need advice from your marshal. He agrees for us to hand over the women?"

"Yes . . ."

"Well, we'll hand them over. For the rest, you can tell him that Canudos won't give in."

"What use is that?" asked Quadrado raising his arm.

"No use. But a man like Pajehu doesn't give in. He kicks the bucket."

Norberto said that he was going to get busy collecting the women. Pajehu remained behind with the doctor who offered him a cigar.

"At General Headquarters," said Quadrado, "they offered me a few good cigars."

"They wanted to bribe you, to get you to talk."

Pajehu took the cigar, turned it around between his fingers and then, crushing it in his hand, threw the fragments on the ground.

"I don't want anything from that scum," he said.

Quadrado looked at him with eyes full of bewilderment. He did not understand that relentlessness with no quarter given.

"They're good cigars all the same," he said, "from the marshal's own box."

"I'll make your marshal smoke one of my own manufacture," retorted Pajehu.

Quadrado began to smoke, blew out a few puffs, and then leaned over to speak confidentially:

"Listen, Pajehu, let us speak seriously. I've seen the troops along the top of the line of hills. You haven't a hope. You'll all be killed if you join battle. If you surrender you'll save your life."

"So you've been entrusted with proposals? All the same you don't take me for a child? Save our life? We know that. They want us to surrender to torture us to death, but a jagunço isn't a slave! We'll fight. We're quite willing to die from a bullet, and not grow moldy in their dungeons."

"Just as you like . . ."

Pajehu rolled a cigarette.

"It's you who'll take them women there?" he asked.

"I said I'd take them."

"You'll come back?"

Quadrado's face stiffened and, in a somewhat solemn tone of voice, he said:

"I'm not a coward. I've proved it."

"All right. I asked you that because we'll need you for the wounded."

"You can rely on me. I'll return."

Norberto had assembled all the women in the big central avenue. Many had been killed in the course of the fights and bombardments, but there still remained more than one could have believed possible. It was a lamentable procession in rags and tatters which stretched from the main square to the foot of the Cannabrava hills. In it were to be seen the bony faces of women like old witches beside faces with the fine features of young mulattas. Here and there was the face of a young mother, pensive and astonished and, in a strange medley, the stern countenances of Indians or halfbreeds, and the laughing faces of negresses.

"Let's get this finished right away," said Pajehu.

Quadrado took the head of the procession and led it toward the heights.

"Come back!" Pajehu shouted to him again.

"On my word!" replied Quadrado.

In the lurid glow of the twilight the sinister procession reached the government lines. Pajehu watched it wind its way on the bare land like a party of pilgrims in the desert. When it had disappeared behind the sierra in the falling darkness, he turned to Norberto.

"Now," he said, "we can have it out among men."

"They'll get us," said Norberto. "But they'll pay dear for it."

Quadrado never returned to Canudos and it was learned later that Sariema, disguised as a woman, had succeeded in reaching the federal lines. So it was that, next year, one could have a shave in his little hairdresser's parlor in the lower town at Bahia.

17. Death of Pajehu

"I KNEW quite well that he wouldn't come back," said Pajehu to Norberto. "He's a softy: not a man like us."

"Pooh!" replied Norberto, "we'll take care of the wounded ourselves."

As between half-breeds, they understood one another. Norberto was a man of about thirty, offspring of the union of a Scottish explorer and an Indian woman. One would have said from his distinctly European features that he had at least eighty per cent of white blood. He was a long, lean, tough, and determined man; and he was capable of eating a pound of meat for breakfast. His hair and eyes were very black, but he had the prominent chin of a man who could command others. Pajehu had taken him as his confidant after the death of João Abbade.

Both men knew that they were going to be vanquished: massacred. Yet they preferred death to enslavement. They had made up their minds to die in the breach, fighting.

Marshal Bittencourt, who had no more practical experience of hinterland warfare than the next, allowed himself to be beguiled by the plan of Captain Figueira, who suggested a charge by the Gauchos down the central avenue with the object of reaching the main square in one swoop. This was the same mistake Moreira Cesar made, but nobody had an opportunity to explain the error. Figueira's idea was that the Gauchos would open the way and would be supported by the infantry, which would deploy here and there in the avenue.

This plan was put into execution two days after the women were handed over.

So the Gauchos dashed headlong down the avenue and in actual fact reached the main square, but the infantry did not succeed in giving them the expected support. The soldiers on foot had hardly approached the first houses when Pajehu threw the lepers into the battle. The same panic occurred as at Cocorobó. The Paraná battalion, which had been given the task of supporting the Gauchos, consisted exclusively of white men, for whom leprosy is terrifying. Whites have not the same familiarity, the same hardness to this disease as colored people. Faced with those noseless and fingerless men of Zé Brandão, they had only one idea: flight. The Gauchos were left to themselves. They fought as men with their solid muscles can fight. But the struggle was unequal. Surging from houses in which they were hidden, the jagunços planted their bayonets in the horses' bellies and then shot the horsemen point-blank.

When Marshal Bittencourt (who was observing from the Canna-brava heights) saw the turn the battle was taking, he realized that there could be no question of taking Canudos by assault: the attack would have to be in mass and general, and the ground con-quered foot by foot.

At one moment he was convinced that the jagunços would yield before an imposing deployment of forces. He knew now that this was a vain hope. The jagunços would not surrender. In his heart of hearts, he agreed with them: he knew very well that, if they surrendered, they would be sent into the swamps or to the railway yards in the fever zones.

But his mission was to finish with them. He regretted this. In his tent on the Favella, stretched on his bamboo mat, he was turning things over in his mind and saying to himself: "What a race of people! What energy! What guts! What men these are! If we had been able to lead them on the right road, what services might they not have rendered to civilization! On these desolate lands, in spite of this corrosive soil, they have created a race whose strength, tough-ness, will, and intelligence do not in any way yield to the better northern races. The jagunço is a victory of man over the sun. If he has been morally deformed, that is only due to difficulties in the transmission of civilization." A decent man and, in his leisure hours, a philosopher, Marshal Bittencourt found no consolation in having to exterminate these enemies. Nevertheless, he had no other alterna-tive. Even if he promised the jagunços their lives, he would not be believed. The eternal obtuseness of men!

Five days later the general assault on Canudos was launched. The troops of eleven Brazilian states took part in it. It was carried out with the bravery and self-sacrifice found only in the tropics. Northern man cannot understand that contempt for death which is found among those who live under the tropical sun. In the north, life is slow and difficult: it is a precious possession. In the south, it is rapid and multiple: it has not the same importance. When a forest is cleared in the north, it requires twenty years to remake it: in the Amazon region, a year. In the south, girls reach puberty at twelve years of age: a population is re-created without difficulty. In the south, death grows tired of mowing down life: men look at death with a quizzical eye.

The battle was terrible. Even in the first clash, the jagunços did not fall back. Each at his post—Pajehu, Norberto, Venancio, and Tranca-Pés with their men—put up a resistance which had something of the implacable in it. Marshal Bittencourt had foreseen this. Hence, the troops proceeded with their advance by laying siege to every house. Here and there the losses were monstrous.

At a given moment the federals issued forth onto the main square and succeeded in deploying; they managed to surround the old church which was, in this place, the principal center of resistance. Pajehu succeeded in escaping by the cemetery. He dashed forward into the little streets of the quarter which extended toward Canna-brava to ask Norberto for help. Suddenly finding himself in the presence of two Gauchos, he threw himself behind a house, drew his pistol and fired four shots. The Gauchos collapsed. Pajehu darted down another little street. On turning the corner of a house he ran into a Negro who was advancing cautiously with his rifle on his hip, his bayonet pointing threateningly. Taken by surprise, the lithe Negro bounded back and tried to bring his rifle to his shoulder to fire. But Pajehu was already on him and with a blow of his head sent his opponent rolling on the ground. With a quick movement he drew his dagger and planted it in the Negro's throat.

Just as he was getting up, two Amazonians threw themselves on him. Fortunately he still had his dagger in his hand and the first assailant fell in the dust with a groan; the other was holding Pajehu by the throat and trying to strangle him. Pajehu succeeded in turning around and, throwing himself flat on his belly, then with a heave of his back he shot his adversary a couple of yards away. The

Amazonian got up and leaped at him like a jaguar. Pajehu dodged him. The man fell headlong onto the ground and the half-breed's dagger went into his back.

At any cost Norberto must be found. How did it happen that this quarter was already invaded by the enemy? Where were the jagunços? Pajehu ran along the tortuous little street and turned left. Three uniforms loomed up in front of him. He felt tired. However, he had the presence of mind to draw his pistol and fire twice. Two men fell. The third had fired at him, but the bullet merely grazed his arm. Pajehu gave a terrific leap and was on the man, but the latter, an officer from São Paolo, had already drawn his dagger. Pajehu saw it in time, seized him by the wrist, and tried to twist it. The officer was strong: he resisted. Then, like a madman, Pajehu leaned toward him and bit his throat. The officer cried out and released his hold. Pajehu's dagger went straight into his heart.

But where on earth were the jagunços? Where was Norberto? Pajehu no longer saw clearly. He wiped his eyes, into which the sweat was running in real torrents, but this only clouded his vision as his hands were dripping with blood.

Anguish began to overcome him, the anguish of a man who felt his strength ebbing. Now the hand which held the dagger was shaking; his muscles were exhausted.

He advanced cautiously, hoping to meet some of Norberto's men. They ought not to be far away. Between the shots which cracked here and there he could hear groans and shouts: "Long live the Conseilheiro!" "Long live the good Jesus!" One more effort and he was going to join them, then he would bring the men down to the church to mop up the square.

In the next street he found himself confronted by a huge Bahian Negro, a man as tall and as broad as Pedrão. Their looks crossed and Pajehu felt that, into his, he had put all his hatred for the black race. He saw the Negro swing his rifle to strike him down with a blow from the butt. Quick as this movement was, Pajehu had forestalled it: he had thrown himself between the soldier's legs and toppled him over. Letting go of his rifle, the Negro seized him by the hair and was drawing Pajehu toward him. With his keen-edged knife the half-breed opened his calf. The Negro gave a jump and let out a cry of anguish. Pajehu turned around and finished him with a slash right in the throat. Then, as if seized by a bloodthirsty madness, he planted his dagger three times in the man's chest.

Pajehu rose on his knees to get his breath: he felt at the end of his strength.

Five uniforms rose in front of him: he could perceive them only as in a fog. He heard some explosions and, pierced by five bullets, he collapsed on the Negro's corpse. He was still conscious of what was happening: he saw, close against his own, the face of the Negro. He seemed to hear a distant cry, like a call in the sierra: "Pajehu!" It was Norberto's voice. Then, nothing more: it seemed to him that he had fallen asleep.

In the little streets the battle continued, bitter and desperate. Norberto, who had repulsed the attack coming from Cannabrava, had not waited for Pajehu to bring down his troops in the direction of the church, which he had seen was surrounded. Little by little the jagunços reconquered the ground. At five o'clock in the evening Marshal Bittencourt gave the order for withdrawal. Canudos remained inviolate.

In his tent on the Favella, the Marshal, who lay on a hammock, which had been sent to help him to bear the hinterland climate, gave his impressions to his general staff:

"We shall win," he said, lighting a cigar. "But what men!"

18. The Last Day

THE SAVAGE GRANDEUR of that last day at Canudos could not be denied. After the death of Pajehu the fights had continued, becoming more and more murderous. The jagunços were holding no more than an area around the old church. That evening they counted themselves. There still remained one hundred and seven.

It was these one hundred and seven men who, during a whole day under a burning sun, were going to stand fast against Marshal Bittencourt's army. Yet they had no more leaders: the Conseilheiro, João Abbade, and Pajehu were dead. There remained only the minor chiefs: Venancio, Tranca-Pés, and Norberto. It was to Norberto that the others offered the command for this supreme struggle.

Let it not be imagined that these jagunços were heroes; they were not men who had made up their minds to be killed for a high ideal. They were men who were defending their skins.

They had regrouped themselves around the church and spent the night piling up rubble with which to make a rampart. On their side, the government troops had refrained from attack and they also were occupied in regrouping themselves. In that maze of streets in Canudos the line of battle could be picked out only with difficulty. And it was practically impossible to know whether the defenders were a hundred or a thousand.

The officers, especially those who had been in the first assaults, explored the terrain prudently, expecting new surprise attacks from one moment to the next. There were none: the jagunços were no longer in a position to attack. They were getting themselves ready to defend the last corner of their town in a fight to the death.

They had chosen a particularly favorable position. On one side, they were under cover of what remained of the walls of the church, which the artillery had pounded fairly well; on the other, of four almost intact houses. In front and to the rear, ramparts made of rubble faced two magnificent fields of fire: the main square and the bed of the Vasa Barris River.

Every man had taken up his position, and each one had at his side half-a-dozen Mannlicher rifles loaded in order that, at certain moments, they could give their fire the intensity of that from machine guns. And they had an adequate supply of ammunition.

Hence, at about ten o'clock in the morning, when the government forces launched a first assault, the assailants were received with a terrible, unendurable fire. However, the attackers were Pernambucans, fine jaunty men who dared to look death in the face. Not a single one succeeded in reaching the parapet wall behind which the jagunços were sheltered. The rifle fire of the jagunços had been so well sustained that all the officers thought they were having to face over a thousand men.

The position of the defenders was then submitted to a violent artillery fire, but the jagunços, ensconced under the houses hardly suffered from it and, when the second attack (led by the Pará battalion) was launced at about 1 P.M., they were all at their posts. A second time the dash of the assailants was broken by a burst of fire of such intensity that the officers were stupefied by it.

A second bombardment with shrapnel shells lasting for more than two hours was more effective. A score of jagunços who had not had time to reach the houses were killed. Among them was Venancio, who received a splinter of shell in the head.

Under cover behind a house, Norberto was counting the dead. There were also some wounded men moaning. Four had been able to drag themselves under cover of the houses and with an end of their dirty shirts were wiping away the blood which ran from their wounds, while others remained laid out under the sun and let themselves die slowly. Norberto suggested putting them out of their misery, but the jagunços did not feel their courage up to it. They were old pals; one couldn't plant a knife in those men.

As the bombardment continued, Tranca-Pés crept over near to Norberto.

"We haven't much more ammunition," he said, "and the men are dying of thirst. I propose that at the next attack we rush out to meet them. We're done for just the same. The sooner it's all wound up, the better it'll be."

"I want to live until the sun goes down," said Norberto.

"Where's that going to get you? As for me, I'd like to throw myself on them, put holes in a few just to show them for a last time what a jagunço is."

"They know that. As for me, I don't fight just for show. I fight for myself. I'd like not to die in the sun. I like the sun, I want to get out of it. Not death with sun in my eyes."

The bombardment ceased. A soldier carrying a white flag advanced toward the middle of the square. From there he shouted:

"Surrender! You have no hope. Surrender. No harm will be done to you."

Tranca-Pés had picked up his rifle. He took aim, pulled the trigger. The soldier collapsed on the ground holding his little white flag. He received the bullet right in the head.

"They're going to be in a rage for that," said Norberto. "You can expect a furious attack."

"That's what's required," said Tranca-Pés.

It was said that Norberto's prophecy would not be fulfilled. The government troops, outraged by the murder of their spokesman, took steps for a decisive action. They had perched a certain number of soldiers on the roofs of houses on the other side of the square: these were good marksmen who directed a murderous fire downward on the jagunços. Norberto was hit in the nape of the neck by a bullet. It was a little after four o'clock in the afternoon and the sun was still very hot.

This time the assault came from two directions. The São Paolo troops attacked from the direction of the Vasa Barris, those of Pará from the main square. Although less sustained, the jagunços' fusillade was still strong enough to repulse the attack. At the moment when they withdrew, the government troops did not know that the jagunços were reduced to six able-bodied men!

"The unfortunate thing is," said a Paulista captain, "that this handful of individuals can still kill a hundred of our men. Let's knock them out with shrapnel."

His advice was taken and the artillery, which had an abundance of munitions, opened fire with a violence which would have been more in keeping when the engagement began. The shells rained on the defenders. Under cover in a house, Tranca-Pés and the five other survivors waited impassively for this fire to calm down, and for the hand-to-hand combat to begin again, when a shell exploded right inside the room where they were. Three men were killed stone dead, and two more wounded. Tranca-Pés, who was crouching against the casing of the door, was the only man unscathed. He had merely a feeling of being poleaxed, deafened. He jumped outside and, with the instinct of self-preservation, lay along the wall of the house.

Little by little he collected his wits and a singular reality occurred to him: he was the last able-bodied man alive in Canudos. On all sides were dead, and wounded men who moaned lugubriously.

From one moment to the next the soldiers would come up to the attack. All the same, he wasn't going to allow himself to be killed like a dog. He rose to his knees and looked at the sun which had just reached the crest of the sierra, and was spreading its vast red curtain over the western sky. The jagunço remained in that position, his mind a blank, but feeling a wish to lie down there and fall asleep.

All of a sudden, moved by an impulse which came from the depth of his being, he bounded unarmed toward the parapet. He climbed on the heap of rubble. Standing upright facing the enemy, with both hands he tore off his shirt to expose his broad brown hairy chest. Then, holding out his arms in the form of a cross, he roared at the government troops stalking forward from the other side of the square:

"Now shoot, you scum!"

There was an instant of hesitation among the soldiers, who were taken aback by the strange apparition. Then, at the command of a sergeant, a volley of bullets laid out on the debris of the church the last defender of Canudos.